C0-AKZ-608

RETURN FROM DARKNESS

RETURN FROM DARKNESS

A NOVEL BY

NINA VIDA

A Warner Communications Company

Warner Books, Inc., 666 Fifth Avenue, New York, NY 10103
A Warner Communications Company

Printed in the United States of America
First Printing: May 1986
10 9 8 7 6 5 4 3 2 1

Designed by Giorgetta Bell McRee

Library of Congress Cataloging-in-Publication Data

Vida, Nina.
Return from darkness.

1. World War, 1939-1945—Fiction. 2. Holocaust, Jewish (1939-1945)—Fiction. I. Title.
PS3572.I29F5 1986 813'.54 85-43174
ISBN 0-446-51225-7

To Scott and Tracy,
my children

Acknowledgments

Before beginning to write this novel, I decided to trace Helene's odyssey. Along the way I met and interviewed people who shared with me their rich and vivid recollections of the past, so that finally Helene and her family became my family.

My deepest thanks to Carlos Talvy, secretary of the Jewish congregation in Barcelona, for taking time from his scheduled appointments to talk to a stranger from California. He was an eyewitness to the plight of European Jews who had hoped to find sanctuary in Spain before and during the Second World War. I'm grateful to him for sharing some of those painful memories with me.

And special thanks to Paco Pascual, our friend and guide in Spain, who went out of his way to fill in the facts about Spanish life during the Civil War.

Deepest appreciation to Bob Euler, Research Anthropologist at Grand Canyon National Park, for heading me in the right direction in my research on the Havasupai tribe, and to Lee Marshall, past chairman of the Havasupai Tribal Council, for his remembrances of Havasupai tribal life in the forties and fifties.

And thanks to Mary Jonssen, Library Assistant at the Museum of Northern Arizona, for responding to letters and phone calls from me with unending patience and good humor.

Thanks to my agent, Meredith Bernstein, and my editor, Fredda Isaacson, for loving the book.

Of course, none of this would have come to anything had it not been for my husband, Marvin Vida, who, with his constant encouragement and editorial help, saw me through.

Nina Vida
Huntington Beach, California
May 1986

RETURN FROM DARKNESS

1939: Helene

I

He sat opposite her in the music room, telling her about Poland as the late-afternoon light of a Berlin autumn day filtered through the Belgian lace panels. Ecru panels, the color of heavily creamed coffee. Elegant and understated. Not harsh and demanding like stark white lace. Stark white lace was better for evening dresses and bassinet covers. And wedding gowns. Helene remembered her wedding. Why should she think of the wedding now, when Maurice had brought the terrible news that Germany had invaded Poland?

Grandmama had helped pick out Helene's wedding gown. Never, Grandmama said, had Berlin seen as important a marriage as that between a Gelson and a Rosenzweig. A genealogist in Munich had traced the Rosenzweig ancestry back to the sixteenth century. It was all in Grandmama's library in a leather-bound, deckle-edged book, a copy of which was in the Berlin Archives of the German National Museum.

"Helene." Maurice drew her back to the present. "We must leave the country now."

"But you said that we had time, that there was no hurry," Helene protested. "I can't be hurried, Maurice. I must think."

Until today there had always been all the time in the world, and suddenly there was no time at all. Hadn't Maurice assured her over and over that the babies would be safe, that the family had the resources to ride Hitler out, that bogeymen had come and gone in Germany and the Gelson family had always survived? When hadn't there been Gelsons in Berlin? Or Rosenzweigs?

"There is no longer any purpose in remaining," said Maurice. "I see patients but have no medicine to give them. I'm no longer even permitted to admit them to the hospital. If they come to me for treatment, all I can give them is advice. I say, 'Don't give up hope,' when I am without hope for them. Now, with the curfew for Jews, I can no longer visit the sick in the evenings. I had thought I could accomplish something by staying, but I see now that it was all wasted effort."

"It was not wasted," said Helene, taking his hand in hers.

"I've tried to do the right thing," said Maurice. "But sometimes the right thing does not make itself clear in time. My choices have put you and the children in jeopardy."

"Count von Kirchner will help us if we stay in Berlin," said Helene. "You must give him more time. He can intercede for us. Special favors might be granted."

"He's done the best he can do under the circumstances. But he has superiors. He is a German officer, not a magician. The time when others could help us in Berlin is past. The time for rational argument, for making sense out of the senseless is over. France and Britain are now in the war, and Hitler has promised to annihilate the Jewish people if this becomes another world war."

"But surely he doesn't mean 'annihilate' in that way."

"No? They say that soon we will be required to wear yellow Stars of David on our clothing. To what purpose, Helene, if not to set us apart? And why set us apart if no harm is to be done us? There is talk of putting Jews in concentration camps. Tell me how they will feed and sustain millions of Jews in camps. You must face the facts and recognize how important it is that I get you and David and Miriam out of Germany."

Helene shuddered. "Maurice, you mustn't look at the dark side. I try not to think of such things."

"We must think of those things. So far our money has insulated us well. We haven't suffered as so many others have. We've been able to buy food on the black market. You have even continued to have the Thursday evening musicales. We've pretended that we could remain in Berlin if we made minor adjustments in our thinking, in our behavior. But now I must advise my patients to use other doctors and, if possible, to leave Germany as soon as they can."

"But what will we do about the house, the pianos, all of the furniture?" said Helene. "And what about the babies? To travel is difficult in the best of circumstances, but to travel with infants—"

"You are not really listening to what I've been telling you, Helene. Possessions are not important now. Your pianos can be replaced. But it is you and the children I'm concerned about. The babies are no longer safe in Berlin or anywhere in Germany. If you want them to grow up, we must leave Berlin. The Count has offered to help us do that. It may be our only chance. Can't you understand?"

"There is no need to speak to me like a child," said Helene, pulling her hand from her husband's.

"Of course you are not a child. And I feel your pain at leaving. But we must face what is happening in Germany, and we must take advantage of Karl von Kirchner's offer of help now."

Helene leaned her head across the tea table to press her brow against her husband's. Her face was oval, its color creamy like the ecru of the lace panels. Her eyes slanted slightly from their brown fullness, and the eyelashes elongated the corners of her eyes so that her face seemed vaguely Egyptian. "I'm sorry if I'm making things more difficult for you," she said. "I'll do whatever you want."

"I know you will." He touched her lips with one finger. "You are my sweet Helene. You must have hope and must stay strong for David and Miriam. Promise me?"

She nodded.

"Here is what we have arranged," he said. "Karl will get us to Italy. Erika and Gunter are ready to leave. The Schneiders are going, as well as the Boorsteins. Gunter has been changing all of our assets into gold and diamonds over the past few months. Now everything is complete. Gunter and I are to take charge of the group; Gunter will handle the financial matters, and I'll tend to any medical emergencies that may arise. And Karl will accompany us to Rome. He has succeeded in arranging for us to meet there with the German Cardinal Otto Feltzman, who will have visas prepared for us. Karl is not sure for what country, but we will be traveling with Vatican diplomatic visas."

"Karl has promised you this?"

"Karl has promised. Everything depends on him, Helene. I thank God every day for his friendship."

"You are a believer in people, Maurice. And because of it I believe in you."

Maurice smiled at her, and the smile softened the worry lines in his face. He was prematurely gray, a forty-year-old who looked older. Still, there were the vestiges of the handsome young man he had been. Wavy brown hair and direct blue eyes. A benevolent manner, an air of authority that inspired confidence in his patients. Many a woman who came to him with a physical complaint found that after a short talk in the consulting room of the clinic, her problem was gone. "It's important to listen well to what your patients say," he used to tell his students in his university lectures. "The mind is the master of the body. Never forget that for a moment."

"When will we leave?" asked Helene as she felt his calm flow into her across the table.

"The day after tomorrow. Karl has arranged for train tickets. He really is a very good friend, Helene."

"For money, one can have many friends, but can we be sure he has the power to do what he says he will do? If he can't help us in Berlin, what makes you think that he will be able to help us in Rome?" she said.

A look of pain crossed his face. His blue eyes flickered momentarily in their deep-set sockets. "At this point nothing is certain; there are no guarantees. I *must* trust."

Helene reached for the silver teapot and poured a second cup of tea for her husband and then one for herself. She was proud that her hand didn't tremble.

"If you say we must leave, we shall leave. I can be strong, too," she said.

"I know you can," he answered.

II

Lisl's tears hung on her roseate cheeks and then dripped down from each side of her double chin. She hugged two-year-old Miriam and three-year-old David close to her, rocking the bewildered children to and fro on her broad lap.

"It's so hard," Lisl said between sobs.

"I know," Helene assured her. "You have been the most faithful friend. We couldn't have managed without you."

Because there had been no time to arrange for the sale of the rugs or furniture, everything would have to remain behind, as though the Gelsons were going away on a short holiday.

"You must take all your uniforms, Lisl," said Helene, "and any of the clothes that you want. And I want you to take for your own everything in the house that you can transport without drawing attention to yourself."

Lisl's eyes opened wide. "I couldn't. Your beautiful things. You'll be back. You'll need furniture. The babies will need their things."

"Maurice wants you to take everything. It will all be stolen by others if you don't."

"The silver?" asked Lisl in astonishment.

"The silver, too," Helene said.

Lisl looked embarrassed now. "I didn't stay with you so that your things would be mine."

"Of course you didn't. I would never think that, Lisl."

Lisl was like a cow, Maurice said, that moved slowly and steadily among the grasses, eating her fill and giving milk as needed, with no real understanding of what was happening in Germany, no sense that the Gelsons and their children were in any real danger. Helene didn't argue with him. His was the superior mind, after all.

Yet she felt that she knew Lisl on a level that Maurice could not. Marika, the governess, had left the Gelsons as soon as the first edicts against Jews were posted in 1936. Frieda, the cook, left soon after, taking Helene's copper pots with her. And the chauffeur, Rolf, left when there was no longer an automobile for him to drive. Only the maid, Lisl, had stayed with the family. The least likely one to remain in the house of Jews, Helene thought. A peasant girl with not much education, someone one would expect to believe what more sophisticated and cultured Germans told her about the depravity and corruption of the Jews. But Lisl was too ignorant or too good to believe anything bad about the Gelsons. She had stayed long past the time when she should have left, endangering her own safety.

Although she had never hugged a servant before, Helene put her arms around Lisl and drew her close, feeling the woman's warmth and solidity as a tangible thing. She envied her identity; she would have given Lisl all the silver and the furniture in exchange for it. But there were the children squirming on Lisl's lap, and Helene knew that Lisl's identity would not stretch to include a husband and two children.

Suddenly the two women were embarrassed by the breakdown of protocol between servant and mistress. Helene moved away; Lisl wiped her nose on her apron and let Miriam and David slide off her ample lap onto the floor.

"Come, we must hurry. Grandmama is expecting us shortly," said Helene.

Lisl bathed the children and dressed them: Miriam in a pink silk dress and matching pink coat with a frilly lace collar, David in a two-piece blue suit with sailor's middy tie. Helene wore her navy serge suit and hat for the last time. That outfit would have to be left behind in favor of the heavier fur-trimmed suit.

Together the two women left the house, each carrying a child in her arms, and hurried along the tree-lined avenue that stretched beyond the stately houses down to the Mitte and yet farther to the *Ringbahn,* where the trains joined Germany to the rest of Europe. Lisl, in her serviceable gray coat and severe hairdo, looked like any other maid helping her mistress with the children.

Helene felt a thrill of excitement at being outside again after the many weeks during which Maurice had not permitted her to leave the house. But Maurice had gone off in the morning with Gunter to make arrangements for the trip and would not be back before evening, and she could not leave Berlin without saying good-bye to Grandmama and asking her one last time to change her mind and come with them.

Helene took a deep breath of the cool autumn air. How wonderful it was to swing legs and arms, to take large chunks of space as she moved. Her muscles sang! She laughed to herself. What melody do we hear when our muscles sing?

The streets were clean and the passersby well dressed. All the buildings were where they had always been—the cinema, the Schiller Schule, where Madame Steller had shouted out the tempo more precisely and accurately than a metronome. "Talents are uneven, young ladies, make no mistake about that," Madame Steller had informed the nine-year-old Helene and ten-year-old Erika as they sat at facing grand pianos. "But to play music together, you must each think of the other, allow for the other's lesser or greater talents. It is not a competition or a race to see who finishes first or who can gain the most applause by playing the loudest or fastest. The purpose in playing music is to make music, nothing more."

Helene looked up at the window of Madame Steller's studio. The reedy sounds of a flute floated down. Madame Steller had died before all the terrible things began to happen in Germany. What would Madame Steller have said had she known that Helene had been housebound for months because Jews were afraid to walk on the streets? Would she have thundered out in her high-pitched musical voice that tempo and musicality were everything, or would she have acknowledged that there was more?

A man passed them, and from the corner of her eye, Helene saw him turn and look at her. Had he thought her pretty, or had he seen "Jewish" written across her face? A woman, bundled in furs, brushed Helene's coat accidentally with her shoulder, smiled, and apologized, *"Es tut mir leid,"* in a low voice. Helene nodded and turned her face away quickly. She checked her reflection in a store window. When she and Erika had been on a concert tour in 1926, Erika's blonde hair and Nordic features had made her immediately identifiable as an Aryan, but people coming backstage had asked Helene whether she was French or Italian or possibly Arabic. No one had ever asked whether she was Jewish. Perhaps they had been too polite to ask that.

David squirmed in Helene's arms, and when she kissed his cool cheek, she felt a tremor of fear at being outside. Maurice would be angry at her for taking the children to Grandmama's. He worried so about everyone and everything. No one else in the world need worry, because Maurice worried enough for all.

She looked quickly around her as they entered the commercial area of Unter den Linden. The sidewalks were full of people here. As they crossed the street at a crowded intersection, Helene thought that she and the babies must be the only Jews on the streets of Berlin.

"A taxi," said Lisl, motioning to the stand across the street.

"Thank God," said Helene.

Once safely inside the taxi with Lisl and the babies, Helene relaxed.

The Tiergarten was ahead, its trees beginning their change to the golds and reds of autumn. Beyond was Grandmama's gabled house, the center cupola, carved in the Italian Renaissance style, visible high above the trees that enveloped the Rosenzweig estate.

Walter greeted them in the high-ceilinged foyer beneath the dome. He was cordial with Helene, as he always had been. His wife, Greta, came from the kitchen and smiled and curtsied to Helene. Then Greta and Lisl disappeared, and Walter, carrying a baby in the crook of each arm, accompanied Helene to the French sitting room where Grandmama waited.

"My dearest Helene." Grandmama called her from the damask sofa by the fire. Her creamy lace gown blended with the perfectly matched pearls at her throat. "How wonderful of you to come," she said, extending her hand to her granddaughter.

Helene held the hand to her lips. "Grandmama," she said, smiling into eyes that sparkled, noting how the full cheeks quivered with repressed animation. There was a photograph on the table beside Grandmama that showed her in her wedding gown, with Grandfather Rosenzweig stiffly straight in a black formal suit, his wavy hair slicked down on either side of his head, handlebar mustaches poking out from the sides of his cheeks. He was gazing lovingly at Grandmama, who was looking at the camera, her round face very much like Helene's except that the cheekbones were higher, the nose was fuller, and the lips were more sensuous-looking. She was turned partly sideways to show off her tiny waist in the wedding gown that had been made especially for her in the bridal salon of the Rosenzweig department store in Berlin.

There was no display of emotion between the two women as Walter placed the two children on the central floral design of the antique Aubusson rug. Then Miriam put one small fist in her mouth and began to cry.

"The children will want milk and cookies, Walter," the white-haired woman commanded in the husky voice that had always reminded Helene of a Russian princess in the cinema.

"Yes, Frau Rosenzweig." As soon as Walter had left the room, Helene burst into tears and fell into her grandmother's arms.

"Now, now, now," soothed her grandmother as she stroked Helene's hair. "Shall I have Walter bring you milk and cookies, too, then?"

After a while the tears subsided.

"Better now?" asked Grandmama.

"A little."

Her grandmother offered her a finely embroidered linen handkerchief. It smelled of Grandmama's distinctive perfume and also of her Turkish cigarettes. Helene wiped her eyes and blew her nose into the delicate fabric. "May I keep it?"

Her grandmother laughed. "Is that all you want from me, a handkerchief? Here, take this; it is a better remembrance." She removed a ring from her fourth finger and placed it on Helene's little finger. The diamond glittered in the lamplight.

"It is better than a handkerchief, my dear Helene, much better." She pulled her granddaughter close to her. "There aren't many things to be grateful for in these terrible times, but I'm thankful that your dear parents are not alive to see this terrible catastrophe. I thought when the influenza took them after the World War that nothing more terrible could happen to this family. And now we come to this."

"Come with us, Grandmama. Maurice wants you with us. I want you with us."

"But where are you going that is any better than this? Who will want to harm an old woman like me? It takes very little food to keep me alive, a small amount of firewood to keep me warm. And Greta and Walter are still faithful."

"But for how long? What will happen to you if they leave? They may have no choice but to leave if the authorities discover them still working for you."

"If anyone can harm those two good Germans, then why should they hesitate to harm this old one, no matter how many bodyguards I have?"

"But you're not an old German. You're Jewish."

Grandmama stiffened against the padded damask.

"I am a German. I was never permitted to be a Russian, but I am a German; make no mistake about that. You are German, Helene. Your children are German. There is no stigma to the Rosenzweig name. Your grandfather's fortune was made honorably. We are not shabby beggars."

"You are Jewish, Grandmama," said Helene in a low voice.

"I am Jewish when I want to be Jewish, not when others declare me to be," said Grandmama. She reached for a cigarette from the gold case next to her wedding picture. She lit it and blew the smoke out in a curling movement of her lower lip. "I raised you differently from the way I was raised, Helene. I wanted to make life perfect for you. I see that I was mistaken. I should not have shielded you from things. When I was thirteen, Czar Alexander II was assassinated by revolutionaries. We lived in a shtetl so small that it had no name. I was one of ten children. My parents spoke only Yiddish, but I knew that to learn to speak Russian was important, that I would be less vulnerable. So against my parents' wishes I played with the Russian children in the adjoining village, and I learned to speak Russian; and when the Czar was murdered, and the Cossacks came and burned the shtetl and looted the houses, I led my brothers and sisters and parents to the farm of a Russian peasant. And I spoke to him in Russian, and he took us in."

"But I speak German," said Helene, "and no one has taken us in."

Grandmama puffed on the cigarette, her lined face softened by a haze of smoke. "Maurice's indecisiveness in leaving Germany worries me," she said after a while.

"You misunderstand him, Grandmama. He had his patients to consider. He didn't want to abandon them."

"You are my grandchild. If I cannot tell you my fears, then who must I tell?"

"You may tell me anything, Grandmama. It goes no farther than this room."

"Good. Whatever I have done for you, it was only because I sought to protect you from ugliness. Since the day that your grandfather found me in the shtetl and married me, I have tried to keep unpleasantness out of my life. And when you were left to my care, I wanted only beauty and happiness for you."

Helene kissed her grandmother's cheek. "You have been wonderful."

"I was not wonderful. I was wrong to keep you always so close to me. And Maurice has been wrong to treat you as though you could not stand in a storm. You can stand, Helene. You are strong." She grasped Helene's arms with her hands. "You are more disciplined than you know. To play the piano as you do requires discipline and strength beyond imagining. You can use that strength now. You must forget whatever past restrictions Maurice or I have imposed on you. You have my permission to be strong, dear Helene."

"I don't know if I can be, Grandmama, and sometimes I'm very afraid," said Helene. "All I know is that my fear at times for the children is greater than my fear for myself."

"That is it, Helene, you must build on that, you must think in that way at all times." She leaned toward Helene and kissed her on both cheeks. "My beautiful granddaughter," she said, "my beautiful Helene."

Miriam began to cry more loudly, her arms outstretched to

Helene. Grandmama straightened up. "And your beautiful children, you are now responsible for them."

Helene picked Miriam up and brought her to the sofa and bounced her on her knee. "Now that there is only Lisl, I have learned to cook a little and to run the carpet sweeper and to help care for Miriam and David. Before, with Marika and Frieda in the house, there were so many people between me and the children. Now I bathe them and help dress them. I no longer feel like a stranger to them."

"Good endings from bad beginnings," said Grandmama.

Helene looked up at her. "Yes," she said.

David pulled at Helene's skirt, his large, dark eyes focused on her face. Grandmama lifted him onto the couch between her and Helene. "You're such a big boy," she said.

"I tell him stories before he goes to sleep," said Helene. "He seems to understand so much more than other three-year-olds. And Miriam has begun to string long sentences together. Count von Kirchner brought her a dollhouse made of tin. Every evening we put the doll to bed in the dollhouse, and I must kiss the doll good night after I kiss Miriam, and then we talk about what we have done during the day and what we will do the next day. That is, I talk and Miriam listens."

"Intelligence is in the Rosenzweig genes," said Grandmama with a smile.

"Brilliance, Grandmama, not intelligence. It is remarkable how attached I have become to the children."

"It is the times, Helene. Everything becomes more precious when we are in danger."

Walter was back in the room with a tray of cookies on a linen-draped tray. The milk was cold and pure in the cut-glass pitcher. He set the tray on a side table and handed each of the babies a cookie.

Grandmama smiled at him. "I do hope there is still a bottle of claret for our lunch, Walter."

"There is, Frau Rosenzweig. Shall I open it now?"

"That would be nice," said Grandmama amiably, her broad face no longer as beautiful as the one in the photograph, but more serene. In the photograph she seemed to be looking at the camera and beyond. Now her eyes focused on things very close to her.

"And we'll lunch in the sun room, so that we can see the gardens," said Grandmama. "The last roses are still blooming."

III

Karl von Kirchner's full Germanic name was Count Karl Wilhelm von Kirchner. He was a colonel in the German Army and the son and heir of Count Maximilian and Countess Mathilde von Kirchner. His title included the 250-acre Von Kirchner estate in the village outside Mannheim, Germany. The grounds were overgrown with weeds, and the iron-filigree balustrade that had been added to the bridge in the eighteenth century was rusted and in need of repair; but the plane trees spread their arms majestically over the estate and the lake and told of the permanence of the manor house and of the family that inhabited it. Portraits of Count von Kirchner's ancestors lined the walls of the cold, sparsely furnished rooms, and over all settled the musty smell of wet winters that had permeated the very stones of the manor house, where exotic forms of algae bloomed forth in the spring.

"There is history in these rooms," Count Maximilian von Kirchner had observed before he went off to be killed in the Great War.

After her husband's death the Countess Mathilde guarded that history jealously. When Karl was in danger of forgetting, she would tell him of their royal relatives in Belgium, of how King Leopold II once held him on his lap and sang to him while Countess Mathilde accompanied him on the piano.

When Count Maximilian was killed, the money dwindled, the fine French furniture was auctioned off, the jewels were sold, and soon there was nothing left but history and portraits and stories of royal connections.

Karl's fellow officers in Group C treated him with deference and called him Count von Kirchner, rather than Colonel von Kirchner, but the only people with whom he felt completely at home were his friends in the Thursday Evening Players. To them he was a talented violinist and a lively and witty friend. Most of the Players and their guests were Jewish. The Count duly noted that fact and then dismissed it. He

considered himself a nominal anti-Semite but certainly with none of the rabid leanings of Hitler or Streicher.

Helene woke from her uneasy sleep feeling drugged, not refreshed by her nap. She kept her head against the cold train window, her eyes closed. Erika was singing a German lullaby to David in a corner of the cramped compartment. On the hat shelf behind Helene's head, Miriam slept, covered with Maurice's overcoat, while Gunter and Maurice talked in low voices on the seat next to Helene.

"What are you whispering about?" asked Helene, shaking the drowsiness away.

"The war," said Gunter. "There is still fighting all along the Polish border."

Helene sat up, suddenly alert. "Will we be affected?" she asked.

"So far the train continues on its way, thank God," said Maurice. "We are far enough from the border that there should be no danger."

Helene was wide awake now. Erika looked at her and smiled, her skin glowing in the dim compartment. Her bobbed blonde hair, clean and shiny, fell straight and neat to just below her ears.

"I'll take David now, so you can rest," said Helene, holding out her arms for the boy.

"We've had a nice time together, haven't we, David?" crooned Erika, her square, pale face close to David's small, olive-skinned one.

She handed David to Helene, who rocked him in her arms. He didn't close his eyes, but stared wide awake up at his mother. Erika moved the children's suitcase from the seat opposite Helene and sat down facing her.

"Do you think he looks very Jewish?" asked Helene.

"You sound like Hitler," Erika said with a laugh.

"No, I'm serious. It's very important. Miriam is fair like Maurice, but David—I don't know—his little face—"

"Don't be a fool, Helene. His face is his face."

Helene stared down at the boy, who appeared to be listening intently to what was said, although she knew he could comprehend only simple language and sentences, nothing so abstract as whether his face looked Jewish or not. It was only his coloring, more like Helene's than Maurice's. Heavy eyebrows for a child his age gave him a serious, almost studious look. As she bent to kiss him on the forehead, the door to the compartment slid open noisily, and the Schneiders' fifteen-year-old son, Rudolph, peered in. "*Herr Doktor,* my mother's stomach is no better, and she says that the aspirin dulled the pain for only a short while."

Maurice reached for his bag, which contained what was left of the hoarded medicines from his clinic. "Then I'll have to give her something stronger," he said.

"She says she is sorry to be such a bother," said Rudolph, "but when she is nervous the ulcer becomes irritated."

"Your mother can't help it if she's sick," said Helene to the teenage boy, in an attempt to remove the pinched expression from his face. Helene had not seen him smile, not even when they had all met at the station in the early-morning hours. David had given him a licorice sweet out of the bag that Erika had bought at one of the kiosks at the train depot, and he had said thank you politely but had held the sweet in his hand without eating it, and only when he thought no one was looking had he popped it into his mouth. He was very thin and tall, as boys are when adolescent growth outstrips their capacity for food.

Maurice walked past Rudolph into the corridor of the lurching train, but Rudolph stood in the compartment doorway, as though waiting for something.

"Come in and tell David a story," said Helene. "David loves stories. Or you can just sit here with us and look out of the window. Maurice will help your mother feel better when he gives her the medication. You mustn't worry so."

Rudolph hesitated. He looked behind him down the corridor to where Maurice had disappeared into the Schneider compartment three doors away.

Now fourteen-year-old Emma Boorstein appeared at the open compartment door and stopped beside Rudolph. She looked past him into the compartment, as though she were unaware of his interested stare. "My mother would like to know if Miriam and David can join us for singing," said Emma.

"Miriam is asleep," said Helene. She turned to David. "Would you like to visit the Boorsteins, David, and sing songs?"

David nodded and put his arms out for Emma to pick him up. Rudolph followed Emma and David down the corridor. He looked sideways at her, a shy smile lifting the corners of his mouth.

Helene sighed. "Who would think that a boy could still be interested in love at a time like this?"

"What better time could there be?" said Erika.

Helene turned toward Miriam to check on her as she slept.

"She sleeps so deeply. Does she always?" asked Gunter at the sound of Miriam's light snore.

"She had a slight fever yesterday," said Helene. "Maurice says that either it is a new tooth or she is catching cold."

When Maurice returned, Count von Kirchner was with him.

"Helene, a seat for Karl," said Maurice.

"Oh, I'm so embarrassed, please forgive me," said Helene, hurriedly picking up toy cars, scarves, gloves, and food that they had brought to eat on the trip.

"I had thought we would take a picnic hamper for the food," Helene explained, "but Maurice said that when it was empty we would only have to throw it away, that paper sacks were more convenient." She folded the sacks into a neat square and placed them beneath her seat.

The Count made no move to sit down in the place she had cleared. He leaned against the frame of the compartment door, his tall, thin body swaying back and forth with the erratic movement of the speeding train. "I have good news on the outcome of the war. Quite good news. The border fighting is almost over. It is now the final phase of the German liberation of Poland. But as a result of the hostilities, there will be a slight inconvenience to us on our trip."

"In what way?" asked Gunter, his nearsighted eyes watery behind the thick lenses of his wire-rimmed glasses.

"We are pulling into Plauen, which is now an Army checkpoint. There will be a routine inspection. The Army must see the documents of everyone on the train before it proceeds farther. I have guaranteed your safety. I guarantee it now. There will be no further military checkpoints between here and Italy."

"How can you guarantee anything against the German Army?" asked Gunter.

"Because you have papers, because the Army respects documents and papers that are in order," replied the Count. "I've told the others not to be concerned, that the danger is to the east, where the fighting still continues. There is no danger in Plauen. When we arrive in Rome, we'll go to the Grand Hotel, and within a day or two you'll see Cardinal Feltzman. The Cardinal is said to be quite sympathetic to the plight of German Jews, since he is German by birth. The appointment has been made. No further arrangements will be required. The Cardinal has it in his power to help you further on your journey. What he will do in that regard I cannot tell you now, but whatever it is, when your destination is firmly known, you'll distribute the diamonds, Gunter, as well as some currency, to each family in your group—and to me, as we have agreed."

The Count looked at Maurice. "Have I omitted anything?"

Maurice shook his head.

"I'm still bothered by the 'J' stamped on our passports," said Gunter.

"You will be traveling with me, a German officer on a diplomatic mission to Rome. No questions should be asked of anyone in my party," said the Count.

"And are you actually on a diplomatic mission to Rome?" asked Gunter.

"Yes," said the Count coldly.

"May I ask what it is?" asked Gunter.

"You may ask. I'll not answer," said the Count.

At Plauen a fog enveloped the railway station and extended out into the fields. Helene peered through the window as they pulled in. The station platform was deserted except for a contingent of thirty smartly uniformed SS men.

The soldiers carried Mauser rifles, while the officers wore side arms. Karl disembarked and walked toward the leader of the group. From the window of the train, Helene could see their expressions as clearly as if they were in her personal dream. Their mouths moved. Karl showed the officer some papers. He pointed to the train and then pointed back toward where the train had come from. The officer smiled benignly at Karl and nodded his head. In his right hand he held one of the papers that Karl had given him, and periodically he slapped the open palm of his left hand with the crisp document.

"What are they saying, I wonder?" Helene murmured to Maurice, whose face was next to hers at the window.

"I don't know."

Karl returned the salute of the officer, then turned briskly and reboarded the train. Maurice and Gunter stood in the corridor waiting for him.

"They aren't satisfied with what I have shown them. They want to examine each family's passport," said the Count, a pained expression on his face.

"Will they board the train?" asked Gunter.

"No. They request that everyone disembark. It is merely a formality."

Maurice opened the compartment door. Helene looked up at him in bewilderment as his eyes darted around the compartment. "What have you done with David? This is no time to play games, Helene. We must present ourselves on the station platform."

"He is with the Boorsteins. Why must we present ourselves? Will they detain us here?"

"Don't ask so many questions, Helene. Just find David."

He never talked to her in this way. He was always so controlled; he complained that she too often verged on the hysterical. But she felt no hysteria now, only cold fear.

"David," she called as she ran down the train corridor, his tiny jacket in her hands. "David, David." A compartment door opened, and Emma Boorstein stepped out, David in her arms. She was smiling. She had not seen what was happening on the station platform.

Helene grabbed David from Emma, holding him tight

against her chest, against her face, breathing in the perfume of him as though she might have lost him forever. "Did you sing, David?" she asked, fighting to get control of her voice.

"I sing," he said, "with everybody."

The Schneiders were now in the corridor. Ruth Schneider was a voluptuous woman who wore a heavy overblouse in an unsuccessful effort to minimize her bosom. She stood bent over, one hand to her stomach, dazed and sleepy from the shot that Maurice had given her. Her son, Rudolph, and her husband, Benjamin, moved to either side of her to help her along.

When the Count had assembled them in the corridor, he explained to them again that it was merely a formality.

"But why are we the only ones on the train to be questioned?" asked Herr Schneider. He was sweet-faced and mild in appearance, a former business associate of Gunter's.

"Because you are the only Jews on the train," said the Count.

"What did you sing?" Helene asked David. She must try to blot out what the Count was saying. The only Jews, the only Jews, the only Jews.

"I can't remember."

Maurice cradled the sleeping Miriam in his arms, and as Helene descended the train steps, she gathered David tightly to her; the air touching her bare arms felt so dank and chill. She had thrown David's jacket around his shoulders and sang in a soft voice to him the Russian folk song that Grandmama always sang. *"Ish-u-mit, i-ku-tit, trip-ni-dash di-ki-da.* Did you sing that song, David?"

"I can't remember."

The Boorsteins followed, Esther Boorstein walking with her head up, her curly red hair a beacon of color in the gray fog. Emma Boorstein had a younger sister and brother by each hand. Behind her, Professor Boorstein stumbled over a bump in the rough pavement. Then came Ruth Schneider, flanked by her husband and son. Then Erika and Gunter. Last, the Count. They all stood in the September fog, shivering as much from nervousness as from the cold. The Count moved among them, patting each on the arm, speaking a few words of reassurance.

The SS officer pointed to Professor Boorstein. "Your name."

"O-Otto Boorstein," stammered the Professor.

The officer laughed. "He has difficulty with his own name."

"Their uniforms are not like Karl's," whispered Helene, but Maurice did not hear her.

"He is a professor of physics," said Esther Boorstein in a loud, clear voice. "He has written books and has lectured in America. His theories are taught in all the universities in the world."

"So it is true that the Jewish women answer when their husbands are addressed, *ja?*" asked the officer in a friendly, joking way. Esther Boorstein put her hand over her mouth and moved closer to her three children.

"I think that you should have stayed in America when you lectured there, *Herr Professor,*" said the officer. Professor Boorstein looked down at his shoes and did not answer.

The Schneiders were next. Ruth Schneider was wearing a bulky jacket over her blouse, but the SS man was looking directly at her bosom. She leaned against Rudolph for support, and her husband stepped in front of her as if to serve as personal camouflage for her breasts.

"Are you sick, *gnädige Frau*?" asked the SS man solicitously.

"It is the excitement of the trip," said Herr Schneider.

"Very understandable, very understandable," said the SS man.

Rudolph supported his mother with one arm while he stared dreamily up at a gray-plumed bird that sat motionless on a telegraph wire next to the train platform.

The SS officer took the passports from Herr Schneider's hand. He looked at the stamped "J," and when he lifted his eyes, his gaze lingered a long time on the partially hidden figure of Ruth Schneider.

The officer then turned to Erika and Gunter Liebermann. He examined Erika's passport and then Gunter's with a look of mock surprise on his face.

"You choose to travel with Jews?" he asked Erika tauntingly. She clung to Gunter's arm for support.

"My husband," she whispered. "We are Germans."

"Ah, Germans. Then that explains it." He laughed. "None of these children are yours?"

"No," answered Gunter, shaking his head. "We have no children."

The officer looked at Maurice's passport next.

"A doctor?"

"Yes."

"You lead these people, do you?"

"Mr. Liebermann and I are responsible for the group, yes."

Karl moved forward now, and walked with the SS man toward the end of the station platform, away from the others. Karl appeared agitated, and the SS man was shaking his head at him.

"We are lost, Maurice, I can feel it," said Helene.

"We are not lost until you can't feel," he snapped back at her.

While the group waited for Karl to return, Esther Boorstein smoothed her husband's hair, and Emma knelt and talked soothingly to the two younger children. The fog seemed to have become thicker as they stood on the platform. Safe and secure inside the train, the other passengers stared out of the windows at them.

Ruth Schneider pulled her heavy jacket more tightly around her bosom and stared absently down the long expanse of railroad track. The fresh air seemed to have revived her so that she no longer needed support to stand. Rudolph and his father stood apart from the others, each with his arm around the other's shoulders, looking up into the sky where the gray-plumed bird had just disappeared.

Count von Kirchner and the German officer were deep in discussion at the far end of the platform.

"You're involved in a criminal mission," said the SS officer arrogantly.

"I am on a diplomatic mission," the Count responded with equal arrogance.

"Then leave the Jews with me."

"I can't. They have documents and Italian entry papers."

"Papers have no meaning to me."

"What has meaning to you?"

"What do they have?"

"Some gold, nothing more."

"You are a liar."

The Count's face contorted, but he said nothing.

"They have diamonds. Jews always take diamonds with them when they run. I will keep two families and twenty carats of the best of the lot."

"Which two families?" asked the Count coldly.

"You choose. It makes no difference to me. But the fat one with the big tits is of some interest, if that fits in with your choice."

The Count turned and walked back to the others.

"The Boorsteins and the Schneiders will take a later train," he told them.

"But I don't understand," said Maurice. "What later train? We were to stay together. How else—"

The Count's look silenced Maurice in mid-sentence. Helene turned and pushed her husband toward the train. "The babies, Maurice. We must guard the babies," she said, on the verge of tears.

"No," shouted Maurice, but Erika was pushing him ahead of her up the steps of the train, with Helene close behind.

The Count put his hand on Gunter's arm, holding him back as the others boarded the train. "I must have twenty carats of diamonds. That is the bargain."

"We will need them in Italy," said Gunter, a stunned look on his face.

"Do you want to join the others?" the Count asked, motioning toward the Boorstein and Schneider families, who were now isolated from the rest of the party.

Gunter fumbled with his trousers and reached inside, pulling out a cloth sack that he wore on a band around his waist next to his bare skin. He studied the stones carefully for size, selected some, put the rest back into the sack, and then turned to Karl again. "Six stones. They are very fine. He gets approximately twenty-one carats."

On board the train Maurice handed Miriam to Erika and fell onto the seat, where he sat breathing heavily, as if he had run a long distance. Huddled with the babies in a corner, Erika and Helene did not dare to look out the window at the platform as the lumbering train engines built up their power. The Count and Gunter were aboard now, standing in the corridor like silent sentinels.

As the train began to move, Helene said aloud, "I must look. I must see it." She looked out the window into the fog. A flock of gray-plumed birds now sat on the telegraph wires next to the platform. Their wings shone like oiled steel in the damp air. Benjamin Schneider still had his arm around his son's shoulder, and he pointed up at the birds on the wire as if to show his boy the beauty of nature. The train was moving faster now. The soldiers in their strange uniforms, with their tall rifles slung over their shoulders, encircled the Schneiders and the Boorsteins, and then soldiers and Schneiders and Boorsteins, with Rudolph and Emma and the two smaller children, moved in a gray mass past the platform and into the fields. As if on cue, the birds swooped away into the sky and disappeared.

IV

Helene, who had slept the fitful sleep of exhaustion before the train stopped in Plauen, was now awake and fiercely attentive to everything that went on around her. Maurice sat in the corner of the train compartment and stared out the window.

"Would you like to lean against me and close your eyes?" asked Helene, her face close to Maurice's cheek.

"I'm not tired," he said.

"Perhaps something to eat."

He turned and looked at her. "Half of our party has disappeared. Just like that. No explanation. And you ask me if I want something to eat."

Helene flushed, but she did not move away. "We must not speak of the Boorsteins or the Schneiders as though something bad has already happened to them. We don't know that."

"I must not talk of them?" asked Maurice angrily. "Are you as insane as the rest of them?"

"Shh, please, Maurice." She began to stroke his forehead.

"Perhaps some water," he said tiredly.

"Of course," she said.

As she left the compartment to get the water, she said to Gunter, "Talk to him, please. You always know how to make Maurice relax."

Tall and muscular, but hampered by weak vision all his life, Gunter had learned to maneuver his way through any situation by sheer force of brains and personality. Besides being an accomplished amateur cellist, he was an inventor who held more patents on radios, toasters, and washing machines than any single man in German history. In 1938 he had been forced by the Nazis to turn his factory over to an Aryan owner, but his sense of humor had not dimmed. If anything, it had become more outrageous, as he sought to obliterate the reality of Hitler's Germany by regaling his friends with tales of women with gargantuan sexual appetites and men with outsized genitals.

He sat down next to Maurice, his hand on his shoulder. "Did I tell you what Bauer told me before I turned the factory over to him?" Gunter peered at him so closely that Maurice's eyelashes almost brushed his cheek.

"No."

"Come, come, Maurice, how can I tell you a story when you refuse to cooperate?"

Maurice didn't answer.

Gunter continued doggedly. "Bauer told me he was sorry that he had to push me out of my own business, but he had five illegitimate children by three women and needed more money than I was giving him. Did you hear me, Maurice? Three women. Can you imagine that?"

"Leave him alone," said Erika, irritated at her husband's insensitivity.

Helene had returned with a cup of water, and she watched Maurice while he drank it. "Do you feel better?" she asked.

"A little."

"What will happen to the others, I wonder?" said Erika after they had been traveling in silence for an hour.

"Maybe they'll be sent back to Berlin," said Helene.

Gunter shook his head. "To what? To where? They sold everything they owned to buy diamonds. Now they don't have the diamonds, and they have no homes to go back to."

"Let's not talk about it. Nothing is solved by talking about it," said Helene. "If we dwell on the fate of the others, we'll be too paralyzed to act in our own behalf."

When the train pulled into the station in Rome, Helene said, "You look much better, Maurice. The color has come back into your face."

"I feel much better," he said, but he was shaky and slightly distracted, as though he were recovering from a lengthy illness.

"If you carry the suitcases, Maurice, I'll manage with the babies myself," said Helene as she gathered up their belongings.

"I'll help you," said Erika. "Don't bother Maurice just yet. He'll be more himself when we get to the hotel. He can take a hot bath and rest, and we'll have dinner. They say that the Grand is divine. All the royalty of Europe stay there."

Rome was alive with people. Mussolini had given a speech early in the afternoon from a flag-draped balcony off the Palazzo Venezia, and the streets still teemed with cars and bicycles and people on foot. The train carrying the Gelsons and the Liebermanns and Karl arrived at the Rome station at three-thirty in the afternoon, and the group walked the few short blocks through the traffic-clogged streets to the Grand Hotel.

"You must not speak to the concierge," Karl cautioned them on their arrival at the Grand. "I will present your passports to him, but with the explanation that you are under protection of the Holy See. No further questions will be asked of you."

The Grand Hotel was an old and ornate building on the Via Vittorio Emanuele, two blocks from the railroad station. Karl turned passports and visas over to the concierge and made sure that everyone was settled in their rooms before he left them. Helene and Maurice's room was high-ceilinged and large and overlooked the Fontana dell' Mose with its four water-spewing lions that guarded the seated statue of Moses. While Maurice lay down fully clothed on one of the two double beds, Helene held David up to the tall casement windows.

"Lions," said David, pointing to the lions.

Miriam cried to be held up to look out the window, too. "See the lions," she said.

Helene picked her up and held her as she had held David. The baby touched her own mouth and then Helene's as if to ask why water didn't jet out of their mouths as it did from the mouths of the lions.

"Because your mouth is too small," said Helene, kissing Miriam's fat cheek as she put her down on the floor, where the baby promptly put her thumb in her mouth and fingered the edge of the tattered cradle blanket that Helene had brought with them from Berlin. "The children are hungry, Maurice," said Helene.

"Let me rest just a little while," Maurice said in a voice flat with fatigue.

"If you don't feel well, perhaps something in your medicine kit will help you. I can fetch it, if you want."

"No, no medicine," he answered, turning his head away. David edged over to the bed and patted his father's face, while Helene sat down beside her husband, her hand on his shoulder.

"You see how much David loves you, Maurice," she said, feeling strange in her new role of caretaker. "I'll draw a nice hot bath for you. Would you like that?"

"Not now. I'd rather rest."

"It wasn't your fault, Maurice."

"I let them go."

"And how could you have stopped them? You're not a superman who has the power to transform events. You're only a doctor." She had never spoken to him so forcefully before.

"Don't turn my own psychology against me," he said, but without anger.

"Ah-hah, you see what I'm doing. That means you're feeling better. Don't let me bully you, Maurice. Tell me what needs to be done, and I'll do it."

"Don't analyze my behavior," he protested. "Let me rest for a while. My brain has been assaulted. My body is trying to adjust to new circumstances, new information. I don't have your resilience. It surprises me, but you have been remarkably sanguine during the past several days. Bovine strength is what you have, like Lisl, like a serving girl."

She kissed him on the cheek that he had turned away from her. "Am I to be insulted, then, being called a cow?" she asked, hoping to joke him out of his despondency. But he had closed his eyes and appeared to be asleep.

Helene picked David up in her arms. "Then what about you, David? Would you like a hot bath?"

"Yes, please, a bath," said the dark-eyed toddler, holding his arms out eagerly.

After she had bathed the children and dressed them in their pajamas, Helene fed them the dinner that she ordered from room service. Eggs and buttered toast and milk with slices of ripe melon for dessert. Then she put them both to bed in the double bed opposite where Maurice slept.

"Dada doesn't feel well," she explained to David as she kissed him good night. Then she sat by the window and inhaled the fragrance of the garden below and listened to the sounds of breathing while her children and husband slept. She felt so safe in this hotel room. So self-contained in this little world. Maurice had said that she had bovine strength, that she reminded him of Lisl. She decided that that was a compliment. She had never seen herself in that way before. But these were crazy times, when people could be thrown off trains like rag dolls into the rubbish. She could no more transform events than Maurice could, but she could be cow-like, like Lisl, sturdy, like the servants who had cared for her all her life.

She turned away from the window to look at Maurice sleeping in the bed, his breathing as regular as it had been in their bed at home in Berlin. What if it had been they who had been left behind in Plauen? Would Maurice have gone off in a corner and sat and left her to cope with whatever future the soldiers had in store for them? Or would he have fought and kicked and beaten anyone who dared to touch a hair of their children's heads?

She leaned her head against the windowpane. Grandmama, she thought, the Cossacks are coming, they're coming again, and Maurice is sleeping and refuses to get up.

The dining alcove of the Grand Hotel was a few steps from the main lounge, with its heavy Italian furniture and brilliant crystal chandeliers. Gunter and Erika had helped themselves from the buffet table and were seated inconspicuously beside a potted palm when Helene joined them.

"How is Maurice?" asked Erika.

"Tired. Very tired," said Helene.

"He must be rested in the morning," said Gunter urgently. "The appointment is for ten o'clock in the morning at the Vatican with Cardinal Feltzman. If the opportunity is lost—"

"The opportunity will not be lost. Maurice is merely tired." Helene spoke with more confidence than she felt.

"The food is lovely," said Erika. "Take a plate. There are salads and beautiful torten. Fill your plate and take some back for Maurice when he wakes up."

At the buffet table there was a small mountain of oranges and apples and late peaches. The leaves of the peaches had been retained, and the fruit mountain looked like a living, growing thing in the center of the table. Helene filled her plate with food and returned to her seat.

"He blames himself, you know," said Helene, staring at the abundance of food on the table.

"Then I should blame myself, too," said Gunter. "I gave the Count the diamonds, and he gave the SS men the Boorsteins and the Schneiders. I was part of the transaction. If you want to assign blame, I bear some of it."

"Perhaps you should have consulted with Maurice first," said Helene. "I think he feels that he has lost control of his life and can do nothing for those he cares about."

"Gunter was in no position to ask Maurice anything," said Erika. "Karl was negotiating over which of us would go and which of us would stay. There was no need to consult with Maurice on anything."

"If he felt so left out of everything," said Gunter, "he could have spoken up. He could have given his place to the Boorsteins, or even the Schneiders."

Helene shivered, thinking of David and Miriam out in the dark fog of the train station at Plauen.

"Darling Helene," said Erika, "please eat something and calm yourself. What's done is done. But there is the appointment with the Cardinal tomorrow, and you'll see, we'll have visas, and Maurice will come to himself again."

Helene looked at Gunter. "What time must we be ready to leave?" she asked.

"If Maurice will meet with me at eight-thirty, we can consider the finances," said Gunter. "We must decide how the diamonds and the gold are to be allotted now that the others are not with us, whether to divide it into thirds, giving the Count a third, now that there are no longer five parts to be considered."

"Maurice will meet you then at eight-thirty," said Helene. "I'm sorry if I worried you about his health or his state of mind."

Gunter waved away the apology. "If we need to explain ourselves to our friends, then what is the world coming to?"

The room was quiet when Helene returned and switched on the light in the small foyer. In the big double bed the children lay sleeping. She bent over them and touched their faces, warm and lightly perspiring, then pulled the covers neatly beneath their chins and kissed each one carefully, so as not to wake them.

"How was your dinner?" asked Maurice from the darkness of the other bed.

"You're awake. I didn't mean to disturb you," answered Helene apologetically.

"You didn't wake me. I've been thinking."

Helene undressed, put on a nightgown, and slid into bed beside her husband.

"Good," she said. "When you're thinking, then I know that you're yourself again. I've been worried about you."

He put his arms around her and pulled her body close against his own.

"You're chilled," he said, running his hands along the coolness of her bare arms. "Let me warm you, then."

She lay atop him, her belly flat against his, her breasts, full and soft, cupped in his two hands.

"I'm sorry," he said.

She kissed him, and he pulled the nightgown over her hips and slowly entered her. She looked down at him as they made love together. "I worried about you so."

"What have I brought you to?" he said, caressing her.

"Shh," she murmured. "I have you back, and we are together."

She moved softly against him.

"Do I give you pleasure?" he asked.

"Yes," she said, "as no one else ever could."

"Tell me of the pleasure I give you," he said.

She held his hand against her sensitive flesh. "Feel how you excite me," she said, moving her hips as he touched her. She let out a small cry of delight, as much for the relief she felt in having him back the way he was as for the thrill of holding him within her.

They lay close together afterward.

"I've been dreaming about the others while I slept," said Maurice. "They appeared one by one, reproaching me for letting them go. But Gunter was there also, berating me for worrying about saving the whole world."

"Gunter was right," said Helene. She kissed him and held him close. "No one can save the world."

He looked down at her, lying so snugly in the crook of his arm. "You are turning out to be the practical one."

"I'm not practical. If you didn't lead, I wouldn't be able to follow," she said.

"I wonder . . ." he answered. His voice trailed off, and he was quiet for a few seconds. Then he said, "Do you know that Otto Boorstein was asked to go to America in 1933 to live and work? Einstein himself invited him. They had worked together at the Institute for Physics for twenty years."

"Why didn't he go?"

"Why didn't he go?" Maurice repeated mechanically. "He said that he could do his work in Germany as well as in the United States and that he was too old to learn to live comfortably in a strange country. Now he won't have to learn anything new ever again."

"Maybe they were going to wait for another train," said Helene. "How can we know, after all, what happened after we went on? Surely Karl would not have left them there if anything bad was to happen to them."

"Karl is not a humanitarian. He is no better than the rest of them. He has come this far because he knows that Gunter and I hold the group's money and that he will share in part of it."

"It is not like you to be cynical," said Helene. She stroked his cheek and smoothed his hair as though he were a child. "God has brought us this far. Even though I'm not religious, I feel His protection around us, as though He were shepherding us along our way."

"I have no faith any longer," said Maurice.

"I have faith, Maurice. Take faith from me. We must be strong. David and Miriam need both of us to be strong for them. They show so much promise. David is such a smart little boy, and Miriam . . . well, Miriam will shine as she grows as no child has ever shone before. I see it in her. You have not noticed, but she is more than a two-year-old. She understands things as well as David does. She can read words in David's books. Can you imagine such precociousness, Maurice, as our daughter has? And she is our creation. And God's."

"In my sleep I confused Rudolph Schneider with David," said Maurice. "Now that I am awake, it becomes increasingly difficult to think of my own two children without thinking of the other children."

"You make me afraid, Maurice."

"Then we'll be afraid together."

V

In 1926 Helene had had a taste of independence. The impresario Frederick Houck made a recording of Erika and Helene playing Mendelssohn's Concerto in D Minor for two pianos and then signed them to a concert tour of Europe. Erika was nineteen, Helene a year younger.

"For the first time in my life, Grandmama won't be able to tell me what to wear or how to stand or with whom to talk," said Helene.

"I leave my granddaughter in your capable hands," Grandmama said to Herr Houck before the tour. Herr Houck was fat and old, and Grandmama, who had been young and beautiful once, knew which men were dangerous to young girls and which were not.

Helene and Erika played the great cities of Europe, and everywhere they went men came backstage, offering gifts, extending invitations, but Herr Houck, true to Grandmama's instructions, was there to turn them away. In Paris Herr Houck had an attack of appendicitis and had to be hospitalized.

"Now is our chance to smoke and drink, to bob our hair and go to parties," said Erika, her eyes twinkling.

By summertime Herr Houck was well enough to report to Grandmama. "I am an impresario, not a chaperon."

Grandmama took the next train to the rehearsal hall in Brussels. "It is time to come home," she said.

"But we've done nothing wrong," protested Helene.

"I'm certain that you have had a lovely time, but I think that it is now time to come home to Berlin. There are, after all, things more important than playing the piano," she said in her Russian-accented German.

Later Grandmama sat on a chair in a corner of the hotel room, wearing her fur coat, smoking cigarette after cigarette in a solid-gold cigarette holder, watching while Helene packed. Erika and Helene and Grandmama returned to Berlin. The following February Erika mar-

ried Gunter Liebermann, and Helene retired from the concert stage.

"A concert career is not appropriate for a young lady," said Grandmama. "Believe me when I tell you that I know what is best for you. Besides, there are women who travel well alone, and there are those who don't."

In the morning Maurice woke early and dressed Miriam and David, and when Helene awakened, her husband seemed to be his old self again.

"Thank God it's morning," said Helene, studying his face for telltale signs of the depression of the day before. "I can be cowlike and strong for only so long," she continued, laughing, "and then I need you back again telling me what to do next."

"Then let me start by telling you that you have time for a long bath while I order breakfast for us."

Helene looked at her wristwatch. She had not wound it since the day before yesterday. "What time is it?" she asked, remembering the promise to Gunter.

"Early. Seven-thirty."

She stretched and sat up in the bed. "Gunter wants to see you at eight-thirty."

Maurice nodded.

David and Miriam stood at the side of the bed, looking at their mother for reassurance in the unfamiliar surroundings of the hotel room.

"Look at how shyly they look at me, Maurice," Helene said with a laugh. "Yes, it's me." She held out her arms to them. David clambered onto the bed, while Miriam could only tug at the bedclothes, one chubby leg extended upward. Helene lifted her up and sat her beside David, and then the three of them got under the covers.

"Where are you?" Helene called, pulling at David's stockinged foot in the darkness beneath the covers. He squealed with delight at the game. "Is this a Miriam I've caught?" asked Helene, now catching the baby in her arms.

"No. I David," said Miriam, scurrying to a far corner of the bed.

Maurice pulled the covers back. "I have three children, not two," he said.

"I like being your child," said Helene as she got up and headed toward the bathroom.

She ran the water into the tub, and as the steam condensed on the marble walls and ran in rivulets into the bath, she stepped into the water and abandoned herself to its luxurious warmth. Propping a towel beneath her head, she lay back, eyes closed, and thought of Grandmama in her lovely lace dressing gown as she served tea on the veranda in the crisp air of a spring day in Berlin. Bone china cups and saucers perched daintily in the kid-gloved hands of her women guests. Everyone came to Grandmama's home dressed as if to greet the Queen of the Netherlands. There were never any loud voices, only the rustle of silks as the ladies moved and the mingled fragrances of exotic perfumes. And Grandmama presided over it all with eccentric charm. She served tea out of a samovar that had once belonged to Catherine of Russia, and she peppered her conversation with Russian phrases while her guests salted theirs with French. She smoked cigarettes and encouraged the other women to learn to smoke also. Of her guests she required only that they be ladies and gentlemen and that the women never wear slacks or utter a word that couldn't be heard in a child's nursery. A world within a world. A place of unreality.

Helene turned on the cold water and splashed her face with it.

"Time to get dressed, Helene," Maurice called from the other room.

The taxicab was waiting in the entry courtyard of the hotel. Erika, Gunter, and Helene got into the back with the babies. Maurice sat in front next to the driver. Helene looked at her husband questioningly.

"Isn't Karl coming?" she asked.

"The appointment is for us alone," Maurice answered, not turning around.

The taxicab let them off at St. Peter's Square, next to a small shop that sold religious medals and reliquaries. Gunter and Maurice each held a baby, and they all walked over the bumpy stones of the huge square toward the Basilica of St.

Peter. An old woman, a heavy shawl around her shoulders, pressed close to Helene. She held a white plaster statue of the Virgin Mary close to Helene's face and said to her in English, "Virgin Mary pray for you." Helene shook her head. The old woman tried the same phrase in Italian.

"Nein, nein, danke," said Helene, walking faster. A group of black-gowned nuns, led by a frock-coated priest, was ahead of them now. The nuns carried bouquets of lilies wrapped in cellophane, and they sang in Italian, their high-pitched voices counterpointed by the raspy baritone of the priest.

Helene looked up at the colonnaded facade of St. Peter's when Gunter pointed to a balcony to the right of the main entrance. "The Pope blesses the crowd from that balcony. We are on neutral ground here. Italy's jurisdiction ends and Vatican City begins at St. Peter's Square."

Gunter and Maurice were in suits, Erika wore a green wool dress and a fitted gray coat with matching hat, and Helene wore the same fur-trimmed suit and hat that she had worn since the trip began. Outside in the square, their clothes showed the effects of the trip. Gunter's dark brown shoes were scuffed across the toes. The collar of Maurice's white shirt looked gray. But as they entered the dark, majestic interior of St. Peter's, the soil could not be seen, and they were indistinguishable from any of the other visitors to the basilica.

"I had forgotten how beautiful it is," said Helene, turning slowly in the filtered light of the apse of the basilica. The arches of the nave of the church floated above their heads and disappeared into the upper reaches of the basilica, lending grace and strength to the delicacy of medieval frescoes and mosaic and glass that hung like a man-made heaven 450 feet above them. Angels and saints and fat cherubs gazed down benevolently from niches in the marble piers. Richly carved wooden confessionals lined the walls, the language of the confessor written in white letters on their fronts. Some had their red lights on, signifying that the priest was within and the confessional was occupied.

"You wait here," said Maurice, handing David to Helene. "Gunter and I will be back for you in a minute." Erika took Miriam in her arms, and the two women stood alone in the center of the basilica, holding the two children. A nun passed them and smiled and said in Italian, "You may sit in the Cappella del Sacramento, if you like, and rest your feet. You will tire if you stand with the children for long."

Helene didn't understand the words, but the nun was motioning with her hand toward the side chapel, and she touched Miriam's chubby leg gently with her other hand.

"*Danke,*" said Helene, and the nun nodded and walked on.

Three elderly religious were in the chapel, on their knees, praying and saying their rosary beads, facing the baroque carved angels of the gilt-bronze tabernacle. Erika and Helene sat down on the last bench in the chapel. A priest was saying Mass, and the three nuns were rising in unison, genuflecting, then rising again. Once, the oldest nun faltered and rested her hand on one knee, unable to lift herself again. The other two offered assistance, but she waved them away and rose stiffly and slowly to her full height.

"No dispensation, even for age, I suppose," commented Helene.

"She has a choice. She chooses to do it that way," answered Erika. "I, as a lapsed Catholic, on the other hand, have chosen the path to perdition."

"Because you're married to a Jew?"

"Yes. The Church considers me a sinner, but still I feel renewed when I'm in a church. I can't explain it. I don't believe it on an intellectual level, but I'm bound to it on a childlike level."

"I feel the same way when I'm in the synagogue. I remember my grandfather telling me to sit up and listen to the rabbi and be proud. But only the cantor's songs held any interest for me."

"We should perform your transcription of Kol Nidre here in St. Peter's," said Erika, looking up at the vaulted ceilings.

Helene laughed. "I don't think so."

"Yes, we could," said Erika. "Up there, you see the niche where the angels are holding the dying Jesus?"

"Yes."

"That's where the cantor would stand. And over there, on that little balcony, would be the flautist and the violinist."

"I can hear it," said Helene. She hummed the melody to

the sound of the imagined flute and violin. "The acoustics would be wonderful."

The chords of the cathedral organ rang out, followed by a chorus of male voices that swelled in volume and filled the basilica, echoing through the apse toward the main altar.

"Look," said Helene, turning to see through the iron grill-work of the chapel.

A scarlet-coated cardinal, his red biretta atop his gray hair, was leading a processional across the left transept toward the center of the basilica. Behind the cardinal marched two white-gowned priests, bare-headed, and behind them followed men in black uniforms with eight-pointed Maltese crosses painted on their capes. One soldier at each corner of the group held aloft a black flag with the same cross displayed on it.

"My God, are they German soldiers of some kind?" asked Helene in alarm. "We are not safe from them even here."

"No, they're not soldiers. You see, the people marching behind them are wearing ordinary clothes," said Erika.

"Then who are they?"

"The Knights of Malta."

The cardinal and his assistants marched to the papal altar, accompanied by the choir music that now reverberated throughout the basilica. The uniformed knights took their places as honor guards on either side of the papal altar. The pilgrims filed into their seats behind the lighted candles of the balustrade of the confession, and the voices sang louder as the organ music dipped and swelled, crescendo upon crescendo. The cardinal stood, head bowed, until the music peaked and the voices were stilled, and then in the silence that followed, he began to give his sermon in German.

"That is Cardinal Feltzman," said Gunter as he and Maurice entered the chapel and sat down.

"Did you talk to him?" asked Helene anxiously.

"We talked to his secretary," answered Maurice. "The Cardinal is aware of our appointment. That much is certain. The secretary knows nothing else about it, but when the Mass is over, we are to have a private audience with the Cardinal in his Vatican office."

"The secretary knows we are Jews?" asked Helene.

"I'm not sure," said Maurice. "We didn't want to disturb anything at this point. The Cardinal is the one Karl said we are to talk to, not the secretary."

Helene shuddered in the coldness of the chapel. "There are so many Germans here, I feel I am back in Berlin."

"They can't harm you here," said Gunter.

"The Cardinal has a kind face," said Helene, "but he is talking about love of country and love of God in the same breath."

"Cardinals are politicians, too," said Gunter. "These are Germans he is talking to. He must not ruffle any feathers unnecessarily. What his private feelings are, we'll soon find out."

Cardinal Feltzman's chambers were in a building adjoining the papal palace. His secretary greeted the Liebermanns and the Gelsons in the walnut-paneled anteroom.

"His Eminence will see you now," said the secretary, who looked very official in his priest's vestments with a large gold cross hanging down against the middle of his concave chest.

"Before you enter, there are certain subjects that I must ask you not to touch upon," said the priest. "Those are: what the Cardinal thinks of the ethics or politics of any world nation, and any questions dealing with the Holy See's position on the refugee question."

"Which refugee question?" asked Gunter.

"Any refugee question," retorted the secretary. "The Holy See, when it deems the time right, will reveal its position on all worldly issues, and it will not discuss them in any manner beforehand. If the subject has been dealt with in papal encyclical or decree, then you can ask me for a proper citation, and I will direct you to where you may read that citation for yourself."

"I see," said Maurice. "Anything else?"

"No. His Eminence is always glad to have visitors from Germany."

The walls of the Cardinal's inner chambers were lined with Flemish tapestries, and his windows opened onto the

Vatican gardens and their precision-clipped hedges. The Cardinal sat behind his desk, and when the group was ushered in, he got up and walked around toward where they stood.

"My name is Gunter Liebermann, and this is my wife, Erika Liebermann, your Eminence."

"And I am Maurice Gelson. My children, Miriam and David. My wife, Helene."

The Cardinal chucked David under the chin and patted Miriam on the head. "You had an appointment with me?" he asked.

"Yes, your Eminence," said Gunter. "The appointment was made for us by Count Karl von Kirchner."

"Ah, yes, I do remember that now. And what was this appointment to be about? You wish a private blessing, do you? Or perhaps I can recommend an audience with the Holy Father on Sunday next. He sees twenty to thirty people in the Sunday audiences, and I can do my utmost to see that you are invited to attend."

Gunter looked at Maurice. It was clear that Karl had told the Cardinal nothing of the purpose of their visit. The secretary stood by the door watching closely to see that his rules for the conversation were obeyed. Maurice blinked rapidly. How were they not to talk of politics or the refugee problem when they were here as refugees?

"We need the Vatican's intercession, your Eminence," said Maurice, hoping to speak before the secretary pulled them bodily from the room. "We have come about safe conduct."

"I beg your pardon?" responded the Cardinal, smiling, his full face wreathed in benevolence.

"The babies," interrupted Helene. Gunter looked at her as though hoping she had the way to express the inexpressible.

"What about the babies, my child?" said the Cardinal.

"We would like to take them away where it is safe," said Helene.

"And where would that be?"

"I don't know."

"But you are German, aren't you?"

"We are German Jews, your Eminence."

"Yes, I see." The Cardinal's smile was fading. He looked across the room to his secretary. The secretary began to open the outer door to the anteroom.

"We were told the Vatican could issue safe-conduct visas," interjected Maurice. "Perhaps to Switzerland."

"Ah, but you see, that is the function of your government," said the Cardinal. "The Holy See does not interfere with the internal affairs of duly constituted governments."

"But we were told, your Eminence—" continued Maurice.

"But you were told wrongly, you see. Someone has made a terrible mistake. I am sorry if you have come a long way to see me on this matter, but I am not in a position to help you. Nobody in the Vatican is in a position to help you. We cannot intervene. You must understand our delicate position in these matters."

"But what will we do, then?" asked Helene in a frightened voice.

"Do? But why must you do anything? You are in Italy on visas, are you not?"

"The visas expire in four more days, your Eminence," said Gunter, "and there is to be no renewal."

The Cardinal shook his head sadly. "You must go to your consulate, then, for assistance."

"Jews have no standing with the German consulate, your Eminence," said Maurice wearily.

The Cardinal's smile had returned. "One thing we can do before you leave. We can give you medals for the children. The medals have been blessed by the Holy Father. I will pray for you all in my evening prayers. The Lord will hold you in his hands and care for you."

The Cardinal kissed Miriam on her rosy cheek. "Would you like a medal, my child?" he asked.

Miriam held out her hand, and he placed it in her palm. "Bless you, my child," he said.

He turned to Helene. "The children appear well and healthy, a tribute to their good care and upbringing. I'm sure that you will continue to care for them well and see to their spiritual health, as well as their physical health. Milk is important to growing bodies, but prayer is essential for inner peace and spiritual growth. We must always be aware that there are certain things that are man's and certain things that are God's, and we must not confuse the two; we must not try to twist the one into the other. It cannot be done, my children. It cannot be done. Man will try to confound you, but with God's help you shall find your way. May his spirit guide you in all your endeavors."

The Cardinal made the sign of the cross over the Jews standing before him, and then the door to the anteroom swung wide open, and the secretary led the visitors away.

VI

The slate-gray Savoia-Marchetti bombers flew first tier, the Macchi fighters directly below them. The airplanes maneuvered in military precision above the heads of the Romans gathered in the Piazza del Popolo, and as though by telepathic communication, the lead bomber tilted its wings and its companion planes bent into the identical arc, the planes playing to each other and to the crowds below, who screamed and cheered at each swoop of the formation. On the reviewing stand stood Count Ciano, with the Spanish Minister of the Interior, Ramón Serrano Suñer, beside him. Ten thousand Italian soldiers marched and strutted past the reviewing stand and the mass of spectators in the piazza.

The outdoor café on the edge of the piazza was filled with people, some standing on chairs to get a better look at the fully equipped soldiers. David stood on Helene's lap, his tiny, dark face turned upward to the sky, fingers pointing at the powerful machines now leaning to the east, toward the Tiber River.

In a corner Maurice sat quietly, his chair against the building, the green and orange awning of the café hiding his face. Erika held Miriam on her lap. Gunter's arm encircled Erika's shoulder. No one had spoken since they left St. Peter's. It was as though they had come from the last vigil at a dying friend's bedside. They couldn't speak of the friend's death just yet. Later they would be able to acknowledge it, to seek out the things that still linked the deceased friend to the living. But now they let the roar of the airplanes and the sight of Mussolini's "volunteer" Spanish fighters fill their brains and numb their senses.

"They're being decorated for the bombing of Barcelona," said Gunter without emotion. "Four days and four nights of bombing. Franco has sent his brother-in-law, Suñer, to decorate the Italian Army for helping him defeat the Loyalists."

"Miriam's cheeks feel very warm," said Erika. The child's rosy cheeks were pinker than usual, and she was perspiring in the cool Roman air.

"Maurice"—Helene turned toward her husband—"Erika is right. Miriam is very flushed. Perhaps we should get back to the hotel room."

"It's not important," he said from beneath the striped awning.

"But if we are to travel, she must not get sick," persisted Helene.

Maurice laughed a tiny, rueful laugh. "Explain to my wife about our travel plans, Gunter."

Gunter turned his face toward Helene, his round gray eyes rounder and grayer behind his spectacles. "Things are difficult, Helene," said Gunter.

Helene held David's legs closer to her chest. "How difficult?"

"Let me explain," said Gunter. He leaned toward her, his voice low. "It is a matter of destination, Helene. Destination is everything now." He glanced quickly at Maurice and then back to Helene. "It would seem that we would do best to separate, try to find our own destinations as best we can. Since the visas are good for only a few days more, if we are to find a destination, it must be done quickly."

"I think you should go by yourselves, then," said Maurice in a quiet voice.

"It might be best," answered Gunter, his voice almost drowned out by the sound of cannon-fire salutes and marching feet as the soldiers paraded before the reviewing stand.

"And the diamonds, we must dispose of them, hide them somewhere," said Gunter. "We can no longer count on Karl's protection. We must think of a hiding place. Later we can come back for them, perhaps even send for them. Who knows?"

"Do as you wish," answered Maurice.

"We must have some money to travel," said Helene, turning again toward her husband. "We must, mustn't we?"

"We must," he answered.

"You will keep the gold coins that are in Maurice's medicine kit," said Gunter. "I will keep some from the suitcase, and the rest will be hidden with the diamonds. I haven't thought where to hide the diamonds, there has been so little time. But in the morning we will decide, and then Maurice and I will go together to the hiding place. We'll both know, then, where it is."

"Perhaps we should each take some diamonds with us," said Helene.

"And do what, trade a diamond for a loaf of bread?" said Gunter. "No, it's too dangerous. When we have made contact with someone who can secure visas for us, we can retrieve enough to pay for the visas, and then, after the war, God willing, we'll come back for the rest."

"God willing," Helene repeated.

Miriam's fever rose in the evening. Maurice seemed strangely apathetic to the baby's cranky cry. Helene took the child into the marble bathroom and pulled an upholstered straight chair up to the sink. She sponged the baby's face and body with cool water and sang to her in a low voice while David played quietly on the floor with his miniature metal touring car.

"David, hand me the towel, please," said Helene. David put down the car and brought a heavy white towel from the stack of towels on the utility table.

"Thank you, darling. You're such a helper, do you know that, David?" she said, blotting Miriam's wet body with the towel. "When you grow up, you'll be a doctor like Dada and help people when they're sick, won't you, David?" Maurice's mood had begun to have an effect on David. While Miriam napped before dinner, David had sat close to his mother on the settee, looking up at her face frequently as if to make sure that she hadn't disappeared.

Too fussy to drink the warm milk that was brought in on the dinner tray, Miriam was put to bed early. Maurice ate nothing.

"Come, David, let me tell you a story, and then you will go to bed, too," said Helene, drawing David onto her lap on the settee. Maurice lay down on the bed and stared up at the ceiling.

"There was a little boy named David." She waited for his usual smile, because all of the little boys in Helene's bedtime stories were named David, and David always smiled at that. "Come on, David, smile for Mama. That's good. Now, this little boy named David was far from home in a land called Italy. In this land called Italy, David was asked by the Queen if he wanted to go on a long voyage."

David nodded his head and began to suck his thumb as he had when he was Miriam's age.

"Now, the Queen of Italy had many people in her country whom she could send on long voyages, but this little boy David, with his big black eyes and his friendly smile, was the one she wanted."

David took his thumb out of his mouth and said, "I'll fly the airplane."

"Of course you'll fly the airplane," said Helene. "So the Queen of Italy said, 'On this voyage I want you to take your sister and your mother and your father, and I want you not to be afraid of anything, because I have an army that will protect you.'"

David's eyes widened.

"'Nobody will dare to hurt David or his sister or his mother or his father,' said the Queen of Italy. 'And to prove that I mean what I say, I want him always to wear this badge. It will protect him wherever he goes.'" Helene removed the cameo brooch that she wore at the neck of her blouse and pinned it to David's pajamas. David put his hand over the brooch and smiled. Helene stood up and tucked a blanket around him, and soon he was asleep.

"You shouldn't tell him stories like that," said Maurice, as Helene sat down on the bed next to him.

"Do you notice how frightened he looks?" said Helene. "He hardly speaks above a whisper. It's as if he thought someone were going to strike him."

"Whose fault is that?"

"Don't talk about fault. He is suffering from the same

thing we all are, and when he looks to you for guidance, it's not there. I feel that way, too; I'm afraid to talk to you now. It is as though you might disintegrate at a word from me." She bent and kissed his cheek. "Come, Maurice, tell me that I need to be told what direction to walk, as you did at home. Don't you remember you used to laugh at me when I could not decide what dress to wear or what to serve at parties or what to give the servants at Christmas?"

"You are living in a dream world, Helene," he said.

"All of life is a dream world, Maurice. You told me that yourself. Tell me again how impractical I am, that you will take hold of the group again, and that we will find a safe place to go with the children."

"There is no group any longer, and I know of no safe place to go."

Her tears fell across his arm. "Please, don't say things like that. I have told David that we would be protected, that all will be well."

"You told him lies, nothing but lies," he said as he turned away from her.

Some time in the middle of the night, Helene awoke. She thought she had heard a light knock at the door. Maurice still slept. She put on her robe and opened the door and looked out into the corridor. Count von Kirchner stood beneath the ceiling chandelier, the gold braid on his officer's cap gleaming in the yellow light.

"*Guten Abend,*" said the Count. "May I come in?"

Helene hesitated a moment. "They're sleeping," she said.

"I'm awake," said Maurice behind her.

Helene opened the door, and the Count walked into the room and sat down in the wing chair next to the sleeping David. Helene stood next to Miriam's bed and rocked the bed gently to soothe the fretful child's cries.

"You have bad news," said Maurice as he sat down on the edge of the bed.

"I come at an inconvenient time, I know," said the Count, "but I feel my task has not been completed until I bid you farewell and apprise you of the fact that your traveling companions have left the hotel."

Helene stopped rocking Miriam's bed. "Left the hocel? You mean that they have gone out?"

"No," said the Count. "They have retrieved their passports from the concierge and have left the hotel."

Maurice looked at the Count. "The diamonds?"

The Count nodded. "Everything is gone from their room. It is quite empty of any sign of them."

"There is a mistake," said Helene in a daze. "Gunter would not leave us and take everything with him. Erika would not let him do such a thing."

"I am sorry to be the bearer of unsettling news, my dear Helene. I also had looked forward to sharing in the diamonds, but in circumstances like this, we must go forward, each to his own plans. Basically, my responsibility to you is officially ended. I did not receive any compensation, but you also did not obtain visas from the Cardinal. We are both disappointed."

"We must remain calm," said Helene. "We must think of something, of somewhere to go."

"I know of no country that will receive you," said the Count.

"Switzerland, is there a chance for Switzerland?" asked Maurice.

"It would be foolish to try," said the Count. "The winter weather has set in already, and the Swiss are detaining refugees in their jails at the border and then sending them back across. There is war now in all of Europe. I know of no country that will allow you entry."

"We have children with us," said Helene, her voice rising. "What do you mean that no one will allow us entry? They must! I have told David that we would be saved."

The Count shrugged. Miriam gave a piercing scream, and Helene lifted her up into her arms. "There, there, it's all right, it's all right."

Maurice sat on the edge of the bed, his head in his hands, while Helene rocked Miriam in her arms and patted her on the back soothingly. "What will the Italians do to us if we stay in Italy?" asked Helene, more calmly.

"Send you back to Germany," said the Count.

"Then you are saying we are doomed?"

"I am saying that I can no longer help you."

• • • • •

She could not sleep. Maurice had said they would sleep, and in the morning Miriam's fever would be gone and the solution to their dilemma would present itself. So she lay beside him. He did not touch her. They were each separate in their minds and bodies. What was he thinking of? Did he have an answer for them that he had not yet finalized? He had dropped so heavily into the bed, and yet she knew that he lay awake beside her.

"Have you thought of anything yet?" she asked him in the darkness. But he did not answer, and exhausted with thinking, she finally slept.

It was the running of water in the bathroom or the metallic sound of a case being opened and closed that woke her. She reached toward Maurice, but the bed was empty. She listened now for the sound of Miriam's raspy breathing. She sat up, her eyes straining to accommodate themselves to the dark room. Miriam was quiet now. Maurice was standing beside the bed where Miriam lay. Helene sank back against the pillows.

"Is she better, Maurice?" she asked. "She had a fever in just the same way in February. Do you remember that? I'm so glad that you are here to take care of her." Silent. It was so silent.

Helene sat upright suddenly, threw the covers back, and threw herself across the other bed, across the still body of her baby.

"What are you doing? Why is she so quiet?"

Maurice moved backward a few steps and then turned toward the settee, where David lay. Helene rushed toward her husband, pushing him against the wall. She grabbed David in her arms and ran across the room so that the beds were between her and her husband. She clutched David's warm body next to her own.

Maurice had regained his balance. As though across a great chasm, he called to his wife from the other side of the room. "It's best, Helene. Miriam is safe now. We can all be safe. Fast, painless." He held the hypodermic up in front of his face. "Our visa, Helene. Here is our visa."

"Maurice, no, no, Maurice, you mustn't. My God, what have you done?"

He had a puzzled look on his face. He gazed down at the baby, then at the hypodermic in his hand. Then he began to cry. Tears coursing down his face, he plunged the hypodermic needle into his arm. Then he lay down on the bed next to his daughter. Giant sobs racked his body for a few seconds, and then he gasped and sat up in the bed, his hands extended toward Helene. When he fell back again, he made no more sounds.

VII

Grandfather Rosenzweig had spent all of 1922 dying. A whole year. He stopped going to his office in Der Bau Rosenzweig and passed most of his days in bed. The house became a small hospital as doctors and nurses visited, bringing breathing masks and oxygen tanks, and testing and charting his vital functions. Grandmama acted as though nothing unusual were happening. She had people in for tea and told Walter to dress Herr Rosenzweig in a suit and place him, tucked in blankets, in a corner of the music room while Helene played for the guests. The mayor of Berlin called at the gabled house twice during the year to inquire after Grandfather's condition. A Mass was said by Grandfather's Catholic employees, and a medal was struck by the city of Berlin to honor Grandfather's philanthropies.

At the end of the year, he died, on schedule, as the doctors had predicted. Grandmama gave up smoking cigarettes for the seven days of Shivah, and Grandfather was buried in the Jewish cemetery with a little sack of soil from Eretz Yisroel in the coffin with him. His death was real and logical. Grandmama mourned but said to Helene, "His was a blessed death."

"David, David," Helene crooned to her son as they sat huddled together in a corner of the room.

"Daddy?" He looked up at her questioningly, his eyes searching her face for an explanation of why his father and sister lay so silently together on the bed across the room.

"Turn your face to me, David," she said when he looked toward them. "Keep your face close to mine."

"Daddy and Miriam sleeping," said David as Helene rocked him in her arms.

"Yes," she said, her tears falling on David's upturned face.

"Daddy and Miriam are tired," she said, holding David tightly. "They are very tired."

There was a clatter of trays in the hall, the sound of knocking on a door close by, then low voices resonating through the corridors as the waiter exchanged morning pleasantries with the occupant of the room next door. Helene shifted position against the wall. David still slept in her lap, his hand clutching the hem of her nightgown. She had not dared to stand up, to walk toward the bed where Maurice and Miriam lay side by side.

The door to the next room closed, and she heard the clink of porcelain bouncing on metal as the breakfast cart continued down the corridor. Then there was the sound of knocking outside their door. David opened his eyes and looked up at his mother. She smoothed his hair and began to cry.

"*Buon giorno,*" called the waiter from outside the door. Helene didn't answer. The waiter put his key into the lock and opened the door and looked across the room to where Maurice and his daughter lay. Then he opened the door wider and pushed the breakfast cart into the room.

"*Buon giorno,*" he said again as he spread the snowy linen on the side table and placed the fresh pink carnation in the center. He set out the children's milk and the pot of coffee, and as he walked around to the other side of the table to place the basket of croissants, he saw Helene and David huddled together on the floor near the bathroom door. Startled, he dropped the basket onto the floor. He looked from Helene to the figures on the bed, trying to comprehend what the scene meant. He had been a waiter in the Grand for twenty-five years. He could figure out a domestic problem or a health crisis instantly. The woman was curled into a corner with the little boy, as though she were afraid of being beaten by her husband. And yet there was no movement that he could discern from the figures on the bed. No movement at all. Helene was looking at him with the same dark eyes as the boy's. They looked like a nice Italian family.

"I'm sorry about the rolls," said the waiter in Italian, "but you startled me. I will bring fresh ones."

Helene didn't answer or make any sign that she understood or even heard him. He approached her cautiously. "May I help you up? I will take the boy first, and then you can stand up, if you take my arm."

Helene didn't answer. The waiter repeated the same thing, this time in fluent French.

"*Oui,*" said Helene.

"Ah, you are French. My father was a Frenchman. A merchant seaman."

She still did not respond. Then he knelt down and picked David up. He walked with him to the side table and poured a glass of milk, and while he held him, David took the glass in both of his hands and drank the milk eagerly. A cheval mirror stood facing the waiter between the window and the side table. As David drank, the waiter studied the reflections of the figures on the bed.

David handed the empty glass to the waiter, who placed it on the table.

"Would you like a bath?" asked the waiter. David stared at him, not understanding the language but soothed and fascinated by the elderly man's calm attentions. The waiter carried him into the bathroom and sat him on a chair while he turned the water faucets on in the bathtub.

"Now, you sit in the chair, and when the water gets high enough, you call to me, and I will help you with your bath. All right?"

David smiled tentatively, understanding the man's gestures though not his words.

"It's all right," said the waiter. "Your mama is here. You wait for me to come back. Okay?" The waiter waved to him and shut the door to the bathroom partway, so that the noise of the running water would obliterate any sounds from the rest of the suite.

"*Prego,*" said the gray-haired waiter. He extended his hand to Helene and helped her to her feet. Together the morning-coated waiter and the nightgowned, barefoot Helene walked toward the bed where Maurice and Miriam lay. The waiter touched Maurice's hand where it rested against the blonde curls of the little girl.

"Ay, ay, ay," the waiter groaned at the touch of the cold, lifeless flesh.

Helene drew closer to the bed. It was as though they were sleeping. So many times she had seen Maurice in sleep before. And how often had she stood just in this way and looked down at Miriam as she slept, all golden curls and pink cheeks. But the cheeks weren't pink now. Helene leaned toward her child. She touched the honey tendrils that lay hidden beneath the thicker curls at the nape of the neck. They felt like softly wound threads of silk. She ran her fingers over the baby's face, feeling the skin, taut and smooth as marble, the nose, so tiny, the lips, still pouty and full. The waiter was kneeling at the side of the bed, his head in his hands. He prayed aloud in a rolling Italian basso.

Helene took her husband's cold, stiff hand in her own warm one. Then she knelt beside the waiter, and with her eyes closed she listened to his voice reciting the prayers.

The waiter stopped and turned to her. "Are you a Catholic?"

She shook her head. "A Jew."

The waiter stared at the bodies for a while. He picked up the hypodermic needle that lay beside Maurice and turned it over gingerly in his hand. "I know no Jewish prayers," he said.

Helene took Miriam's hand in hers; the fingers were stiff and unyielding. She kissed them. *"Shema Yisroel adonoy eloheynu adonoy echod."* It was the only Hebrew prayer she knew. "Hear, O Israel; The Lord our God, the Lord is One."

"My name is Pietro Maldini," said the waiter.

"I am Helene Gelson."

Pietro laid the hypodermic needle on the bedside table and sat down on the opposite bed, his hands between his knees. "What has happened here?"

"I'm German. From Berlin. We had hoped to find help in Italy to escape the Nazis, but our money has been taken and our Italian visas expire in two days. There was nowhere for us to go, no one to help us, and my husband despaired for our lives." She shivered as she spoke. "He has been depressed, without hope, inconsolable. Perhaps I knew that this was possible. Perhaps I even felt for one moment when he held the needle in his hand that I would let him kill David and me also and be done with it."

"But you did not."

"No. Something in me prevented it."

"You know no one in Italy, no one to go to?" he asked.

"No one."

Her eyes never left Miriam's face as she talked. "My husband was a good man, a doctor. He could not have done this if he were not out of his mind."

"Their clothes?" asked the waiter when she had finished. "We must not leave them unclothed. It is only respect."

"Yes, I will help you," said Helene.

She turned away from Miriam and walked to the closet. Maurice's suit hung there alongside Miriam's pink dress and matching coat. Helene brought them to the bed and placed them across Maurice's feet. She trembled as her fingers brushed against his cold flesh.

Pietro went into the bathroom. "The water is high enough, I see," he said to David. He turned off the water. "But you must wait until I finish helping your mother. Then I will come back, and you will have a fine bath."

Pietro took two towels and soaked them in the warm water of the bathtub, then wrung them out and carried them back to where Helene stood looking at the bodies.

"You are doing very well," he said, handing her one of the towels. Pietro removed Maurice's pajamas and cleaned the body with the wet towel.

"She is our baby, Miriam, only two years old," said Helene, looking down at Miriam. Pietro said nothing, and then Helene knelt down beside the bed and carefully removed the baby's pajamas. The skin was alabaster smooth to her touch. It was not her baby's skin.

Pietro dressed Maurice. He tied his tie and combed his hair and put on his shoes and socks. "A very handsome man," he said, standing back to view the body.

Helene struggled with the buttons of the pink coat, then the hat framing the expressionless face. She bent close to Miriam's mouth. "She knows so many words," she said aloud. "She is so quiet, when I know she longs to talk to me."

"I will bathe and dress the boy while you get ready. The maid will be here soon and will find them," said Pietro.

"We have no place to go," said Helene from her position beside Miriam's body.

"There is room with my family."

Helene started to cry again. Pietro patted her shoulder and then went into the bathroom.

"Such a big, strong boy," said Pietro as he washed David's legs. "You're going to help your mother from now on. I can see that."

When David was dressed, Pietro brought him to Helene. She had put on her suit, but her eyes were puffy from crying, and her hair hung in tangles around her face.

"I will tell them I have to go home, that my wife is sick," said Pietro, "and then you and the boy will go home with me. But your hair—you must walk through the lobby," said Pietro. "You will have to retrieve your passport. You must not draw attention as you walk through the lobby of the hotel." Helene stood like an obedient child while Pietro combed her hair.

David had not said anything to her, but she saw the fright in his face as he glanced at the bodies on the bed.

"Come here, darling," she said, holding her arms out to him. "You must say good-bye to Dada and Miriam."

She walked to the bed with David in her arms.

"Remember how I told you about the Queen of Italy?"

David touched the cameo that Pietro had removed from his pajamas and pinned to David's shirt front. He nodded, but the fear was still in his eyes as she held him close to his father's body.

"Dada and Miriam are not going to go on the voyage, David," said Helene. "See how peacefully Dada is sleeping." Her voice broke. "Would you like to kiss Dada good night?"

David nodded and reached toward Maurice's cold cheek and kissed it. Then he touched Miriam's face but pulled his hand back quickly and looked at Helene.

"That is what it means to die, David. We just go to sleep. That's all."

• • • • •

Pietro's apartment was in a thirteenth-century fortress on a hill looking down at the equestrian statue of Marcus Aurelius. From the apartment there was a clear view of the Coliseum and the grass-covered Circus Maximus, and out beyond to the crumbling Aurelian Wall and the ancient gateway to Rome. The fortress, like the Coliseum and the Circus Maximus and the Wall, was now only a vestige, a reminder of Rome's past. Washing hung from the windows of the fortress like disheveled battle flags, and cooking odors floated from the windows of its tenement apartments. Women called to their children playing in the narrow, dirt-littered streets below.

In addition to Pietro and his wife, Anna, their son, Errico, and his wife, Rosa, and their four young children lived in the apartment. Pietro and his wife slept in the only bedroom. Errico and his family occupied the large, square, cold room on the other side of the corridor. During the day, when the washing, cleaning, and shopping were done and the Roman streets were alive with people below, Anna and her daughter-in-law leaned out the shuttered windows, and while the old Victrola that Pietro had bought Anna on their wedding day in 1899 scratched out tinny music, they gossiped with their neighbors at the window next to theirs. Ever watchful, Anna interrupted her conversation to shout words of caution whenever the children playing on the street below grew too rowdy.

Later, when the lights of the city came on, Anna and Rosa prepared the evening meal in the kitchen they shared with the neighbors in the apartment to their left. Their daily routine almost never varied. Pietro talked about Mussolini and Hitler with Errico, but talk of politics was uninteresting to Rosa, and Anna was more concerned with the outcome of her cousin's hernia operation and how they would find room for the new baby that Rosa was going to have in March. Those concerns were all she could manage and all she could think about when Pietro brought the German woman and her child home with him and told her to set two more places at the dinner table that evening.

"You're crazy. We barely have enough for ourselves,"

snapped Anna. "The woman looks rich. Get her a room in the hotel."

Helene and David stood in the corridor at the entrance to the kitchen. She wore her fur-trimmed suit, and David his blue suit with matching coat and cap. Helene's dark eyes appeared to be rimmed in kohl, they were so deep-set, so dark and tired-looking. She seemed not to understand what Anna and Pietro were saying.

Rosa came into the kitchen from the outer room. She looked at the well-dressed visitors for a few seconds, then turned her back on them and went to the sink and began to grate cheese for dinner.

Pietro sighed. Anna was more and more difficult to communicate with. She no longer saw beyond the walls of her fortress apartment. She encountered the outside world only in the market, on the streets below her window, and at Sunday Mass. She had grown fat and gray, and was concerned only with how well her family ate. She monitored their slop pail in the downstairs toilet. Constipation was to her a life-threatening sign. To move one's bowels and to eat well were God's commandments. Why else would He have given human beings stomachs and appetites? For Pietro to explain to Anna what was going on in the world beyond her windows was a monumental undertaking. Until now it had never seemed important. All Anna knew of politics was that they ate better now that Mussolini was in power and that a neighbor woman had said that Mussolini was a miracle worker who had halted the flow of lava on Mount Etna before it destroyed an entire village that lay in its path. To Anna, then, Mussolini was not a politician, but a messenger sent from God to guide the Italian people to more food and better bowel movements.

Pietro, however, read the newspapers. In the beginning he and his son, Errico, had been sure that Mussolini would bring back Italy's greatness, the greatness that they were reminded of when they gazed out at the Aurelian Wall from their window. But now Mussolini talked of a war with Britain, and he had already sent planes and money to bomb Spain in a war in which he didn't belong. And the clumsiness of the goose-stepping Italian soldiers as they attempted to imitate Hitler's precision troops was an embarrassment to Pietro, who read about Italy's shortage of uniforms and military equipment in the clandestine newspapers that now circulated around Rome. It was even said that when newsreel footage of the strutting Mussolini was shown in the cinemas, the people jeered and hooted at him in the darkness of the theaters.

All this was impossible to tell Anna. She did not understand the significance of the racial laws, that problems were being created where none had existed before. There had never been a problem with Jews in Italy. The Jews lived like everyone else. They looked like the Italians, they talked like the Italians. They were Italians. And now Mussolini was saying that the Jews were not Italians at all, but were of an inferior race that must be driven from Italy, and that no good Italian should have the slightest pity for their plight. Mixed marriages were now forbidden, as was Jewish service in the armed forces, the teaching of non-Jews by Jews, and Jewish ownership of defense factories. Civil service administrations, banks, and insurance companies had to fill their jobs with non-Jews.

Piux XI had spoken up only once in behalf of the Jews, in the Vatican newspaper, the *Osservatore Romano.* He had accused Mussolini of imitating Hitler, and in retaliation Mussolini had unleashed Count Ciano on the Pope and on his apostolic nuncio. Capitulation came from the Vatican in the form of an announcement that the racial problem was indeed a fundamental one for Italy. Pietro did not fret over the Church's cowardice. He had long understood that the Church's position was that Jews were good only when they were Catholics.

"The woman and her son will stay here with us, Anna," said Pietro firmly. "They have no place to go." He used his authoritative voice with her when it was absolutely necessary that she accept an order.

Anna looked from him to Helene and David standing forlornly in the corridor. She contrasted her own lumpy figure in the cotton housedress, a dirty apron tied around her waist, with the figure of the slim, well-dressed stranger in front of her. The woman looked like the models in the pages of the fashion magazines that Rosa sometimes bought at the market. Hearing Pietro's tone of voice, Anna changed her expression from one of belligerent outrage to one of grudging obedience.

"Come, come," said Pietro to Helene. "You are welcome here."

In the quietness of the Roman night, Pietro lay beside his wife in the deep, muslin-covered feather bed. Helene and David were asleep on a borrowed mattress on the kitchen floor. There was the muffled sound of crying from one of the grandchildren across the corridor.

"I don't understand why she must stay here," said Anna.

"Then we will throw her outside." Pietro sat up in the bed and pulled the covers off his wife's rounded belly.

"Pietro, you are a crazy man." She yanked at the covers, smoothing and pulling them up around her neck.

"Then I am a crazy man," he said, lying back down again. "We will go to sleep now that we are agreed I am a crazy man."

"Who is she?"

"She is a German. Her husband was a doctor."

"Her husband? And where is he now? Why is she looking for charity when she dresses in furs and has a husband who is a doctor?"

"Why do you ask so many questions? You never want to know anything, and now you will not shut up with the questions. It is late. I am not as young as I once was. I cannot work all day and not sleep at night. Give me peace, Anna, please."

There was silence for a while. Neither of them slept. Finally, in a very low, conciliatory voice, Anna asked, "I will not call you a crazy man, then. You are not crazy. But you have never brought strangers into our house before."

"Times are different, Anna. It is time to bring strangers into the house."

"Then this is a political thing you are doing? Is she a spy?" Anna sat up in the bed at the thought of a spy sleeping in her kitchen. "My God, my Christ, she is a spy," she exclaimed. "You and your newspapers and your endless talk of politics, you will get us killed."

"Go to sleep," said Pietro. "She is not a spy. Will you be calm and compose yourself if I tell you the truth?"

"I swear, as the Holy Mother is my sacred protector."

"Then I will tell you. She is a Jewess. This morning her husband killed himself and murdered their two-year-old baby daughter because he feared there was no place in the world that would take him and his family in."

There was a sharp intake of breath next to him, and Anna reached for her rosary beads that hung on the corner post of the bed. She held the beads in her hands and began to tell them in a rapid, staccato voice.

Pietro stopped talking. After the telling of the tenth bead, Anna's recitation broke off as abruptly as it had started. "But she is alive. Why did he not harm her and the boy?"

"She prevented him from killing the boy. She broke the spell. Then he ended his own life."

"Mother of God, Mother of God, where are you in these perilous times?" cried Anna. "Mother of God, sweet Mother of God." She chanted and prayed at the same time.

"The Church is quiet, Anna. The Mother of God is with you and me here in this bedroom. The woman is strong. She looks frail, but she is not. She and I bathed the bodies. I dressed the husband in his suit. She dressed the baby as if she would take the child to meet the Pope. She cried in the beginning, but then there were no more tears. We left them lying together. Before we left, she held the boy up and showed him his father's face one last time. She had him touch the bodies so that he wouldn't be afraid."

"Oh, my God, what test the Lord has put her through. She doesn't look able to carry a sack of potatoes. How will she survive? And now with the child to look after—"

"She can stay in Italy for only two more days, then her visa is no longer good. We have talked already. Spain is not in the war yet. Errico will drive her to Naples in the truck tomorrow. He will arrange for her to cross to Spain. Perhaps a fishing boat will be willing to take her through the Strait of Bonifacio so that she can get to Barcelona. Without papers she has nowhere to go, but she thinks that maybe in Spain she will have a chance. I cannot discourage her."

"Of course not, of course not," said Anna. "Errico must do everything he can. And so must you. And she and the boy will eat well in the morning. I will see to that. And I'll pray to the Holy Virgin tonight to see to it that the boy does not remember any of this when he grows to be a man. He will never have a restful sleep in his life if he remembers any of this."

"That may be so, Anna. But you had best pray that he grows to be a man, and don't concern the Virgin with the kinds of dreams he will have."

VIII

Grandmama had invited Maurice to dinner in 1928. He was a young doctor, just opening his practice, and friends of friends said that he had a shining future and attended the opera regularly, and therefore would be just right for Helene.

He arrived, his pleasant face clean-shaven and smiling, with just enough of an air of diffidence to endear himself to Grandmama immediately. She seated him at the head of the table, with Helene on one side and Erika and Gunter on the other.

"How does a doctor reconcile himself to pain and suffering?" asked Erika across the candlelit table.

"I'm afraid there is no such reconciling," said Maurice. "To reconcile oneself is to accept one's inability to heal." He spoke well but with the air of someone who had made an effort to learn to talk easily.

"When Helene's grandfather died, I did not count it an inability to heal, but a call to God," said Grandmama.

Maurice looked embarrassed and said, "But that is often the case with the old and the infirm. I speak of those in their younger years."

"But you do not equate yourself with God?" asked Helene. It was the first time she had spoken, and Maurice looked at her with a penetrating gaze.

"This is a conversation best left to philosophers, not physicians," he said. "My promise is to promote life."

"At whatever cost to you?" asked Erika.

"At whatever cost to me," said Maurice.

Helene slept fitfully during the night. Often she reached over to touch David, who lay next to her. They had slept in their clothes, covered by one of Anna's hand-sewn quilts.

The borrowed mattress smelled of urine, and the floor on which it lay was cold and hard. Once in her dreams she heard Miriam call to her, and she had a surge of joy, of indescribable relief. I knew it hadn't happened! How could it have happened? Miriam's fingers touched Helene's lips. Miriam's breath flowed warm and sweet against Helene's face. "Mama is here, darling, Mama is here."

Helene sat suddenly upright on the mattress. "Miriam!" She shouted the name.

"It is me, Pietro," said the old man, his hand on her arm.

"What?" Helene asked, startled. She looked around the dingy kitchen. Anna stood at the sink slicing bread on the drainboard. It was not yet light, and the single overhead bulb illuminated only the area where Anna stood.

"Is it time to leave?" asked Helene, remembering.

"Errico is dressing," said Pietro. "It is a long ride to Naples. Anna is preparing food for you to take with you. You and the boy must have breakfast before you leave."

"The thought of food sickens me," said Helene.

"It will sustain you," said Pietro. "But this idea you have that when you get to Spain you will be safe is one that may be erroneous. You may not be accepted there any more than you would be anywhere else in Europe. I have been up for two hours talking to the neighbor across the hall, who runs a newspaper concession in the Via Veneto. He reads the papers all day, and he is the one we go to when we need to resolve a point of information. I asked him what he would do if he were a Jew with no papers except a German passport marked with a 'J.' He said that a Jew with a German passport is a Jew with no passport at all, that it is the same as being a stateless person, a refugee, and that even if the passport were valid, Eastern Europe is closed to that person, as well as Britain and France, since they now are fighting Germany. He says that Salazar in Portugal has made a pact with Hitler to turn back any Jews who seek refuge in Portugal but that America or South America are possibilities if you fall within the quotas."

"But how can we get to America without travel papers?" said Helene.

"He admits that that is a problem to be considered. I told

him that you have in mind that Spain will take you and the boy in."

"And what did he say?"

"He says that Franco is reeling from civil war and that it's a great risk to attempt to enter without papers."

"But there is a possibility that we can enter?"

"That is a fragile reason to take such a perilous trip. Spain fights her own war now, and from the newspapers, I see that things there are confused, particularly in Barcelona, where the boat is to take you. Conditions are very bad. There is chaos, no food. Franco hunts the rebels down in the streets and kills them by the thousands every day. How can you hope that they will take in refugees from a different war?"

"In all that furor maybe Spain won't notice us when we arrive," said Helene wanly. "Your friend is probably right that it is perilous to try to enter Spain."

"But you will still try?" asked Pietro.

"I have to try," said Helene. She kissed David on the cheek. "Wake up, David. Are you hungry?"

He stretched and opened his eyes.

"Remember Pietro?" asked Helene. "You slept in Pietro's house last night."

David put his arms out to be held. "My baby boy," said Helene, gathering him to her.

"The toilet is downstairs," said Pietro. "We have running water, but the plumbing is broken and needs fixing." He made a gesture of helplessness with his hands.

Helene carried David down the stairs to the toilet. She pulled David's pants down and put him on the homemade commode that sat next to the nonfunctioning toilet. "You must do something in the toilet now, David. We have very little time before we must leave."

David sat on the commode and looked around at the grimy walls while Helene washed her face and dried herself with a limp-looking towel that hung on a peg on the wall.

"Where are Dada and Miriam?" asked David when he was finished.

"In heaven," said Helene, her face turned away. She

washed him in silence and combed his hair, then he waited while she used the commode. They left the toilet and started up the steps. Halfway up, Helene sat down and pulled David onto her lap.

"Dada and Miriam are in heaven, David. You remember that I told you about heaven before."

"Is heaven in Berlin?" he asked.

"It might be," she said.

"In Grandmama's house?" he asked.

"Maybe in Grandmama's house," she said weakly.

When they reached the top of the stairs again and entered the kitchen, the mattress was standing upright against one wall, and the square wooden table was set for breakfast. There were slices of buttered bread on a plate, with a pot of cherry preserves and a plate of eggs scrambled with bits of sausage and onion.

"Sit down, sit down," said Pietro, picking David up and and putting him in one of the chairs while Helene sat down in another one.

Errico entered the kitchen, his wiry body neatly dressed in work clothes and a heavy wool sweater. He said, "*Buon giorno,*" without looking at Helene's face, and then sat down and began eating from the plate that Anna set before him.

Anna brought a steaming cup of coffee to the table and put it down in front of Helene, then said, "Pietro has told me of your troubles. This is your house. We are a poor family, but we are civilized, and we obey the commandment to succor those whose fortunes are not as great as our own, for then we will be blessed in the sight of the Lord." All of this was said in rapid Italian, while her arthritic fingers made several signs of the cross.

"She is saying that she is sorry she was unfriendly to you last night," interpreted Pietro as he took a seat at the table.

"Thank you," said Helene, looking up at Anna. "You are very kind."

Anna did not move away from the table, but continued to stare at Helene and David. David ate hungrily, but Helene merely sipped the coffee that Anna had brought her.

"How do you bear it?" asked Anna finally. "Why do you

not tear your hair and scream because you have lost your husband and child? Did you not love your husband? Was the child not of your own body perhaps?"

Helene looked at Pietro.

"She says she extends her sympathy to you and wishes to comfort you," said Pietro.

Helene looked down at the table. Tears filled her eyes, but she wiped them away quickly. The tears seemed to satisfy Anna, though, and she went back to the sink.

Before they left, Anna handed Helene a bandanna filled with bread and sausage and dried fruit. "I'm sure that Jews also pray to God," said Anna, "and you must pray that you will be able to care for your son and that God will give you strength to be a good woman, and maybe one day you will find another husband and have another child to replace the one you have lost."

"She says that David is a beautiful child and that you must keep yourself healthy and sane for his sake," said Pietro.

Helene nodded. "Thank you very much for everything. I could never repay you."

Anna moved tentatively toward her, and then Helene held out her arms, and the two women embraced and cried together for a few moments before Pietro told them that it was time to leave.

Errico lifted David onto his shoulder, and Pietro took the small suitcase and the black satchel. Anna cried into her apron and watched from the window as they emerged from the stairwell down below and walked across the narrow street to where Errico's old truck was parked.

Pietro opened the passenger side of the truck, and David slid across the seat toward the steering wheel. Then came the suitcase and the satchel on the floorboard beneath David's feet. Helene held her hand out to Pietro. There was the sound of coins falling into place in his palm. Pietro cleared his throat and looked pained.

"I would refuse this because what we are doing has nothing to do with gold coins. You understand that?"

Helene nodded her head. "I understand."

"But I will not refuse it. It is not my place to refuse gold when we have so little money."

Helene's hand closed Pietro's fingers over the gold coins. "This is not payment, Pietro. I can't pay you for this. It is for the truck, for the gasoline, for Errico's lost wages today."

Pietro kissed her on both cheeks. "I apologize for Italy, for Mussolini," he said. *"Arrivederci."*

"Arrivederci."

Errico spoke no French at all. The 120 miles from Rome to Naples was driven in silence. They stopped once at a small café in Capua, next to the remains of the Temple of Mithras, where the escaped gladiator Spartacus is said to have prayed for aid during his revolt against the Roman Senate. Capua had the stillness of an archaeological dig rather than the electric tension it must have had when Hannibal camped there while waiting to battle the Roman legions during the Carthaginian wars.

Errico waited outside in the truck while Helene took David to the toilet at the rear of the café. When they came out, the proprietress of the café offered David a sweet wrapped in tissue paper, and Helene bought a bottle of milk for David to drink in the truck. "Is it much farther?" Helene asked when she and David were back in the truck.

"Farther?" Errico repeated, puzzled.

"It's not important," said Helene.

"Ah, farther. Napoli?"

"Yes, Napoli."

"Le quattro."

Helene understood. Four o'clock in the afternoon. She opened the bottle of milk and poured some into a mug that Errico had in the front seat of the truck. She handed the mug to David, along with a crust of the bread from Anna's bandanna. She broke off a piece of sausage and wrapped it in a chunk of bread, which she handed to Errico, who took it and ate while he drove. Helene ate also. Her stomach gnawed at her. Even in grief, the body continues its demands, she thought. How marvelously efficient the body is, fingers and legs and arms moving effortlessly, voice sure and steady and intelligible to others. The woman in the café could not tell by looking at Helene that she was a madwoman and that a long wire coil ran from the top of her head to the back of her heels and that it was the coil that held her in place, telling the muscles what to do, controlling the facial expressions so that no one could see that she was insane with grief.

"Vesuvius," said Errico, pointing to the volcano that soared into the sky from the east shore of the Bay of Naples.

"Yes, Vesuvius." Helene nodded.

"Napoli," said Errico, pointing down below them to the Bay of Naples.

The road wound down from the hills toward the small harbor of Piccolo Sant' Angelo. There, fishing boats bobbed atop the azure water while fishermen mended their nets on the docks.

"Look at the boats, David, look," said Helene, holding him up on the seat of the truck.

Errico pulled the truck onto the dirt road leading to the dock, then left Helene and David in the truck while he walked down to where the boats were moored. Helene held David close to her on the seat as he pointed excitedly to the colored banners flying from the masts of the fishing boats. Helene felt no worry, no emotion. Errico would ask the fishermen if one of them could take a woman and child across the Mediterranean Sea to Barcelona. The fishermen would say either yes or no. The wire coil had no control over that.

Errico was back. He held his hand out to her, palm up. "*Quanto?*" he asked.

Helene measured out some gold coins from the black medicine satchel. The coins were dwindling. She placed five coins in Errico's open palm. Ten gold coins remained in the bag.

Errico turned and walked back down to the dock to negotiate with the owners of the boat. After a few minutes Errico waved toward the truck that it would be okay.

IX

Once they were out of the Bay of Naples and into the Tyrrhenian Sea, the winds began to blow. Salvatore and his son Marco owned the boat. Salvatore, who spoke a little French, came down below to check on how Helene and David were faring in the choppy seas.

"If you sleep you won't feel the rolling as much," he said. Water ran from his oilskin sou'wester and jacket onto the floor of the cabin. He looked too old to be battling the sea in rough weather. His hands were big and callused, and his face was grooved and lined by years of exposure to salt and sun.

"David doesn't feel well," said Helene. She sat on the edge of the bunk with David's head in her lap.

Salvatore bent down and pulled a pail from under the bunk. "Little boy, just vomit into this," he said.

"He doesn't understand French," said Helene, feeling nauseated herself. "If we could have some soup or crackers, something to help us settle our stomachs—"

Then Marco was on the steps, leaning into the door of the cabin, calling to his father. The boat tilted on its side, and David and Helene were thrown to the floor, but Salvatore steadied himself in the doorway by holding on to the metal frame of the opening. Helene looked up at him. She was so disoriented she could not tell whether the boat was still upright or not. Marco ran back up the steps, and Salvatore followed. The pail had rolled into the corner with David and Helene, and they both leaned over it and retched.

Gradually the boat righted itself until Helene and David were no longer pinned against the wall of the cabin. She got to her feet and carried David to the bunk and placed him beneath the covers, tucking the blankets in around him. His eyes were already closed in sleep. Next to the bed was a basin with a towel and a drinking glass, and in the cabinet below was a bottle of water. She poured some of the water into the basin and washed her face and hands, then filled the glass with water and drank it. Her heart raced wildly as she clung limply to the side of the basin. Lean forward so you don't faint, she had heard Maurice say, so she bent forward until she felt her heartbeat slowing down. When she felt able to move, she filled the glass again and brought it to the bed, lifted David up, and held the glass to his lips.

"You must drink some water, David," she said, remembering Maurice's lectures to her on how rapidly children become dehydrated with vomiting or diarrhea. David didn't open his eyes, but when the water entered his mouth, he swallowed.

"Good boy, David. I love you, David," she said, then began to cry. She lay down beside him, and, drained and empty, they both slept.

In her dreams Helene wandered empty streets searching for Miriam's blanket. Miriam would not sleep without the blanket. Maurice, where is Miriam's blanket? You know she cannot sleep without her blanket. Then Helene heard a scream. Someone was screaming so loudly that it awakened her just as she was about to recover Miriam's blanket. Helene sat up in the bed. David was pulling at her arm and calling to her. The wire coil had somehow become tangled in her sleep. She pulled David into the crook of her arm and talked to him softly. "I'm sorry, David. It was a bad dream. I'm all right. Go to sleep, David, go back to sleep."

When he had fallen asleep again, she lay, eyes open in the darkness, feeling the roll and sway of the boat now as a soothing rhythm. Dreams were so strange, she thought. How real Miriam and Maurice were to her in dreams.

It would be a relief to walk onto the deck and feel the sea breezes on her face. David would be safe down here. The wind had died down. There would be no more seasickness. She imagined she could feel the gentleness of the breeze already as she swung her legs over the edge of the bunk and stepped down onto the planks. They creaked beneath her weight, and David moved in his sleep. When she was sure that he was soundly asleep again, she put on her jacket and shoes and walked out of the cabin and up the steps to the deck. She was right, the breeze was refreshing. She didn't mind the chill in the air. She hadn't been able to breathe below. Leaning against the railing, her forehead against the cold steel of the lower mast, she looked down into the water. Was she capable of doing what Maurice had done? Could there ever be anything horrible enough in life that she could do what he had done? With just a little effort she could climb onto the railing and jump into the inviting blackness of the water below. She could visualize herself doing it, could see her legs moving slowly, cautiously from rung to rung and then feel herself teetering momentarily at the top before she let go and fell free into the sea.

She backed away from the railing. The door to the pilot's cabin opened, and Salvatore walked out onto the deck holding a cup of hot soup out to her. "Go on, take the soup while it's hot," he said. He smelled of fish and diesel oil and perspiration. His grimy hand was firm and steady around the steaming cup.

"It was so close below," she said, taking the cup from him. She sat down on the nets, and he watched her while she sipped the soup.

"When the boy gets up, I'll take him into the pilot house and show him how the boat works," said Salvatore.

"He'd like that."

Salvatore pointed out into the darkness with an oil-smeared finger. "Corsica and Sardinia are ahead, and between the two islands is the Strait of Bonifacio. When we pass through the strait, we will be in the Mediterranean Sea. On the same course lies Barcelona, Spain."

"Have you ever brought anyone on this trip before?" asked Helene.

Salvatore held up two fingers.

"Were they refugees?" she asked.

"You mean Jews?" said Salvatore.

Helene looked down at the vegetables floating in the soup. "Yes, Jews."

"Yes, they were Jews," said Salvatore. "One family of a mother and father and three little girls. Another one of just a husband and wife."

"Do you know what happened to them? Did they land without any difficulty?"

"We landed both times at night, as we will land with you. Both times were in 1938, during the heavy fighting in Spain, and the docks were filled with soldiers. The man and his wife ran along the docks. There were no children to hold them back, and the soldiers didn't stop them. The other family we let off, and when we moved away, I heard gunfire, and I saw the wife fall. We made for the open sea, and I was occupied with the boat and didn't see what happened to the man and the three little girls."

Helene shivered despite the hot soup. "You take a risk also by going so near to shore with us."

Salvatore shrugged. "I take a risk by going fishing in deep water also. I have fallen into the water and been chased by sharks. I have been burned when the engine on my boat caught fire. My other son fell overboard and never came up. He was a fine swimmer, and there were no sharks around. God is the only one who knows where my son's body is. And still Marco and I continue to fish. I don't worry about things like that."

Helene nodded. "The soup makes me feel better."

"Good," said Salvatore.

"When will we reach Barcelona?"

Salvatore looked up at the stars. "Tomorrow night at approximately this time."

The fishing boat moved noiselessly through the deep waters of the outer harbor. In the distance the lights of the city of Barcelona flickered weakly, barely illuminating the statue of Christopher Columbus that stood guard at the harbor's mouth.

"It will soon be dark, then we'll dock," Salvatore said to Helene. He pointed to the shadowy shape of land slipping by the porthole of the cabin. Helene looked out.

"Barcelona?"

"Yes," said Salvatore. "It's very quiet, no noise of gunfire, but that means nothing. They know that we are out here, and without others to shoot at, they may put all their attention on us. That is why it must be very dark before I get close to the dock, so that we can come in without being noticed." He turned and left the cabin.

Helene washed David's hands and face and wiped the vomit stains from his wrinkled wool coat. Then he stood patiently while she put the coat on him and set his cap atop his curly hair. As she washed herself at the basin, she glanced at him. Black eyes and little face almost lost in wool. She tugged at his cap when she had finished at the basin. "You look so grown-up," she said at his serious expression.

He put his hand in hers.

"Sometimes you look so wise that I think you should tell me what to do, David," she said, kissing his cheek.

She put on the fur-trimmed jacket that she had worn since the day she left Berlin. She had bought the suit in Paris in 1936 at a couturier on the Rue de Rivoli. Germany had been getting grimmer daily as Hitler's new regime was put into place, and Maurice had thought that a spring vacation in Paris would revive their spirits. It had. They had laughed as though starved for laughter. They had explored the Left Bank as though they had never been there before. Arm in arm they had walked the tree-shaded boulevards, stopping to sip coffee at outdoor cafés. Maurice had bought a watercolor from a street artist in Montparnasse, and when they brought it home, they had had it framed and had hung it at the top of the stairs next to the Tintoretto that Grandmama had given them for a wedding gift. The watercolor and the Tintoretto and the house they hung in were lost. Miriam and Maurice were lost. David, who had been conceived that spring in Paris, might soon be lost. But the fur-trimmed suit, traveled in, slept in, used as a blanket, remained.

Helene picked up the suitcase in one hand and the satchel in the other. David, muffled in clothes, watched her.

"You will have to stay close by me, David. I can't carry you now. You will have to walk. Do you think you will be able to do that?"

"Yes."

"Good."

When they reached the deck, David ran to the railing and peered out at the lights of the harbor. Salvatore took the bags from Helene and placed them on the starboard side of the boat, and Helene joined David at the rail to look out at the shoreline. There was enough moonlight for them to see the statue of Columbus on its giant pedestal, facing the Mediterranean. A freighter sat near the entrance to the harbor, its lights blazing, illuminating the bombed-out buildings along the inner loop of the harbor. Soldiers with machine guns stood in the doorways of gutted buildings. More soldiers stood guard along the deserted quay, amid the twisted metal and upended wooden pilings that were all that was left of the Barcelona docks.

"We Italians bombed the city day and night for over two weeks," said Salvatore sadly. "This is all that remains."

Winches clanged and machinery whirred as the freighter's cargo was unloaded. Men's voices echoed across the makeshift loading dock as they shouted to one another.

"You see the way they run in every direction," said Salvatore. "Since the city fell to Franco, all the experienced dockmasters are dead or in hiding. I remember Barcelona Harbor as one of the great ports of call in the world. Now it is a rabbit warren filled with hungry Loyalists and anarchists and communists, but it is lucky for you that the freighter is here, because their attention is diverted."

"Then I thank God for the freighter," said Helene as she watched the unloading operation.

Salvatore picked David up in his arms. "You won't forget about how to steer a boat now, will you?"

David smiled at the unfamiliar words.

"Take care of the little boy," Salvatore said to Helene as he put David down on the deck.

"I will," said Helene.

The fishing boat slipped by on the shadowy side of the freighter's superstructure. Marco was at the wheel in the pilot's cabin while Salvatore stood on deck and with hand motions guided the boat's path through the darkness.

"Mama, look," said David.

"Shh, darling," said Helene. She pulled David close against her so that her skirt muffled the sound of his voice. The boat was so close to the freighter now that Helene could make out the faces of the soldiers standing guard. The light played on the ruins of the buildings, highlighting every broken timber and every bullet mark. No one noticed the fishing boat as it glided past the freighter, through the boat basin, and into the inner harbor. At the upper end of the inlet, to the north of Las Ramblas, the boat skittered along the edge of the docks, weaving in and out of the waves before they broke against the pilings.

When they were close enough, Salvatore threw a rope and tied it fast to the remains of the dock. He tossed the suitcase and the satchel up onto the dock first, then turned to Helene and offered her his hand.

"You will go first and then the boy," he said.

The boat drifted toward and away from the dock. Only the tether kept it from traveling too far away from the landing. Salvatore held tight to Helene's hand, and as the boat slapped against the dock, he lifted her up. She took one step onto the top rail of the boat and the second step onto the wooden plank that hung beneath the dock, and then both feet were on the dock, and she was clinging to a buttress as the boat moved back again, away from her. Even in the darkness she could see David's eyes. He stood in the middle of the deck, splashed with ocean spray, staring up at her.

"David," she whispered as he floated away from her. She felt that she was going to faint, watching him move away rather than toward her. Then David was in Salvatore's heavy arms, and the boat was being pushed toward her again. She held out her arms.

"Don't leave, David," she whispered again. Salvatore, with David in one arm, reached for the dock, as if by his own strength he would steady the boat, and at that moment, straining as far across the water as she could, Helene caught David into her arms.

"I've got you, David," she murmured, clasping him to her, kissing his cold face.

Salvatore waved up at them from the deck of the boat,

then pulled the rope free, and the boat floated back away from the dock. The motors were started, and soon the boat was gone from view.

"Are you very cold?" Helene asked the wet and shaking child. For answer he opened his mouth so that she could see his teeth chattering. She sat him on the dock and pulled off his wet jacket, then opened the suitcase and took out a heavy sweater, which she pulled over his head. "You'll feel warmer in a minute," she said, holding him close to her until his shaking subsided.

"Can you walk now?" she asked after a little while.

"Yes."

Helene looked around her. The streets leading from the harbor seemed quiet except for an occasional figure hurrying along a side street.

"You must stay close to me, David," she said, picking up the suitcase and the satchel. He followed behind her as they walked along the ruins of the dock. She looked down the Paseo de Colón to see whether she could see the spires of a church or a cross. If she could find a church, someone there could direct her to a synagogue.

Near the statue of Columbus was a small square, and to the left was Las Ramblas, a wide promenade extending from the harbor to the center of the city. Along the sides of the promenade were streets lined with stores and cafés, all of which were shuttered or barricaded or bombed to the ground. No traffic moved on the streets. A group of men huddled around a bonfire on the corner of Calle Carmen. A prostitute, her thin arms dangling from beneath her sleeveless chemise, lounged against the wall behind them. Down the street stood the church of Nuestra Señora de Gracia.

David had begun to lag behind, and every few steps Helene needed to stop and wait for him to catch up. "Just a little bit farther, David," she said. "Not too far."

The church was locked. Helene knocked on the wooden door and pressed the outside bell. In a few seconds the door was opened by a priest.

"The church is closed this evening," said the priest.

"I don't understand," said Helene in German. "I don't speak Spanish."

The priest stepped from the church and stood on the landing in front of the door. He glanced at David and the suitcases that Helene had placed against the stone threshold.

"The synagogue," she said. "Could you please tell me where the synagogue is?"

"*Sinagoga?*"

"Yes, *sinagoga*," repeated Helene.

The priest's movements were rapid now. He looked down the street, satisfying himself that no one was watching the church doorway. Then he picked up the suitcases and pulled Helene and David into the church, shutting the blackened wood door quickly behind them.

The church smelled of centuries of burnt votive candles. There were no windows to let out the ancient air.

"You have come by boat?" asked the priest as he led Helene and David through the church, past the tabernacle that held an ivory-carved statue of the Virgin Mary, candles guttering at her feet. At the vestry the priest sat Helene and David down on an oak bench. "*Barca?*" he repeated, making a wavy motion with his hand.

"Yes, *barca*," said Helene. "The *sinagoga*, can you take me to the *sinagoga*?"

"*Sí, la sinagoga*," said the priest. "*Espere usted, por favor*," said the priest, and then he left.

Helene waited nervously for the priest to return. He is a man of God, she said to herself. Why would he want to call the soldiers? She watched the door anxiously. Through it would come either the priest or soldiers.

After a long while the priest returned accompanied by another man. He wore an overcoat, and his shoulders and body were so massive and outsized that he dwarfed the vestry and everything in it. He was smooth-shaven and Levantine-looking, with a straight, high-bridged nose and full, sensual lips. His dark hair waved back from his forehead in a thick, unruly shock, and his dark gray eyes under heavy brows matched his thick hair.

"My name is Antonio Katakis," he said in German. "Father Girón tells me that you are looking for a synagogue."

"Yes."

"Don't be frightened," said the man. "I didn't mean to

frighten you. Everyone in Barcelona knows me, Tonio Katakis, originally of Salonika, Greece. I am the secretary of the Jewish Committee in Barcelona."

"But you speak German."

"And English and French and, of course, Yiddish. Father Girón says that you came by boat."

"We came from Naples."

"A dangerous trip and a dangerous time to be arriving in Barcelona."

"Tell me where else we can go, and we'll go there," said Helene.

"No, no, you did right, you did right, and you're fortunate to have come to Father Girón. He is a good Christian, a just man."

"But can David and I stay in Barcelona? I will stay nowhere that there is danger to David."

Tonio looked at David. "There is no place in Europe that is not a danger to Jewish children. And no, if it were known that you were here, you would not be able to stay in Barcelona either. Soldiers patrol the streets looking for black marketeers and for signs of Loyalist resistance, and they also look for illegals, people with no visas."

"We are so exhausted. If we only could rest awhile."

Tonio reached down and lifted David up in one arm and then picked up the suitcase.

"Take the satchel," he said, "and follow me."

X

Erika and Helene at school, giggling in Fräulein Gusick's lecture hall. Erika and Helene watching Marlene Dietrich dance in Joseph von Sternberg's The Blue Angel *and later telling Grandmama that they had attended a piano recital at the concert hall in Charlottenburg. Erika and Helene on a Berlin street passing a man in a tall black hat, long black coat, and full bushy beard with side curls. Both of them laughing and pointing and making faces at the black-clad figure's back. Erika and Helene in the zoo in the Tiergarten, and Erika turning suddenly from the monkeys to stare at Helene and then to ask, a thoughtful look on her face, "But what is a Jew?"*

The rabbi's wife passed silently in and out of his study, placing dishes of food on the lace-covered table for Helene and David. Her face impassive, she spooned portions of fried potatoes onto their plates. She was short and gray-haired and wore an old silk dress protected by a heavy cotton apron. On her feet were well-worn men's carpet slippers. She said a few words to Tonio in Greek and then walked into the adjoining room, where twelve men in hats and prayer shawls stood before a portable bimah, chanting and weaving in unison.

"The Rebbitzen is sorry that she has no milk for the boy," translated Tonio. "She also apologizes that she serves you nonkosher sausage. But food is very scarce. Even bread is rationed now. Milk can be procured only on the black market. If she had known there would be a child coming today, she would have made arrangements to buy milk for him."

"It isn't important. I don't observe the laws of kashruth," said Helene. "We can eat everything. You've been very kind to us. David could have walked no farther than the church."

"I hope you're not still afraid of me."

Helene shook her head. "I'm not afraid of you."

"Good. So this is David, but what is your name?"

"Helene Gelson."

"If you don't want to talk, I'll be silent," he said, staring intently at her.

"No, I want to talk," she said. "If I tell you what has happened, then you will be in a better position to advise me. It won't be easy to tell you, and it won't be easy for you to hear, but I'll tell you what has happened to us from the time of our decision to leave Berlin."

Helene told the story slowly, so as not to leave anything out.

"You were fortunate to have the Count for a friend," said Tonio as she recounted the journey to Rome.

"Yes, in that we were fortunate, but I must tell you about Maurice." She rushed through the story scarcely pausing for breath, as though when she came to the tragedy, the ending might be different. But how could it be? And with the words came tears, and all the horror crashed down upon her again.

Tonio rose from the table and went into the other room to get the Rebbitzen.

"She seems little more than a child herself," said the Rebbitzen to Tonio as she stood in the doorway looking at Helene, not touching her, not coming near her to comfort her. "But there are so many like her; she is not so special. Worse things have happened. Why don't you take her to the Jewish Committee offices; she can stay there with you for at least a few weeks. Here there is no room, and the soldiers come daily to make sure that our small family has not grown since the last time they were here."

Helene had wiped her eyes and was cutting David's food for him. She listened to Tonio and the Rebbitzen talking in Greek, and she knew that they were talking about her and David and deciding what to do with them.

Tonio sat down at the table, and the Rebbitzen disappeared again.

"She speaks to you in Greek?" asked Helene.

"Yes. The largest Sephardic community in the world is in Greece," said Tonio. "When the Spaniards expelled the Jews in 1492, Greece was the most convenient place to run."

Helene looked around the study. A young girl sat at a desk typing, light brown hair caught up in a snowy-white bandanna. She wore thick-lensed eyeglasses, and every once in a while she looked up from the typewriter and smiled at Helene.

"The Rebbitzen is afraid that if you stay here, you may endanger the Jewish community in Barcelona," said Tonio. "There are very few Jewish residents here. Before the Civil War, maybe a hundred fifty families. When we pray, we break the law, but usually the Spaniards look the other way. Sometimes they don't. The Jews are still in Spain on sufferance. Nothing has changed. Prayer services are held here in Rabbi Theonikis' apartment when a minion can be assembled, but if it was thought that rescue efforts were conducted from here, prayers would have to cease."

"I don't want to cause anyone any harm," said Helene.

"Of course not, of course not, and you shouldn't worry that you cause harm by being in Barcelona. It is for me to worry now how to help you while you are here."

The voices in the other room grew louder. Helene could not understand the words of the prayers. The books on the shelves had strange writing on their spines, and from the intense man opposite her she had learned that there were Greek Jews.

"I am Jewish, and these people are Jewish," Helene said. "I have never thought about being Jewish especially, until the Nazis came to power. Now I find that there are many things I don't know about it. How do you come to be here?"

Tonio smiled. "I was an attaché to the Greek embassy in Barcelona when the Spanish Civil War broke out. When the embassy closed, I stayed on. I intended to go back to Athens in 1937, but then the Jews started coming over the Pyrenees, and the Jewish Committee asked me if I would stay and help, so I stayed."

"Have many come here from Germany?" she asked.

"Hundreds. And now they begin to come from France and

Eastern Europe as well. They come through the mountains, in snow up to their hips, with no food, no clothes, half dead. They fear the concentration camps that the Germans are building. At first we thought the snow and the cold had deranged their minds to such a degree that they were possessed of demonic visions of the destruction of the Jewish people, but rumors have come to us from the east that their fears may be justified."

"David and I will never go to a camp," said Helene flatly.

"There are camps in Spain, too," said Tonio. "They are actually prisons."

"In Spain? For the Jews?"

"For Jews, for Loyalists, for political refugees," said Tonio. "Miranda de Ebro is the one closest to Barcelona. Even there the Jewish prisoners are mistreated by the non-Jewish prisoners. It is very bad."

"For the men in the other room, being Jewish is important," said Helene. "But for David and me, it is only a burden."

"For them it is a burden also, but they refuse to admit it. The more they are pushed, the closer they wear their religion. They wrap themselves in it. Here in Barcelona, where there is hardly any food, some would rather sicken and die than break the kosher laws."

"But isn't it God's commandment that the preservation of life is more important than obedience to religious law?"

"So, I see you do know something about Judaism, after all," said Tonio, smiling.

Helene pulled her passport from the satchel and put it on the table. "Is there anything that can be done with a passport like this? Is it possible that I can obtain a Spanish visa or entry permit, something that will enable David and me to stay in Barcelona without going to prison?"

Tonio picked up the passport and looked at it, then tossed it back onto the table. "The law changes daily, sometimes hourly. Sometimes the same law is interpreted in many ways. Franco is split in his attitude toward the Jewish people. On the one hand he sees them as the accursed Jews, the people that Ferdinand and Isabella threw out of Spain. But then, when he sees the Germans and the Poles mistreating those same Sephardic Jews, he protests that they are murdering Spaniards, and for the moment he forgets that he is talking about the accursed Jews."

"Then what will happen to us here?" she asked.

"You must expect to stay in hiding until you're discovered."

"And what did the rabbi's wife say to you about me?"

"She thinks the safest hiding place for you for a while would be with me at the Jewish Committee Center."

"What is that? Do you mean there is a place that actively helps people like us?"

"No, no, nothing so official as that. For the most part, all we can do is watch helplessly. Franco has banned Jewish welfare agencies from operating in Spain, but we work on promises. We try to keep people out of prison. We wait for the passports that the Joint Distribution Committee promises to send us."

"Then you are breaking the law by hiding us."

"Of course."

"But you will do it?"

"Of course."

Tonio's apartment occupied two floors in a building on Calle de Rocafort. The downstairs was the offices of the Jewish Committee. Desks lined the walls. Behind the desks were maps of the world, red pins outlining the various Jewish populations. Telephones rang endlessly, and a steady stream of visitors and refugees flowed through the outside door, to be stopped and questioned by the armed guard in the inner courtyard and then to be admitted inside. Tonio's private quarters were upstairs. The bedroom contained a bed and a dresser and boxes and filing cabinets that were the overflow from downstairs. A small bathroom held more boxes. The kitchen converted into a darkroom so that the photographs of the refugees streaming through the Jewish Committee offices could be developed and kept with the refugees' dossiers in the bulging file cabinets.

Tonio removed his personal belongings from the bedroom and put them in the adjoining kitchen, where he slept on a cot between the stove and the sink.

Helene and David stayed upstairs and out of sight for several days after they arrived. The only time they saw anyone was when Tonio brought them food or knocked on the door to the bedroom to be allowed to walk through to use the bathroom.

"I feel that I want to do something to help," said Helene at the end of the first week of hearing the telephone constantly ringing in the downstairs offices. "David is very quiet. No one will notice that there is a child with me if I come down and help the others."

"Nobody will notice anything in the general confusion of the office," agreed Tonio, "but sometimes we are visited by the authorities, who want to see that we are not exceeding our function as a clearing house."

"We can't stay upstairs forever."

"Your knowledge of German and French would be useful," admitted Tonio. "Just remember not to talk to Spaniards who come inquiring after relatives, nor to anyone who looks like an official of the government."

Sixteen people worked in the offices of the Jewish Committee. The lines of refugees began forming before seven in the morning, and everyone was too harried to pay much attention to Helene and David. She was given a desk and the assignment of recording the names, ages, and country of origin of each member of the refugee families. She was not to give advice. If there were any questions, she was to call Tonio or Leah, a sharp-featured French Jew who had lived in Barcelona with her Catalan husband since 1912, to provide answers.

Most of the refugees who came to the Committee offices seeking help were eventually arrested by the Spanish authorities and taken to the Barcelona jail. From there some were sent to Miranda de Ebro prison, while others, with enough money for bribes, quietly bought permanent visas.

"I'm too busy to think of myself or David when I'm working," said Helene to Tonio after a few days. "Thank you, Tonio. It is a blessing not to think."

There were incidents.

"Where are you from?" Helene asked the thin man who stood in line in front of her. He coughed spasmodically, caught his breath, and said, "Riga, Latvia."

"A Litvak," said the woman standing behind him. "He should get at the end of the line."

"We are Litvaks," protested several of the others in line. "We are Litvaks."

The man bent toward Helene to give her the information on his family while she strained to hear him over the arguing going on behind him.

"And we are Sephardics," said an elderly man in a dirty but well-tailored suit. He squeezed himself in next to the man from Latvia and shoved a worn and creased piece of paper into Helene's face. "Do you see what that says?" he asked. "It says the Pasteur Institute in Paris has proved that we Sephardim are really an Aryan people and do not belong to this rabble."

"Please," said Helene. Men began to shout at each other in the line, and the man from Latvia turned around in time to receive a blow to the head from someone behind him.

Tonio was there in an instant, along with the guard from the courtyard. Several people were knocked down in the fray, and Tonio's head was cut, but finally all was quiet.

"You're Jews," he screamed at them. "Tell Franco whether you are Ashkenazic or Sephardic and see whether he cares."

Later Tonio said to Helene, "It's human nature. They fight over the small things, because the big things are so unmanageable."

One morning a commotion downstairs woke Helene from sleep. She reached for David, and he was gone. "My God," she said as she ran in her nightgown to the head of the stairs. A woman stood face to face with Tonio, who held David in his arms. The woman was screaming, the veins standing out in her neck.

"If you have room for them, then you have room for others up there, too," she screeched.

"David," called Helene softly, so as not to frighten him further.

When Tonio saw Helene at the top of the stairs, he put the child down, and David ran up to his mother.

After he had calmed the woman down, Tonio came upstairs. Helene had dressed and made the bed, and she sat on the edge of the bed with David next to her.

"I must go, Tonio. It isn't fair to you or to the others."

"I will decide what is fair and what is not fair here. The woman was distraught. I cannot take the whole world in."

"But you made an exception for me."

"I did." He sat down on the bed next to her. "If I had money, I would buy papers for you and David, but there is no cash. Supplies are donated, and workers volunteer their services. We are without funds except for operating expenses. If only we knew what Franco's intentions really are with regard to the Jews. He says that he will remain neutral in the European war, but who can say?"

"The woman who screamed at you might call the authorities, and they'll find me here," said Helene.

Tonio rubbed his eyes with his hands. "It will gain her nothing, but you're right, she might call them."

Helene put her hand on Tonio's arm, and when he turned and looked at her, she saw something in his eyes that she had not intended her touch to evoke. She took her hand away.

"I talked to a priest in the Cathedral La Seu yesterday," said Tonio. "Up until now conversions under situations of duress were suspect. Neither the Church nor the authorities were much impressed by them. But now the Bishop has offered baptism to Jews with Spanish visas. He sees it as a service to God to put his imprimatur on such conversions." Tonio paused. "But you have no visa."

"I have a diamond," she said, showing him Grandmama's ring on her finger next to her gold wedding ring. "Will this be enough to buy visas for David and me? I think it is two carats, but I can't be sure."

Tonio looked at the ring and then turned away. "To attempt a bribe in Barcelona is a risk also. It is possible that there aren't enough carats in the ring or that the attempt will be made to the wrong person. So far no one knows that you're here. It would be best to keep the diamond as a last resort, for something more certain."

"What would baptism do for us, if we had visas?" asked Helene. "Would we be legal, then, if we converted to Catholicism?"

"You would have the rights of any other citizen. Nobody pays any attention to birth certificates in Spain. It's your baptismal certificate that they want to see. With it you would be permitted to work anywhere you wanted in Spain, if there were jobs. Without it you can become a shopkeeper, if you're lucky enough to have money. Or you can leave the country. There are no laws against being a Spanish Jew, if you can prove you were born in Spain. But then again, Spanish Jews have no baptismal certificates either. And so it goes, round and round."

"Then a baptismal certificate stops all questions?"

"All questions, if you have a visa along with the baptismal certificate. Without that, it's all academic anyway."

Helene began to prepare for the moment when she and David would have to leave Tonio's apartment. The scene with the woman had put her on guard. During the day she watched for the presence of someone official, a soldier who looked in her direction or a person, perhaps, who stood in line and stared at Helene in a strange manner.

"It won't happen that way, Helene. It never happens in the way that we anticipate," said Tonio.

She would awaken in the middle of the night bathed in perspiration, certain that David was gone, too, that somehow Maurice had reached from beyond the grave and snatched David away from her. And when she realized that David was safe in the bed beside her, she would lie awake thinking of what she would do when the moment arrived that she and David had to leave.

"Where will you go if you leave here?" asked Tonio.

"I haven't thought it through," she said. Meanwhile she and David lived from day to day.

In the sixth week the moment came. She sensed, rather than heard, the notification of her expulsion. It was four-thirty in the morning when the door to the bedroom opened. Tonio stood in the doorway in his bathrobe, hair more disheveled than usual. A lit cigarette dangled from his full lips.

Helene sat up in bed immediately. She touched David's warm body protectively.

"It has been reported to the police that an undocumented woman and her child are living here," said Tonio.

"How long before I must leave?" asked Helene. Tonio turned and tossed the cigarette into the sink behind him, and then he walked into the bedroom and sat down on the foot of the bed.

"Tomorrow morning someone will arrive to take you to the police station for questioning, and from there you will go to Miranda de Ebro. No further visas are being granted to refugees from the Greater Reich. The prisons are so overcrowded that they have begun to deport German Jews to Germany."

"No, David will not go back to Germany. You haven't been in Germany. I have. It's impossible."

He turned his head slightly away from her. "What can I do? There is nothing I can do. I'm powerless to do anything for you and David."

Helene leaned toward David and kissed his smooth cheek as he slept. "He is only a little boy," she said. "So many bad things have happened to him, and he is still such a little boy."

Tonio reached toward her, his hand almost touching the white skin of her breasts above the bodice of the nightgown. But he didn't touch her.

"May I stay?" he asked.

"Yes."

"The boy is sleeping," he said.

Helene picked David up gently and placed him, still sleeping, in Tonio's arms. He carried him to the cot in the kitchen, and when he returned, he shut the door behind him. Helene switched on the small lamp on the bureau next to the bed. As Tonio leaned against the door watching her, she got out of bed and walked to him. He opened his bathrobe and pressed her body against his bare flesh.

"You're such a good man, Tonio. I'll never forget your goodness," said Helene, closing her eyes against the image of Maurice's ghost.

He kissed her, exploring her mouth with his tongue. Slipping the straps of her gown off her shoulders, he cupped her breasts in his hands and kissed the smooth flesh. "Since the first day in the church, I've thought of you this way," he whispered as he lifted her in his arms and carried her to the bed.

Tears misted her eyes as he laid her down gently on top of the coverlet and gazed at her nakedness. "Tonio," she said.

"Shh, it's all right now. I'm here with you," he said, lying down beside her and encircling her with his arm.

"I would not have killed myself. I would have stayed alive for you, Helene," he said, touching her belly with his fingertips. He ran his hand over her nipples, then kissed them. "I am glad he didn't stay alive for you, Helene, and that it is I who touch you now, I who hold you in my arms and caress you."

His hand touched the softness above her open thighs. "The feel of your skin makes my heart burst," he said.

She lay back against the pillows, her knees up and apart. She guided his hand to the spot that always took her to a place beyond caring. He was telling her that he loved her.

"Stay with me, Helene," he said, his body atop hers. "Stay, stay, stay," he said as he moved in and out of her. She held his head close against her breasts and tried not to hear what he said.

In the morning she dressed David and packed her few belongings, and while Tonio slept, she left the apartment.

XI

Helene had rarely noticed other people's children before she had her own. There were no younger cousins in the family when she was growing up.

"Babies are so adorable," Erika would say as she stopped on the street to admire a child in a perambulator.

"I find them more curious than adorable," Helene would reply, not understanding what attraction other people's children had for anyone else.

"Wait until you have your own," Grandmama warned. "You'll see."

"But I really have no interest in children," Helene protested, "no patience for them."

"You don't need patience, Helene," Maurice told her as part of his campaign to begin a family. "There are servants who are paid to have patience."

"Then why have children at all?" she asked.

"For the future," said Maurice.

The thirteenth-century Cathedral La Seu faced onto the Plaza Cristo Rey, its two towers soaring above the Gothic Quarter surrounding the plaza. Helene stood at the edge of the square and looked up at the cathedral's facade, concentric Gothic arches embellished with serpentine swirls in the style of the Berbers who once ruled Spain. Guarding the arches were statues of saints that grew out of the stone and reached heavenward. A jagged crater gaped, ugly and raw, in the center of the plaza near the cathedral's steps, a souvenir of the Loyalists' anticlericalism, when nuns and priests were executed, Church property was confiscated, and churches were burned to the ground during the recent Civil War.

A slight rain was falling, glazing the dusty cobblestones of Puerta del Angel and washing the faces of the saints. A young man in a beret and work clothes sat on the stones of Puerta del Angel, his back against the wall of the cathedral, and played a battered guitar. His music, a blend of Catalonian words, Jewish melodies, and Arabic rhythms, echoed through the winding medieval streets. He nodded his thanks and kept singing as a woman dressed in black homespun bent and put a piece of bread into the empty cigar box at his feet.

At the entrance to the cathedral, at the top of the steps, a priest stood talking to a crowd of people gathered around him. Helene hesitated a moment, looking down at David, who was listening intently to the music. She knelt and straightened his coat, letting her hands rest on his thin shoulders. "How long can we run from the Jew-haters, David? You know that I love you, don't you?"

He nodded his head up and down.

"It's a very cold day today," she said, shivering in her wool suit. "Not a day to go to prison, is it, David?"

He shook his head no.

While Helene and David had stood listening to the music, the square had begun to fill with people. They clustered in family groups. In each, someone held an infant. Helene turned around to look at those who had gathered near her. The people were poorly dressed but clean, and each baby wore a handmade white dress.

The rain was coming down harder now.

"*Señoras y señores, vengan ustedes con sus niños,*" the priest shouted to the crowd as he motioned for them to follow him inside. Helene held David by the hand, and they moved with the group up the steps and into the cathedral. Once inside, the priest was joined by two other priests. Helene turned to the woman standing next to her.

"*Baptême?*" asked Helene in French.

The woman looked puzzled for a moment, and then noting the similarity to the Spanish word, she smiled and bounced her baby higher on her arm to show her off to Helene.

"Sí, bautismo," answered the woman in Spanish.

The noise of the crowd reverberated throughout the cathedral. Babies cried. Helene felt herself being pushed along. She bent and scooped David up in her right arm and maneuvered him and the two suitcases past the crypt of Santa Eulalia into the cloister of the cathedral. In the cloister they waited at the closed door to the Chapel Santo Cristo de Lepanto while one of the priests talked to the assembled families. Helene understood a word here and there, enough to comprehend that they were being told how to behave and how to respond inside the chapel. David felt heavy on her arm. "Put your arms around my neck, David. That's right."

The priest had started to call out names. There were shouts from the crowd of people in front of the chapel door as their names were read. Occasionally someone said something, and the rest of the people laughed, and the priest motioned for them to be quiet. The cloister was empty except for the babies and their families waiting to be admitted to the baptismal chapel. Within the garden in the center of the cloister was a lake surrounded by flowering shrubs, where two majestic swans swam side by side, their feathers a stark white against the gray stones of the cloister walls. Above the door to the chapel was the inscription *"Adoremus in Aeternum Sanctissimum Sacramentum."*

Helen felt as though she weren't there at all. She could not understand the language. Nobody paid any attention to her with her suitcases and the three-year-old child in her arms. She desperately wanted somebody to know why she was there, to understand why she was doing this. Tears filled her eyes. "I love you, David," she said, her lips close to his face.

The door to the chapel opened, and as the people pushed forward, the priest turned some away, telling them that there was room only for parents and godparents. The chapel was filling rapidly.

"Bitte," said Helene in German as she felt herself being shoved to one side, away from the door. One of the priests had started to shut the left-hand side of the door. People dropped back now. Helene took the last few steps at a run.

"*Bitte*," she said, pointing to David. The priest smiled at her, not comprehending. Helene's heart raced. He was shutting the right-hand door now.

"*Bautismo*," she said, repeating the word the woman had said to her.

"*Sí, bautismo*," said the priest, stepping aside so that Helene could slip through the narrow opening.

There were seats for all those who had managed to get through the door into the chapel, and Helene and David sat in the rear near the iron grille that gave onto the main cathedral. Some of the relatives who hadn't been able to gain entry to the chapel now stood against the grillwork, their faces pressed against the iron. A fourth priest, in an embroidered robe with a white velvet cape around his shoulders, entered the chapel from an adjoining room. He began to recite what sounded like a prayer to Helene. The people around her were kneeling, their heads bowed. A baby's piercing cry interrupted the prayer. The priest stopped talking; the baby's cry stopped, and the priest resumed his incantations. When he had finished, another priest moved to the high priest's side, and a litany began between the priest and the congregation. The priest's resonant voice filled the chapel as he exhorted the faithful to respond to his supplications. At each pause in his litany, the people responded, as if in one voice, "*Sí, lo creo*," and the priest intoned, "*Yo bautizo*."

The litany was mystical. "Yes, I believe" from the people, "I do baptize" from the priest. Helene didn't need to understand the words to comprehend that the assembled parents and godparents were being asked if they believed in Jesus Christ—"*Sí, lo creo*"—that they were being asked if they believed that they must renounce Satan—"*Sí, lo creo*"—that they were being asked if they believed that their children would be forever after safe in God's hands—"*Sí, lo creo*."

"*Yo bautizo*," said the priest after them.

"*Sí, lo creo*," murmured Helene.

"*Creen que Dios crea todas las cosas en el mundo?*" asked the priest.

"*Sí, lo creo*," repeated Helene, along with the others.

The litany continued, and the words of the priest and the

responses of the congregation soothed Helene. It was so simple. *"Sí, lo creo,"* and David would no longer be a Jew.

Finally the chanting stopped. A few words of instruction were spoken by the priest in white, and the families stood up and formed a line. Helene watched intently as the first couple in line walked to the altar. The mother handed her infant to the priest in white, and he dipped the baby's head in the baptismal font and then handed the child to his assistant, who wiped the child's head with a towel while the father lit a white taper and inserted it in a standing candelabrum at the side of the altar.

At last it was David's turn. Helene shoved the suitcase and the satchel under the bench and carried David to the altar.

"It won't hurt, David," she whispered to him. "It's like a game."

The priest bent David's head to the font, splashed the water across his forehead, and then passed him to his assistant. The priest handed Helene a blank baptismal certificate and a taper. After she lit the taper and placed it in a holder next to the others, she looked at the flame momentarily. She felt that she should stay and say a brochah over the candle. A Jewish prayer to negate the Catholic holy water.

"Gracias," she said to the priest, who had already turned to the next infant.

"See, it was a game. Was that fun, David?" she asked as she retrieved the suitcases from beneath the bench. She held the baptismal certificate close to her as they walked to a bench near the crypt of Santa Eulalia. "Sit here, next to me," she said. "Is your head still damp?"

"Yes." He touched his hair with his fingers.

"Now you're like all the other children who were here." She pressed her lips against his face and held her arms around him until he began to squirm.

"Now, let's see." Blinking back her tears she stared at the baptismal certificate in her hands. There was a blank line marked *"Apellido."* She knew so few Spanish names. She looked around her, searching for names, any names that would change David from a German Jew into a Spanish Catholic. The plaque above the baptismal chapel said "Santo

Cristo de Lepanto." She bent her head and wrote "Juan Lepanto."

"Stay here, David. Don't move. Promise me you won't move."

"I won't."

She put the satchel with six gold coins in it beside him on the bench. The remaining two coins were wrapped in a handkerchief and pinned to the inside of her skirt. She walked across the cathedral, beneath the dome, to a carved-wood confessional. She sat down, her face near the screen.

"Do you speak French, Father?" she asked.

"Yes, my child."

"Will you hear my confession?"

"Yes, my child."

"Forgive me, Father, but I have taken what does not belong to me. I was entrusted with the child of a wealthy family who fled Spain during the Civil War. The parents entrusted me not only with the child, but with their gold as well. Now they have asked me to send the child to them, but I have spent the gold, except for six coins."

"What is it you ask of me, my child?"

Helene shoved the baptismal document beneath the grate.

"I leave the child in your care, Father, and I ask your forgiveness. The child is a baptized Catholic. Pray for me, Father. Pray for the child."

Helene stood behind a column in the shadowy nave of the cathedral and watched David as he sat alone on the bench, his feet swinging back and forth beneath the cold stone seat. She held her hand to her mouth for fear that she would cry out to him to run to her. He did not yet suspect anything. She could pull him into her arms, and they would run away together again. She shook her head, the tears streaming down her cheeks. She had no choice. "Maurice, I have no choice," she whispered in the gloomy silence. "You had a choice, but I have none."

David was looking up at the ceiling, counting the angels in the stained glass of the clerestory windows. She would remember his face, and she would find him again. He would not be lost to her forever, only separated from her for a little while.

Two nuns emerged from a side door of the basilica and walked purposefully to where David sat. One nun knelt so that she looked directly into David's face, and her hand stroked his hair gently. The other nun stood with her arms folded and watched solemnly.

"That's it, David. Let the nuns love you," whispered Helene, and then she turned and ran across the mosaic floor, down the stone steps, and out into the street.

XII

After Helene and Maurice were married, there was the excitement of setting up a new home, of learning to be a wife. There were luncheons at Grandmama's and shopping to do and concerts to attend. When they had been married two years, Helene gave a recital for the benefit of wives of veterans of the Great War. After that there were more benefit concerts, and soon she was in demand in all the music salons in Berlin.

Maurice was delighted with Helene's renewed career. It was just small enough and manageable enough to provide her with something to do while he was busy with his growing practice and university teaching.

"My dear Helene, you waste yourself in Berlin," said Herr Houck after one of Helene's recitals. "To pursue a career, one must tour. I can arrange concerts in Europe, and when you are well known here, I will take you to America."

"Insanity," said Maurice when Helene told him about it. "What Herr Houck proposes goes against your nature, Helene. I know you better than he does. You do not have the fortitude to pursue a career away from the home."

Grandmama concurred. "You will destroy your marriage. You must not lose Maurice. Never forget, Helene, that men are the ones who must face the world. Women merely nurture."

Helene stood in the shadow of the jewelry shop across Las Ramblas and listened to the volleys of gunfire that came from behind the gray stone building on the corner of the Plaza Cataluña. The plaza was the hub of the city, accessible from any direction. Helene watched the people, the citizens of Barcelona, as they marched in support of the Franco regime. "*Vae victis*"—"Woe to the vanquished"—came back to her from that long-ago time when Fräulein Gusick lectured to her class on the Roman Wars.

She looked around her, feeling bereft but certain that she had done the right thing. David was safe. She would say that over and over to herself. David was safe.

She twisted Grandmama's diamond ring around and around on her finger. Now she would use it to gain time before the police found her. She would move from place to place if she had to. And when the money from the ring ran out, she would make plans again. But David was safe. David was safe.

Crowds of people bearing signs that said "*Muerte a los Judíos*" marched angrily around the plaza, shouting and waving their arms in the air. Helene understood the word "*Judíos,*" so similar to the German "*Juden.*" She also understood the look of hatred in the people's faces, and she recognized the German uniforms as soldiers crisscrossed the streets and the alleys leading to the Plaza Cataluña and blended with the Nationalist troops who stood at parade attention in front of the gray stone building.

She opened the door to the shop. A middle-aged man in a shabby black suit sat at a desk writing by the light of a single overhead bulb. The jewelry cases were empty. The man stood up suddenly and pointed toward the door. "*Cerrado,*" he shouted. Helene ignored him and moved toward the single light. She was inside. She would not go out so easily into the dangerous streets. She held her hand under the light so that its beams caught the facets of Grandmama's diamond ring.

"*Pesetas,*" she said, her eyes searching the man's long, thin face. He hesitated. She took the ring off her finger and placed it in his hand.

"Josep, *listo,*" came a voice from the rear of the store. The man looked anxiously at the front door. He walked quickly to the door and locked it, then flipped a switch on the wall, and the single light went out. Now the jewelry store was in darkness. Suddenly the shop was filled with men in heavy sweaters with workmen's caps on their heads. They seemed all to be talking at once with an air of urgency. Helene could see the man she had spoken to walking toward the rear door, where the figures had come from. He held Grandmama's ring in his hand.

"Parlez-vous français?" she asked, panicked that he might walk out of the store with the ring.

"No," the man replied. The others were pulling backpacks from beneath the counters, and the small shop was rank with the odor of their unwashed bodies as one by one they tied on their packs and filed out the rear door of the shop. The man with Grandmama's ring paid no attention to Helene. He had dismissed her as being of no importance. And then she began to scream. The cry came from deep within her, a scream of desperation, of hurt and sorrow beyond remedy. It released something within her, an energy that she hadn't known she possessed. She held her hands to her head and let the scream fill the shop. There were shouts and the sound of running feet on stone pavement in the alley, the noise of motors being started, and the man silenced Helene's mouth with his hand and pulled her along with him through the storeroom, past the mattresses that lined the walls. Then they were out in the air, his hand was no longer on her mouth, and she was being pulled up into the rear of the truck by two of the men in sweaters, who had rifles slung on their shoulders. When the truck lurched forward, Helene was flung into a corner. A woman in a man's overcoat, her head draped with a black woolen shawl, pulled Helene close to her. She put her fingers to her lips for silence, and then the truck was roaring down the alleys behind Las Ramblas, headed for the Pyrenees.

The woman in the black shawl emptied Helene's suitcase of clothes while the truck bounced along the bomb-damaged road on the way to the border.

"Arregla con estos," said the woman, handing two sweaters and three pairs of stockings to Helene. Rummaging through the suitcase, she picked out Helene's nightgown and toiletry kit and slipped them into her own cloth satchel. At the next bridge the woman tossed the suitcase and its contents out the back of the truck into the river.

Josep, the man who had taken Grandmama's ring, sat near

the rear canvas flap of the truck. When the suitcase tumbled into the water, he moved over the packed bodies to where Helene sat staring at the clothes in her lap, a numb expression on her face.

"Put them on," he said in French, although he had said he did not speak French. "It's bitter cold now in Port Bou." He looked the other way while the woman helped Helene put on the extra pairs of hose and layer the sweaters beneath the fur-trimmed jacket.

"The border is closed. We're going to travel on foot through the Pyrenees to southern France," said Josep.

He handed her a thousand-peseta bill. "For the ring," he said. "You will need it when we leave you off in Port Bou."

As the truck jounced along the rutted roads, Josep's face was enigmatic. The only emotion she had seen him display was in the shop, when he had shouted at her. Now, in the truck, he was in command. There was no need for shouting.

"But I can't go with you to southern France. Spain is the only place where I might survive," Helene protested.

He looked at her curiously, then removed the diamond ring from his pocket and studied its old-fashioned setting.

"You are a Jew?" he said.

Helene pulled her passport out of her inside jacket pocket. Josep looked at it with its stamped "J" and tossed it back in Helene's lap. "We'll be joining the Republican guerrillas in Perpignan. We could let you out on the road now, but it's more dangerous here than in the city if you do not have the appropriate papers. Do you understand?"

"I understand."

"The soldiers patrol in trucks. And you are a woman alone." He glanced at her slender figure.

"I understand."

"You may stay with us, go as far as we go. I don't think you want to join the guerrillas and fight Franco, do you?"

The woman in the man's coat and the shawl was smiling and nodding at Helene as though she understood the conversation.

"I don't know. I don't know," said Helene. "Who fights whom is so confusing, and that I'm here in this truck with you—"

"I'm sorry for that," said Josep. "I had no time to explain. The truck had come and could not stay parked for more than a few minutes without someone noticing it. There are thousands of us in the Pyrenees. You are welcome to join us."

At Port Bou the truck stopped and let them out. They set out in the darkness, walking through the low grasses, moving silently and steadily. As the grades grew steeper, the heels of Helene's walking shoes began to slip against the rocks of the path. There were three women in the group, besides Helene, and fifteen men. No one complained of the pace, although the women began to lag behind as the air grew thinner and the climb steeper. Bushes and gorse tore at their clothes as they left the flatlands below and ascended the slopes toward the mountain passes. Helene was glad that the woman had thrown the suitcase away. There was nothing of value left in it. She felt free and unfettered climbing with the others, as though she had a purpose, that by putting one foot in front of the other, she was doing something for herself. There was a reality to the climb, an importance to it, as though something vital would be accomplished by her arduous efforts. Fight alongside the Loyalists? She had never thought herself capable of fighting anyone. But if she could stay with Josep and the others, it would be better than trying to hide in Barcelona.

They hiked the whole night, stopping once to relieve themselves in the bushes. It had begun to snow, light patches of white floating in the black night. The air was frigid, but Josep urged them on.

"If you walk, you will stay alive," he exhorted them.

Helene felt a painful stab in her chest with every breath. Everything now was blotted out of her consciousness except the act of placing her feet solidly on the path so as not to slip. When they had walked ten miles, it started to snow heavily so that the path was slippery beneath their feet, and it was difficult to see where they were going. Josep had them walk in single file now while he looked for firm footholds in the snow. The woman who had thrown away Helene's suitcase offered her one end of her black shawl, and they helped pull each other along the precipitous slope.

Suddenly the caravan stopped. Josep shouted back at them

not to move forward, that there was a gorge below. A six-foot-wide bridge spanned the great empty expanse beneath them. The snow-covered trestles of the bridge gleamed treacherously in the light of the stars.

Josep stepped onto the bridge cautiously. He held the railing as he tested the ability of the bridge's timbers to hold both him and the weight of the snow. Helene watched him, glad of the respite. She rubbed her hands briskly on the woman's shawl, and then she rubbed the wool back and forth across her face to bring the blood to the surface. The woman chanted a prayer as Josep walked across the creaking ridge.

"Vámonos, uno por uno," he called to them when he had reached the other side. They started across the bridge, one at a time. The sun was coming up, casting a golden-mauve shadow on the landscape below them. They crossed the bridge slowly, and as each person reached the other side, a small shout of victory went up from the rest. Helene didn't understand the Catalan they spoke, but she understood that they were, as she was, forced to flee their own country.

Gradually the stars began to recede as the sun rose. It was easier now to see where they were walking. A stone farmhouse was ahead of them, smoke curling from the chimney. Josep motioned again for them to stop. The woman with the shawl smiled at Helene and pointed to herself.

"Sofía."

"Helene."

They huddled together beneath the black shawl, stamping their feet in the deep snow to keep from freezing. Ahead of them the sharply etched hillside dropped down into icy mists. Across the canyon, atop a craggy col, there sat what looked like an ancient castle, battlements facing the gorge, serrated roofs highlighted against the sawtooth mountains behind it. Helene breathed deeply. There was never such a beautiful place as this. She had done the right thing. David would live to see beautiful places like this.

Josep didn't come out of the farmhouse. Dogs came out and surrounded the group, as though herding a flock of sheep. Then came the armed soldiers in their gray uniforms. One of the soldiers barked sharp commands in the cold morning air. The men dropped their guns and backpacks to the ground. Sofía fell to her knees in the snow and crossed herself, as if preparing for death.

Helene looked around her. These were not German soldiers. She was not a Republican guerrilla. It was all wrong. It was not meant to be this way.

Then Josep emerged from the farmhouse, two officers behind him.

Helene ran up to him and clutched at his arm. "What has happened? Who are they?"

"French troops," said Josep, pain in his face. "They are sending us to a camp in Saint Cyprien. They don't want us waging war on Spain from French soil. We are finished."

When Helene fell back away from him, one of the officers looked at her speculatively.

They were herded into the farmhouse and fed bread and a small portion of cheese. Then the processing began. Each one of the group was called to a table in the corner of the farmhouse, and papers were looked at, questions asked. When each interrogation was completed, the person was segregated from the rest of the group.

Josep and Helene sat next to each other away from the others. "My passport, Josep, they will look at my passport," said Helene in a low voice.

Josep didn't look at her. In the dim light his hawk nose and thin face were an expressionless mask. "It is up to them what they will do when they see the passport. France is at war with Germany, and you carry a German passport."

There were only five people left to be interrogated. Helene rubbed her face with her hands, trying to think, trying to plan. "Should I destroy the passport, Josep? Would that be better, not to have any papers at all?"

He looked at her now, and she could see the sadness in his eyes. "The camp at Saint Cyprien is a concentration camp. If you have no papers, they will send you there with us."

"I don't know what to do, Josep. Help me."

"Show them the passport. Who can predict what the French will do?"

When Helene's turn came, the officer glanced up at her dispassionately and then examined her passport on the desk in front of him. "You are a German Jew?" he asked, his small mustache moving as he spoke.

"Yes."

"You are an enemy alien in French territory."

"Yes."

"Why are you here with Spanish Loyalists?"

"It was an accident."

"I see." He looked at her passport picture for a long time. "A very nice photograph," he said. "Passport pictures are rarely so flattering."

Her heart was racing. "Thank you," she said.

The officer sighed. "You have given me a special problem. It has been a while since I have seen Jews coming over the Pyrenees. But to be going in this direction, well, it is unusual. A few months ago I would have let you go. A German passport would have meant nothing to me. But we are at war with Germany now. It is a different situation. You cannot stay in France."

"I must not go back to Germany," she said. "I have sacrificed much to get out of Germany. Please don't send me back. I have a little money—"

The officer's eyebrow went up. "This is not Spain," he said. "Keep your money to yourself."

He closed the passport and put it atop a pile of documents. "You may sit with the others," he said.

"Sit with the others? Does that mean that—"

"It means nothing."

That night Helene and the Spaniards slept on the wooden floor of the farmhouse, close together near the fire for warmth, while the soldiers drank cognac and sang French folk songs into the late hours of the night.

In the morning the Spaniards were sent by truck to Saint Cyprien to be interned in a French concentration camp. Helene was put on a train bound for Germany.

XIII

The appointment was for three in the afternoon in General Victor Paulen's office at the Berlin Regimental Barracks. Count von Kirchner arrived at precisely 2:45. The guard at the gate looked at the Count's papers and then telephoned to someone within the compound.

"You are early," said the guard as he put the telephone receiver down and handed Karl's papers back to him.

Karl replaced his papers in his pocket. "I must stand out here in the cold, then, for fifteen minutes?" snapped the Count. He had trained himself to deal with underlings in a brutally dismissive manner so that he could be assured attention would be paid to him when he dealt with them again. It did not come naturally to him. He preferred to be charming, to be at his ease and to make others feel at ease also, but there were certain postures that he had learned to adopt in order not to be shoved aside. The new German Army required that one assert oneself.

The guard was on the telephone again. When he hung up, he saluted the Count stiffly. "My Colonel, General Paulen asks that you proceed to his office and wait in his private sitting room."

Karl gave the Nazi salute and walked briskly through the gate and across the field.

General Paulen's adjutant greeted him effusively when he entered the General's waiting room. "Colonel, it is very good to see you back home again," said the lieutenant. "The General has been waiting eagerly to hear your report. Did you enjoy your stay in Rome?"

"Rome was very crowded; the streets were dirty and littered," said Karl.

"And the weather?" persisted the lieutenant, playing out his part of the interested subordinate.

"And are you really interested in Italian weather?" retorted Karl, "when I am half dead from the Berlin cold?"

The lieutenant, a pale young man of no more than twenty-two, blushed lightly. "The General is engaged at the moment. If you will come with me to his sitting room, I'll bring you a cup of hot tea. Would you like your tea with milk and sugar?"

"With brandy would be fine," answered Karl, relaxing his guard for the first time since he had arrived at the barracks.

The lieutenant led the Count to the sitting room. It appeared to have been decorated by a woman. A French settee, upholstered in light blue damask, sat opposite a small grand piano, whose top was engulfed by a red silk shawl upon which were pictures and flowers and millefiori crystal bibelots arranged in artistic fashion. The red of the shawl was repeated in the central motif of the Persian rug that covered the wood floor in front of the settee.

The Count drank his tea and smoked a cigarette; then he walked around the room, looking out the windows to the parade grounds below. He walked to the piano and picked up a millefiori paperweight and held it up so that the red and blue and yellow canes sparkled from within their glass cage. His mother had a collection of millefiori that had been handed down to her from her own mother, the Baroness von Blendheim. She kept them in a French vitrine at the Von Kirchner estate in Mannheim.

The door opened behind the Count, and General Paulen entered the room, followed by the rotund figure of Field Marshal Göring. "My dear Karl, I am so sorry, but I have been in a meeting with the Field Marshal," said the General.

Karl stood up to his fullest height and gave the Nazi salute to the fat man who stood facing him, his chest heavy with medals. "Field Marshal," Karl said when he had snapped his arm down at his side again.

"Your mission to Rome was successful?" asked Göring as he settled his plump body onto the delicate settee.

Karl looked at the General and then back to the Field Marshal.

"The Field Marshal had his hand in everything, Karl. After all, he and Count Ciano are old friends. Any time we send messages to Count Ciano, the Field Marshal is told about it."

Göring looked up at the two men, who stood stiffly near the grand piano while Göring lounged against the settee.

"You and Count Ciano have many friends in common, I hear," said the Field Marshal conversationally.

"Yes. The Count's cousin is married to my mother's sister's child," said Karl.

"Ah, quite impressive," said Göring. "Isn't that quite impressive, Victor?" he asked, turning to the General.

"Yes, it is. Count von Kirchner and his family are a credit to the Fatherland."

"Count Ciano has sent me some beautiful religious relics that the Italian Jewish community had presented as gifts to him." Göring laughed when he said the word "gifts."

"The Count has exquisite taste," agreed Karl, "and he is a very generous man."

"Then you talked of mutual friends and relatives, did you?" asked Göring, a touch of envy in his voice.

"We mentioned my mother, the Countess Mathilde. He asked after her health. We talked of school friends."

"So you went to school with Count Ciano, did you?" Göring's eyes were bright, as though from fever.

"Yes, Herr Field Marshal."

"If the Field Marshal would like to join us for a brandy—" interrupted the General.

Göring placed one bejeweled hand on his rounded knee and lifted himself with effort from the down cushions of the settee. His face was momentarily hit by a beam of daylight from the window. Around his hairline the skin appeared lighter than it was on the rest of his face, and what seemed to be flecks of powder showed on the shoulders of his uniform.

Göring walked to the door and then turned and looked at the opposite wall above the settee.

"Victor, I have a painting that belongs with that French sofa. A Vermeer. I could let you have it for a price. You will excuse us, Count, if we talk about art in private for a moment?"

"Of course," said Karl, bowing stiffly. The General and the Field Marshal left the sitting room, and Karl was alone again with the blue damask and the millefioris. He felt agitated, as though too much had been said to the Field Marshal, and that somehow the conversation in the General's office now did not deal exclusively with Vermeers and blue damask sofas. There was always this problem, of talking too much, of risking revealing too much, and perhaps because of it having to perform duties that were not in line with the duties of a German officer.

After ten minutes the pale-faced lieutenant opened the door and said, "The General will see you in his office now."

The office was as austere as the sitting room was frivolous. General Paulen sat behind a massive, square, unornamented desk that held no pictures and no paperweights. Venetian blinds at the windows reduced the glare of sunlight on all-white walls. The wood floors were polished to a high gloss, and Karl's shoes slid slightly as he walked across the floor to the straight leather chair at the side of the General's desk.

"So, Victor," said the General, as though he were greeting him for the first time. "Sit down, sit down."

Karl sat down, his back straight and not touching the backrest of the chair.

"The *Führer*'s message was delivered to the Count, then?" asked the General.

"Yes, *Herr General.*" Karl reached into the briefcase that he carried with him. He pulled out a sealed manila packet and handed it to the General. "Count Ciano also sends his personal regards to the *Führer.*"

General Paulen leaned back in his chair and stared silently at Karl for a few moments. "And you saw Count Ciano and spent a few days visiting friends in Rome—nothing else?"

Karl felt himself falling into the pit that he had feared.

"I saw friends, yes. I have many friends in Rome, *Herr General.*"

"Yes, I know."

Karl waited for a few seconds, and then he spoke.

"Am I to be assigned to Army Group B now that the war has started?"

"No, not Army Group B."

"But I was told that my next assignment would be Group B."

"There has been a change of duty for you. The Field Marshal and I were talking about it before you arrived. He is very impressed with you, Karl. He feels that you could better serve the Fatherland in a noncombat position, that a man of your quality and cultivation and connections should be seen more and not be hidden in the ranks of the Army."

Karl was wary, careful not to show his apprehension. "What is the assignment to be?"

"I am not at liberty to say. Your orders will come very soon from Himmler himself."

Karl felt himself grow cold. "Then it is to be a political position," he said. "I beg Your Excellency's indulgence, but I have never involved myself in political affairs. I have felt that my vocation is in the Army as a soldier. I would hope that the Field Marshal understands that my background and training have not been in political affairs."

"Well, be that as it may, the Field Marshal is recommending you to Himmler, and you will accept. The Field Marshal does not recommend lightly, and he does not accept refusals when he does recommend. And I might tell you that the Field Marshal has told me in strictest confidence that the *Führer* is planning to create the special rank of *Reichsmarschall* for him within the next few months. It would be well not to antagonize him in any way."

"That may be so," said Karl, "but I feel that as a German soldier and as a citizen I have the right to appeal any decision that takes me out of the ranks of the Army."

General Paulen's eyes were as icy as Göring's had been feverish. "You say that you visited friends in Rome. I have information that you attempted to smuggle a group of Jews out of Germany. I also am advised that you were unsuccessful in that attempt. Am I correct?"

Karl's back touched the back of the chair now. How much did the General know about Rome and what went on there?

Karl's voice did not betray him. It was still strong and steady. "Before I answer, may I ask where you have received your information about this so-called group of Jews?"

General Paulen stared into Karl's eyes, measuring his truthfulness. "A lieutenant in the *Einsatzgruppen* in Poland reported to the chief of the security police, Reinhard Heydrich, that a Colonel von Kirchner had given his protection to several Jewish families attempting to leave Germany, that the lieutenant had had to take the matter out of your hands and resolve it himself, and that all the Jews were resettled somewhere in Poland."

Karl's body relaxed imperceptibly in the chair. The General didn't know about the Gelsons or Gunter and Erika. "Yes, your facts are correct," answered Karl.

"Good. I promised the Field Marshal that you would present no problem to us, that you were an obedient soldier willing to go wherever you were assigned."

Karl stood up and saluted the General. The General had gotten his Vermeer, and Karl would not be punished for the Jewish episode.

As the General escorted Karl to the door of the outer office, he put his arm paternally around his shoulder.

"I'm sure I will be content in my post," said Karl.

"Of course you will. You will be a soldier, no matter where you are." He patted Karl's shoulder affectionately, as one who has no advantage to lose. "Remember, Karl, the enemy is not only on the battlefield. You must be valorous, for the enemies of the Reich are all around us, and we must meet them wherever we find them."

The two men shook hands, the lieutenant looked up from his desk and smiled knowingly at Karl, and the appointment was over.

XIV

In 1939, the British closed the door to Palestine for Jewish refugees.

In 1939, Jews were not permitted entry to Argentina, Brazil, Colombia, Nicaragua, France, Belgium, Holland, or Switzerland. The United States quota was filled until 1941. Great Britain's quota was filled, and her colonies now refused to admit Jews.

In 1939, 20,000 Jewish children, needing temporary haven, were refused entry to the United States. The American Legion lobbied against their admission on the ground that the bill would only open the door to Jews who were mental deficients and communist infiltrators.

In 1939, the Nazi-occupied countries refused to let their Jews out. The Jewish people were now caught between those who didn't want them and those who didn't want them.

Hitler had free rein.

Helene was given back her passport, and two French soldiers were assigned to escort her to the German border. The soldiers played cards with each other to pass the time, and they shared their food with her.

"This is where we leave you," they said when the train reached the border at Strasbourg.

"Over there you can buy a ticket on the German train," said one of the soldiers, pointing to the German border depot.

Helene reached into the pocket of her jacket and pulled out the pesetas. "I have no marks to buy a ticket," she said.

"I'll take the pesetas," said the soldier. "This is enough to buy a ticket."

Helene looked at the marks the soldier had handed her.

This was all that Grandmama's ring had come to, enough marks to buy her a train ticket back to Berlin.

She walked slowly across the railway tracks between France and Germany. The French soldiers watched her as she walked.

"*Au revoir,*" the soldiers called out after her, but she did not turn and did not answer.

The German guard at the depot looked at her passport and grinned. "Welcome back to Germany," he said.

The journey was an internal one. Helene didn't see the landscape outside the train window, and she paid no attention to the soldiers at the depots along the route. She felt removed from danger. The worst that anyone could do to her had already been done. There was no longer any fear. She felt like a piece of paper buffeted by the wind, insignificant in the landscape, merely one of many such pieces of paper.

The train stopped at small towns along the way, but she had only the gold coins, and there was not enough time to cash one to buy food. To still her hunger she left the compartment periodically and walked down the train corridor to the water dispenser near the restroom, where she drank water until she felt her stomach distend with liquid. By evening she felt light-headed from hunger, and she lay down on the seat in her compartment, her jacket folded beneath her as a pillow. She fell into a peculiar waking sleep in which her eyes were partially open, but she saw nothing and heard sounds only as at a great distance.

She awoke to the sound of the compartment door sliding open. A stout woman entered, filling the compartment with her girth and the smell of her cologne. Helene's eyes opened momentarily. The train was stopped at a station.

The woman removed her coat and hat and placed them on the shelf above the seats. Helene turned her head away, not wanting to awake from her dream state.

"My, my, the German winter does not disappoint us this year," said the woman, bending over Helene to see more clearly out the window. "Look, it's snowing, and barely December yet."

The woman was hardy-looking and jovial, and now the scent of yeasty dough broke through her cologne.

"Ah, you're sleeping. I apologize if I disturbed your sleep," the woman said.

"I'm awake," said Helene, sitting up straight in the train seat. "Are we near to Berlin?"

"Very soon we will arrive. The conductor said half an hour."

Helene felt the woman's eyes on her, studying her torn stockings and the stains and pulled threads and furless patches on the once-beautiful fur-trimmed suit.

"You have had an accident?" asked the woman.

"I have had an accident, yes."

"You live in Berlin?" asked the woman.

"No."

The woman looked at her suspiciously. "You look to me to be French, or is it Italian? It's so hard to tell nowadays."

"Yes, I'm Italian. I will be visiting relatives in Berlin."

"It is a beautiful city, Berlin, isn't it, with the cafés and the parks? I have never been to Rome. I would like to visit some day."

"Yes, you should do that. It is very beautiful."

"The Germans and Italians both understand the same things," said the woman emphatically. "No more Jew stores, no Jew banks, no Jews to poison the minds of our children, to trick us into losing the greatness of our country. It is because of the Jews that Germany has suffered so in the past. We have let ourselves be seduced by the Jewish money god. It is in purity that we shall regain control. Just as the Italians now seek to make themselves pure, so will the German people. Do you agree?"

The woman's face was an ordinary face, flushed now with ideological fervor. She didn't appear to Helene to be a monster. This was casual conversation, joined to talk of the weather. It offended no one, because one knew full well that a Jewish face could be spotted in a moment. There were diagrams in *Der Stürmer.* The shape of the lips would be so, the shape of the nostrils would flare so, and even the lids of the eyes would have a particular shape. Heads were a giveaway. The brow would be a certain distance from the hairline, and the ears would begin at a spot no more than a finger's breadth from the line of the upper cheekbone.

The woman smiled benignly at Helene, waiting for an answer.

"There were many people on the streets in Rome," said Helene.

"That is a curious thing to say," said the woman.

Helene turned away. "I'm sorry," she said. "I have been very ill, and I am not yet recovered."

At a bank near the railway station Helene exchanged a gold coin for marks. She bought a small purse to keep the money in, and a comb for her hair. As she walked along the crowded sidewalks of the Leipzigerstrasse, past the smart-looking women who darted in and out of the stylish shops and elegant department stores that lined the boulevard, she was conscious of her own bedraggled appearance. Christmas trees with blinking colored lights winked from every window. People laughed and called to each other as they shopped for the Christmas holidays.

Helene stopped to read the headlines on a newspaper. "USSR invades Finland." Below the war story was an article titled "Nobody Else Wants Jews Either." The story quoted Dr. Goebbels as saying: "The countries of the world love the Jews so much that Malta has volunteered to take 7, Jamaica 5, Ceylon and the Bahamas 10 each, and Gibraltar and the Leeward Islands one Jew each. Let them all be silent when we take it upon ourselves to settle the Jewish question for all time."

Helene shivered beneath her layered sweaters and jacket.

"*Entschuldigen Sie, bitte,*" said an elderly man as he walked around her. A few people turned to look at her in her ripped jacket and stained skirt. She moved backward toward the brightly lit shop window, out of the way of traffic, then turned around and looked into the shop window. Honeyed cakes formed a pyramid on a revolving stand. Helene watched the cakes spin around. There were small linen-covered tables inside, and people were eating cake and drinking hot chocolate. It would be warm inside, and she could clean herself up a little and get something to eat.

She walked in and hurried past the people who stood at the pastry counter buying holiday cakes to take home. In the rear of the shop, she entered the small bathroom and locked the door behind her. She leaned over the sink, breathing hard, although she had not been running. When she had regained her composure, she pulled off the ripped jacket and dropped it into the trash bin beneath the sink. She wet a paper towel and rubbed it across the spots on her wool skirt, then washed her face and combed her hair. She looked at herself in the mirror. There were scratches on one side of her cheek; she could not remember what had caused them. Her dark eyes stared back at her. David's eyes. She stood at the sink and let the tears fall for a few minutes. Then she washed her face again and went out into the pastry shop and bought a cream-filled pastry and a cup of hot chocolate.

Afterward she left the shopping district and walked quickly to the tram stop. She got on and paid the fare, then rode to within half a block of her house. The snow had stopped, and the streets were icy. She felt the wet cold seep through her layered sweaters. As she approached the house, she heard the sound of piano music and singing spilling out into the street. A path between the leafless rows of birch trees took her to the door.

She heard people singing carols in the drawing room of the house as she walked up the steps. From where she stood at the side of the door, looking through the stained-glass insets of the bay window, everything seemed the same as she had left it. Potted geraniums were placed beneath the windowsill, where they could catch the morning sun. The *bureau-plat* that had belonged to Maurice's mother was just where it had been, between the grandfather clock and the Renaissance-style bookcase.

The two Steinway pianos still faced each other on the small raised stage where she and Erika had played so many duets together and where the Thursday Evening Players had staged their musicales. Maurice always sat on a folding chair to Helene's right side and turned pages. Gunter sat right near the footstool that held the sheet music, in the middle of the stage, his cello between his legs, his near-sighted eyes close to the cello's neck. Count von Kirchner stood off to the rear, a little distance from the others, his violin tucked beneath his aristocratic neck. They were playing a Brahms quartet. The Count had practiced well. His glissandos were as smooth as a pane of glass.

Helene blinked. The Thursday Evening Players disappeared. A middle-aged woman sat at one of the pianos playing Christmas music. Several people in evening dress sat on Helene's sofas, drinks in their hands, as a maid passed canapés on the silver butler that Grandmama had given Helene when David was born. A little girl of about five years of age sat near the ceiling-high Christmas tree and fingered the ribbons of the brightly wrapped gifts arranged beneath the tree.

The knot in Helene's stomach made her feel dizzy with pain. Just as she reached her hand out to steady herself against the frame of the window, a man on the sofa looked up toward the window. Had she made a noise? Helene could see his face clearly. A stranger. A perfect stranger sat on her sofa and ate canapés off Grandmama's silver butler. Strangers lived in her house.

The man got up from the sofa. He was walking toward the door. Helene straightened up and moved to the far end of the covered entry and stepped down the two steps to the walkway that ran toward the rear of the house. Then the door opened, and the man looked out. He walked a few feet farther toward the head of the stairs and looked directly at the spot where Helene stood. She didn't move. He rubbed his arms briskly against the cold air, then turned and went back into the house.

Grandmama's house was dark. Helene watched it from across the street. The cold was stinging now, and her head throbbed. The only light shone from the servants' cottage.

Helene ran across the street toward the cottage. She felt weak with relief that Walter and Greta were still here and had seen to Grandmama. She would smother Greta with kisses and apologize to Walter for thinking that he would run and leave Grandmama to the Nazis.

She knocked, and the door opened. At first Walter stared at her without recognition, his eyes cold and his bearing stiff and proper. And then suddenly he changed. He looked away, his body bent in paroxysms of sobbing. Greta came running into the room at the sound. "Frau Gelson," she said. "How did you come here?"

"We'll talk later," said Helene. Greta moved to one side of Walter, and Helene to the other, and together they led him through the small living room into the kitchen and helped him into a chair at the kitchen table.

"Here," said Greta. "Drink the brandy." As Walter drank the glass of brandy, Greta turned to Helene. "To see you reminded him of Frau Rosenzweig."

Helene sank into a chair next to Walter and put her head on her arms. Greta stroked Helene's hair but said nothing.

Walter drained the glass of the rest of the liquor and wiped his mouth with the back of his hand. His hair was grayer than it had been, and his strong, straight back was bent over.

"Frau Rosenzweig is gone," he said weakly.

Helene lifted her head. "Gone where?" she asked, her voice low and flat.

"*Ich weiss nicht,*" said Walter helplessly. Greta patted his shoulder.

"*Still,*" said Greta to her husband.

She turned to Helene. "He suffers much from this. The police came one afternoon two weeks ago. Frau Rosenzweig had just awakened from her nap. She said that she would take tea in the sun room. I didn't want to interrupt her. She had had a cold that had settled in her chest, and she didn't sleep well at night. For a few nights I slept in the bedroom adjoining hers, and I would listen for her cough, and when she called, I would bring her tea and help her to the bathroom. So when the police came, naturally, I felt that she must not be disturbed. And so I told the officer so. But he pushed me aside. He said that punishment would come to me for protecting the old Jewess. When Walter came from the pantry, where he was polishing the silver, the policeman shoved him out of the way and walked through the house to where Madam Rosenzweig sat taking her tea. She greeted the policeman very graciously, and then she excused herself to get dressed. She put on a blue shantung suit with a simple silk blouse and had me comb her hair. Before she left, she sent me back to her closets to fetch her blue felt hat with the gray feathers on it. So beautiful, your Grandmama," said Greta, and she began to weep.

With a despairing cry Helene ran her hands through her hair again and again until it stood wildly out from her head. Greta snuffled and continued talking. "The policeman bowed to Madam Rosenzweig when he saw her dressed so fine, looking so much like the great lady. He offered her his arm. He said that it was a formality, that they wanted to question her about the Rosenzweig family holdings. I sat up all night waiting for her to return, but she never did."

Helene looked around the small kitchen as if somewhere in the corner her Grandmama hid in her fine suit and blue hat with the gray feathers on it.

She stared at Walter and Greta for a few moments, Greta in tears, Walter murmuring something unintelligible. Then Helene ran from the kitchen, through the cottage, and across the rose garden to the gabled house. She pushed open the door to the sun room and ran through the silent mansion.

"Grandmama, Grandmama," she called, as she had called so many times when she returned home from school. She stood at the door to Grandmama's bedroom. Grandmama's lace dressing gown lay across the satin coverlet of the bed. Her perfume bottles and powders sat on the gilt tray on her dressing table. At any moment she would come out and ask how the lessons went, what French verb could she conjugate today.

Helene moved through the pantry into the kitchen. The copper pots still hung gleaming on their hooks above the worktable. She ran her hand along the edge of the sink, feeling its solidity. It was here. Grandmama wasn't.

Greta had entered the house and was behind her now, trying to comfort her. She was offering her something to eat, urging her to sit down in a chair.

There was nothing that could be done. Those who went to the police station never came back. Nothing was more final than that. And yet Grandmama's presence was all around her. It was in the gleaming pots, in the lace dressing gown, in the faint smell of her perfume that lingered still in the very air of the house.

"Evil times," said Greta. "I am so ashamed, Frau Gelson. I cannot understand how anyone could harm such a *gnädige Frau* as Frau Rosenzweig. I have prayed to be able to understand how that could happen, that they take an old lady from her home and never bring her back."

The circle was closing. Helene was completely alone now. The enemy surrounded her. She took Greta's hand and let herself be led back to the cottage.

Grandmama's bed enveloped her. She could feel the impression of Grandmama's body in the mattress. There was warmth beneath the down covers. She slept and dreamed and awoke and pretended that Grandmama was away on holiday. Greta came and brought her meals and warned her that she must leave before the Gestapo came back. Helene told Greta about Maurice and Miriam, and Greta sobbed and went away, and Helene slept again. In the chaos of her nightmare-filled slumber, Helene heard the sound of automobiles in the drive and a shrill scream that could only be that of Greta in pain. Helene sat up in the bed. Was it now her turn to endure what others had endured? Was it now her turn to feel physical pain? Heavy boots tramped through the house, doors were slammed, and drawers were opened and closed.

"And who is this?" demanded the booted figure in the doorway. Helene reached for her passport on the bedside table. The policeman approached the bed and pulled the passport out of Helene's hand. He looked at it and then threw it on the bed. "Get dressed."

Two other Gestapo men came to the bedroom. Helene walked toward the dressing room to remove Grandmama's nightgown and to put on her clothes.

The first man caught her by the hair and pulled her back toward the bed. "Dress here."

She had no underwear on beneath the nightgown. She turned her back on the three men. Her modesty was all that remained to her. Did she fear physical harm less than she feared that they might look at her naked body? No, she decided as the nightgown slipped over her head. Her body no longer belonged to her. She would have to remember that her body was now in the hands of others. Only her thoughts remained her own.

As she reached for her clothes on the chair next to the bed, she picked her underpants up in her hands and looked at them, making note of the way the side seams were joined to the waistband, the way the material was gathered.

Then she felt herself being pushed against the down quilt. One of the policemen held her back arched against the side of the bed, her legs spread out on the floor in front of her, while the second policeman, standing by the side of the bed, entered her. When he had finished, he slapped her across her bare breasts, the flat of his hand leaving a red imprint on her skin. The bedroom was turning like a kaleidoscope. Truly it wasn't her body that this was being done to. The second man took his turn, and when he had finished, he spat in her face. "Filthy Jew cunt."

She closed her eyes and tried to free her mind from the torture chamber that Grandmama's bedroom had become.

"Come, open your eyes, *Mädchen,*" said the last Gestapo man. She opened her eyes and screamed with pain as he thrust into her rectally. She felt that she would explode with pain. The other men were laughing. The more she screamed, the louder they laughed.

Finally the torture was over. One of the men stayed with her in the bedroom while the other two went through the drawers and closets of the house gathering up jewelry and whatever else looked valuable.

"I need to use the toilet," she said. The policeman followed her into the bathroom and stood watching while she urinated. She got up from the toilet, unsteady on her feet. She leaned against the washbasin and splashed her face and body with cool water. The man now lounged against the wall and watched her disinterestedly. If they can do these things to me, then I must have no modesty or fear before them, because they are like the animals in the forest. We are not of the same species. It is an accident that the beasts have been allowed to escape from the forest to prey on human beings.

He followed her back to the bedroom and watched her while she dressed. She put on her clothes slowly. The muscles in her back ached as she moved, and her pelvis felt as though someone had tried to tear her in half. The policeman didn't talk to her. But, then, animals didn't speak the same language as human beings. And if they attempted to, she thought, it would be curious to hear animals that could talk, and we would marvel at how exquisitely they mimicked our words, but it would mean nothing in human terms.

She looked into the mirror. Her eyes were dry. She had no tears for herself, no pity for her bruised body. It was an accident that she had been here when they arrived. It was an accident that she had been born a German and a Jew. She touched one cheek, which was bruised and swollen where her face had been shoved against the bedpost. It was strange how she had not felt the injury at the time. There were so many injuries and insults at the same time, how could she have isolated a single pain? The bone beneath the eye socket felt different to her fingers, as though the cheekbone had been broken.

The Gestapo finished their looting of the house, and when everything they wanted had been loaded into boxes for transport, they pushed Helene ahead of them to the waiting car. The cottage door hung open, but there was no sign of Greta or Walter.

Helene was taken to the Gestapo headquarters in Berlin, where she was placed on a bench in a room with twenty other women. She sat there for ten hours. No one came with food or water, and the only toilet facility was an overflowing bucket standing in the corner. Then she and the other women were taken out and put in an open truck and driven to the countryside, north of Berlin, through forests clean and white under soft blankets of snow, to a medieval town called Fürstenberg. Steepled houses dotted the rolling hills above the town. The lake lay placid and serene as it had for centuries. Fishermen fished from their boats, and the townspeople took the fresh air on country walks. The truck stopped at the shore of the lake. Helene looked out. A high concrete wall surrounded by barbed wire faced the lake. They were told to get out of the truck and wait.

After half an hour the gate was opened, and Helene and the others were marched into the women's compound of Ravensbrück Concentration Camp.

XV

Count von Kirchner's orders came in mid-December. At first he was dumbstruck that such a thing could be possible, that he, a German soldier, would be assigned to be co-commandant of a concentration camp. He telephoned General Paulen immediately upon receiving his orders, but the General was not available and did not return his call. That was ominous. It meant that to appeal to anyone in higher authority not only would be a waste of time, but could possibly be dangerous. Strange stories had been circulating about the camp system, and Karl had closed his ears to them. He wanted nothing more than to be left to do his job as a soldier and to survive the war. But now he was to be forced to listen.

He spent his last weekend on leave with his mother, Countess Mathilde, in Mannheim. They played bridge, and he promised to visit her as often as he could now that he was to be assigned to duty in Germany. He didn't tell her what the duty was, because he was not exactly sure what it was himself.

A driver picked him up in Berlin and drove him to Fürstenberg. Commandant Koegel awaited him at his home in the SS residential section of the camp.

He greeted Karl warmly and showed him around his house, which was furnished with rare works of art and antiques. "Everything you see has been bartered for," said the Commandant. "I cannot use everything that we retrieve from the prisoners, and the inventorying is not very perfectly performed, so I find myself with an excess of gold rings at times and a shortage of Old Masters." The Commandant laughed. "Other people have the opposite problem, so it is a simple matter of adjustment and accommodation."

Karl listened with interest. So this was what it meant to be a commandant of a concentration camp. Perhaps there were worse things that could have happened to him. If someone had to, as the Commandant said, "retrieve" gold rings from prisoners who had no need for them, it might as well be Count Karl von Kirchner as anyone else.

Luncheon was served on the Duncan Phyfe table in the dining room of the Commandant's house. Two women prisoners, quiet and unsmiling, wearing white maids' uniforms, served the lunch.

"It is really not bad duty here, Karl," said the Commandant as they sipped liqueurs and smoked cigars in the drawing room after their meal. "We run a privileged camp. We have an Austrian countess, a French noblewoman, and a countess from Poland. There are many artists, musicians. Himmler has it in his mind that we may be able to use them in the future in some way, perhaps as political hostages. The possibilities are intriguing, my dear Colonel."

"So it would appear." Karl didn't know how candid to be with his new superior. He could possibly be as pleasant and unassuming as he appeared, but without knowing more about him, it would not do to reveal oneself fully.

"I'm still perplexed as to why I've been assigned here, *Herr Commandant,*" remarked Karl. "It does seem out of the realm of my experience, which I always thought fell more within traditional Army boundaries. Of course, I don't object, you understand. I am at the command of the *Führer,* wherever he chooses to send me. But still, it is a matter of some curiosity to me, as you can well imagine."

"Of course. I understand perfectly," said Koegel. "And you are aware, I'm sure, that Field Marshal Göring recommended you to Himmler personally. The Field Marshal felt that your presence could allay fears that Ravensbrück was other than a detention camp for political prisoners. We all agreed—I, most of all—that your breeding and position in one of Germany's oldest families will serve to blunt the attempts of those who would impugn our efforts to run this camp as efficiently as we can. Although at present the camp is underutilized, we have just received our first shipment of Gypsy children and their mothers, and it is anticipated that as the war progresses, there will be more and more prisoners, and it will be mainly your duty to present a smiling face, as it were, to the townspeople of Fürstenberg and to whoever should care to know what goes on here."

"Then I will be involved in liaison work from within the camp?" said Karl.

"Yes. You will have an office next to mine, and in my absences you will act as full commandant. All procedures have not been put into operation yet, as the camp is still new. The camp is designed to house fifteen thousand women, and at present we have two thousand two hundred ninety. It will be our duty to use the prisoners' labor to produce SS uniforms and other textiles needed for the war effort. Any ideas you can contribute to help the camp operate more efficiently will be most welcome."

"Will I have contact with the prisoners at all? I have never had experience handling captive people."

"No, no, don't worry, my dear Colonel. If you care to have contact, you may. But I can assure you that with the exception of the special group, the rest are Poles and Jews. Not a very appetizing lot."

The Commandant laughed at his own wittiness. Then he called his adjutant to drive Karl around the compound, to show him where the commandant headquarters was and where his office would be. The Colonel and Karl shook hands, and as a parting remark the Colonel said, "I must stress to you again how very impressed with you the Field Marshal is. He thinks that men of your quality should be seen more and not hidden in the ranks of the Army. You must do your best to live up to his high opinion of you, Colonel. And you must remember that the work you do here is as vital as that done by any soldier in defense of our Fatherland. You can destroy the enemy in Ravensbrück as well as anywhere else."

"I will do my best," said Karl, not sure what the word "destroy" was meant to convey.

"Good," said Koegel. "Heil Hitler."

"Heil Hitler."

The commandant re-entered the house, and Karl was taken by car on a tour of Ravensbrück. He was shown the newly constructed barracks, as well as the SS activities work center and the SS booty storage and SS residences. The camp overwhelmed his senses. The ingenuity of its design. They kept prominent women in special quarters, the Commandant had said. Gypsies and Jews and communists were housed apart and wore blue uniforms with gray stripes. There was still an air of cleanliness and newness about the place. It was the beginning of an adventure for Karl, one he would not have chosen himself but one that might enrich his status ultimately and perhaps draw more attention to him than if he had performed heroically on the battlefield.

By the time the tour was concluded and he had been returned to his new living quarters, he was exhausted but quite content. Everyone had treated him cordially. There had been no need to exert himself with the adjutant. His position as co-commandant of Ravensbrück obviously earned him instant respect. He ate dinner with the Commandant and his adjutant and several of the women prison guards. During dinner they were entertained by a string quartet from the camp. As a reward the musicians were taken into the kitchen after the concert and given cake and ice cream. Later one of the women guards, Obersfehrin Ilse Blucher, asked Karl if he wanted her to join him for the night.

"Thank you, but no," he said.

She looked at him strangely.

"I have a wife in Berlin," he lied.

She smiled and looked up at him coquettishly. "So? I find you very attractive. Your wife won't miss the part of you that I take."

The look on her face told him that he must not refuse this gift. He must not make an enemy of anyone who would be likely to help him in the future.

"And I find you very attractive also," he said.

Her smile was radiant, with large white teeth between moist lips. "We'll go to your room, then?"

"We won't be disturbed?" he asked.

"We won't be disturbed. Who would disturb the co-commandant of the camp when he is with someone whom he finds attractive?" she said.

There was nothing else he could say that would deflect her ardor without making her suspicious, and he could not explain that the reason he did not want to sleep with her had nothing to do with her at all. Perhaps when he knew her better and found her trustworthy, he would tell her the reason. For now he took her arm, and they walked together to his quarters.

XVI

It was the Gypsy children, with their black-olive eyes and their sad faces, clinging to the skirts of their mothers, who made Helene realize the enormity of what had happened to her. There were Davids all around her. She had saved him from this, but there he was in the lowered lids and smooth, sallow skin of the Gypsy children. Some nursed at their mothers' breasts. Others sat close to their mothers' warm bodies, instinctively aware that danger lay but a step away.

They arrived together, Helene in the morning, the Gypsies that afternoon. They went through the processing together, swirls of colorful skirts and jangling metal bracelets, bandannas of silken threads, and Helene's skirt and sweater, all exchanged for shapeless uniforms of blue with gray stripes. Then the assignment to barracks and the pandemonium as the two hundred Gypsy women and their children looked for space to live in.

"Is this bed taken?" asked Helene of the woman sitting on the edge of an upper bunk, her skinny legs dangling over the empty bed below.

"Help yourself," said the woman.

Soon the barracks was filled. Women milled around between the occupied beds, confused looks on their faces.

"It reminds me of a game we played as children," said the woman in the upper bunk.

"It makes no sense. I don't understand any of this," said Helene. She called to a woman who stood with a baby in her arms and two little boys tugging at their mother's unfamiliar striped uniform. The Gypsy woman looked at Helene, not understanding.

"What are you doing?" asked the woman in the upper bunk.

"I want to give her my bed," said Helene.

"She will find a bed. Take care of yourself first. The guards will come and get the overflow and take them to another building."

The woman was birdlike in appearance, with tiny hands and feet and thick black hair flecked with gray. She spoke German with a cultured accent but not a German accent.

"French?" asked Helene.

"*Oui.* Which do you prefer to speak? German or French? Or if you'd rather, we could talk in Lithuanian, Italian, or Russian. I speak five languages. There are mostly Poles here at the moment, but as the war goes on, I expect to use them all."

A guard came and herded the excess Gypsies out of the barracks. Helene sat down on the bunk. "You are a professor of some kind?"

"Francesca Mojica, born in France, taught philosophy at the University in Cracow."

"Helene Gelson, German. Born in Berlin."

"German, and they put you here with the others? What have you done? Political crime or racial?"

"Racial."

Francesca nodded knowingly. "I myself am a Catholic, but my husband is Jewish. I don't know if I'm here because of my husband or because I'm a Pole or a Frenchwoman or because I preached socialism to my students."

"It doesn't really matter anyway," said Helene.

"It matters a little more for those like you. It is much harder here if you are Jewish."

"Where is your husband?" asked Helene.

"By now I hope he is in Palestine. Without that hope I could not bear it here."

"You have no children?" asked Helene.

"None, thank God. Do you?"

"No," said Helene.

It was difficult to sleep that night. The Gypsies made noise all night long, trying to settle the children down, trying to find some way to be comfortable in the two feet of space assigned to each person. Helene held her fists against her ears, trying to blot out the sounds of the children, trying not to share the fear that the Gypsy mothers felt for themselves and their babies.

At three-thirty in the morning, at the sound of a whistle outside the barracks, Helene moved her head against the rough mattress ticking and opened her eyes. It was pitch black in the barracks. She heard the noise of women getting up and of children crying. And the whistle continued to blow.

"You must get up," said Francesca from the bunk above Helene's.

"Where are we going?" asked Helene. She sat up on the edge of the bunk and rubbed the back of her neck where the muscles ached. There were bruises on her arms and legs, and her right cheek had swollen so that her eye was shut in the folds of the surrounding black-and-blue skin.

"To the factory. Hurry. What's the matter with your face?"

"They beat me," said Helene.

"Well, hurry, or that will seem but a mosquito bite."

Helene had slept in her uniform, the only clothes that she had. She waited in line to use the toilet outside the barracks and to splash cold water onto her bruised face.

The moon still shone overhead as the assembled women stood in rows outside their barracks. The women's breath made frosty clouds around their faces. They shifted from leg to leg and rubbed arms and faces with stiff fingers to battle the cold that entered through the thin fabric of their uniforms. Facing the women was Obersfehrin Blucher, wearing a thick-woven gray uniform on her short, compact figure, the eagle insignia of the SS on her sleeve. She held her chin with her hand and appeared to be waiting for all the women to arrive.

A latecomer ran from the toilet toward the waiting women. She clutched her stomach with one hand and held the other hand to her rectum. As the woman drew near enough, Obersfehrin Blucher reached out with her foot and tripped her, and she went sprawling on the muddy ground. As the woman lay flat on her stomach, the guard placed the toe of her shoe near the woman's face, a slight nudge. Helene held her breath. The foot was motionless, as was the woman's body, and then the guard gave a small hop, just as if she were playing hopscotch, almost a lighthearted skip on one foot. With the other foot she began to kick at the woman's stomach. The woman screamed in pain as the blows came one after the other. Helene turned her face away. She could not stand to look or hear. If she looked and if she heard, then she would have to lie down next to the woman and feel what the woman was feeling.

"Don't be shocked," said Francesca. "The women guards are worse than the men. If you want mercy, don't ask it of an SS woman. And try to stay with the group. Don't stand out. Don't be conspicuous."

After being given a cup of black coffee and a piece of hard black bread, the women were marched across the camp to the textile factory. Helene, who did not know how to operate a sewing machine, was put to work pulling the heavy bolts of fabric to the pattern-cutting tables, sweeping up the scraps from the floor, and putting them into buckets according to the sizes of the scraps. The workers worked in an airless building and were given nothing to eat all day. At four in the afternoon they were marched back to their barracks and made to stand at attention while the evening meal was given out. It consisted of turnips and potato peelings cooked into a watery soup, a two-inch piece of sausage, and a chunk of black bread.

In the evening the barracks was bedlam. Children cried. The Gypsy women chattered in Romany, their voices blending into the cacophony of Polish and German and French. Four Frenchwomen across the aisle from Helene were talking about chocolate soufflés.

"The cream must be absolutely fresh," said one.

"There can be no substitute for real butter," said another.

"And the eggs, ah, the eggs," rhapsodized yet another, "they must be no older than four hours. But, most important, all the ingredients must be exactly at room temperature."

Helene lay in her bunk and felt sick to her stomach.

"Actually," said Francesca, continuing her conversation of

the day before, as if a whole day had not intervened, "I was a very conscientious teacher. I let my students read Nietzsche's *The Will to Power*, as well as Marx's *The Communist Manifesto*."

"Is everyone insane here, or is it only me?" asked Helene, sitting up on the edge of the bunk and looking at the chaos around her. "A woman is beaten for having diarrhea; we're herded into barracks and fed watery soup and made to work in a factory like slaves; children are imprisoned for the crime of having been born; and when we have a moment of peace, these women talk about mythical soufflés as though they were expecting company for tea at this very moment. And you, you prattle on about your political convictions."

"Ah, I have an idea," responded Francesca. "In the morning we storm the camp; we take the SS guards prisoner; we set the dogs on them, aim the machine guns in the other direction. Let them feel how it is for a change, eh?"

"At least recognize what is happening here."

"But your 'here' is reality. We'd rather not be in this reality if we can escape in our minds. You'll see, you will accept it as the norm very shortly. Everyone does. Everyone. The SS guards come here not understanding the reality of the imprisonment of innocents any more than we understand the concept of being held here against our wills. But soon we all understand what is expected of us. They are here to discipline, we are here to be disciplined. Our acquiescence gives them license to be brutal. Their brutality sends our imaginations in search of escape, if only through exchanging recipes."

"Then it's hopeless. We'll stay here until we are worked to death," said Helene.

"Some have left. Not many, but there have been a few. But they're the elite, the ones who are housed in the concrete buildings on the other side of the camp. Sometimes they get out because of who they are or because somebody pays for them to get out. It's hard to say. We have no contact with them. All we hear are rumors."

Francesca disappeared and returned in a few minutes with a bit of cloth that she had soaked in water. She offered it to Helene.

"Put this on your cheek. It will take the swelling away."

Helene took the cloth and put it to her eye. "It's very kind of you. I'm sorry I talked to you the way I did."

"Why should you be sorry? Because you want to protect what few feelings you've got left? See this arm, the way the elbow is twisted? That's because it was broken and not set in a cast. It has healed crooked. The day of my arrest I got this. So you got something else. Everyone here has something. Don't apologize. If you feel like it, you can tell me your story. If you don't, you won't. We're not here to match stories anyway. We take one day at a time, hoping to get enough rest and enough food to carry us forward for another day. Terrible things, much worse things, are happening other places. We hear stories every day from the new people coming in. Be glad you were brought here instead of to some other camp."

On the way back from the factory the next day, Helene looked across the field toward the concrete buildings. She squinted in the late-afternoon gloom at the figure of a man in an Army uniform. He turned his head to look at the women marching back to their barracks.

"You know that man?" asked Francesca, watching Helene's face as she gazed across the field.

"I'm not sure," said Helene, still staring at the shape of the man, at the way he stood.

"Yes," she said, "he is someone I knew in Berlin."

"He's the new co-commandant of the camp. He came right after you did. We don't know very much about him yet. He's not through finding his way around. If he is a friend, I wouldn't expect too much from the friendship in this place."

Suddenly Helene felt the urge not to reveal herself, not to let him see her. Suddenly the familiar figure was someone else, someone she could not know, could not envision in these circumstances, someone seen through a stranger's eyes, described as a co-commandant of a concentration camp. A concentration camp. This place.

Francesca looked at her interestedly. "Tell me something about him, who he was before the war, how you know him."

"He's Count Karl von Kirchner. Very old German family, a very sensitive and cultured man. A musician who also writes poetry in the style of Browning. He belonged to a chamber music group that met at our home on Thursday nights. He lived in Berlin, as we did. Our home was one of the most beautiful in the city. I lied when I said I had no children. I could not bear to see the Gypsy children and think of my own Miriam and David. Karl loved our children. If he had had it in his power to help us, he would have." Helene's voice broke.

"Where are your children now?" asked Francesca.

"My husband killed himself and our little girl. Miriam was her name. I gave David away to the nuns in Barcelona."

"Must not cry here," said Francesca. "Think of something else, something interesting, something amusing. Tell me about Berlin in the early days. What was it like?"

It did no good. He had seen her. Clear across the field, in the darkening afternoon, he had seen her and had caught her eye. They had looked at each other across the field. She walked on with the others, but she could feel his eyes still staring after her. Perhaps Francesca was wrong. Perhaps he could help her here. He could not possibly be aware of what kind of place he had come to. And if he was aware of it, she knew that his would be a voice of sanity, that he would help to save lives as he had attempted to save lives before.

"You're shivering," said Francesca. "It's only the second day. Your body and mind are rebelling now."

"You analyze everything too much," said Helene, trying to free her lips and shoulders of their spasmodic movements.

"It's my training. It keeps my mind occupied. You must learn some tricks, too, or you will go mad with your thoughts. So, then, what about our Count, you think you know what kind of man he is?"

Helene shook her head, as much to rid herself of the trembling as to answer Francesca's piercing question.

"No, I don't know what kind of man he is at all."

XVII

*When Helene was small and awakened with what Grandmama called a "*schwarze Nacht*"—"black night"—it would be long minutes before she realized that she was really in her own bed, in her own bedroom. The terrors were so real that she would stare into the dark of the bedroom, fully awake but still within the dream. Grandmama's prescription was always warm milk and reassuring hugs, and in the morning there were instructions for Greta to prepare more puddings and milk dishes and fewer fried foods for Helene's delicate digestive system.*

"Grandmama, why do we dream bad things?" Helene would ask.

"God gives us bad dreams, because to wake up makes us appreciate life."

Ravensbrück was a schwarze Nacht, *but there was no awakening.*

She was in the Count's office. He had called for her. She stood near the door, fully aware that she had not bathed in two weeks, that her clothes smelled, that she smelled. He made no move this time to approach her, to kiss her hand, as he had so many times in the past, before the nightmare began. There were candies in a dish on his desk. He offered her some. She took a handful and looked at him quizzically before she lifted up the edge of her shapeless dress and emptied the candies into the gathered hem.

"For the Gypsy children," she said. "A Christmas treat for the children."

His eyes showed no pain at talk of the children, he who had brought gifts to Miriam and David.

"You understand, Helene, that I cannot do anything for

you here. If you were a Pole, I might possibly be able to see to it that you received better treatment. But Jews . . . My behavior is watched as closely as any prisoner's. If it were to be known that I was friendly with a Jewess, that I tried to help her, I would be severely disciplined."

"May I sit down?" she asked, feeling the exhaustion of the last twelve-hour shift and the meager food.

"Certainly." But he didn't move toward her to help her into the chair. She was an apparition, a thing to be dealt with as charily as possible. Economy of words, economy of motion so that no human contact or human touch would pass between them.

"Terrible things are happening in this place, Karl. You could stop them without helping me personally. The children are hungry. Their mothers tear their hair for ways to see that their children survive. Perhaps a little more food for the children, at least?"

"The camp has been set up by Himmler. All we do is run it as efficiently as we can with what he gives us. Don't think me an unfeeling man, Helene. But men are dying on the battlefield. Brave, strong men. No one is exempt from suffering in these times."

She stared at him, studying the face, trying to remember him as he was when he sat in her home, so charming, so jovial, so eager to entertain, to please. "Then why did you call me here?" she asked.

"To tell you that I couldn't help you. I want no unexpected, unexplained contact between us. I don't want you to tell people that you know me or to expect any favors from me because of our past friendship."

"Then the friendship is a thing of the past," she mused, more to herself than to him.

Karl's brow shone with sweat, although the day was cold and bleak. "This pains me also."

Irrationality piled upon irrationality. Her captor was pained. But nightmares are like that, she thought.

He moved as though he were about to go to the door and open it. If he did, whatever opportunity she had to help the Gypsy children would pass.

"Please, one minute more," pleaded Helene. "In his despair

Maurice killed our baby and then himself. Can you imagine that he could ever do such a thing, Karl, a man like Maurice, so loving of everyone, so mindful of duty? Can you envision a despair so great that he could do such a thing?"

"You will have to leave now," said Karl abruptly.

"Please, my head isn't clear these days," she said. "I don't accuse you. It wasn't your fault. It was Erika and Gunter. When you left us that night, Maurice and I felt that there was no hope, no escape for us."

"But you didn't kill yourself," said Karl.

"Perhaps I'm the coward and not Maurice," said Helene. "I cling to life past all logic. Even here in this place I try to live, to eat, to sleep, to wake up the next day. I think of David, and I have hope that he will live through the war. You remember David. Such a quiet child. I always worried about David much more than I did Miriam. I thought that people would take advantage of him when he grew up. Do you remember when he—"

"I cannot help you," said Karl dismissively.

"You were a friend to us. I understand your position in this matter. It is quite clear that you have to do your duty, but perhaps something could be done for the Gypsy children, because they cry so pitifully. I feel such anguish for them and their mothers. My sorrow can't be as real as theirs is for their children, but I grieve for my own, and in my grieving I am with the Gypsy mothers."

"Don't, Helene, there is nothing I can do. I am sincerely sorry."

"Nothing you can do, or nothing you will do?"

"It's the same thing. I won't argue with you. It serves no purpose."

"But I'm in the grip of a paranoia. I feel that I'm a German, and yet Germans have hounded me to this place. Surely you who are in such an exalted position can give me explanations. Why are you here, Karl? Why am I here? Why are Maurice and Miriam dead? Explain the unexplainable to me. I sit here beseeching you to help me understand why this place exists at all. It seems a small favor to ask of a friend, that he clarify something when he has the power to do so."

"You assume that I have more power than I do. I am at

times as mystified by what has happened as you are. I tried to help you when I could, but it is no longer possible. I share your grief about the children, but I am a German soldier first. I do what I'm told to do. There is no other way."

"There are other ways in civilized societies."

"I don't recognize those ways," snapped Karl. "I will not be a party to treachery against my country. You will see, when it is all over, there will no longer be a need for camps like these, and things will go back to normal once again. You will be able to return to Berlin and resume your life."

She smiled at him wistfully, filled with sadness for both of them. She had never known him at all. They no longer were able to speak to each other in a common language. He would have her return to a Berlin that had caused the destruction of her family. It was as if they had each taken a long journey to the center of the earth, and where he had found Nirvana, she had found nothing but molten lava.

He was speaking. "I can tell you that conditions at Ravensbrück right now are as heaven compared to other camps. But there is talk of bringing in more transports. Things will change. You will consider the food you have now a bounty, and the crying of the children you will remember as sweet music."

"Then they'll all die," she said quietly.

"If they must, then they must," he answered.

In the early months of 1940 the transports of people to Ravensbrück became more frequent. With each succeeding transport the rations were cut, and then cut some more, and yet cut again. Six hundred now slept where three hundred had before. And Helene's periods had stopped. She had lost count of how long ago they had stopped.

"No one has periods here," said Francesca wisely. "It's the food. The body needs protein and rest, or you can't have periods."

But then nausea came on her unexpectedly, so that she couldn't keep down the hard black bread and the watery soup. One afternoon while dragging a bolt of cloth across the factory floor, she felt the need to lie down, to rest, to dim the lights that danced behind her eyes. When she awoke, Francesca was bending over her.

"Up, Helene. You will be sent away if you don't get up."

"I can't get up. If they send me away, then I can rest."

"Help me," hissed Francesca to a Polish woman at the sewing machine closest to where Helene lay.

Wordlessly the woman and Francesca dragged Helene to a hiding place behind the bolts of fabric, where she lay, undetected, until she had recovered enough strength to resume her work.

That night in the barracks Francesca said, "I can get something for you in the infirmary. It is not exactly for abortion, but it can be attempted."

Helene dreamed that Maurice was by her side, holding her hand. "Now," he said.

She squeezed his hand and pushed, but there was nothing.

"Now," he said, "now, now."

The water flowed between her legs, but nothing came.

In the morning she was flushed with fever, and she leaned on Francesca's shoulder at the roll call. Three hours into the shift, standing against the wall of the factory toilet, Helene passed a macerated lump of tissue. She held the bloody mass in her hand. It was too soon to tell whether the eyes were blue or not. She laid the remains of the fetus gently in the corner with the piles of garbage, and then she leaned against the wall and breathed deeply. She had just delivered herself of a dead baby, she told herself. Where had the feeling gone that she could no longer cry over the death of a child? She walked stiffly back to the factory floor. Francesca looked up at her anxiously. Helene nodded as she walked past. The potion had worked. She felt her old hunger returning, and she began to think of the bread and soup that waited for her at the end of the shift.

XVIII

The bitter December wind whipped through the city streets and entered the open windows of the Barcelona jail as Martita waited her turn in the unheated corridor. Waiting was one of Martita's learned specialties. She had waited, tilling the fields with her two daughters, while her husband, Raul, was away fighting with the Republicans. The months passed, and she received no word from him. Her patient waiting was rewarded at the end of a year when a letter arrived from her brother Ernesto, telling her that he and Raúl had been captured by the Nationalist forces.

"The pain I feel is like no pain I have ever felt," wrote Ernesto. "The devil could not have devised the punishment that I have had to face. Raúl and I and the others were told that we were to be executed by firing squad the next morning in a field near Toledo. We prayed together the night before. By morning I had made peace with myself and was ready to die. Then Raúl and I were separated. Five captives, including myself, were given rifles. The rest of the prisoners were marched toward a farmer's field and lined up facing us. How can I tell you, Martita, what it was like to shoot those men, to see my compatriots shoot Raúl, who was like a brother to me? What choice did we have? How can I live with what I have done?"

Now the Civil War was over, and Ernesto languished in jail, starving and filthy, existing on bits of potatoes and confined with thirty men in a cell that had been designed to hold two. The date of his scheduled execution was known only to his jailers.

"You five can go in," said the soldier to the first group in line. Martita took David's hand in hers, and together they walked through the open doorway to Ernesto's cell. When she was close enough, she picked the child up and held him against the cold iron bars. Her arms were dry-skinned and sunburned from long hours of working in the fields, the hands those of a peasant, short nails and fingers permanently stained by the red loam of the Spanish earth. Her clothes were gray and shabby; her black hair was pulled back severely against her head and wound into a knot at the nape of her neck. Her only ornament was a pair of thin gold wire loops in her ears.

Each of the men crowded against the bars to see if the visitors were for him. The women who had been let in began to wail at the sight of the emaciated prisoners and the overpowering stench of human waste and unwashed bodies. Martita pressed tightly against the bars. She would not relinquish her space to anyone. She was allowed but this one visit a week, and she would not be pushed aside. The soldiers watched carefully to be sure that nothing was passed through the bars to the prisoners.

"Ernesto," shouted Martita. Her brother sat on the straw-covered floor, one knee up, his hand resting limply across his knee, his head bent. He had not rushed to the bars when the others did. He looked weaker and thinner than when she had visited him last.

Ernesto looked up at her and at the child, whose face was puckered up against the cold iron bars like an old man's. He raised himself slowly and walked to the space that Martita had staked out as her own. She turned her head and smiled flirtatiously at the soldier who was watching their movements intently.

"My son," she said proudly to the soldier. She kissed David on the head but did not move him away from the bars.

Ernesto was close enough now that she could smell his sour breath and see the yellow in the grounds of his eyes. He wore no shoes, his pants and shirt hung loosely on his body, and he clung to the bars to support himself.

"Hands away from the bars," ordered the soldier, moving toward them.

Ernesto stepped back, his hands in the air. "*Mira*—see, I am away," he said.

The soldier moved back to where he was.

"What do you have here?" asked Ernesto, pointing at David.

"My son. Do you like him?"

"You have no son. Where did you get him?"

"Sister María Blanca gave him to me."

"I told you, you must not take anything ever again from the Church."

"But she is our sister."

"And she is a cleric. And the clerics have destroyed the hope of our people. They gave us the blood of Christ when what we needed was land."

"Come as close as you can," Martita said in a low voice. Her brother's ravings had caused the soldier to turn his head away in disgust. Martita slipped the sausage quickly into David's hand and then thrust his tiny fingers between the close-set bars. Malnutrition had dulled Ernesto's reactions. He looked at the sausage without moving.

"Quick, take it," whispered Martita. Ernesto moved more quickly now, as though suddenly awakened. He took the sausage in his hands and hid it in the pocket of his pants.

"The soldiers guard the orange groves," said Martita, "and they shoot anyone who tries to pick the fruit. People starve in our village, Ernesto. Sometimes there is food to buy but no money to buy it with. In Valdepeñas the wheat harvest was small because there still is so little water, and in some places the soldiers set fire to the fields before we could harvest it. And when we took what we had left to market, we were forced to sell to those who were with the Nationalists. They gave us very little money, and then they took our wheat and resold it in the cities and on the black market."

"All this is to explain why Sister María Blanca has given you a child to keep," said Ernesto angrily, "and you, who are hungry and starving, have kept him. Let the Church feed the orphans of the war. If you keep him because his hand is small and can pass me food through the bars of the cell, then I must counsel against it. As your older brother I instruct you that your duty is first to feed your own two daughters and then yourself, not to take in orphans that the Church should rightfully keep and care for."

Martita put David down on the ground next to her and held on to his hand. "He is a very quiet child, Ernesto. He hardly speaks, and when he does it is in German, and I don't understand what it is he is trying to tell me. Only once has he cried. He called for his mamá, and he cried, but other than that one time, he is as you see him now, an old man's expression on his round face."

"I can show you many quiet children who have old faces and cry for their mamás. Why must you choose him?"

"He came with gold, Ernesto, two pieces of gold. That is how I got the sausage for you, from the *estraperlo,* the black marketeers. How else would I buy anything, with even bread rationed and with no money to buy the necessities of life? Gold, Ernesto. For one gold piece I received four thousand pesetas."

Ernesto looked at David and then at Martita. He wobbled unsteadily on his feet, thinking of what Martita had told him. "The Church gave you this child, along with two pieces of gold. Peasants have no use for gold. They hope to corrupt you, to make you dependent on luxuries, to remove the strength that you have and that no gold can give you. They want to defeat you by making you like them. You must give the child and the gold and pesetas back before the Church taints you with its evil ways."

"The Church is good, Ernesto. It is Christ's church. The clerics cannot destroy that."

Ernesto waggled one skinny finger at his sister, his weak body fed now with the fuel of his passionate hatred of the Catholic Church and anyone and anything that contradicted his anarchist beliefs.

"You do not understand their ways, Martita. I do. I am your brother. I tell you to take the child back to Sister María Blanca and to return their poisoned money."

"Shh, shh, Ernesto, you will make yourself faint. I understand perfectly well. I know that they gave me the gold for a reason, and that was so I would take the child away and care for him. I also know that if they gave me two pieces of gold, then there was more gold they kept and did not give to me. But that is all right. I understand what has happened. The boy was left in the cathedral by a woman. He was left with a baptismal certificate given to a child by the name of Juan Lepanto. But the boy is not a Catholic."

"He is a baby. How can he know whether he is a Catholic or not?"

"No, no, now it is you who do not understand. It is his *pene.*" Martita's eyes swept the front of her brother's pants. He looked down at his fly and then up again. Now he understood what his sister was trying to tell him.

"It is cut, like the *pene* of Jewish babies," she said.

David tugged at her hand, his face turned up toward Martita's.

"*Pobrecito,*" she said. "What story could he tell, Ernesto, eh?"

"Hide him well, Martita. Franco is not so much in love with the Jews either. You could have trouble if someone finds out."

Martita patted David on the head with her earth-stained fingers.

"Nobody will find out. Juan is my son now. He will take Raúl's place in the fields. He will grow to be a big and strong man, a Spaniard. No one will have reason to look at his *pene.* And the Spanish woman who will love him will know he is a Spaniard and Martita's child. He has the face of a Spaniard, don't you think, Ernesto?"

"You are a fool, Martita."

The soldier was calling to them that it was time to leave. Martita and Ernesto looked at each other now for a long while, as the other women were led, crying, away from the cell.

"Will you be back again?" he asked.

"If you are here, I will be back," she said. And then she turned, and with David clutching her hand, she followed the others out into the corridor.

1943–1945: Tonio

XIX

"He is a man, like any other man. Speak to the man, Tonio, and he will listen. If at times his eyes appear to look through you and past you, as though he has not heard a word you have said, don't let it fool you. He hears you. He hears you very well, and he understands quickly. No subtleties escape his understanding."

The black sedan sped past the shaded trees along the road outside Madrid. Radigales, Spanish Consul General in Athens, sat nervously smoothing the leather of his briefcase against the fine worsted of his trouser leg as he spoke in short, staccato bursts of Spanish.

Tonio, in his shabby gray suit, sat next to him and smoked cigarette after cigarette, listening intently to Radigales' words. Tonio had made an attempt that morning to dampen and comb his wild crown of hair and to smooth his ferocious eyebrows, but now the wind from the open car window had blown the dampness away and returned his hair to its natural bloom. His giant's body and halo of hair gave him the appearance of a powerful biblical patriarch in a frayed business suit.

"I don't mean to contradict Your Excellency's assessment of our chances," said Tonio, "but if Hitler was unable to convince him at Hendaye in 1940 to join the war on the Axis side, it doesn't sound as though he will be an easy man to deal with. After all, we have no Morocco to offer him as spoils of war."

"True," agreed the Consul General. "We have nothing to offer him in material terms, but we can help him in the eyes of the Allies. He reopened the border to refugees in April only because Churchill and the Americans threatened him.

He is a man who looks to the future, no matter what excesses he engages in in the present. He was not deaf to Churchill's promise that if Spain provides a haven to save innocent lives, its help will not go unrewarded when the war is over."

"I want to believe that you're right," responded Tonio.

"We have to be right in this. Too much is at stake."

Both men fell silent for a while, Tonio smoking and watching the countryside through the car window. It was a drizzly May day. No people walked along the lanes of the highway. There was only the car and the sound of the tires on rutted pavement and the charged atmosphere between the two tense men as they drove along the road to El Pardo palace.

"One other thing," said Radigales suddenly. "His expression does not change. It is a tactic of his. It is meant to disarm those who come to joust with him. By appearing not to hear, he hopes that you won't think so hard or try so hard to convince him of your position. But that is death. With that blank gaze he can finish you, and you will never know at precisely what moment he administered the fatal blow to your mission."

At a curve in the road just outside Madrid, in an area covered with lush green vegetation, the driver of the sedan stopped the car alongside high iron gates. As Tonio leaned out the open window, he felt the rain pelting his face. There was an opening in the gate, and behind the gate a heavily fortified guardhouse. Soldiers of the Guardia Civil, in their green uniforms, were on duty at the guardhouse, and every few feet along the winding road that disappeared into the trees stood a member of the Guardia de Franco, Franco's elite corps of bodyguards, each armed with a submachine gun. Tonio glimpsed Moorish buildings beyond the trees as the sedan drove through the open gate and stopped when a soldier leaned into the driver's window to inspect the documents of the occupants. Telephone calls were made, and conferences were held between the leader of the Guardia de Franco and the soldier who had come to the window to talk to the driver.

"Is something wrong?" asked Tonio nervously.

"Calm, calm. We must be calm. Everything is in order, my

dear Tonio," said Radigales. His face was flushed, and his hand trembled as it rested on the back of the front seat.

The soldier waved them through, and the sedan lurched forward and down the machine-gun- and tree-lined road toward the sixteenth-century palace.

"It is rumored that Franco's grandmother was a Jewess," said Tonio tensely.

"Perhaps. In any event, it is not something that we can depend upon to be of benefit to us."

At the visitors' entrance to the palace, another contingent of the Guardia Civil stood at attention. The driver stayed behind with the car, and the Consul General and Tonio, flanked by ten rifle-armed men, were led through the arched portico and along a marble entry hall whose walls were lined with the paintings of Velasquez, Murillo, and Goya. The sound of the men's boots echoed through the halls. There were no voices. The troops moved in practiced, precision fashion. The leader of the corps walked directly behind Radigales and Tonio, whose steps had fallen in with the cadence of the soldiers who escorted them to the meeting with Franco.

"*Estamos,*" said the leader to Radigales. A carved interior door faced them. The men had stopped and were now aligned on either side of the door. The leader of the group moved forward and opened it. "*Sigame,*" he said to the Consul General and Tonio, and motioned for them to enter. Radigales entered first, followed by Tonio and three of the armed guards. The door closed behind them.

El Caudillo Francisco Franco was seated at a carved refectory table, a sheaf of papers in his hand. He looked up as the men entered. Tonio stood behind Radigales and watched the other man's movements, not wanting to make a false step. The room was high-ceilinged and ornate, with gilded Mudéjar carvings along the slope of the ceiling. The windows behind El Caudillo looked out over the palace gardens. A long carved-oak credenza behind Franco's desk held pictures of his wife and daughter and grandchildren.

Tonio felt better now that they were finally in the room with Franco, now that the moment had come. For him the anticipation, the pondering of all the imponderables, the endless "what-ifs" that Radigales and he had engaged in since Radigales' return from Athens the previous week had been the torturous part. Action held no fear for Tonio. In movement he was at his best, he could think more clearly, and his instinctive reactions were truer than at other times. He felt soaringly happy to be here. All the planning and doubting had come down to this meeting with the bemedaled man in front of them. This was where it would be decided, here in this room, with the dictator of Spain, the man who had had the cool audacity to keep Hitler waiting at the border at Hendaye for three hours.

Franco stood up and walked around to the front of his desk, a small, slightly potbellied man with a brush mustache and masked, drooping eyes.

"Caudillo," said Radigales, bowing from the waist.

"How are you, Sebastian?" Franco's voice was high-pitched, almost squeaky.

"Very well, thank you. Tired, but otherwise well."

Franco looked at Tonio, unsmiling. Tonio felt himself suddenly conspicuous as the only Jew present. He smoothed his wind-blown hair with one hand and straightened up so that all six feet three inches of him towered above the others in the room.

"Caudillo, may I present Antonio Katakis, former secretary to the Greek embassy in Barcelona," said Radigales.

Tonio bowed, as he had seen Radigales do. Franco merely nodded his head. An elderly servant entered the room with a tray of wine and *tapas,* which he set down on a library table in the center of the room. Radigales waited until Franco had seated himself once again behind his desk, and then he sat down in one of the Napoleon campaign chairs facing Franco. Tonio hesitated a moment and then sat down in a chair next to Radigales. Franco's bodyguards stood at attention, two at the door, two at each side of the window behind Franco, and one across the room, beneath a portrait of the Generalissimo in his brown military uniform, mounted stiffly upon a pure white stallion.

"I have been rereading the letter that I told you about, Sebastian," said Franco. He put on his reading glasses and read aloud:

"'In the name of the executive committee of the World Jewish Congress, I address myself to Your Excellency to beseech you to express kindly to the Spanish government our deep gratitude for the refuge that Spain has accorded to the Jews coming from the territories under the military occupation of Germany. We understand all too well the difficulties of the situation, and we know the great effort that this war represents for the economy of Spain. We are doubly grateful for the permission given to the refugees to remain in Spain until such time as permanent residence is found for them, a problem that could be long and difficult to resolve during the conflict.

"'The Jews are a race that possesses a great memory. They will not forget easily the opportunity that has been given to save the lives of thousands of their brothers.'"

Franco removed his reading glasses and looked at Radigales. "That was written by Rabbi Perlzweig of the World Jewish Congress to Ambassador Cardeñas in Washington. Let it not be said that the Franco regime does not act with Christian charity."

"Of course not, Your Excellency," said Radigales. "No one will ever say that in my presence. I would not permit it."

Tonio could see that Radigales was straining to gain a position in the conversation as Franco was attempting in advance to effectively block any criticism of him or his handling of the refugee question.

"Good," said Franco, leaning back in his high-backed chair.

"But Your Excellency is aware of the question about which I have come, I'm sure. It is the plight of the Greek Jews. In particular, the Sephardic Jews of Salonika."

Franco raised his hand to interrupt Radigales. "You have not come here to talk about Sephardic Jews. My position is very clear on that. Count Jordana has wired the American Secretary of State that we will accept all refugees henceforth."

"Respectfully, Your Excellency," persisted Radigales, "the problem is not with those who are able to arrive here safely. The problem is in obtaining the release of the Jews of Salonika who are now in German custody, those who can trace their Spanish lineage to their ancestors' expulsion from Spain in 1492."

"I have performed my duty in that regard," said Franco. "Those who did not declare their Spanish citizenship according to the 1924 decree must now accept their fate. Ambassador Vidal in Berlin has done all he can to see that those attempting to register later will be supplied with transit visas, if possible, to other countries, but we cannot allow all Jews who claim some connection to Spain to come and settle here indiscriminately."

"These are not all Jews, Your Excellency," said Radigales patiently. "Already forty-two thousand Jews of Salonika have been deported to Auschwitz, to a fate at which we can only guess. It is only one small group that we are interested in at this moment. Five hundred eleven Sephardic Jews have been arrested by the Germans in Salonika. They have not been deported as yet. They await word from you that proof of Spanish citizenship will save them. Time is critical. The Germans have set the evacuation to Auschwitz for June 15, 1943. We have a list of those who can prove Spanish lineage. It only remains for Your Excellency to intervene concerning visas and a guarantee of transportation out of Greece. Perhaps we could supply them with visas to Morocco. And we need not stamp each entry visa; they could travel on a collective passport so that valuable time will not be wasted."

Franco's face mirrored no feeling at his Consul General's impassioned arguments.

"I'm sorry to be so emotional, Your Excellency," said Radigales. "These are emotional times."

Franco did not reply to the apology. "They have murdered forty-two thousand Greek Jews in Auschwitz, you say?"

"It is rumored that mass extermination is carried out in the Eastern European concentration camps," replied Radigales.

"Hitler would kill Spanish Jews, then, too, is what you are telling me?" asked Franco quietly.

"He would not pay attention to the difference if we do not, Your Excellency. There is a chance to save some by declaring them Spanish citizens. It is a chance."

"How would this be accomplished in time, before the date that they have set for their evacuation?" asked Franco.

Radigales turned to Tonio. "Tonio—Mr. Katakis—is a native of Greece, Your Excellency. He is willing to act as an intermediary between the Spanish government and the Germans in behalf of his fellow Jews. He is willing to travel to the camps with them, if need be, to see that the rescue is completed. The Germans have already conferred on him the status of a neutral negotiator, but if he is given the imprimatur of the Spanish government, he may travel through Europe with impunity as the designated representative of Spain."

"There are others to be saved also, Your Excellency," interjected Tonio, sensing that the time to speak had come. "Give me the power to stretch and bend the proof of Spanish citizenship, and I will be an arm that will do more Christian charity for Your Excellency and the Spanish people than you ever dreamed of."

"I have no particular love for the Jewish people, Mr. Katakis," said Franco, "but I also have no love for the murdering of Spanish citizens solely because of their religious beliefs."

Tonio felt a surge of joy at Franco's qualified retort. El Caudillo would go along with the plan to save the Sephardic Jews.

"You have my permission to act quickly in behalf of the Sephardim of Salonika," said Franco. "Do not let the Germans outmaneuver you. They will not push my patience too far. They still hope for my help in the Balearics. Visas, collective or otherwise, as they wish. If Hitler needs more bodies for his funeral pyres, let him murder Germans and leave my Spaniards alone."

XX

On the morning of Tonio's arrival in Salonika, the Spanish Vice-Consul, Otto Beressa, met him at the railroad station.

"Radigales isn't with you?" asked the short, gray-haired man as he led Tonio to the waiting taxicab.

"Radigales is still in Berlin," answered Tonio, tossing his suitcase into the taxi before he and the Vice-Consul got in.

"That's ominous. He was to be back in time to screen those who've applied for visas." Beressa licked his thin lips nervously.

"There were delays and missed appointments."

"It is most difficult, Tonio, most difficult. The deportations have been scheduled and canceled and then rescheduled each time there's a new communiqué from Berlin. The people are dying not once, but a thousand times."

Tonio closed his eyes and leaned his leonine head back against the taxi seat. He hadn't slept in thirty-six hours. He and Radigales raced the clock in everything they did. When they had been informed that the German Foreign Ministry had not received the message that Franco was willing to accept the 511 Jews, he and Radigales had flown to Berlin to deliver the message in person.

"Spain will not abandon the Greek Jews," Radigales had shouted at Foreign Minister von Thadden.

"Then let Spain send Spanish ships to Greece to get them," the Foreign Minister had shouted back.

"I'm sorry, I apologize," Radigales had said. "We can all appreciate how short our tempers have become. Please forgive me."

"Of course. And I sympathize with you," the Foreign Minister had said.

Radigales had continued, his diplomatic self now firmly in control. "Would it be acceptable to the Foreign Ministry if

Swedish ships run by the International Red Cross were to pick up the Greek Jews at a convenient Mediterranean port?"

The Foreign Minister had thought a moment and then grudgingly said, "It would be acceptable."

Tonio had flown from Berlin to Stockholm to speak to the Spanish ambassador, who had agreed that the Red Cross was the most logical agency to transport the Jews. That evening, when Tonio had returned to Madrid, there was a message from Radigales informing him that his trip had been for nothing. The Germans had vetoed the suggestion.

"There's bad news about your wife and her child," said Beressa. "They were deported two days ago."

Tonio sat up, wide awake.

"They were included in a transport of Portuguese Jews."

"And the Greek undersecretary did nothing to stop it?" demanded Tonio so loudly that the taxi driver turned around to look at him.

"There was nothing he could do, Tonio. There was no proof that the child was his, so, of course, the Germans wouldn't let her stay. And Madrid wouldn't give an answer as to her citizenship status. You and Radigales, the only two who could have done anything for her, were gone. I'm sorry, Tonio, truly sorry. Tragedies abound. I know that is no consolation to you."

"Yes, tragedies abound," murmured Tonio, thinking of the pretty auburn-haired woman who had left him six years before and come to Greece to bear the Greek undersecretary's child. He had not thought of her in a long time. The pain he felt now was an abstract pain. Andrea and he had long ago severed whatever connection had existed between them. All that remained was dimming memory and an occasional curiosity about her and the child she had borne. What she looked like. If Andrea was happy with her Christian Greek.

He shook his head to rid himself of the thought of the auburn-haired Andrea and her faceless child. "This is an exercise in futility that Radigales and I are engaged in," said Tonio, his eyes bright with uncontrollable fury.

"And I also. But I'm not as young as you and Radigales," said Beressa. "Sometimes I think a younger man should replace me, someone more forceful perhaps. The Germans sense my weakness, I'm afraid."

"You are better than any three Germans they can pit against you," said Tonio angrily. "Don't blame yourself, Otto. It was not your fault."

At the Jewish Community Hall, several hundred people were lined up outside the front door waiting to make their daily report to the German authorities inside. The main recreation room of the community center had been converted into offices, complete with desks and file cabinets and telephones. The children's nursery had been taken over by SS Lieutenant Colonel Karl Adolf Eichmann, while his administrative assistants occupied the small elevated stage.

"All this in order to destroy Jews," said Tonio as he and Beressa walked across the busy hall to Eichmann's office.

Eichmann smiled and rose to greet Tonio. He had the manner of an insurance executive, pleasant and faintly ingratiating. "Good to see you back, Tonio," said Eichmann.

Tonio shook Eichmann's hand, feeling the skin against the skin of his own hand. He never ceased to marvel at the ordinariness of the man, at the fact that his handshake was no different from any other handshake. Was this the man from the Death's Head unit at Dachau? Surely not. At any moment he would reach into his desk drawer and bring out a preprinted insurance form, and all the people in front, waiting to be logged in like so many sacks of turnips, would disappear back to their homes, back to their lives.

"I have heard from Ambassador Altenburg in Athens this morning," said Eichmann. "He says to delay the transport, that Franco will take his Jews in. Is that your information also, Tonio?"

"Yes. The Consul General and I were with Franco two days ago. He gave us his promise."

"So you have the ear of Franco?" said Eichmann in admiration. "To persuade him is not an easy thing to do, I'm told."

"He is concerned with the fate of all Spanish citizens," said Tonio.

"Yes. Spanish citizens," said Eichmann, his voice tinged with sarcasm. "I'm happy to hear that he is willing to receive them. And I might add that he is welcome to them. Then we won't have the paperwork to do on this group again. We were fully prepared to go through the orders again for a transport to a camp in eastern Poland. This news saves me many man-hours." Eichmann hesitated a moment and then said, as though as an afterthought, "Of course, there is still the question of transportation. We refuse to pay for railroad transportation for your Spanish Jews. If Franco wants them, he will have to provide his own transportation."

"Radigales is clear in his orders to me. The Spanish government is firm that it is the German government's responsibility to provide transportation; that if it weren't for your policy against the Jews, none of this would be necessary."

"But it is not my policy, Tonio, any more than your government's policy is yours. We are all servants in the end, aren't we?" asked Eichmann.

Tonio didn't answer.

"In any event," continued Eichmann in his businesslike way, "my function is to see that things run as smoothly as possible, with as little expense as possible. And I don't want you to think that any of this is personal, because it isn't. I like you, Tonio, and you're a Jew. Ergo, I don't hate all Jews, by any means. It is merely a political situation that we are involved in."

"We need some more time," said Tonio. "We have to think of a way to bring the Sephardim to Spain."

"There can be no more extensions," said Eichmann firmly, all attempt at pleasantness gone. "My presence is needed elsewhere. This matter in Greece must be cleared up now."

"But it is only a matter of time," insisted Tonio. "I'm sure that we will be able to take them off your hands when Radigales gets back."

"I'm sure you will be able to. But in the meantime, and as a temporary matter, the five hundred eleven will be sent to the new detention camp at Bergen-Belsen. They will be kept separate from the rest of the prison population. We want no harm to come to Spanish nationals, even if they are Jews. We understand your country's position on the matter, but you must appreciate ours also."

Tonio's mind was racing. Bergen-Belsen. He had never heard the name before today. "Where is this Bergen-Belsen, and when will they be sent there?" he asked.

"It is near Hannover, Germany. We occupy half of an old Wehrmacht prisoner-of-war camp. We have built a model camp that will be used for prisoners in transit, for exchange of prisoners, and for temporary detainees, such as your Sephardic Jews. Your Jews, in fact, will be the first to be interned there. They are brand-new facilities."

"There will be no problem retrieving them when the transportation is in order?" asked Tonio.

"No, no, no problem at all," said Eichmann. "You bring your visas, and your railroad cars or trucks or buses—even bicycles, if you'd like"—he laughed—"and you may have your Jews."

Radigales returned the next day to the news that the 511 were to be sent to Bergen-Belsen. "All for nothing. They will never survive a camp," Radigales said to Tonio as they sipped coffee in a café around the corner from the Jewish center. "I don't care what kind of camp Eichmann says it is, they will never survive it."

"They need not all go," said Tonio cagily.

"Tonio? You have an idea?"

"I have an idea."

As the Sephardic Jews showed up at the Jewish Community Hall for the daily roll call, Tonio and Otto Beressa stood around the corner watching the people pass.

"Those three," said Beressa, pointing to a tall, dark-haired man and his slender wife and teenage son. Tonio waited until the three had entered the building. When they exited, he followed them; a short conversation ensued. The man nodded. The woman held Tonio's hand and looked up into his face as he explained what they were to do.

By the end of the day, Tonio had approached 150 people whom he thought were suited for escape.

"It is set for this evening," said Beressa as he and Tonio parted at the Spanish embassy in the late afternoon.

"You are a strong man, Otto," said Tonio, gripping the older man's hand in his. "Better still, you are a good Christian."

When Beressa entered his office, Eichmann was waiting for him.

"I hope I haven't startled you, Señor Beressa, but I'm leaving for Berlin in the morning, and I know you will want to know what I have decided."

Beressa's hands shook as he sat down at his desk. "Perhaps it is Radigales you should inform about your plans, rather than me. He is the senior consulate officer."

"No, I will leave my message with you. By midnight tonight all Sephardic Jews will be rounded up and taken to Bergen-Belsen."

"Rather than tomorrow?"

"Yes, rather than tomorrow." Eichmann was looking at him strangely, or it might have been an illusion created by the lamplight shining off Eichmann's glasses.

"I will inform Radigales," said Beressa quietly.

"I know that you will."

Beressa sat in his office until after dark. His wife called from home asking why he had not appeared for dinner, didn't he know what time it was, was there no end to the lengths he would go to for his Jews?

"I will be home when I've finished my work," he said. When he was sure there was no one left in the consulate, he exited by the rear entrance and walked the few blocks to the small hotel where Tonio was staying.

"Now. We must move now, Tonio. Eichmann came to my office. Either he knows something or it is merely a whim of his, but all will be rounded up at midnight tonight and sent to Bergen-Belsen."

"He knows something," said Tonio, pulling on his overcoat. "You go home, Otto. You have risked enough today. I'll take care of it."

Tonio took a taxi to the home of the first people on his list. He gave them the names of two others on the list while he raced to the next house. By ten in the evening all on the list had been informed of the plan, and by ten-thirty on the dark railroad siding three kilometers past the Salonika station, 150 Jews stood and waited.

At eleven o'clock in the evening, Eichmann and his aide arrived at the home of Otto Beressa and were shown by a servant into the drawing room of the Vice-Consul's home.

"I'm missing a hundred fifty Jews, Beressa," said Eichmann as he faced Beressa across a highly polished library table. "I won't be angry if you will merely tell me what you have done with them, where you have hidden them."

"What are a hundred fifty Jews to you, more or less?" asked Beressa, smiling at his own boldness.

For the first time, something resembling anger distorted Eichmann's features. "You are a small man, Beressa. You don't think in very grand terms. You're right. What are a hundred fifty Jews more or less, when I've got so many? But tell me, I'm curious to know where you have hidden them."

"You give me more credit than I'm due, Herr Eichmann. I am merely a Spanish diplomat, doing my job as best I can. I, like you, initiate nothing. I merely follow orders."

Eichmann stared at him blankly for a few seconds. "Tell me why you fight so fiercely for these Jews," asked Eichmann. "What can it matter to you what becomes of them?"

"I am a religious man, *señor.*"

"Religion has nothing to do with it. This is a political matter," said Eichmann angrily.

"To you it is a political matter. To me it is a religious matter. We all act out of our own convictions."

Eichmann smiled. "You think that God is watching out for these Jews, do you?"

"Yes."

"He has not done a very good job in the past, has he?"

"I have no answer for that," said Beressa, grim-faced.

"Well, I have an answer for you, my dear Vice-Consul. I shall find those Jews, and when I do, I will see to it that the person responsible for their escape is dealt with severely. And if it should turn out that that person is also a Jew"—

Eichmann shrugged—"perhaps someone you and I both know . . ."

"I understand, *señor.*"

"Good. I'm glad that you do."

Tonio paced up and down the railroad tracks. Beressa had made the arrangements. The Italians refused to deal with Tonio. They would work only with a Christian who was a high-ranking official in the consulate. There were to be no Jew tricks, the Italian general had told Beressa earlier that day.

At 11:05 a six-car train passed by the main station at Salonika on its way to Athens, carrying a troop of Italian soldiers home on leave. The conductor made no signal that he would stop. Until the last moment Tonio thought that he would not stop. The train roared out of the distance, a black and magical steed come to snatch 150 miserable Jews away from Eichmann's net.

"Stop, damn you, stop," muttered Tonio under his breath.

When the train was five hundred yards away, Tonio detected a difference in the sound it made as it sped over the tracks. It was slowing. The people standing on the siding did not talk, they hardly breathed. They watched the train, guiding it to a stop with their eyes and their hearts.

As the train slowed there was the squealing of tires on the pavement. In the darkness of the train platform the people huddled together. They had brought nothing with them but the clothes they were wearing. One of the men turned toward Tonio at the sound of the car screeching to a halt a few yards away.

"Quick, there is no time," said the Italian lieutenant as he hung from the train steps. He reached down and took a little girl up into his arms. Other hands reached down all along the length of the train, pulling the men, women, and children up into its steel fortress.

Eichmann and two of his aides were running across the weed-strewn field toward the platform. Tonio lifted the last child up to its mother, and then he began to run parallel to the tracks toward the dark of the field opposite the siding.

"Are you coming?" the lieutenant called to Tonio.

"No, you go on," Tonio answered as he ran. "And God be with you."

Eichmann strode into Beressa's office shortly after the Spanish Vice-Consul had arrived. He paced back and forth in front of Beressa's desk without speaking for a few minutes, then opened the door and stared out into the embassy reception area. All the while Beressa worked at the papers on his desk as though Eichmann were not there.

"You may ignore me, Herr Vice-Consul, but we are both fully aware of the reason for my visit this morning," said Eichmann.

"Indeed?" asked Beressa, his eyebrows going up in surprise.

"Indeed. They have escaped. All of them."

"I'm sorry, but I don't understand," said Beressa. "Who escaped?"

"Play your games, Beressa. The Spanish government is trying the *Führer*'s patience."

"You must speak to Radigales when he returns," said Beressa calmly.

"I will speak with Radigales. But I'm speaking to you now. Where is Antonio Katakis?"

Beressa thought for a moment. "I believe that he is on his way to Madrid. Yes, he is on his way to Madrid at this moment."

Eichmann stared stonily at the Vice-Consul for a long while, and then he said, "All right. It is of no consequence. The Jews will show up. They always do. And remember that I still have three hundred sixty-one who are now on their way to Bergen-Belsen for safekeeping. You may play at being heroes for now, but your Jews will not be safe for long if I am not shown some concrete evidence that Spain will send for them."

When Eichmann had left, Beressa sat for a long while at his desk. Tonio had achieved the impossible, snatching Eichmann's property from beneath his nose. Property. It was insanity, pure insanity to think of people as property, and yet how else to explain the rationale behind visas and transportation and protocol and politics and contradictory captures and releases of human beings? Beressa's head ached as he tried to sort out exactly what he and Eichmann had said to each other in their short conversation. Eichmann suspected Tonio, but if he had actually seen him at the train station, he would have said so. No, he had come to bluff his way through. He was angry that he had lost 150 Jews, and he was looking for someone to blame. And yet he was holding 361 Jews for conditional repatriation to Spain. It was a paradox, a man-made irony. Radigales would laugh when he tried to explain it to him. Beressa sighed and looked at his watch. Not yet time for lunch. It was scarcely ten o'clock, and yet he felt exhausted, as though he had spent a week at his desk. No one would miss him if he closed the office for the day. He picked up his felt hat and put it on. He switched off the office light. And the papers that he had peered at so intently during Eichmann's visit, the sheets that held the names of 150 Greek Jews, he threw into the wastepaper basket.

XXI

It was now September 1943, and Helene had been in Ravensbrück for almost three years. No one any longer pretended that this was a model camp for political prisoners or that anyone who entered would ever leave alive. Each night Helene watched the skies for a sign. But the stars remained fixed. No change. The crematoriums were installed in Ravensbrück, and yet the sun came out in the mornings. The Gypsies and their children disappeared, and the moon glowed just as brightly as ever it had during those innocent Thursday-night musicales in Berlin. The Polish women were taken by the Nazi doctors to the Ravensbrück "infirmary," and their healthy limbs were injected with gas gangrene in order to test the efficacy of new drugs, and yet the earth did not tilt discernibly. Every inch of ground was covered by bodies, living and dead, and the air stank with the smell of burning flesh, and not once did God send a sign that He saw.

Francesca walked beside Helene. They were weightless. Their feet left no impression in the soft earth.

"I must show you what I have hidden when we return to the barracks this evening," said Francesca.

"Is it food?" asked Helene.

"No, it isn't food."

Beyond the tents that now held the overflow of prisoners was a hilly rise. Obersfehrin Blucher's girlish figure was outlined against the smoky dawn, a uniformed man next to her. There was the sound of pistol shots.

"Look," said Francesca.

Helene raised her head. She was light-headed with hunger.

Her feet carried her forward with the others, but it took the utmost concentration of will to remain upright. Her eyes could see, her feet moved, and she heard and spoke. That meant that she still lived.

"Karl," said Helene, suddenly confused. This was Blucher's job. Karl was not one of them. He played music and wrote poetry in the style of Browning.

It was a man's hand that was raised, not the feminine hand of Ilse Blucher. Blucher was pointing, and in Karl's hand was the pistol. To Helene it was nothing more than a curiosity that the pistol should be in Karl's hand and that he should be shooting the women at whom Blucher pointed. Helene looked away, and now she walked more deliberately. She felt the need to press her feet more deeply into the earth, to prove that she was still alive and capable of working. For between her footfalls and Karl's upraised arm, she knew there was an unfathomable connection.

The boards of the floor of the barracks were rotting in places from the dampness. The edge of one piece of wood curled up slightly beneath the tier of bunks that Helene and Francesca occupied.

"Look here," said Francesca as she pulled the board up and slid it to one side.

Helene got down on her knees and peered into the dark pit beneath the floor.

"I'll show you," said Francesca excitedly. She took a scrap of bread from her pocket and held it down into the hole. There was no light in the barracks, but as Helene stared at Francesca's fingers, she discerned the shape of a small, thin hand.

"My God," she said, and moved away from the hole.

"She's mine," said Francesca as she held her water-filled tin cup down for the child to drink. "Come, don't you want to see her?"

Helene sat on the floor away from the hole, holding herself with her arms and rocking from side to side. "No, I don't."

The other women in the barracks lay lethargically in their bunks and paid no attention to the open hole in the floor.

"Where did you get her?" asked Helene.

"She's a Gypsy child. Someone had her hidden before I got her. It was the day that the last of the Gypsies were killed. Her mother was one of them. The child never speaks, which is fortunate. Otherwise she would have been discovered by now. She appears to be about eight years old, but she is so tiny, it's hard to say."

"I can't look at her," said Helene. "To think of her beneath the floor all this time . . ."

Francesca placed the board over the hole again. "I have no name for her, but it gives me pleasure to care for her."

"You need the food for yourself," said Helene. "You're so thin now, I don't know how you stand upright."

"Giving the child food keeps me alive," said Francesca, her eyes bright.

Helene knew now of the presence of the child, but she could not make herself go near the hole in the evenings when Francesca picked up the loose board and handed the child the scraps of food. The Gypsy children had been gone for a long time, and they and Miriam and David had receded into memory. If she were to go near the hole and to look at the child and to touch her, there was a danger. Feelings were a danger.

"You are wrong not to come and see how nicely she takes the food from my hand," said Francesca. "When we leave this place, I will take her to Palestine to show to my husband."

"She is not a pet dog," said Helene. "She is a child."

"Then if she is a child, why will you not look at her?"

"I cannot," said Helene.

Helene held the bowl to Francesca's lips. The frail body had already expired. Only the ethereal voice remained. They, who had propped each other up and cared for each other for three years, were alone among the thousands. They were the last. All those who had come when they had come were gone.

"I give the child to you," said Francesca.

Helene wanted to argue with her, to dissuade her from leaving her, but there was not enough energy for that. She held Francesca's limp body in her arms long after there was any need, long after the ethereal voice had been quieted. And in the evening she dragged her friend from the barracks and laid her next to the stack of bodies outside the barracks door.

All during the night Helene thought of the child beneath the floor. There was no sound, and yet the child must be hungry. Helene had the ration of food that Francesca had not eaten the day before. She had hidden it in her clothing so that no one would steal it. If she lifted up the board, she would have to look at the child. If she lifted up the board, she would have to give the food to the child.

In exhaustion Helene fell asleep. In her dreams she walked and walked about the camp searching for a safer place to hide the slice of bread that she had saved, but everywhere she looked someone was standing guard. By the latrine, no one is standing guard at the latrine, she said to herself in her dream.

The distance to the latrine was so long that she had to crawl the last few feet. Women came in and out of the latrine, but no one noticed Helene sitting in the dirt holding the piece of bread.

After a while a woman stopped and tapped Helene on the shoulder. "I have seen others like you here. You are dying."

In the morning, before roll call, Helene pulled the board up and held her hand in the hole beneath the floor. Why am I afraid? What makes me wait until others have failed before I act?

There was the sound of movement below and then the touch of tiny fingers on her own as the child took the bread out of her hand. Helene recoiled from the child's touch.

"No, come back," she said as she sensed the child moving away. "My name is Helene. I will bring you food again this evening."

After the evening rations of bread and watery soup had been given out, Helene drank half the soup and ate a small portion of the bread. She looked longingly at the remaining piece of bread, and then she pulled the board out where the child was hidden.

The child grasped Helene's hand again and then took the bread and soup and began to eat. Helene kept her face close to the hole, close to where the child and the sounds of the child were. Her heart pounded in her chest. Why am I afraid? she asked herself over and over again. She could hear the noises the child made as she drank and chewed. Little sucking noises. Helene bent closer so that she could see the child as she ate. The child was black with dirt, so it was difficult to tell what she looked like in the darkness that surrounded her. There was the smell of excrement everywhere. Then she saw her very clearly, face and body caked with dirt, face pinched and dark, hair matted to her head. Only her eyes were human, glowing in the darkness. Helene choked in fear at her glimpse of the child, but she forced herself to continue watching.

Helene had heard Francesca talk to the child in French, but she had never heard the child answer.

"Has anyone ever given you a name?" asked Helene in French.

There was no answer.

"I will call you Sara," said Helene. "Sara, wife of Abraham. Miriam, sister of Moses," she said softly. She touched Sara's rough cheek, and she felt a tear roll down the child's face. "I will take care of you, Sara," she said.

Helene replaced the board quickly. She smoothed the splintery edges of the board with her fingers, touching the wood gently and carefully. A child lives there in a pit beneath the floor. Sara lives there. Sara. Helene began to cry. And while she cried, she remembered that she had not cried in three years.

It was yet another morning, like so many mornings that had gone before. Someone shook Helene roughly in her sleep. Helene opened her eyes. No one else was stirring in the barracks yet.

"Get up," said the woman guard.

Helene looked frantically around her. It was her turn to

die, and there was no one to entrust the child to, no one who would open the boards and feed scraps of food to the child.

"A moment," she pleaded, trying to think of what to do.

"No moments. Now."

The guard marched her out of the barracks and across the field, toward the hilly slope where she had seen Blucher and Karl. But why was she now alone with the guard? No single prisoner was worth a guard's time. Perhaps she wasn't going to die. They reached the hill, and they continued walking. Perhaps. Perhaps.

And then they were in the building where the SS guards lived. And it was light and airy, and there was the sound of music being played on a phonograph. She was taken to a shower and given a bar of soap and a towel and a clean uniform. She looked at the soap in disbelief. She wanted to run back to the barracks and scream, "Look at what I've got. Have you ever seen such a thing as I've got?"

The guard waited outside the door. Helene stood beneath the shower, her face turned up toward the water, and felt that now she could die happy. She was clean. She had forgotten what it was like to be clean. Her skin felt sore beneath the force of the water. She sat down on the floor of the shower stall and let the water run until the guard came in and told her to get dressed.

She was taken to a small anteroom and told to sit in a chair and wait. She looked around her. Fifty women could sleep comfortably in this anteroom, she thought. The desk and chairs could be removed, and there would be a clean, new space to live in. She pulled her long brown hair back so that it fell behind her ears. It had been three years since she had been alone, since she had sat in a chair, since she had been clean, since she had touched her hair and wondered what she looked like.

The door to the anteroom opened, and a tall man in a heavy overcoat entered, followed by an SS man. The SS man turned and left, and the door closed behind him. She felt dizzy. She let her head drop between her legs so that she wouldn't faint. His arms were around her. He was crying. She lifted her head up and looked at him. It was strange that he was crying.

"It's how I look that makes you cry," she said, touching her blue-veined forehead with one thin hand.

As he hugged her to him, she felt as if he were crushing the bones of her arms, which were almost visible beneath the skin. She groaned in pain.

"My God, my God," he said over and over again.

He pulled his chair close to hers so that he could support her frail body against his own sturdy one. Her lack of response alarmed him, and he searched her face anxiously for a sign that she was not yet beyond the living. He had seen those before in the camps he had visited, the *mussulmen,* the walking skeletons, those who had reached a point beyond pain or hunger or human contact. He touched her arms gingerly where the bones almost jutted through the thin covering of skin. She knew him. He had seen the recognition in her face, but her almond eyes were feverish above her tautly drawn cheekbones, and there was a vacancy in her expression.

"Helene," he said, and again "Helene," as one does when trying to awaken someone from sleep. "You must not stay here any longer. I'm going to arrange for you to leave here."

"I don't understand how you found me here. No one knows where I am," she said.

"It is only an accident that I found you," he said, trying not to betray his anguish as he looked at her emaciated form.

"This is all an accident," she said absently.

"Franco has finally given permission to search out all Spanish Jews and to assert their rights as Spanish citizens," said Tonio.

She looked at him, not comprehending.

"Your name," he said slowly. "I found your name on the camp's roster. At first I didn't believe that it could be you."

"And is it?" she asked in confusion.

"Helene, listen. You must listen carefully to me."

She closed her eyes. "I'm listening."

"The Spanish Jews are being moved to Bergen-Belsen. They will be kept apart from the other prisoners there until

Franco can arrange to bring them back to Spain. Your name will be on the list of those to be moved to Bergen-Belsen."

She did not respond.

"Do you understand?" he asked.

"I'm not Spanish," she said.

"You will be Spanish for the Germans," said Tonio.

"Have you brought me something to eat?" she asked, suddenly alert.

Tonio released her and searched through his pockets. "I have only this," he said, handing her a remnant of a candy bar wrapped in tissue. She snatched it from his hands. Then she turned the hem of her fresh uniform over and poked through the threads until there was a hole large enough to slip the tissue-wrapped candy through.

"It's for Sara," she said contentedly.

"Who is Sara?"

"My daughter."

"Yours? Born here?"

Helene shook her head. "Her mother was a Gypsy. She died in the first year. Sara is my daughter now. I named her. Francesca called her 'the child,' but I gave her a name. Sara."

"It's a beautiful name, biblical, like the wife of Abraham."

"I love Sara like I loved Miriam and David. I have to stay here with Sara. No one can care for her like I can care for her. No one will watch out for her like I do." There was a delusionary edge to her voice.

"Where do you keep Sara?" asked Tonio gently.

"In a hole in the floor beneath where I sleep. No one knows she is there. Karl doesn't know she is there. If he knew, he would shoot her like he did the other children."

"Then we will make Sara Spanish, too, Helene," said Tonio softly. "You see what power Franco has?"

Her eyes were bright and attentive suddenly. "Can he make everyone in the camp Spanish?"

Tonio clasped her to him again. "It's not possible, Helene. Nothing more than this is possible."

"This is what I have inherited, Herr Katakis. It is not of my making. I took over from Commandant Koegel. This camp was never intended to hold this many women. Things get out of control. And then the decisions come from above. Himmler himself is in constant communication with me. Nothing happens that is not in full accordance with Himmler's directives."

Commandant Suhren paused and blinked his thin-lidded blue eyes rapidly.

Tonio placed the list of names on Commandant Suhren's desk. "These are the people who I have determined are deserving of the protection of the Spanish government."

"You come in here and look through my lists of prisoners' names, and then you pluck some out and tell me they are Sephardic Jews," said Suhren angrily. "These are not all Spanish names on this list. How can you tell that they are Sephardics? I must have some proof."

Tonio sat down at the desk and began to write on a piece of paper that he had taken out of his pocket.

"There is your proof, my signature. I vouch for the names. I sign the list as a duly appointed representative of the Spanish government. The seal is there, and here is a copy of the letter from Generalissimo Franco directing that all Spanish nationals be treated in every respect as Spanish citizens."

Suhren took Franco's letter and read it quickly and then handed it back to Tonio.

"What do you want done with them?" asked Suhren, forcing himself to be civil. "I see there are fifteen here. We have no accommodations to keep them from the rest of the prison population until they are released."

"A train will be sent to take them to Bergen-Belsen to be held in special custody," said Tonio.

"When will that be?"

"Within the week. Final travel arrangements are being made for a group that is there now awaiting repatriation. When they are safely gone, we will send for the fifteen who are here."

"It's a lot of trouble for a few people," said Suhren.

Tonio ignored the remark. "You will notice there is an unnamed child on the list, approximately ten years of age. A girl. I have been informed by one of the other Sephardics that she is the child of a deceased Sephardic woman."

Commandant Suhren nodded knowingly. "Of course, a Sephardic child. And you have the names of the deceased parent, of course? Perhaps I can help make up a name for you."

Tonio would not let himself be bullied. The man was not sure of his power. He was less sure of Tonio's power.

"The name has been forgotten," said Tonio. "But the mother entrusted her to the care of the others when she died. She is recognized by the others as a Sephardic child. There is no question about that."

Suhren's face was impassive. Helene had said that she would not leave without the child, that she could not leave without the child. Tonio would not accept anything but complete agreement from Suhren, because if Suhren balked, or refused, Helene would refuse to leave, would stay behind and die with the child.

"The child is hidden in the barracks," said Tonio, his eyes boring into Suhren's. "Find her. I hold you responsible if anything happens to prevent her arrival in Bergen-Belsen along with the others."

Helene and Sara were moved to Bergen-Belsen, along with thirteen Sephardic Jews whom Tonio had found in Ravensbrück. They were kept in a special barracks while it was decided how and in what manner the Spanish government would claim them. While they were there, they were given treatment reserved for privileged prisoners. Ample food, rest, and medical care.

Helene never tired of looking at the child. She reminded her of David, with her big, dark eyes and round, olive-skinned face. At first Sara kept her eyes covered in the sunlight and never moved away from Helene's side.

"She is a beautiful child," the other prisoners said as Sara grew healthier before their eyes and began to grow again.

"I love you, Sara," Helene said over and over to the child, and Sara responded by beginning to talk.

Helene counted days now, where before she had not known what year it was. Six months passed, during which time negotiations continued for their release. The Swiss agreed to allow passage of the fifteen prisoners through their territory, provided that the Joint Distribution Committee gave the Swiss a guarantee that they would maintain the prisoners while they were on Swiss soil. At the end of 1944, when release appeared imminent, 155 Jews who had tried to escape a Nazi roundup in Athens were brought to Bergen-Belsen to join the other Sephardics.

"The numbers are wrong," said Commandant Kramer on Tonio's fourth visit to Bergen-Belsen.

"The numbers are correct," protested Tonio. "I have given you document after document verifying the number of Sephardic prisoners. I have also presented verified documents that the Swiss will permit the prisoners' transit through Switzerland and that the Joint will pay for their food and transportation."

"Then the names are incorrect," persisted Kramer.

"You must release these people before they die of typhus," said Tonio.

"They are my responsibility," shouted Kramer. "Do you understand that? My responsibility. I have not created what Bergen-Belsen is, and I do not condone that the population of the camp doubles and doubles and yet doubles again. Because the war is being lost, they send me prisoners. Because the railroads to Auschwitz are bombed, they send me even more prisoners. It is my responsibility to see that they are properly identified, that they are kept here until I receive further orders. Nothing more. I owe nothing to Franco, and I do not believe your documents."

"I am willing to take one hundred seventy of them off your hands," said Tonio cajolingly.

"I cannot guarantee their safe conduct through Europe to Spain."

"Then take them as far as Hendaye. The Spanish government promises to take over at the Spanish border."

"Eichmann has not given the orders yet," said Kramer stubbornly.

"Right now our Spanish consul in Athens, Sebastian Radigales, is in Berlin assuring Foreign Minister von Thadden that the JDC will pay all costs," insisted Tonio.

"Then let Eichmann tell me that himself. I cannot take it upon myself. I just cannot."

While negotiations droned on, conditions in the privileged camp at Bergen-Belsen began to deteriorate along with those in the rest of the camp. In April 1945, as the fall of Germany became more certain and the Allied forces approached Bergen-Belsen, Helene and Sara and the rest of the Spanish nationals were jammed onto a train with 2,200 other prisoners. Sara clung to Helene's body as they sat in a corner of the train and people cried out for water as the train rolled along the railroad tracks for the third day. There were explosions in the distance. The train stopped once when the track suddenly ended, and then the noise of hammering steel against steel began outside the locked cars as the train's crew worked to repair the bombed-out section of track. But no one brought food or water to the people packed inside. The clanging of metal stopped, and the train started up again. Helene spoke soothingly to Sara in French.

"See how bright the sky is," said Helene. The light entered the train in ribbons between the train's wood-plank sides.

Sara hid her face against Helene's shoulder. She was the size of a six-year-old rather than a ten-year-old, and her black eyes bore a look of perpetual fright.

"Come, come, it's all right now," said Helene soothingly. "What more can happen to us, Sara? Only good things can happen to us now. We will be free. Do you understand what that means, to be free? That means we will have our own house, and you will have a place in the house all your own, with a bed of your own. And you will have all the food you want, and you will eat when you want to and sleep when you want to; and you will walk outside, and no one will follow you or tell you not to walk where you want to walk. And there will be books, and you will go to school and learn to read the books. And the stories in the books will make you happy. I will never permit sad books to be brought into the house. And there will be only laughing. No crying, never any crying."

Suddenly the train was screeching to a stop. Through the

slats of the floorboard, Helene saw sparks flying up beneath the train. She held Sara close to her as everyone around them began to scream and shout and pound on the sides of the car. The train skidded out of control along the tracks in a catapulting, headlong motion, metal wheels on metal tracks producing a sustained high-pitched squeal. Helene closed her eyes. Now her time had come, now God's plan for her was ended. Why had He made her struggle so to stay alive if He was to take her and Sara in this way?

The train hit the abandoned truck with an explosive force that rumbled through the chain of cars, snapping the cars back and forth and tossing the people violently against first one end of the car and then the other. Legs and arms tangled together. Then there was silence, except for the low moan of the injured.

Helene felt Sara's arms still around her neck. She was alive. She could feel her warm breath on her lips. They clung to each other, not moving, waiting for the train to start, for someone to come. But no one came, and the night turned into day.

Sara slept in Helene's arms, and when she awoke, Helene said, "Listen to how quiet it is."

And Sara listened. There was no sound of the train crew, no sound of anyone fixing the train so that it could move again.

In the afternoon Helene heard the noise of trucks pulling alongside the train.

"Are you alive in there?" asked a brawny American as he pulled the door to their railroad car open.

Sara began to cry at the sound of the strange language.

"Don't cry, Sara, don't cry. Now is no time to cry," said Helene, hugging the child to her.

"We are here," Helene shouted in French back to the American.

"Well, I'll be damned."

1945–1946: Will

XXII

February 4, 1945

Dearest Peg,

I've been in transit and haven't had a place to mail letters from so am sending this batch of ten all at once. I only hope that when the Yalta meeting is over, I'll be attached again to Ike's staff. At least that way my mail finds me. Wherever Ike goes, the mail is never far behind. This has been a rest, though. Slogging through the mud was beginning to feel good. I guess Boss Luce was right to mix up the *Life* staff a bit. Sort of an enforced vacation, not having to worry about getting your butt shot off while you're standing in the middle of the fire zone snapping off pictures. No, don't worry, haven't even come close to me yet. And here I am with Roosevelt and Churchill and Stalin, photographing them eating and talking. The three don't seem as cordial to each other as they did at Teheran. I guess now that the military strategy is history, they're beginning to look at the pie that's looming in front of them and wondering who's going to get the biggest piece.

Roosevelt looks gray. That's the only color to describe him. I've sent my negatives of the first day on their way back to the States, and it's my feeling that Roosevelt will be dead before the shots show up in the next issue of *Life*. That scares the hell out of me. Stalin will be too big for Winnie to handle by himself.

Enough about that. So you miss me, do you? Words can't tell how I feel. Every night, no matter where I am, I think of you and Katie snug at home, safe, and I thank God for it. There is a whole new bunch of guys here from *Look* and *Saturday Evening Post,* and anyone and everyone I can corner I show the snapshots you sent me of Katie on her new bike. That makes it not only her seventh birthday that I've missed, but now her eighth. Besides that, it's been two months since any mail's caught up with me. Yes, that was a groan. And a complaint. And a whine and a whimper.

What else? I love you, can't wait till this damn thing winds up so I can come home to you and Katie. Don't listen to my pessimism about Roosevelt, Churchill, et al., too closely. You're the only one I tell how I feel about things. And, after all, they are only feelings. Roosevelt will probably outlive us all.

I love you.

Your Will

March 7, 1945

Dearest Peg,

Hanging around with the politicians at Yalta, I had forgotten what it was like to really be at war. Ike brought me up short when he sent me off to join Combat Command "B" of the 9th Armored Division. He said, with that country-boy smile of his, "Will, how'd you like to take some real photographs?"

Which accounts for what I got on film this morning at the Ludendorff Bridge near Remagen. Bill Hoge, commanding "B" Company, decided to take the bridge, which was still intact. He sent a second lieutenant onto the bridge, bold as brass, and when the German guard on the other side got a load of him, he tried to set off the charges he had stashed beneath the bridge. No soap. Another German jumped into the fray, lit the fuse, but nothing much happened in the way of an explosion. Meanwhile I'm snapping, jumping, snapping away as if my life depended on it. I can always feel when the deathless picture is in the making.

Anyway, an American, a Sergeant Drabik, crosses the bridge and is the first American fighting man to set foot on the right bank of the Rhine. Behind him are a combat engineer and three sappers, who begin tearing the charges from the bridge's girders and throwing them like candy canes into the river. What a sight. By this evening we've got 8,000 Americans, give or take a few, on the bridgehead. In the process they've taken 51,000 prisoners. A dejected, tired-out, and finished bunch of soldiers. Got a German corps commander along with the regulars, too. Seems the commander stumbled across these men and asked why they weren't fighting, and it wasn't until an American MP touched him on the shoulder that he realized he had fallen into the middle of a concentration of POW's. Can't get too angry at the German fighting man. He looks too much like us.

Got a stack of letters yesterday. One even from my brother. Second one this year, and all he does is complain about his job at Lockheed.

It was interesting that Gruber called you about the fashion layouts I did in Paris in 1939. Doesn't he know there's a war on? Anyway, tell him I don't think I'm interested in fashion photography any longer. I think I'll just stay on at *Life* and see where the wind blows me. It makes life more exciting than seeing which way the hems fall.

I love you. I miss you. Kiss our daughter for me. Keep writing!

Your Will

March 24, 1945

Dearest Peg,

I did something today that I hope I never have to repeat. I joined General Ridgway's XVIII airborne corps and, along with four airborne divisions, parachuted into the enemy battery positions. The fighting was fierce but didn't last long. I lost a camera bag with yesterday's rolls in it somewhere in the field where I landed. We had to scramble to take cover. Major-General Miley thinks the operation was a success overall. Losses minimal. Fifty wounded, 31 killed.

Can't think, I'm so exhausted. I love you.

Your Will

April 13, 1945

Dearest Peg,

Heard about Roosevelt's death today. Everyone strangely apathetic about it, as though all emotions have been amputated by this damned war. Nothing much can shock me, after all the death and dying.

Some things of the past week that have kept me up nights: Joined an American division near Oranienburg. Still can't believe I really saw what I saw. We'd heard rumors of camps where they were keeping political prisoners and Jews—mainly Jews I now find out. The damn war's nearly over, and the Germans start marching the half-dead prisoners along the roads, heading nowhere in particular, just so they won't be left in camp when the Allies arrive. A place called Sachsenhausen and its sister camp, Ravensbrück, threw 40,000 men and women out on the roads. The first inkling I had was when we started seeing bodies at the side of the road. It was raining heavily, but it looked like most of them had been shot when they couldn't go any farther. If we'd only made it here sooner, most of them would probably still be alive. I'm still trying to sort it all out in my mind. I don't understand the meaning of any of it. It brings into question my whole idea of the German mentality. A lot of the stories we've been hearing the past year about death squads and crematoriums are beginning to fit after what I saw at Oranienburg. And, of course, there was no one in charge; the SS had disappeared by the time we found the remains of the prisoners. Maybe 2,000 are still alive out of the 40,000, and there's no one to put on trial, no one to grab ahold of. Some children were among the prisoners. I've thought of you and Katie every moment since then.

I love you.

Your Will

April 17, 1945

Dear Peg,

Yesterday we entered Bergen-Belsen, two days after the British. General Patton looked like he was going to faint. He had to be helped to walk to his jeep, where he held on to the steering wheel and vomited in the dirt.

I won't tell you what it was like, because I can't. Bodies as far as the eye could see, some living, some dead. Walking corpses. Mass graves were bulldozed by the British. Five thousand bodies in this grave, 4,000 bodies in that grave, and so on and on and on. Even with the best medical care and food brought in, it's estimated that at least 1,700 a day of those who remain will die within the next few weeks.

I'm sending you a picture I developed this afternoon. It's not a picture of the camp. You'll see those pictures everywhere you turn in the next few weeks. It's a picture of the camp commandant, Kramer. I photographed him like you would photograph a rare species of animal. He strutted around afterward, proud to be the center of attention, while a short distance away was a stack of children's naked, dead bodies, waiting their turn for disposal.

I'm bone weary, Peg. Mainly I'm weary in spirit. A kind of malaise is settling in on me that makes me not want to take any more deathless pictures. My heart and my eye are wounded. All I want is to take you and Katie somewhere where it's peaceful and quiet, and where my camera eye will stop replaying the horrors. I want to be where people are good to one another. I need my faith restored. But deep down in me there's a fear that something vital and innocent that I need to have to be a functioning human being has been forever lost.

I said that the photograph of Kramer was as of a rare species of animal. Not so rare. There are countless more just like him. Most of them have taken off their uniforms and disappeared. That may be the scariest thing of all.

Kiss Katie for me.

Will

XXIII

Will needed a shave. He ran his hand through the red hair that flopped unevenly across his forehead. He hadn't had a haircut since he left Cyprus, and he didn't care. He was on a train bound for home. It was 1946, the war had been over for a year, but still the train was filled with servicemen. A Marine dozed in the seat next to Will, his shoulders straight even in sleep.

Will looked down at his wrinkled battle fatigues, the same ones he had been wearing when *Life* had assigned him to the Allied Military Government to photograph the displaced persons camps that the Allies had set up throughout Europe. For the first time since Will had been sent to cover the European campaign, *Life* had paired him up with a journalist, Mark Horngood, and together the two of them had roamed among the human remains of the camps, Mark writing of what he saw while Will photographed it. Then, for five weeks running, *Life* ran a serialization of the story. At the end of the series, Lindinauer, *Life*'s Berlin Bureau Chief, suggested that they zero in on a typical refugee family and follow their progress through the displaced persons camps, and he would reserve another three weeks' space in the magazine for the story.

"It's too close to the bone, too personal, too soon after the events," Mark Horngood objected. "Haven't these people been subjected to enough without us following them around, watching and waiting to see what shore they wash up on?"

"Do it," said Lindinauer. "I don't care how long it takes or how much money it costs. And if it hits raw spots, so much the better. That's what our readers want to see. Just do it."

So Will shot five hundred rolls of seventy-millimeter film,

and Mark wrote sixty thousand words on them. The words had been shipped off to Lindinauer in Berlin to be edited and were now on their way to New York, but the film still lay wrapped securely in toweling in the safety of Will's camera case. He had checked his duffel bag with the conductor but would not relinquish possession of the battered leather case that contained his Ektar Combat Graphic and the five hundred rolls of film chronicling Ora and Sam Abrams' travail from concentration camp to displaced persons camp to the final Jewish detention camp on the island of Cyprus. Not even during the last few days in San Francisco with Mark Horngood had Will let the camera case out of his sight.

"Powerful stuff, images," Will said to Mark the night before they parted.

"More powerful with words attached," said Mark.

"Yeah, but words don't stay in my mind like those damn pictures do," said Will.

On the train platform in San Francisco, Will and Mark hugged each other. "Watch that film with your life," said Mark.

"You sure you don't want to come home with me, spend some time with Peg and me in Lawndale, California?" asked Will. "Quietest town in America."

Mark shook his head. "I'm still feeling a little subhuman, still not quite up to socializing with regular people yet. I feel so angry all the time, and I can't seem to get a focus on exactly what I'm so angry about."

"I feel the same way," said Will.

"I don't think your in-laws or your wife would want to have to deal with *two* battle-scarred *Life*rs. One's just about enough."

"I guess so," said Will. He patted the camera case that was slung over his shoulder. "We did a good job."

"The best," agreed Mark.

"We did them justice, don't you think?" asked Will, his face sad and hopeful at the same time.

"We called it like it was," said Mark.

When they waved at each other as the train pulled out of the station, Will was alone with the photographs that replayed themselves endlessly in his mind's eye. He tried to divert himself, to perk himself up, to distract himself from that part of him that remained with Sam and Ora Abrams. He was going home, he told himself. Peg and Katie were waiting at his father-in-law's house. There was going to be a party to welcome him back. Be happy, for Christ's sake, he said to himself angrily. You're going home.

Will looked out the window at the passing landscape. Nothing made sense to him anymore. He had always prided himself on his practical approach to life, on his even nature, on his love of a good joke, on his readiness to join in mindless revelry. Suddenly he remembered that he hadn't heard the sound of his own laughter for a year or more. He touched his fingers to his throat as if to reassure himself that he still had the capacity to laugh if he wanted to.

All the seats in the train were taken. Two sailors sat on their seabags in the aisle. A group of Marines leaned against the rear wall of the compartment and watched a crap game in progress on the floor next to the washroom. Will looked at their faces. They were all happy to be going home. They were joking and laughing. Why couldn't he be that way? Why had he photographed onto his mind every grim frame that his camera lens had seen so that the funniness of life could no longer reach him? He felt the absence of Mark with an acuteness bordering on pain. When Mark was with him, he knew that someone shared what he was feeling, and somehow between the two of them, their feelings were diffused and made more bearable.

"The trouble with you guys is you've been brainwashed by the Zionists," Stan Bingham had said at the journalists' award dinner at the St. Francis Hotel the night before Will left San Francisco. "It's really very clever how they get you to feeling like a Jew yourself. See, sympathy is the name of the game. Without sympathy they haven't got a pot to pee in."

Will stood up and stared at the writer from *The Saturday Evening Post.*

"Sit down, Will, it's okay," said Mark from the other end of the table. Someone was in the middle of a speech. Will's voice rang out over the speaker's words. "You goddamn prick," he said. He swung at the same time, hitting the writer in the left eye. Mark was out of his seat instantly, and he and another man helped the writer away from the table toward the men's room. The speaker had stopped speaking. There was a quietness in the banquet hall. Will was breathing heavily and staring after the writer as he was helped out of the room. "Come back here, you prick, you goddamned prick. Weren't you there, you fuckin' bastard?"

While Will sat drinking in the bar, Mark picked up their joint award for journalistic excellence in a continuing series. Then they walked back to their rooms at the Sir Francis Drake. They didn't mention the writer from *The Saturday Evening Post.* Will bought a bunch of violets from an old woman on the corner of Post and Geary. He sniffed at them while they walked to the hotel.

"Violets don't smell," said Mark.

Will continued to sniff at them. "They'll be dead by tomorrow," he said suddenly.

"Put them in a glass of water when you get into your room," said Mark.

Will took one last sniff and then tossed them out onto the cable car tracks in the middle of the street. He stopped walking and stood and looked at the flowers. Mark stood beside him, not saying anything. A cable car rounded the curve of the hill. Will watched its path toward the flowers. In a few minutes the cable car had passed, and the flowers lay mashed into the crevices of the steel rods in the street. The two men turned and walked silently up the street.

The train's air had become thick with smoke. Will felt that he would stop breathing if he sat there any longer. He stood up, and holding his camera bag close to him, he walked through the crowded aisles toward the rear of the train. There should be a club car somewhere to the rear where he could get a drink and clear his head, he thought. He walked slowly, stepping over sleeping bodies. It was quieter here toward the rear of the train. He opened the door to the next compartment, and when he entered, he immediately sensed the stillness surrounding him, the absence of conversation, the lack of movement. Everyone was in uniform, and in the dim light everyone's skin had the color of rich red earth.

A muscular man in a Marine uniform stood just inside the

door. He wore no cap; instead, around his forehead and circling his shiny black hair was a headband of homespun red and yellow cloth.

"Is the club car back here?" asked Will.

"The other end of train," said the Marine, no expression on his face. His black eyes above his high cheekbones glanced at Will and then away again.

Will made no move to open the door to retrace his steps. The quiet of the compartment was soothing after the din of the other sections of the train. He stood near the door next to the Marine, feeling the train sway and vibrate beneath their feet.

"Were you in Europe?" asked Will finally.

"Yes," answered the Marine, not turning his face toward Will again.

Among the men sitting silently in the compartment there were other headbands.

"American Indian unit?" said Will.

"Yes," replied the Marine, his profile broad-nosed and Eskimo-like where the full cheeks disappeared into the generous mouth.

"Cherokee unit?" asked Will.

"No. Navaho and Havasupai."

"And you?"

"Havasupai."

The man responded as spoken to. He offered nothing. He did not seem so much bothered by Will's questions as distant from them.

"I've heard of the Navaho, but not of the Havasupai. Where's your tribe located?"

The Marine turned his face toward Will for the first time. "On the Colorado River of the Grand Canyon. 'Havasupai' means 'people of the blue-green water.'"

The Indian's hair shone sleek and thick beneath his headband. "We spoke on the radio in Havasupai language so the Germans would not understand the messages."

The Indian spoke in short sentences punctuated by long silences. The silences could be taken for aloofness or disinterest, but Will sensed that they reflected a reluctance to reveal himself to a white man. Will studied his features. He had rarely seen Indians except in Hollywood movies. And then they were always on the wrong side of the fight.

"Well, shake my hand," said Will, extending his hand to the Indian, who looked at it for a few seconds and then took it and squeezed it firmly.

"My name's Will Mathison."

"I am Elgin Jones."

"Is that your real name?"

"Bureau of Indian Affairs name."

"I see. I was at the Grand Canyon when I was a kid. Your tribe actually lives down there?"

"Yes. By the Colorado River."

"How do you get down there?"

"There is a trail down from the Hualapai Indian Reservation. It is three hours on horseback or seven hours on foot."

"It sounds isolated."

Elgin nodded.

"How the hell did they find you to put a uniform on you?" asked Will in astonishment.

"Gold miners explored the canyon and found us in 1882."

Will shook his head in wonderment, and the two men were silent for a while.

"Did you hear about what the Germans did to the Jews, Elgin?" asked Will abruptly.

"I saw a camp," said Elgin.

"What did you think about it? I mean about the Germans. What do you think of the Germans?"

"The Havasupai are peaceful people. We trade with the Pueblo Indians—the Navaho and Hopi. We are brothers to the Hualapai. We tend our fields and ride our horses through the canyons. When we were able to roam the high plateaus in the winter, before the reservation was made, we killed food only to be eaten. When someone was hungry and we had food, we fed them. Whatever child was in our home when there was food to be eaten, we gave the child food to eat. Our old people are very wise. There is beauty in the lines of the old ones' faces."

Will listened quietly. There was civility in the Indian's circuitous answer, dignity in his subtle rebuttal to the question about German barbarism.

"Then the Havasupai people have much to teach us," said Will.

Elgin's eyes were on Will's, strong and steady. "We are not perfect. We are locked onto five hundred twenty acres and not allowed to hunt the high plateaus any longer. The missionaries come and tell us to pray to their gods. The Bureau of Indian Affairs takes away the power of our tribal council to make decisions. Our children are sent away to the Indian school nine months in every year. All of this angers us. Our men drink too much and fight too much, and there is much despair."

"But you wouldn't murder the white man because of it? You wouldn't be like the Germans?"

Elgin shook his head. "We are men, not animals. We have lived in the Grand Canyon near the waters of the Colorado since the twelfth century. The white man has been with us for only fifty-five years. We have patience."

"You must be happy to be going home," said Will. "As for me, I can't make up my mind if I'm happy to be going home or not. It scares me what they don't know at home about what's happened. I'm a photographer for *Life* magazine, and I don't have to tell you what kind of pictures I've been taking lately."

Elgin nodded his head.

"Home for me is a small town in California called Lawndale. Not much happens in Lawndale. My wife's family are Mormons."

"The Mormons have visited us in Havasupai also," said Elgin.

"Yeah, well, then you know what I mean. Swell folks, the greatest, the salt of the earth, as the saying goes. But the Church is their main preoccupation. I mean, if I talked for four hundred years about the war in Europe, they'd never connect it with themselves. Does that make sense?"

As soon as Will asked the question, he realized that the Havasupais must be even more parochial in their thinking than the Lawndale Mormons, so what the hell was he thinking of trying to unburden himself to this strange Indian?

"Being with your family will make you happy," said Elgin. "People understand more than you think they will understand."

Will looked at him in surprise. "They do, don't they? There's no need to explain every little thing, is there?"

"No," said Elgin.

"Have there been any journalists down in your village, anyone writing up the story of your tribe's problems?" asked Will, warming to the man.

"You mean like in *Life* magazine?" said Elgin, a small smile on his lips.

Will laughed. "Yeah, like *Life* magazine."

"Not yet," said Elgin.

Will nodded. "You're a pretty sharp guy, Elgin Jones. Talking to you has made me feel good—real good."

For the remainder of the trip, Will and Elgin stood in the darkened compartment together, speaking occasionally, feeling relaxed in each other's company. As the train pulled into Union Station in Los Angeles, Will wrote his name and his father-in-law's address on a piece of paper and handed it to the Indian. Then he picked up his camera bag and slung it over his shoulder. Impulsively Will took off his *Life* photographer's badge and handed it to Elgin. "If you ever find yourself lost in Lawndale, California, look me up," he said. "And who knows? Maybe *Life* will send me into the Grand Canyon to take a few pictures of you and your tribe sometime."

Elgin took the pin and affixed it to the front of his uniform. He then removed his headband and in bold printed letters wrote his name on the cotton material: "Elgin Jones, Havasupai Village of the Grand Canyon, Arizona."

Elgin handed the headband to Will, who placed it over his own red hair. "How do I look?" he asked.

"Like a Havasupai," said the Indian.

Will hesitated at the open door of the compartment as the train stopped. "You go to Arizona from here?"

"Camp Pendleton for mustering out," replied Elgin. "Then to Arizona."

"Well, good luck to you," said Will, shaking Elgin's hand for the last time. Then he jumped down onto the station platform, his camera bag slung over his arm and the red and yellow headband securely on his head.

XXIV

"So you think you've had it so tough. Listen, working at Lockheed on the graveyard shift has been no bed of roses either." Will's brother, Glenn, had him cornered in the kitchen, between the refrigerator and the welcome-home cake that Will wasn't supposed to see until Katie lit the two candles on it and Peggy carried it into the dining room and put it on the round oak table. But now Will was in danger of putting his elbow into the cake as his brother persisted in telling him how hard he had had it.

"Oh, Will, you saw the cake," said Peg as she walked into the kitchen, Katie following close behind her. "Katie and I wanted it to be a surprise."

"That's okay, isn't it, Katie?" asked Will as he bent down and hugged the towheaded girl. She had none of Will's freckles and red hair, and yet her coloring was brighter and more vivid than that of her white-skinned, flaxen-haired mother. Will took Katie by the hand, and the two of them walked out of the kitchen, leaving his brother standing at the sink.

"Get me away from him, Peggy, or I think I might just kill him," said Will in the hallway between the kitchen and the dining room.

"He's not so bad, Will. He's been so generous with Katie and me while you were gone. He really means well."

The living room of the small frame house was filled with relatives and neighbors. Peggy's father in his Sears mail-order suit was sitting on the couch with a stack of *Life* magazines on his lap, while his friends from the Lawndale stake of the Mormon Church looked over his shoulder at Will's photographs.

"And does Mervyn have to show everyone those damn pictures?" Will snapped.

"He's proud of you, Will, that's all. He doesn't mean you any harm."

Katie pulled her hand away from Will's and scampered over to her grandfather and climbed up on the sofa beside him.

"See the pictures your daddy took, honey bun," said Mervyn proudly.

In one long stride Will was at the couch and had put his palm over the magazine that lay open on Mervyn's lap. "She doesn't need to see that stuff, Dad."

Mervyn looked up at his son-in-law in surprise. "But it was the truth, wasn't it, son?"

The phone was ringing in the kitchen. Peggy ran to answer it, and then she came back into the living room. "It's Ernest Gruber," she said, making a face. "You're not going back to work so soon, are you?"

Will didn't reply. He walked into the kitchen and picked up the telephone. "Ernest, how are you?"

"Terrific. Why haven't you called?"

"I wasn't ready to call you yet."

"But I need to make the arrangements. I can get a house for you not far from London. You can put the kid in school. Your wife will be happy. There's plenty to do. Shopping, sightseeing. I want a blow-by-blow of the United Nations as it's being organized."

"Peggy doesn't want to live in London."

"It won't be for long. They've bought the Flushing Meadow site, and you'll be back in New York by next year."

"Peggy doesn't want to live in New York either."

"Look, Will, I know you've had a rough assignment, but we need you in London. I'm afraid I'm going to have to tell you to go, not ask you."

"An ultimatum?"

"I'm afraid it is."

There was silence on Will's end of the telephone.

"I need an answer," said Gruber.

"I'll let you know," said Will, and hung up.

• • • • •

Peggy stood in the doorway of the bedroom, her normally colorless cheeks flushed with the excitement of the day. She was very quiet and shy and resembled her mother, Lucy, more now than when Lucy was alive.

"Come to bed," said Will.

Peggy turned off the bedroom light and got into bed beside her husband.

"I can't get used to having you here," she said.

"It's been ten hours. Aren't you sick of me yet?" The warmth of her body flowed to him through the sheer cotton plissé nightgown.

Her mouth was on his, lips parted, soft flesh of her mouth against his. "I'm so glad you're here, Will. I almost stopped believing you'd ever come home."

"I'm here, Peggy," he said, lifting the sheer cotton up over her shoulders so that her smooth breasts and belly lay pressed against his bare skin.

He could feel her heart beating against his chest.

"Katie was so excited all day," she said. "I was so excited all day." Her legs twined around his, and the flesh between her legs was moist to his touch.

"Did you miss it while I was gone?" he asked, moving his penis slowly back and forth across the moistness.

"I thought about it every day," she said, her breath coming in little spurts.

"Two and a half years, and nobody has touched you?" he asked, sliding gently into her. She shivered slightly in his arms.

"Nobody," she said, holding his penis and guiding it in and out of her. He turned her on her back and looked at her lying on the bed. The daughter of Mormons, raised in a small California town an hour from Los Angeles and a world away from Bergen-Belsen. She took his hand and put it against her upturned breast. He bent and kissed the breast, his tongue lingering over the nipple. He felt an urgency and an anger and a desire for her that he had never felt before.

"God, I've wanted to do this for so long," he said, thrusting deeper into her. She twisted from side to side on the bed, bringing him into her, soothing and placating his anger and desire and urgency with her simple sensuality.

"God," he said, "I had forgotten. How could I have forgotten?"

"Shh," she said. "Don't stop. You haven't forgotten."

Peggy lay in his arms, and they talked. They had really not had a chance to talk since he had gotten home. There had been Katie to pay attention to and Mervyn's questions to answer. And the telephone had rung off the wall from the minute he had arrived.

"What did Gruber want?" she asked.

"He wants me to go to London."

"What did you tell him?"

"I didn't tell him anything. I wanted to talk it over with you first."

Peggy kissed him. "I love you," she said.

"It was very bad in Europe, Peg."

She looked up at him with her clear blue eyes. "You told me that it was," she said softly.

"No, I didn't tell you how it was at all. I meant to a thousand times, but there weren't words enough. The last spread, the one we did about Sam and Ora Abrams, has depleted me. Finally, it was the one story that drained my reserves and left me dead inside."

Peggy hugged him to her. "You're not dead inside, Will. You're alive, and you've come home to me and Katie, and we love you." She began to cry in a way that he had seen Lucy cry when Mervyn spoke sharply to her.

"I haven't told you about the Abrams yet. I need to tell you about them."

"I'm listening," she said.

"Sam was twelve when they took him to Auschwitz. He remembers his mother and father and eight-year-old brother standing with him on the station platform when they got off the train. His mother was patting his hair and had just said something to him. When he turned around, his family was gone.

"Ora was fourteen when she was given to a Gentile family in Berlin to be hidden. She never saw her own family again. When she was fifteen, she was discovered and sent to

Ravensbrück. She was sterilized. In Auschwitz the doctors made an incision in Sam's upper thigh, and into the wound they stuffed pieces of straw mixed with cloth. When the leg swelled up and turned blue, they treated it with experimental drugs. When the camp was liberated, the first thing that had to be done was to remove his leg.

"I followed them through the bureaucracy, Peggy. Mark and I were with them as they went through the refugee camps after the war, trying to get to Israel. And every door locked to them. We left them again behind barbed wire on Cyprus, looking at Palestine—what they call Eretz Yisroel—but not able to get in. Two kids, really. Married. Him missing a leg and God knows what else. And she can never have a child like Katie."

"Don't, Will, stop it, don't tell me any more about it." She was holding her hands to his lips to stop the flow of ugly words.

He held her in his arms and cradled her like a child. "I want back what I had, Peggy. I want it back so bad, I think I'll die if I don't get it."

She kissed his eyes and his mouth. "You won't die, Will. I'll go wherever you want. If you want to go to London, I'll go to London with you."

"I can't go back to Europe. Not now, anyway. Europe is a hideous place. There is no beauty there any longer. It's a festering sore, a gangrenous wound. It's everything that is perverted and rotten. All you've ever known is Lawndale and your father's feed store and the bright faces of the third-graders you teach at Lawndale Elementary. I've seen piles of rotting third-graders all over Europe."

Peggy began to push him away, but he caught her by the arms and pulled her back. "I'm sorry," he said. "Don't be afraid. I didn't mean to tell you everything so fast, but I need you to understand how sick I am."

"You're not sick," she said.

"Yes, I am, Peggy. I'm sick, and I don't know how to cure myself."

XXV

Will was finding it difficult to respond to people. He couldn't seem to make small talk anymore. He especially couldn't talk to anyone who asked him about what it was like in Europe. And were the pictures really the truth, or had they been doctored up by some magic of the photographer's art? And was it true that six million Jews had been murdered, or was it just so much Zionist propaganda? Because everyone knew that the Jews had had their eye on Palestine for a long time, and what better way to get it than to exaggerate their misfortunes? Sure, they must have suffered some. All of Europe suffered. They weren't so special in their suffering, were they? As hated as the Jews were, you couldn't blame them for fudging a little bit on the figures, now, could you?

Mervyn's fellow Mormons came to the house to leaf through the stack of *Life* magazines that sat on the coffee table in front of the couch in his sunny living room and to ask the big-time war correspondent who had his by-line on the great *Life* magazine what it really had been like in Europe. Their faces were open in their curiosity. They asked their questions guilelessly, not understanding that each question acted as a punch to Will's stomach.

"I realize that small minds have trouble comprehending things," said Will angrily to the last woman who asked if his pictures were real and whether there truly had been such things as concentration camps. The woman began to cry, and Peggy took her into the kitchen and gave her a glass of buttermilk and a homemade brownie and told the woman that Will was taking medication for his nerves and not to mind him because he didn't mean what he said.

Later that day Mervyn gave Will a stiff drink of Jack

Daniel's. Since his wife, Lucy, had died and his allegiance to his fellow Mormons had become more fraternal than religious in tone, Mervyn had taken to keeping liquor in the house and occasionally having a drink before dinner.

"You've got to understand these people, Will," said Mervyn in the slow and ponderous way he had of talking. "These folks don't mean you no harm. They're just curious is all. Folks have told stories about you for the last five years, and now here you are, setting on my living room couch, and they just wanted to see if you was real, that's all. They don't mean no harm to you or to Jews or to anyone else. They're good people, Will, God-fearing people who go to church regular. People like you and me, Will."

"Nobody's like me anymore," retorted Will, feeling the liquor softening up his anger.

"You'd be surprised. They have tragedies in their lives, just like anyone else. Just because they live in a small town don't make them ignorant people, Will. You speak kindly to them, they'll understand."

"I'm out of kindly words. Don't have any to give them," said Will.

Mervyn shook his head. "Then you better find a way to get some, son. You got a wife and daughter to worry about. You can't go hiding in the bedroom every time someone comes in here wanting to talk to me. And they do, you know. Sometimes they just want to talk to me. Don't think you're so all-fired famous that no one comes in here to talk to me anymore."

"I don't like them asking me questions, that's all," replied Will.

"It's human nature, son. They wasn't there. They want to feel it. Pretty hard to believe what's in those pictures without they got somebody telling them that's the way it was."

"I'll find another place to stay," said Will.

"No, you won't neither. You'll stay right here. I want to watch and see that you got your head on straight before you leave this house. I ain't sending my daughter and granddaughter off to live with some maniac."

Will looked at him in astonishment. "You think I'm behaving like a maniac?"

"Damn close to it, son, damn close to it. If I had to make a choice between you and a maniac, I'd be hard-pressed to do it, I can tell you that."

The Grand Canyon lay below them at Mather Point, red and brown and green carvings in stone, cathedrals in granite, and far in the distance the blue-green of the Colorado River, the canyon's architect. Will raised his Graflex to his shoulder and peered through the viewfinder.

"Will, do you think you should stand so close to the edge?" Peggy called to him from the safety of the path. He didn't reply, merely kept his lens trained on the thin ribbon of water in the canyon.

"Women tend to worry about such things," said a man at his side. Will did not turn to look at the man, but began to shoot a succession of shots of the river and the fantastic rock shapes that sat poised in the same positions they had been in for millions of years.

"Will, please," called Peggy again.

Will put the camera back in its case and stood looking at the canyon and feeling the April breeze, cool but with trails of warm air mixed in it. He glanced at the man at his side, a tall man in a Windbreaker, with wire-rimmed glasses interrupting the blandness of his smooth-shaven face. The man was staring out over the canyon, his face in profile to Will.

"I'm sorry, did you say something to me?" asked Will.

"Ah, you were occupied by the camera," replied the man. "It was nothing. I was merely noting that your wife is much like mine. She worries about small dangers."

Will turned around and looked back to the path where he had left Peggy standing, holding Katie tightly by the hand. Next to Peggy a woman with straight yellow-blonde hair cut in bangs across her forehead knelt with her arm protectively around a little girl, a child a few years younger than Katie.

"It makes the person feel very small, eh?" asked the man amiably.

"Yes," said Will, noting the man's heavily accented English.

"You use the camera very well. You are a professional, perhaps?"

"Photographer for *Life* magazine."

"So? That is very interesting. Perhaps I have seen your pictures, then?"

"If you read *Life*," replied Will impatiently. He had left Mervyn's living room behind. There was no need to humor anyone here on the edge of the Grand Canyon, nor would there be any necessity to talk to anyone once he and Peggy and Katie had arrived at the Havasupai village.

"You are here for a special reason, yes? To photograph the Grand Canyon for *Life* magazine?"

"No," said Will, hoping to cut the conversation off.

"I am sorry, I have talked too much perhaps," said the man, and he turned away from the edge and walked back to the path. Will felt oddly chastened. The man had meant no harm, had only been trying to make friendly conversation. He had asked him no painful questions. Jesus, Mervyn was right, he was a maniac.

"You're rid of me, Mervyn," Will had said the day the letter arrived from Elgin Jones.

"If I could stop you, I guess I would. Ain't no place to take a wife and baby."

"They won't scalp us. The chief has extended his invitation to me personally." Will handed the letter to Mervyn, who took it and read it quickly and then handed it back to Will.

"Pretty educated for an Indian, I suppose," he said.

"He was in the Marine Corps, Mervyn."

"If you say so."

"I say so."

"What about your boss?"

"Gruber? I told him I was having a nervous breakdown. Told him I was going for a cure on an Indian reservation. I told him I was going to do a picture spread of the Indians. He said he wanted me to go to London. I told him I'd sell the spread to *The Saturday Evening Post*. He said he'd changed his mind, he'd buy it, and to forget about London for the time being."

But it was Peggy who had surprised him. He had thought he would have to do a selling job, would have to persuade her that it was a safe place to take Katie.

"When are we leaving?" she had asked.

"That was easy," he said.

"You wanted a fight?"

"No. A few questions, maybe."

"I trust you, Will."

The arrangements were made. They arrived at Grand Canyon Village by train on April 2nd. They would spend a few days at the El Tovar Hotel on the south rim of the Grand Canyon, a treat for Peggy, a last luxurious few days with a bathtub and room service and leisurely walks along the rim.

Will turned and walked up the path toward Peggy and Katie.

"Will, these people have a cattle ranch not far from Hermits Rest," said Peggy as he approached. "They're staying at El Tovar like we are. Isn't that nice? I've asked them to have lunch with us in the dining room."

Will grimaced. The woman was smiling at him. The little girl beside her looked exactly like her husband, brown hair, brown eyes, none of her mother's blondeness.

"Erika, this is my husband, Will Mathison."

"How do you do?" she said. He nodded. Close up she wasn't as pretty as she had been at a distance, and her eyes darted nervously from her husband's face to Will's.

"My husband, Gunter Liebermann," she said. Gunter held out his hand to Will. The sleeve of the Windbreaker pulled back with the motion of his arm, and the blue numbers on the forearm were exposed for a fleeting moment. Will looked into Gunter's eyes behind the glasses. His eyes had followed Will's to the blue numbers. Will cleared his throat and turned toward Peggy.

"I think it would be a nice thing to do, to have lunch together at El Tovar," said Will pleasantly.

They sat near the window of the dining room, looking out past the lawn to the low stone wall that ran along the rim of the canyon. Alexa, the Liebermanns' six-year-old daughter, was showing Katie the kachina doll that her parents had bought her that morning at the Hopi House.

"How are you going to get to the Hualapai Hilltop from here?" asked Gunter. "Although it is in the canyon, there is no road from here. You must go back to Williams and then through the Hualapai reservation."

"We're meeting someone tomorrow who's taking supplies to Hualapai Hilltop," said Will. "We'll go with him, and then we'll be met with horses up on the plateau."

"If there are problems with your plans, we also leave tomorrow. We would be glad to take you as far as Hermits Rest," said Gunter.

"Is there a way into the Havasupai Village from there?"

"There is, but you must have a guide to take you down. It is a horse trail only part of the way. Then you must go on foot."

"I appreciate the offer," said Will.

"It is nothing," said Gunter.

Their food came, and the conversation became stilted. Will wanted to talk to Gunter about the blue numbers on his arm but couldn't bring himself to say anything.

"Is there a school for Alexa near your ranch?" asked Peggy.

"I teach her myself," said Erika proudly.

"I see," said Peggy.

"Will you be in Havasupai Village long?" asked Erika.

Peggy looked at her husband.

"We haven't talked about it that much," he said.

"Your daughter will miss school, no?" asked Erika.

"I have a lesson plan with me," said Peggy. "I teach third grade in Lawndale, California."

"California," repeated Erika. "We have never been to California."

"Where have you been?" asked Will, seizing the opportunity.

"Germany," said Erika in a low voice. "I was born in Germany."

Will looked at Gunter, waiting for him to speak. He pulled back his shirt and fingered the blue letters on the back of his forearm. "I was born in Germany, too," he said slowly.

"I did a series on the concentration camps," said Will, his voice trembling slightly.

"So?" Gunter's eyebrows went up.

"Of course, photographing them was not like being in one," Will added hastily.

Gunter did not answer for a while. Then he said, "When you have time, come to visit us. I will not talk of sorrowful things. Erika and I have put that in the past. We do not talk of what cannot be changed. You were curious. I have showed you my arm. I was in Auschwitz. I will not talk to you about it again."

Will picked up the glass of water at his place and downed it rapidly, feeling like the outsider he really was. He couldn't look Gunter in the face just then. He had not meant to pry. He wanted only to express sympathy, to form a connection with someone who understood what he understood.

"We will be friends together, then. Yes?" asked Erika, breaking the awkward silence.

"It is possible," said Gunter.

XXVI

Will woke up at five in the morning and watched the sun come up over the rim of the Grand Canyon, its rays illuminating the shadowed crevices and outlining the buttes and peaks of the gorge. He had begun to relax here, to feel the possibility of peacefulness within himself again. At six o'clock he woke Peggy and Katie, and while they dressed, he went down to the hotel kitchen to buy a box lunch to take with them on their journey.

It was a short walk from the El Tovar Hotel to where Sam Wickes waited next to his pickup truck.

"Sam Wickes?" asked Will.

"The one and only," replied Sam.

"I'm Will Mathison. My wife, Peggy, and daughter, Katie."

"Pleased," Sam said, doffing his ten-gallon hat momentarily and revealing the permanent groove that the hat had made on his thick gray hair.

"When they told me we were going to be met by the Havasupai Indian agent, frankly I expected to see an Indian," said Will, helping Peggy and Katie into the front seat of the pickup truck.

"Sometimes I feel like an Indian," replied Sam Wickes as he loaded the Mathisons' luggage onto the back of the truck next to the boxes of supplies. "Been living with them too damn long, I guess."

Will got into the truck next to Peggy, who held Katie on her lap. Sam Wickes, face burned coffee-colored by the sun, threw the tarpaulin over the load in the open bed of the truck, secured it, and then got into the truck. He looked sideways at his passengers on the seat beside him.

"Brought everything with you from the hotel, did you?" he asked, with the accent on the "ho."

"Everything that was ours," replied Will.

Sam turned and looked through the rear window of the pickup for traffic as he pulled out of the dirt area next to the Santa Fe Railroad terminal. A red and black cotton scarf wound around his deeply lined neck. He wore a deerhide vest over his cotton shirt, worn-down-at-the-heels cowboy boots, and dusty work pants held up by a Navaho belt inset with sea-blue turquoise stones.

"At the prices they charge folks, you shoulda helped yourself to a little something extra," he commented as they left the railroad station and the horse corrals behind and began the drive that would take them out of the park.

At 9:00 Sam pulled into a gas station in Seligman and filled the truck with gasoline. Seligman, which popped up out of a twenty-mile stretch of dry and desolate Arizona highway, sported a run-down motel, a café and gas station, and a few dilapidated houses. Peggy and Katie went to the ladies' room in the gas station, and Will picked out four Orange Crushes from the red cooler in the office.

"It's really dirty in there," Peggy said to the scrawny man who ran the gas station when she returned.

"Probably hasn't been a lady used it since 1936, I don't suppose," replied the attendant reflectively.

Will paid for the drinks, and they all got back into the pickup truck, and in four blocks Seligman was behind them and the highway had taken over again.

"How long have you been Indian agent to the Havasupai?" asked Will as they drove.

"How long? Let's see, left Bullhead City in '25 to look for gold in the Superstition Mountains. Had my fill of that and then wrangled steers in Kingman for a spell. Must have been '30—yep, it was '30 when I first went down to the Havasupai. Haven't left it since, except to get supplies or to attend an Indian powwow."

"Elgin spoke of you as if you were an Indian," said Will.

"I'm the only white man to live with the tribe. I suppose that qualifies me as an Indian. We've had missionaries in the village at times, and Bureau of Indian Affairs people snooping around making sure that no one leaves the reservation to hunt up on the plateaus. Every now and again we have a white schoolteacher, but they never stay that long. Right now the school's closed again."

"Peggy's a schoolteacher. Maybe she can help out while we're there."

"No pay, you know, unless the Bureau sends you. The tribe can't afford to pay a teacher," said Sam.

"Oh, I wouldn't need to be paid," said Peggy. "I'd like to do it."

Sam glanced at her and then at Will. "How long did you say you were staying?"

"We haven't decided yet," he replied. "I have a commission to do a photo layout on the tribe and Havasu Canyon. It all depends on how long it takes."

Sam looked back at the road and shook his head. "It's not easy living down there."

Will looked at him in surprise. "Elgin said it was a beautiful place to live."

"Oh, it's beautiful all right. Probably's got some of the prettiest waterfalls anytime, anywhere. And there's no blue like the sky above Havasupai Village, and no green as green as the willow trees in the springtime. Even the weeds have a green that's like no color I've ever seen before. Probably never been a sound so reassuring as when the breeze blows through the canyon in the spring and you hear the sound of the leaves and feel the spray from Havasu Falls in your face. No cars down there, only horses. And they don't bother none, just their whinnying or the dust they kick up out of the red earth is all."

"That doesn't sound like a hard place to live to me. I've just come back from Europe."

"Served in the Big One, did you?" asked Sam.

"Photographed it."

"Didn't pay that one too much attention," said Sam. "Don't always get a newspaper delivered into the village. And didn't mean too much to me when I did get one. Only thing I noticed was when Elgin and a few others put on a uniform. Sure made me laugh, I can tell you that. They couldn't even vote, but the government sure didn't care about that. Anyhow, the whole thing was like as if someone's talking to you about goings-on on the moon. Know what I mean? Got enough of my own to handle right here, right now, to worry too much about anything else. But come to think of it, there's some folks living up near Hermits Rest had something to do with the war. Didn't ask him too much about it. Don't like to nose into people's business."

"We met the Liebermanns in Grand Canyon," said Peggy. "Have you been to their ranch?"

"Rounded up a few horses that got loose from the corral up at Haulapai Hilltop is all. Seemed like hospitable enough folks, I suppose. Gave me a drink of water one time. The mister keeps to himself pretty much, but the lady is nice enough. Must have come out of the war with all their money. That ranch is the biggest in Mojave County. Three thousand head of cattle, nine range hands, a house as big as a train station."

"Sounds like you got pretty friendly with them," observed Will.

"I just notice things, that's all. Don't make a point of it. It just happens."

"Why do you say it's hard to live in Havasupai Village?" asked Peggy with a concerned look.

"Not hard, really. I exaggerate some. Always has been a failing of mine. Some folks say they feel like they're in jail down there. Mind you, I've never felt it myself, but it's not hard to see why they would say so. I suppose it's beautiful enough if you don't mind that there's only one way in and one way out, or that the walls of the canyon lock you into a few miles on the canyon floor, or that in the winter those walls cut out the sunlight so that there's daylight for only four hours a day and what there is of it is cold and damp. And there's no store down there, only what I bring in or what the mailman brings in. In the summertime the Indians grow their own food, but in the winter they depend on what's brought in. It's ruined their diet, all that white bread and potato chips. But when they try to go hunting up on the slopes in the winter, the National Park Service is on their necks about spoiling the canyon, as if two hundred thirty-nine Indians could spoil the goddamn Grand Canyon. The Bureau of Indian Affairs is always sticking their nose into things, telling the Indians what they can do and what they can't do. It's no wonder they stay drunk most of the time."

"How do they get the liquor?" asked Will. "I thought it was against the law to have liquor on an Indian reservation."

"Sure enough is. As near's I can tell, it's the mailman. Now, mind you, there's no proof. But I don't bring it in. I know that Elgin don't bring it in. Mail comes in by horse train two times a week, Tuesday and Friday nights. Wednesdays and Saturdays the young bucks are drunk off their heads."

"Why do you stay?" asked Peggy.

"I've been trying to figure that one out myself for quite a few years now. Meantime they made me a member of the tribe, so I feel like as if I owe them something. They need a white arm to beat up against the BIA with. The Bureau don't pay a whole lot of attention to what the Indians have to say. So I stay, and we fight together to get their hunting lands returned to the tribe."

Will felt himself being pulled into another world. It was strange that he didn't resent Sam for not caring about the Second World War. He had been ready to fight the whole Lawndale Mormon stake because they didn't share his agony over the concentration camps. Why did he hold them to a different standard than he did Sam? Why did he excuse unequivocally Sam's ignorance and indifference to what was one of the great horrors of the twentieth century? He looked at Sam's face. There was nothing hideous or inhuman or unfeeling in the weather-beaten face. On the contrary, it was a face that gazed on the Havasupai Indians and called them brothers. There was a great philosophical question being raised here, thought Will, but the heat of the day had begun to fill the pickup from the open windows, and there were only cows grazing for as far as he could see, and he was moving bodily from the twentieth century into some unknown time warp where waterfalls fell cleanly into hidden pools, and newspapers that told about genocide and atom bombs went undelivered, and the fate of 239 Indians provided the fulcrum upon which the earth turned.

They turned off the main highway at Peach Springs, and now the road was a dirt road, rutted from the rains of the past winter. Here and there a load of gravel had been dumped to fill in a particularly deep pothole. They drove on, speaking only occasionally, and stopped at Frazier Wells so that Katie could use the outdoor privy. Then the road began its upward ascent to Hualapai Hilltop. There were no cows to be seen here, and the air was cooler and blew with gale force across the high plateau.

Two hours later, at Haulapai Hilltop, Sam pulled the pickup into a parking area next to a couple of beaten-up pre-war automobiles.

"We're here," said Sam, opening the door and jumping down. Will helped Katie and Peggy out of the pickup. Katie ran toward the hitching rail that faced the gorge below.

"Be careful," Peggy cried out as the child ran along the windswept rise.

"She needs to move her legs," said Sam. "It's no fun for a youngster to be cooped up in a truck for five hours."

Seven horses were tethered to the rail. An Indian boy of about ten years of age sat atop his pony at the mouth of the trail. His long black hair beneath its blue headband was whipped by the wind. His buckskin shirt was tucked into long twill trousers that were wrapped in yellow doeskin chaps. From behind the Indian boy a horse and rider rounded the steep rise of the trail and rode toward where Sam and the Mathisons were standing at the corral.

"Will Mathison," the Indian called in greeting as he alighted from his horse and tied the reins to the rail.

"Elgin," said Will. Then the two men were clasping hands like old friends. "Peggy, this is Elgin Jones."

Elgin stared awkwardly at Peggy for a few seconds and then called to the young boy who sat watching from his pony while Katie patted the pony's sleek flank. "My son Lee," Elgin said.

"Now we know everybody," said Sam, "let's load this stuff onto the horses and get goin'."

Elgin picked Katie up and sat her atop one of the horses while Peggy watched worriedly. "She's only eight," she said. "Her feet don't fit into the stirrups." But Katie's face was ecstatic. She bent low over the horse's neck and whispered to him and caressed his coat.

Elgin adjusted the stirrups so that they fit Katie's feet, and then he said, "She will ride well."

When the packhorses were loaded with the supplies, Elgin tied the three horses together and led them to where Lee sat on his pony. Lee took the reins of the lead packhorse and began down the trail.

"It's so steep," said Peggy uneasily. "I rode as a girl but not since then."

Elgin nodded and picked out a black bronco that had stood contentedly at the rail without moving or whinnying as the other horses had done. He held the horse while Will helped Peggy to get on. Elgin slapped the rear of the horse, and the horse began to follow the pack train down the steep trail.

"I'd like to keep an eye on Katie," said Will as he got on the horse that Elgin had selected for him.

"Elgin will keep her in front of him," said Sam. "He won't let anything happen to her."

The caravan began down the rock-strewn trail, which was wide enough for only one horse to pass and had a sheer drop of a thousand feet on their right-hand side. The odyssey had begun. Will's camera bag was around his neck. Once past the switchback trail he would open the case and begin to record Havasu Canyon.

Elgin had greeted him with a warm handclasp but had given no explanations of where they would go, when they would go, or how they would go. He had merely got them on the horses and set them moving down the trail with all of the western gorge of the Grand Canyon laid out beneath them.

After an hour, when they had traversed the most treacherous part of the trail and were on the flatlands, Will began taking pictures of the cathedrals of red-rock sandstone that loomed two thousand feet above them. They rode steadily and soon were in the washes, where the redbuds were in bloom, their branches heavily laden with magenta blossoms. Will felt a thrill at being here amidst the silence and aloneness of the remote canyons. The sun peeked in and out of the wash, and he half expected someone to shout,

"We'll cut them off at the pass." But there was no sound except the soft whoosh of the wind through the cottonwood trees, blowing the fluffy cottonwood seed like swirling snow around them and layering the ground with a downy blanket. Will thought of asking to stop to eat the box lunch he had picked up before they left Grand Canyon, but neither Peggy nor Katie had complained of hunger, and he, caught up in the beauty around him, promptly forgot his own.

1946–1956: *Juan*

XXVII

To the north the town of Puerto Lápice, its white signpost proudly proclaiming the site where Don Quixote laid siege to the windmills of La Mancha. To the west Almagro and its splendid seventeenth-century Dominican Monastery of the Assumption. To the south Valdepeñas, dry, its land seared brown by the sun, silvery-gray clouds holding tight to the rim of the high plateau. Not a beautiful or historic town in the sense of filigreed monuments or literary pretension. More a place of obstinacy, where wheat and barley and grapes grow despite the drought-plagued land. A hardy place, its people as tough as the grape vines that bear fruit in the summer and are pruned to the nub in the winter, with brown roots exposed and branches that look dead to the eye. Valdepeñas, a town where four thousand people were killed in the Civil War in 1937, and where wine is still made, and where an iron sculpture of Don Quixote sits incongruously on the edge of the main road, in the middle of nowhere, telling the casual traveler nothing about its meaning. The sculpture and the rusting trucks and cannons in the gullies, and the newly electrified power plant, are Valdepeñas' monuments.

Martita's house sat at the end of a red-dirt road leading to the Sierra Morena mountains. Sheep grazed on the hills behind the house. The land ran smoothly up to the tree-dotted slopes in the distance. In the fall, when the harvest was over, the poplar trees turned to yellow and red.

Juan ran ahead of the two girls, his long legs and ten-year-old body effortlessly climbing the hill. He slowed down once to look behind him. Thirteen-year-old Isabel had stopped and was rubbing the sole of her bare foot. Eleven-year-old Luisa, fierce black eyes gazing determinedly ahead of her, kept a steady pace along the rocky path. At the top Juan sat down on the dirt and looked below at the gold and white, ocher and violet checkerboard of cultivated land. His body had grown so much in the last year that the peasant pants he wore came to the middle of his calf, and his bare toes, wiggling in the loose red earth, no longer could fit into the sandals he wore when he worked in the fields. Martita had promised that when the harvest money was in and Don Carlos had been paid for the rent of the land, there would be money for sandals for Juan, a Holy Communion dress for Luisa, and silver earrings for Isabel.

"Hurry, it's coming," yelled Juan at the two girls as they struggled up the slope. He spoke Spanish, but occasionally a word would come to his mind that wasn't Spanish, and with the word he would have strange feelings, feelings he couldn't explain. When he asked Martita what the words meant, her brow would furrow, and she would say that he needed to pay more attention in church, that Satan was trying to get hold of his mind.

Luisa, her round brown face grinning, dropped into the dirt next to Juan. Then Isabel, limping, made it to the top.

"I don't see it," said Luisa.

"There," answered Juan, pointing a finger at a black speck that moved across the patterned landscape.

"It looks like a worm with smoke coming from its head," said Luisa with a laugh, holding her grimy hands to her mouth as she watched the train.

"It's the *talgo;* it's faster than any other train," said Juan. "Tomorrow morning it will be in Barcelona."

"How do you know so much about where the train will be tomorrow?" taunted Isabel with the superiority of age.

"One day while I was working in the olive grove, the men told me."

"Where is Barcelona?" asked Luisa. Although she was a year older than Juan, she treated him as an older brother. Isabel at thirteen knew nothing compared to what Juan, who worked with the older men in the fields, could tell her.

"Barcelona is far away to the north, near the ocean," he answered.

"Did you see the ocean when you were in Barcelona?" asked Luisa.

"I don't remember," said Juan. "I want to remember, but I cannot."

"God makes it so orphans don't remember things," said Isabel knowingly.

"Why would he do that?" asked Luisa, puzzled.

Juan held the stick as though he were a man. The men all towered above him, but he swung the stick just as they did, and the thwacking of his stick against the branches of the olive trees was as distinct and as satisfying a sound as that made by the hundreds of other sticks that flailed the trees and caused the olives to rain down on the canvases spread beneath the trees. The workers had started the flailing of the trees at dawn. At noontime Isabel came with a dish of stewed chicken, which Juan ate when the overseer told them to take the noon rest.

In the afternoon Don Carlos came out of the large white-washed adobe house and walked down the lane to the olive grove, where he stood and watched the men in silence as they worked their way through the grove, gathering the olives. He and the overseer talked together for a while, and then Don Carlos, in his white pants and hand-sewn leather boots, walked back to the house.

Don Carlos had asked Martita to bring the boy when she came to pay the rent. The money from the harvest had not been enough to get a Holy Communion dress for Luisa and silver earrings for Isabel and also to buy new sandals for Juan. So Juan stood in Don Carlos' heavily draped library in his bare feet. His face was washed, his hair had been slicked back by Martita. His smooth forehead, where the sun had not tanned it, was a soft golden-olive color, and his big, expressive eyes shone large in his child's face. Martita kept him behind her so that Don Carlos wouldn't notice that the boy had no shoes and that his pants came up almost to his knees.

"There has not been much rain," said Don Carlos.

"No, *señor,* and the harvest was not as good as I had expected," answered Martita. "With just the boy and myself and the little help that the sisters can give me, I can cultivate only enough to keep us alive."

"You need a husband," said Don Carlos seriously.

"I had a husband, *señor.* And a brother. Both gone. And for what?"

"Ask God for the answers to those questions. You and your husband saw what responsibility it is to make the land prosper and to feed your family from it. It was a good lesson for you, Señora Hurtado. The land was given my family by God. There is a natural order to things. We are not meant to upset that natural order capriciously."

Don Carlos Mendes de Salceda spoke quietly. There was no need for him to be loud to get attention. There was never any doubt that his listeners heard what he had to say, whether they were the students who sat in his lecture halls at the University of Barcelona or the peasants who paid him rent to till his land. He was a small man with a narrow head and little brown eyes that saw everything. His hands were those of an aesthete. It was said that he was the guiding force behind the new university system that Franco was attempting to build on the ashes of the one he had destroyed. Don Carlos had always steadfastly supported Franco, and when fifty percent of the professors at the University of Salamanca had been shot during the Civil War and the entire teaching staff of the University of Barcelona had fled for their lives, he had seen it as an act of retributive justice sent from God.

Martita handed a packet of pesetas to Don Carlos. "It is not the entire amount. I will ask you to lend the money to me till next season."

Don Carlos walked to a carved oak cupboard in the corner of the library and placed the money in one of the drawers. Then slowly he began to walk around the library, pausing to look out the windows at the olive grove down the hill. He stood at the window awhile, then turned to the bookshelves and pulled out a book from which he read aloud.

"The Opus Dei is an association of the faithful who,

through their specific vocation, devote themselves to seeking Christian perfection and exercising the apostolate in their own sphere, each in the exercise of his profession or worldly task, to bear witness to Jesus Christ and thus to be in the service of the Church, the Supreme Pontiff and all souls."

He snapped the book shut and looked at Martita. She crossed herself as though he had been a priest reciting a prayer from his breviary.

"Where did the boy come from?" asked Don Carlos, walking around behind Martita to see Juan more closely.

"He is an orphan, *señor,* a poor unfortunate child of the war. His parents left him in the care of my sainted sister, Sister María Blanca, who, of course, being a religious, could not keep him."

"And so she gave him to you as a present, did she?"

Martita looked at the floor. "*Sí,*" she said in a low voice.

"I have watched him working in the olive groves," said Don Carlos. "He is very quick for his age, very alert. The overseer tells me that he can rely on him more than the men to understand and obey. He also tells me that the boy counts the bundles of olives and retains the numbers in his head. The overseer values his ability, but the workers think the child is bewitched."

"Bewitched? *Por Dios,* he will not play with numbers again," said Martita anxiously. "I will beat him if he dares to do such things again. He is only a child playing games. How can he be bewitched? He lives with me and my two daughters. Surely I would have noticed if someone had bewitched him. Look at this child, Don Carlos." She shoved Juan in front of her and held up his face for Don Carlos to see. "He is a poor peasant child. Who would want to bewitch him?"

"Calm yourself, *señora,*" said Don Carlos. "The men are superstitious. I put no credence in what they have to say. But it has occurred to me that it is a sin against God to let go to waste such intelligence, even if it be found in a peasant child."

"A waste," said Martita quickly. "I agree, Don Carlos, it would be a waste." She clasped Juan close to her again.

"I see that you have been looking at the books on the

shelves," said Don Carlos to Juan. "Come here to the window so that I may see you in the light."

Juan walked toward the window. Although he was barefoot and his shoulders had taken on the musculature of premature hard labor, there was a certain elegance in the way the child carried himself, in the way he moved. In his face was an alertness when a person spoke to him.

"How old are you?" asked Don Carlos.

Juan looked at Martita momentarily and then answered in a clear voice. "Ten years."

"Your name?"

"Juan Lepanto."

"And are you a Catholic, Juan Lepanto?"

"*Sí, señor.*"

"And have you accepted Jesus Christ into your heart and soul as your redeemer, without whom life is not worth living?"

"*Sí, señor,*" answered Juan, falling easily into the catechismal interrogation.

"Do you remember anything of your parents?"

Juan hesitated. A strange word floated in his head again, but Martita had said that that was the work of Satan, and if this man was a priest, as he appeared to be, then he would beat him if he spoke of satanic things.

"No, I don't remember them," said Juan finally.

"Good. Would you like to be able to read the books in this library, Juan, and to be an educated man when you grow up? Perhaps even to become a priest?"

Juan glanced over at the leather-bound books that covered the walls of the dark and musty library.

"I would like to read, *señor,*" he said.

"And to become a priest, if Jesus calls you to the priesthood?"

"*Sí, señor,* if Jesus calls me, I will become a priest."

Martita crossed herself again and pressed her fingers to her lips as a sign of devoutness. Don Carlos turned toward Martita. "I have not seen your house. Is it sufficient to house the boy, as well as your own two children?"

"We manage, *señor.* It is a simple house, a main sleeping

room, which we all share. There is a courtyard in the center of the house, where I keep the chickens. And across the courtyard is where I cook the meals. We have no bathroom. We bathe at the well and take care of our other needs as best we can."

Don Carlos grimaced at the description of Martita's house. He shook his head. "No, no, he cannot stay there. If his education is to be complete, he must live here with me."

"But, *señor,*" Martita protested, realizing finally that Don Carlos did not mean merely to help with the boy. He meant to keep him.

"Now, now, I will not take him from you. He will be here in the house, where you can see him and talk to him when you want to," said Don Carlos.

"But the grapes, the chickens—who will help with the barley in the spring? I am a woman alone, *señor.* I will never be able to pay you for the rent of the land if you take Juan away."

"We shall make an adjustment, *señora.* You owe me nothing more for this year. As for the coming year, you shall have Juan's earnings."

Martita's eyes opened in surprise. "Juan's earnings?"

"Yes. To be a student is work, just as laboring in the fields is work. If Juan works well, and his progress is satisfactory to me, I will pay you what you would have earned from the cultivation of your barley field."

Martita flushed with pleasure. She ran to Juan and grasped his face in her hands and kissed him wetly on both cheeks. "Juan, Juan, God has sent you to me. It is a sign."

She looked up at Don Carlos. "Jesus has touched him, Don Carlos. He is a special child of Jesus. I can feel it. I know that his parents are in the arms of our Savior at this very moment and that they thank our dear Lord for guiding their child's footsteps to your own loving arms."

She kneeled at Don Carlos' feet in prayer. "Dear Lord, hold and keep this saintly man alive and in good health so that he may continue to be your holy and devoted servant and so that he may guide more poor unfortunates to Jesus Christ through your good offices. Amen."

XXVIII

On the day following Juan and Martita's visit to Don Carlos, Martita rose early and heated water to wash Juan's cotton pants and shirt. When they were washed, she spread them on the gorse bushes near the well, and by the time the sun had risen, the pants and shirt were dried and stiff. She awakened Juan and sent him to wash himself while she kneaded his scratchy clothes in her hands so that the fibers were softened enough to wear. When Juan returned from washing, he dressed and then walked holding Martita's hand through the field and up the path to Don Carlos' house.

"You must remember, Juan," Martita warned him as they walked, "you are to dress and undress alone. Do not permit Don Carlos to see your private member. Can you remember that?"

Juan looked up at her with a puzzled expression on his face. "I will remember. I do not understand why, but I will remember."

"See that you do," she said.

"If he sees it by accident, what will happen to me?" asked the worried child.

Martita laughed and tousled his head with her brown hand. "He will die of shock, because then he will know that he has brought a Jew into his house."

As they drew near to the rear door of the house, Martita stopped and kneeled down beside the boy. "You are a good boy, Juan. You have worked hard for me. I have not given you the things that a child deserves, but then I have not given very much to my own two daughters either. This is our chance, yours and ours. Don Carlos can be a generous man, but first he demands obedience. You understand?"

Juan nodded, his face serious.

Martita smoothed back the long hair that hung down on his forehead. She brushed the toweling lint from the shoulders of his rough-spun shirt.

"But I'm not going away? I will still be here where I can see you?" he asked.

"Of course, of course, you foolish boy. Martita is always here for you, but it will not be the same again. From this morning on you will belong to Don Carlos. And that is as it should be. He is paying handsomely for you, and it is just that you should be his property. You will visit me when he permits it. But from now on, Graciana, Don Carlos' servant, will see to your needs." Martita held tight to Juan's shoulders and pulled him close to her face so that her mouth was inches away from Juan's and he could smell the acrid-sweet odor of olive oil on her breath.

"Listen to everything that Don Carlos says to you, but do not believe everything, because he is a man of rigid and unbending ways who does not understand the life of the peasant. He does not see that our lives are hard because of men like him. He knows only that it is God's will that we suffer and die. He will teach you many things that are very important. He will make you a priest. Not a humble priest like Father Alcarona, but a priest in Salamanca, or even Barcelona, where you will have *poder*. Do you understand that? Power? Like Don Carlos has here in the village, that is what he plans for you."

Tears welled up in Juan's eyes.

"Cry? Who cries who has such a great opportunity?" said Martita brusquely. "If I could, I would dress Luisa or Isabel in boys' clothing so that Don Carlos would notice them and give them the opportunity he gives to you." She sighed heavily. "But that is not to be. It is you he has chosen."

Juan threw his arms around Martita's neck.

"You cry now and finish with it, because you will not cry in Don Carlos' house. You hear?"

"Yes," said Juan through his tears.

Graciana accepted Juan from Martita's hand.

"*Adiós, muchacho,*" said Martita.

"*Adiós,*" answered Juan.

Martita left the kitchen, and Graciana closed the door after her.

"You will bathe before you see Don Carlos," said Graciana, staring at Juan's bare feet, washed just before he left on the walk to Don Carlos' house and now soiled with the dirt of the earthen path through the field. Graciana opened a door and pulled out a heavy wooden tub, which she set on the floor of the large kitchen. She filled two vats with water and put them on the stove to heat. Juan looked around the kitchen at the gleaming copper pots that hung by iron hooks from the wood-beamed ceiling. He had never seen a kitchen like this, with its tile floors that were cool beneath his bare feet. Or the great windows that looked out onto the fields. Or the cooking pots that sat on the workbench next to the hearth ovens.

"Come, come, your clothes," said Graciana impatiently.

Juan turned to look at her.

"Your clothes. You cannot bathe in your clothes."

"I will do it, I will bathe myself," he said, remembering Martita's warning. She had said not to show himself to Don Carlos, but was not Graciana an extension of Don Carlos?

"A peasant boy and modest?" She laughed. She poured the heated water from the two vats into the wooden tub and then handed a thick white towel to Juan. "There is soap next to the tub. Wash your ears, and be sure to push back the foreskin of your penis and wash it carefully. Has Martita taught you the ways of personal cleanliness?"

"Yes," he said, afraid to reveal that Martita had never said anything to him about his private member until this very morning. And what was a Jew?

"When you have finished, put on your old clothes. I have nothing else to give you to wear."

When Graciana had left the kitchen, Juan removed his clothes and stepped into the water. He had bathed at the pump that morning in cold water and had rubbed himself dry with a square of muslin that Martita kept hanging from a nail on the outhouse next to the water pump.

Now he sat and soaked in the warmth of the water. That he was here was a wonder. He did not know yet what it all meant, if his coming was to be a good or a bad thing. Martita said that it would be good. But Martita was not always right. She was rough and outspoken and hit him without justification at times, but he knew that she would not want harm to come to him. And she had hugged him before she left him at the kitchen door this morning.

He held the bar of soap in his hand. It felt creamy and soft, not like the soap that Martita made on the kitchen stove. He lathered the soap up in his hands and washed his face and ears and rinsed them. Then he looked through the water to his private part, which seemed to lie floating in the water between his legs. Graciana had said to make sure he pulled back the foreskin and washed carefully. He pulled at his penis, turning it this way and that. Finally he stood up in the tub and let it hang down so that if there were a foreskin on the side or underneath or near his navel, he would be able to find it. But try as hard as he could, he could see nothing to pull back or tuck in or clean under.

He sat down suddenly when he heard Graciana's footsteps returning. She opened the door. "Not finished yet? Hurry. Don Carlos wants to see you." Juan waited until she had left and closed the door, and then he got out of the tub and stood dripping wet on the cold tile floor. He wrapped the heavy towel around himself. The touch of the towel was soft and comforting. Martita was right. Don Carlos had a house with many good things in it.

Don Carlos was waiting in the dining hall, seated at one end of the long refectory table. At the other end Graciana had set a place for Juan. Graciana had her hand on Juan's shoulder as she brought him to where Don Carlos sat. "He has bathed, *señor,* but his clothes, as you can see, are the same."

"That will be taken care of," said Don Carlos. "Measure him, and I will see to it that clothes are sent for him from Madrid. And measure his feet carefully, especially the width, because his feet, having been unaccustomed to wearing shoes, will be unnaturally wide and difficult to fit."

Graciana and Don Carlos talked over Juan's head, as though he were not there at all. He looked from one to the other's face. Finally Don Carlos caught his eye. "Sit down. Graciana has brought you your breakfast."

Graciana led Juan to the end of the table and sat him down, then took the linen napkin from the side of the plate and spread it on Juan's lap. She stood at Juan's side, prepared to monitor his manners. After all, he was a peasant and had never eaten at Don Carlos' table before. There was no way to predict how he would behave.

"It is all right, Graciana, leave the boy alone," said Don Carlos. "We will eat together, and he will watch me and learn."

Graciana shook her head. She had misgivings, but Don Carlos had spoken, and she never disobeyed. She turned and left the two of them together in the cold dining hall whose heavy draperies kept out whatever sunlight there was outside.

Don Carlos bowed his head and clasped his hands together. "Let us pray," said Don Carlos.

Juan bowed his head exactly as Don Carlos had and listened to the rolling sounds of grace being said in Don Carlos' fine Castilian accent.

When Don Carlos had said "amen," he glanced up at Juan and gave him a silent signal to commence the meal. Juan stared at the plate in front of him. He had never seen food like this for breakfast. There was a slice of ham and soft-cooked eggs and a hard roll that had been split and spread with butter that dripped, yellow and melting, along the smooth crust. To the right of the plate was a small porcelain dish with fruits of every color and description in it. A tall glass of milk was to the left of the plate, its sides frosty. He lifted the glass and drank deeply of the milk. Most days he was lucky to have a piece of dry bread for breakfast.

Don Carlos had put his fork down and was watching Juan eat. Suddenly Don Carlos shouted, "Stop."

Juan looked up at him, his eyes wide.

"Like so," said Don Carlos, picking up his knife and fork and demonstrating how to cut the ham. "You do not pick the food up with your fingers. Never. Keep your eyes on me now."

Don Carlos began to eat, slowly and methodically, not appearing to enjoy his food. It seemed he ate only to instruct

Juan in the manner of eating. Juan gulped down what was in his mouth and watched Don Carlos' hands avidly.

"That is how you must eat," said Don Carlos, putting down his fork again. "We will eat our meals together until you have learned your manners. Then you will eat alone. I take my meals in my study."

Juan looked around the huge dining hall and tried to visualize himself eating his meals here alone.

"So, Juan, your education begins today," said Don Carlos. "Do you undertake this new life with proper humility and with devotion to God and adoration of Christ Jesus?"

"Yes, I do, *señor.*"

"Speak more loudly. I didn't hear you."

"Yes, I do, *señor,*" said Juan, his small boy's voice echoing in the great dining hall.

"Your schedule will be devised by the week. There will be catechism in the morning. Then I will tutor you in reading. First you will learn to read and write in Spanish. Then, when you have progressed satisfactorily, you will study Latin and Greek. You will read Ovid and Homer. And you will study English."

Juan looked at him blankly, wanting to eat more of the breakfast that was congealing on his plate but afraid to take his eyes away from Don Carlos' face. The primary rule in this house seemed to be to pay strict attention to Don Carlos.

"When Professor Baranca is able, he will travel here from Barcelona to tutor you in mathematics and theology. Your days will be strictly regulated here. Breakfast will be at six a.m. Then you will bathe and dress, and you will present yourself in my study, where I will tutor you for an hour. The rest of the morning until lunchtime you are to spend in your room studying the books I will give you and going over what I have taught you in the study session. You will have lunch at twelve noon. Then you will retire to your room for a two-hour siesta, after which, if I am available, I will teach you to ride. I have picked out the horse for your first lesson in horsemanship. This will provide you with necessary fresh air and exercise. When we return from riding at four p.m., lessons will resume in my study until five o'clock, after which you will retire to your room to study the lessons. You will have dinner alone at eight in the evening."

Don Carlos watched Juan's face to see that the instructions were being listened to, or, if they were not absorbed yet, then at least the groundwork for absorption had been laid.

"As for Martita," Don Carlos continued, "it would be best if you did not see her for several months, until I am sure that your routine is well established and that her influence on you is diminishing."

Juan felt his appetite leaving him. His eyes fell from Don Carlos' face. He felt that he was going to cry at the table. Then maybe Don Carlos would send him back to Martita, where it was at least warm and there was human companionship.

"Did you hear me, Juan?" asked Don Carlos, shouting across the table.

Juan raised his tear-filled eyes. "Yes."

"Good. There will be periods of time when I must be in Barcelona at the university. At those times you will go to Barcelona with me. You will have a room there, and our schedule will go on much as it does here. Of course, there will be no riding in the afternoons, but perhaps there will be others of your own age with whom you may talk."

"Others?" asked Juan, his tears drying on his cheeks.

"Yes," answered Don Carlos. "If you are to be a priest and an important man, you must learn the ways of others of your kind. It will not be enough that you see one man and his life. You must see many men and their lives in order to be educated."

Don Carlos put down his fork and wiped his mouth with his napkin. Then he stood and pushed his chair away from the table.

"Finish your breakfast. Then go to Graciana so that she may measure you for your clothes. And when that is accomplished, we will begin your first lesson."

Martita stood below the path leading to Don Carlos' house. She watched Juan and Don Carlos on their horses as she had watched them every afternoon since the day three years before when Juan had gone to live with Don Carlos. Juan had grown. He was now thirteen. He promised to be a tall man, broad of shoulder. His dark hair blew in the breeze as he rode, and his eyes were no longer frightened. Martita watched while Don Carlos rode toward the stable, leaving Juan to ride alone for a while longer. When Don Carlos was safely out of sight, Juan rode through the field to where Martita stood.

"Luisa complains that you spend very little time with us," said Martita, patting the horse while Juan tied him to a tree.

Juan grinned. "It is not so easy to escape from Don Carlos as you would suppose."

"I notice that you escape when you please," said Luisa, suddenly appearing.

Juan pinched her cheek and began to chase her along the path to the cottage, the two laughing and squealing like the children they were.

Martita followed behind them toward the house. Things had been better these past few years. Her debt to Don Carlos had been eliminated, and there was more food and better clothes. She had even been able to take Isabel and Luisa to Barcelona to visit Sister María Blanca. And it was because of Juan. Juan was Martita's lucky charm. Her life had changed since she had found him. And she need not have worried that Don Carlos would make of him a duplicate of himself, because where there was coldness in Don Carlos, there was warmth in Juan. The lessons and the strictness of Don Carlos' training had refined Juan and separated him from Martita and her family only in superficial ways. He spoke, dressed, and conducted himself as Don Carlos did, but without the icy coldness. It was still Martita that Juan came to for a respite from the sterile isolation of Don Carlos' house. That Juan read books and had elegant manners and had met important people in Barcelona could not be questioned, but there was an uncertainty in the boy still, an unsureness of who he was or where he belonged that was clear to Martita. That uncertainty drew him back again and again to be a part of her family. Yet in his thinking he was strong. He did not lack physical courage, nor was he any longer afraid of Don

Carlos. He had learned the lessons that Don Carlos had taught him better even than the Don himself had anticipated, and he had also learned the weaknesses of the Don, as Martita had learned them. In many respects Juan was as much Martita's son as if she had borne him herself, in the way he hid his cleverness, in his cautious mistrust of others, and especially in his quiet refusal to pledge himself to the Don's way of thinking.

Martita heard laughter coming from within the cottage, and now Luisa's teasing voice. If Juan were to marry Luisa, Martita would be content. But for that he would have to give up the vocation that Don Carlos had chosen for him and also any claim to Don Carlos' fortune. Martita sighed. The arranging of lives was a difficult occupation and not always successful. Besides, she had the feeling that Juan would not marry Luisa, priesthood or no priesthood, fortune or no fortune.

XXIX

The lecture hall in the philosophy department of the University of Barcelona was stuffy, and there was much sneezing and coughing as Don Carlos spoke to the students. Outside it was cold and dreary after the morning rain. Inside, the smell of old boots and wet raincoats mingled with the sharp scent of mentholated cough drops. Juan looked around him at the rapt expressions of his fellow students as they listened to Don Carlos lecture. At nineteen Juan appeared older than he was. Years of laboring in the fields as a child had made his upper torso muscular, his waist firm, and the sun had permanently robbed his skin of its olive pallor and replaced it with a deep, weathered tan. Only his large brown eyes gave away his age. They were clear and unworried. His face had a sensual cast to it, with the nose faintly aquiline and the head well shaped with thick, dark-brown hair. He resembled Spaniards who had the blood of the Arabs and Jews in their veins.

Juan had heard the lecture before, but Don Carlos liked to see him in attendance, and Juan hoped to ease the strain that had existed between them lately by acceding more readily to Don Carlos' wishes. It was not that Juan did not respect Don Carlos, but he had begun to read things that disputed Don Carlos' beliefs. Books on the shelves of the university library dared to disagree with the tenets of the Opus Dei. Of course, they were removed as soon as the professors discovered them, but by then Juan and others of the students had already been contaminated by their radical contents.

"Spain must return to her former glory," Don Carlos told his class. "There has been too much talk of change, of progression, of liberalism. Liberalism to me means immorality,

"This is very nice," said Sister María Blanca as the waiter seated them at a table in the corner. Sister Angelina nodded. She had taken a vow of silence. Juan had never heard her speak, but she smiled and coughed and sometimes giggled in amusement. She used her hands and her face a lot to indicate her feelings. Sister María Blanca never left the cloister without her.

"Your term will soon be over?" asked Sister María Blanca.

"We have our final examinations next week, and then Don Carlos and I will return to Valdepeñas."

The waiter brought the menus, and the nuns looked over the bill of fare. Juan reached into his pocket and took out the money that Martita had sent him from Valdepeñas. He had no need of the money. Don Carlos saw to whatever he needed, but Martita would be offended if he were to send the few pesetas back to her. It was a gesture from her to remind him that there was still a connection between them.

"For the poor," he said, handing the money to Sister María Blanca.

"It is appreciated," said the nun, taking the bills and placing them in the small purse that hung around her waist.

"And are you content with your studies, Juan?" she asked.

"I think so. I have too many questions, though. At times it angers Don Carlos."

"You must not anger him. He is your benefactor. You should praise God every day Who brought you to his attention."

"The trouble is that he educates me, and in the educating I become smarter, and there is a problem in that."

Sister María Blanca's white face blended into her starched white wimple. Her upper lip was grooved, and little white hairs grew in the grooves. The waiter came and took their order. Sister Angelina pointed to something on the menu, and Sister María Blanca told the waiter what Sister Angelina would have to eat.

"He wants me to be a priest. He talks about it as though it were a reality," said Juan.

"You have not told him otherwise, I hope."

Sister Angelina glanced from one face to the other. She

was a mirror of Sister María Blanca's emotions. Sister María Blanca looked alarmed now, and so did Sister Angelina.

Juan shook his head. "No, I haven't, but I know the time will come."

"It need not come. He need not know."

Juan looked at her with a shy smile. "A Jewish priest, Sister?"

"You are not Jewish. You were baptized a Catholic. I saw the baptismal certificate. I personally handed it to Martita." Suddenly she put her hand to her chest in dismay. "Martita has lost the certificate?"

"No. She keeps it in an iron box beneath her bed," said Juan.

Sister Angelina crossed herself in relief.

"You've grown tall and strong, although a little thin, I think," said Sister María Blanca. "You look like a Spaniard, you speak like a Spaniard, you were baptized a Catholic. You'll make an imposing priest."

Juan leaned across the table and said in an urgent voice, "Tell me, did you see her?"

"Who?"

"The woman who called herself my nurse. Did you see her?"

"I have told you over and over again, I saw no one. Father Jaime sent me to fetch you on the bench. By that time she had gone."

"Did she say she was a Catholic?"

"I can't remember. Yes. She gave confession. She professed to be a Catholic."

"Would you have known if she was a Jew? I mean, can you tell if someone is a Jew by looking at her?"

"I suppose you can," said Sister María Blanca in confusion. "Yes, I'm sure you can."

"Then that settles it. You can tell by looking at me that I am a Jew."

"You are not a Jew. You are a baptized Catholic. Never tell anyone that you're a Jew, because it's a lie. You are not. The Church will not permit it to be so." Sister María Blanca's grooved lip quivered with emotion.

Juan reached toward her and patted her hand reassuringly.

"They say there are Jews in Spain, but I've never seen one outside my own mirror. Do they all hide behind baptismal certificates as I do?"

Sister Angelina gasped in horror at the blasphemy.

Sister María Blanca shook her head reprovingly. "You are still young, Juan. You'll understand more as you grow older."

"That doesn't answer my question. Have you ever seen a Jew whom you knew to be a Jew?" he asked almost angrily.

"No," she said with a pout that complained louder than words that she had been badgered into the answer.

"All right, then, we'll change the subject," said Juan.

Sister Angelina looked grateful, and Sister María Blanca's eyes darted around the restaurant, lips pursed.

"Don't you want to ask me about my friends, Sister?" asked Juan teasingly.

"Yes, tell me about your friends," she answered, only slightly mollified.

"Well, my *colegio mayor* is dedicated to the Opus Dei. Some of them are my friends. We study together, but they are very serious, more serious than I am. Their lives are already bound up tightly with the Church. Even though some of them will be teachers and lawyers and doctors, their personal lives are secondary to their religious ones."

"That's something you should learn to emulate," said Sister María Blanca, seizing the opening. "It's not enough to glory in your own intelligence, for that is what you do when you emphasize your personal self and think little about your inner life."

Juan grinned. Sister María Blanca was herself again. He was sorry that he had pilloried her. She was very dear to him. He would watch his tongue with her, too, in future.

"Yes," she said, warming now to the subject, "you are much too fun loving and casual about important matters, Juan. Piety is a trait that you need to cultivate."

A private banquet room had been opened off the main lobby of the Barcelona Ritz. Before the dinner began, Don Carlos and Juan joined a group of men in the lobby. They sat on deep gray velvet banquettes set against the gilt-mirrored walls. Waiters in white coats and white gloves brought trays of appetizers and placed them on the low French tables in front of the banquettes. Tall, leafy potted palms created the illusion of private space as the men talked.

"Generalissimo Franco has agreed to appoint Don Diego Manero as Minister of the Interior," said Don Felipe León de la Madrid. He smoked a slim cigarette in a silver cigarette holder and had been introduced to the others as the president of the Banco Nacional de España.

"We'll see to it that our newspaper reflects the voice of the Opus Dei in the matter of his appointment," said Don Antonio Paco de Aragón.

The priest at the end of the banquette looked questioningly at Juan and then at Don Carlos. Don Carlos had been about to say something to the owner of the newspaper, but instead he caught Father Sincero's eye. "Pardon me, Father?" said Don Carlos, as if he were unaware of what the priest's look meant. He would force Father Sincero to verbalize his concern, get it out in the open so that it could be laid to rest now.

Father Sincero looked uncomfortable, and then he said, "The boy. Should the boy be here when we discuss these matters?"

Don Carlos turned and put a fatherly arm around Juan's shoulders. "You mean Juan Lepanto, Father? Is this the boy you mean?"

The others looked at Father Sincero and then at Don Carlos and the boy.

Don Carlos smiled benignly. "Juan is not just a boy, Father Sincero. Juan is one of us."

XXX

At the beginning of Juan's last year at the university, he earned honors in English, French, and philosophy. He and Don Carlos had declared a truce of sorts. Don Carlos grudgingly admitted that Juan's rationalism was of the first order but insisted that his pointed questions in the lecture hall were not in keeping with someone who was destined for the priesthood. Juan, for his part, promised to listen more and speak less about controversial matters when he was with the other students.

"It is not I who demand that you watch your tongue," Don Carlos admonished. "It is all those who would stop your career before it begins. You must understand the enormity of the fight over Spain's soul that is taking place in the university. And you must be on the side of Jesus. That is the winning side, the side that Franco blesses and that the Church ordains."

Juan waited on the promontory of the Parque Güell, beneath the mosaic stalactites Gaudí had created as a paean to his untrammeled spirit. The park descended from the promontory in tiers, each tier bordered by an extravaganza of curvilinear benches decorated with bits of glass and pottery shards and pretty pebbles. It was an appropriate place for the students to meet. Gaudı had been as much a revolutionary as they were.

Juan watched the blue-uniformed children from the Sagrada Familia school as they played stickball on the tier below him.

"*Bueno,*" said a voice behind him, and then a hand grasped his warmly. "These are my friends," said León Rosario, motioning to the three young men who were still climbing down the hill behind the park enclosure. "Pedro, Martín, and Sandor," he said, introducing the others.

Juan shook hands all around. León walked to the rim of the enclosure, where he could look down at the lower tiers toward the Gaudı memorial cottage at the entrance to the park.

"Good. We can talk freely here," said León. He led the group to the mosaic benches that abutted the forest of blooming plants on the far side of the enclosure. "Juan, you're a fortunate man that we've chosen you."

Juan shook his head. "You choose me for nothing. I have come to hear what you have to say only. Nothing more. When I've listened, then I'll tell you whether or not I have been chosen."

"Well spoken," said León, puzzled with the response and unsure whether they had been wise to invite Juan into their inner circle.

"You've taken honors this year," said León, leaning close to Juan, trying to take the measure of the muscular, aristocratic-looking young man opposite him. León's compact body moved nervously as he talked. His eyes were a greenish-blue and appeared to stare through Juan, as though to see inside him. His clothes were those of a conservative university student, slacks and white shirt, tie and wool pull-over sweater. Although he was small and slight of build, his intensity radiated and cast an aura of urgency over the meeting. He didn't talk like the typical university students, whom Juan thought were little more than parrots, listening to the lectures and at examination time repeating the information back to the professors exactly as it had been given to them. They appeared to have no thoughts of their own, no opinions.

"We've watched you for a long time now," León said. "You're not like the others. It impresses us also that you are the protégé of Don Carlos and yet you question his authority. That is a commendable trait."

"I've promised to be less eager in the classroom. If you're

interested in my stirring the students from their apathy, you have miscalculated," said Juan.

"No, no," said León forcefully. "On the contrary, we prefer that you be less vocal. If you join us, you are to make yourself nearly invisible. Only in that way can the work be done effectively and without detection by the authorities."

Juan looked at the other three. Their faces were serious. He didn't know whether to laugh or to be alarmed at what he heard. "Conspiracy to change the university? Is that your aim?"

León smiled engagingly. When he smiled, his earnest, pale face with its clear blue eyes became handsome.

"No, not a conspiracy to change the university." He paused. "Perhaps a conspiracy to change Spain."

Juan stood up. "You have been misled, then."

"Don't go yet. Let me finish what I've come to say," said León, his smile gone. "Your Don Carlos is a member of the Opus Dei."

"Yes."

"Do you understand the purpose of the Opus Dei, Juan?"

"It is an organization of honorable men, a Catholic action group. I understand that much."

"Ah, then you understand nothing, my friend. We are Catholics—Martín, Sandor, and Pedro—all Catholics. I spit on the Opus Dei."

Juan sat down on the bench. He was curious but also wary. "*Dígame,*" he said. "Tell me more."

"The purpose of the Opus Dei is to return Spain to the thirteenth century. They are a group of fanatics who want to control Spain so that they can remake it according to their private, mystical vision. They control the largest banks. They are filling the university chairs. They sit behind Franco as he keeps us from breathing the air of freedom."

Juan squirmed now on the bench. He didn't want to hear the words. They were ominous words that pulled at his logic and reason and made him think in traitorous ways. "Don Carlos is my benefactor," said Juan finally.

"Of course. So much the better. We ask you to do nothing to hurt your benefactor. We ask you to act for Spain."

"How would you have me act for Spain?"

"Help us. We see that books are circulated, that newsletters are distributed in the streets. We hold meetings where discussion is free, where ideas are talked about, where plans are made for the future of our country."

"I see. Then you're communists."

"No, not communists, nor anarchists either. We are questioners, just as you are." León paused, watching for the effect that his words had on Juan.

"I can't help you. Don Carlos watches me. My activities are scrutinized. I'm to leave for Salamanca to begin theological studies next year. I can be of no use to you whatsoever."

"But you can, Juan, simply by being who you are and by knowing the people you know. How can we counteract the enemy if we don't know his actions? You can report his actions to us, Juan. You can act for freedom."

Don Carlos and Juan arrived in Valdepeñas for the winter vacation. The olives were in the process of being harvested. The grapes had been pulled from the vines. The quietness of this place welcomed and enfolded Juan and removed him from the strain he felt in Barcelona.

Martita had begun to age. Juan noticed it on this visit particularly as she sat in front of the open fire in her house and told him about the events that had occurred in Valdepeñas since he had gone away. Isabel and Luisa had gone to Toledo for the harvest festival and would not be back until the early-morning hours.

"They have gone by bus. When the festival is over, the bus will return to Valdepeñas," she said, her eyes as black as ever but now rimmed with feathery lines. "It may come back tonight, or perhaps in the morning hours. There is no set time."

Juan's large body filled the upholstered chair, and his long legs sprawled out on the plank floor. Martita got up to refill his wineglass. "It is this year's grape, not yet ripe but good enough, eh?"

"Very good," he said as he leaned his head back against the worn chair. Don Carlos had given the chair to Martita so that Juan would have a place to sit when he came to visit her. There was no other furniture except for the table and chairs where Martita served the meals. The table had been built by Raúl before he went to serve the Loyalists. It was made from the wood of the local poplar tree, which was spongy but long-lasting.

"Valdepeñas is a peaceful place," Juan said, savoring the warmth of the fire and the mellowness of the wine.

"Soon you'll be finished with your studies, and you can come back here and be a gentleman like Don Carlos."

"Not if I enter the priesthood."

Martita looked up in surprise. "Surely you won't do that for him?"

"He expects it."

"But you don't want it?"

"I don't."

"Then let him be disappointed," said Martita with a toss of her head.

"It's too complicated."

"I see nothing complicated about it. He did a good deed for you and for us. We are all alive and happy. Now you must go on with your own life as you see fit. He may speak of Jesus, but he is not Jesus. He does not have the power over you that you give to him."

"There are other things that you don't understand."

Martita responded sharply. "I understand what is important. That is what I understand."

When Juan returned to the house, Don Carlos had retired for the night, and the servants had left and gone back to their homes. Juan read for a while in the library, and when he felt himself nodding off, he closed the book and went to his room. The house was cold, as Don Carlos liked to keep it. He said it was a small mortification of the flesh always to be a little cold.

Juan removed his clothes and lay down on the bed and pulled the thin white cotton coverlet over his naked body. He tried to think of nothing, to empty his mind of its preoccupations, and soon he was asleep.

It was still dark when he awoke to the screech of the owls hooting in the olive grove and the murmur of voices in the still night air. He lay awake listening to the voices, not able to hear the words clearly enough to understand what was being said. There were footsteps now in the house. They hesitated at his door. The door opened. He lay still, his eyes accustomed to the dark. There was a flash of white fabric in the dark, like a sudden burst of light, then the sound of swishing skirts, and clothing dropped to the floor. He pulled back the thin coverlet, and then he felt the softness of her as she pressed herself against his body. He ran his hands slowly up and down the curve of her back as she moved against him. She straddled his body. He could see her breasts outlined in the dark; he could feel the softness within her. He touched the tips of her breasts, and she moaned and moved sinuously from side to side. He sat up with her so that they were facing one another, and they held each other tightly, and he pushed deeply into her. She was holding his face and kissing him, and then they came together.

"Luisa," he said.

They slept in each other's arms, and before daylight she rose and dressed again in the flamenco costume she had worn to the festival in Toledo. He watched her as she dressed. Her black curls were still caught up in the tortoise combs, but tendrils had fallen along her neck and at the sides of her face. There were traces of rouge and smudges of mascara around her eyes. Her cheekbones were high like Martita's, but there was still the softness of the child in her features.

"You will soon be finished with school, and then I won't have to leave before dawn," she said, pulling her underskirt up around her waist.

"I'll be going to Salamanca, Luisa, not coming back to Valdepeñas."

"Don't tell me that, Juan. You will never be a priest. You will come back here and marry me."

"I'm only twenty, Luisa. Even if I came back to Valdepeñas, I would not marry."

She pulled on the second petticoat and buttoned it.

"And I'm twenty-one, and I must marry soon, or it will be too late. Isabel will be a *soltera*. Everybody says so. She is twenty-four and not yet married. That is past the time for someone to pick her. At the festival already I could feel that the boys no longer looked at her in that way. But if you don't want to come back to marry me, there are many who will."

She buttoned the frilly red blouse and walked to the bed. "Then you won't be unhappy if I no longer come to your bed, Juan? For if I marry, surely my husband would not permit that."

Juan laughed and pulled her toward him. He pushed the tendrils back and kissed her on the forehead.

"That is your answer, a kiss like you give a sister? I wasn't your sister when you held me and thrust your *pene* into me. You must make a decision, Juan. You cannot always expect me to give myself to you if you promise me nothing in return."

She stared down at him. He was smiling at her indulgently.

"Aaah," she exclaimed, stamping her heel as the flamenco dancers did. With a flounce of her skirts, she turned and was gone.

XXXI

Juan pulled a heavy sweater over his shirt and tie, tossed his book pack onto the bed in his dormitory room, and ran across the campus to Don Carlos' quarters.

"We were to have lunch together today," said Don Carlos reprovingly when Juan arrived, out of breath. Juan smoothed back his black hair that had been tossed about by the wind, then sat down in a chair by the fire. Don Carlos stood at his desk, which was covered with books and papers and newspaper articles. The door from the office and reception room into Don Carlos' bedroom was open, revealing its austere furnishings: a chest of drawers and a straight pine chair on one side of the neatly made bed, on the other side an end table upon which lay the Bible, and above, on the stark white wall, a carved wooden crucifix.

"Have you eaten? It is three o'clock," said Don Carlos, looking at his watch.

"No, *señor,* I lost myself in the books, and when I looked up, I realized that I had forgotten our appointment."

"It is of no importance," said Don Carlos. There was always the formality between them. They rarely said anything to one another of a personal nature, and then only about such matters as dental appointments or school assignments.

"I have hardly seen you since we returned from Valdepeñas," said Don Carlos, his pale brown eyes regarding Juan soberly. As Don Carlos had aged, his profile had come to resemble the faces of the Hapsburg rulers in their portraits by Goya: exaggerated thinness of jaw and lip, unflattering elongation of the beaked nose, a weakening of the undershot chin.

"I've been studying," said Juan.

"It is studying that I want to talk to you about. Or, rather, the people with whom you study."

Juan started to speak, but Don Carlos held his hand up for silence.

"No, now hear me out. You are young still, not yet out of your boyhood, still in need of my guidance in these matters. There are some influences in the university that are unwholesome ones. We are aware of their presence, and evil will be rooted out in due time. In due time. But until that happens, I must protect you from contamination."

Juan looked at him in amusement. "They are not evil, *señor,*" he said evenly. "You misunderstand."

"I misunderstand nothing," said Don Carlos angrily. "It is you who misunderstand. You are here by my sufferance. You remain here by my largess."

"Why?"

"Why? Because I see something of worth in you. A keen intellect, a quick grasp of things, the making of a leader perhaps."

"But you decry my intellect. You won't permit me to use it. You own only half the truth, *señor.* There are others who supply me with the other half."

"Then is it too late to save you?" asked Don Carlos.

Juan looked at the older man hunched in the chair opposite him.

"But you have saved me, *señor.* Without you I would still be living in Martita's house, unable to read, fit only for a life in the fields."

Don Carlos shook his head sadly. "No, I have not saved you. Only Christ has the power to save you. And you have turned away from him. I fear that the forces of evil and liberalism now own your soul."

León tossed the twine-wrapped pamphlets to Juan and began to chase him down the alley behind the Barcelona wharf. Sandor, walking behind them, yelled, "Wait up, you *locos.* This is not a game."

But youthful exuberance and joy at being in the open air

away from schoolbooks gave a playfulness to their mission. They darted in and out of alleys, watching for the soldiers who stood in the doorways of the public buildings along the Barceloneta port area. Juan stopped once at a street stand and bought a cupful of chestnuts that an old woman was roasting over an iron stove. Tiny seafood restaurants lined the meandering streets, and in the cul-de-sacs of the streets, where the delivery trucks parked, the kitchen help sat together and cleaned shrimp and shelled peas into gleaming steel bowls in preparation for the evening paella.

"León, over here." Juan called León to the window of the turn-of-the-century Siete Puertas restaurant. It resembled a house, with its starched curtains at all the windows and its hanging glass lamps casting a soft glow from within. Black-coated waiters with pomaded hair moved from table to table, listening attentively and then bringing trays and bowls of steaming Catalonian delicacies. Juan peered through the glass of the front entrance at the table laden with the famous sausages of Barcelona. "We can finish later," he said. "I had no lunch today. Besides, when we leave, we can drop a few pamphlets on the front step as a gift."

"The trouble with you, Juan," laughed León, "is that you don't have the true revolutionary spirit. You are too easily swayed by your stomach."

"According to Don Carlos, right now you and your evil friends are locked in deadly battle for the control of my spirit, of which my stomach is only a small part."

The laugh left León's soft, handsome face. "You have told him about La Marcha?"

"No, I told him nothing," answered Juan, turning away from the tempting food. "But nothing escapes him and the regents."

Sandor caught up with them. "Two more blocks, and then we're through. We can cover the public buildings on the Paseo de Colón. There's the post office building and the museum. Then we'll come back and have a late lunch."

Sandor had begun to grow a small beard as a symbol of his contempt for university regulations. In La Marcha he was one of the more militant members, one of a minority who felt that the students were in danger and that they should be armed. León was the calming influence. "After all," he would say, "one need only look at us to see that we are merely students and that what we do is nothing more than schoolboy pranks."

They turned down the street toward the ocean front. At the post office they stopped and ran up the steps to where a soldier, no older than they were, stood with a machine gun in his hands. The soldier stared straight ahead, his booted feet spread apart, the gun in his hands poised and ready.

"*Señor,*" León called, and when the soldier turned at the distraction, Juan pushed open the post office door and threw a few pamphlets toward the people who stood in line with their packages. From the bottom of the steps, Sandor motioned to them to hurry. The soldier turned now to the door as it swung closed, a look of confusion on his face. Juan was running down the steps two at a time, León behind him. A post office employee opened the door and waved the pamphlets at the soldier.

"*Alto,*" yelled the soldier, raising the machine gun to his shoulder.

At the sound of the command to stop, León turned and ran back up the steps. He had dropped the rest of the pamphlets in the dirt, and now he held up his hands to show that they contained nothing more. He walked toward the soldier, who was taking aim with the machine gun.

"León, come back," yelled Sandor, pulling a small automatic weapon from his pocket and waving it in the air.

Leon looked at the gun in horror. The soldier had seen it also. "It's only a game," León shouted at the soldier, but the soldier was not listening.

"León, he'll kill you. It isn't safe," shrieked Sandor before the bullets ripped through his body and then through León's.

Juan began to run, erratically and with no sense of purpose or destination. But there were other soldiers, and they were young and strong also. Along the Paseo Pujadas, where the old men sat on benches and talked endlessly about their solutions to Spain's problems, a young soldier finally caught up with Juan.

• • • • •

"There is a defense," said Don Carlos when he visited Juan in the Barcelona jail. Juan sat in a chair in the white-walled visitors' room, where two armed soldiers stood guard at the door. Don Carlos looked nervous and frightened. He had never seen the inside of a jail before, nor seen a gun at close range. He had spent the Spanish Civil War in Paris.

"Don't be afraid, Don Carlos. They only shoot at you in the street."

Don Carlos pulled his chair close to Juan's. "I say there is a defense. Your age. You were unaware that the boy was armed. Youthful energy led astray. Children playing at revolution."

"It is not play when two students are killed," said Juan. He made a fist and held it up and shook it at the soldiers. "The rage I feel is not a child's anger, Don Carlos."

"It is unfortunate, but it has happened," said Don Carlos. He looked uncomfortable at Juan's violent show of emotion. "No one but God himself can explain the meaning behind it. The parents of the dead students will mourn, but perhaps this will teach the others the consequences of excess and so prevent more deaths."

"It will warn them of nothing, *señor*," said Juan. "It will only steel them to fight on. But you needn't worry about me. This has never been my fight."

"No, of course not. Your devotion is to Christ. You will go to Salamanca as we had planned."

"I said it was not my fight. I am not a Spaniard; I can never be a priest. I cannot fight for the Opus Dei. I can only look on from the outside."

"You're upset, unable to think. Of course you can be a priest. What insanity has taken hold of you?"

After all the years of keeping his Jewishness hidden from Don Carlos, Juan decided that here in prison, with Don Carlos staring at him as if he were a madman, he would tell him. "The little boy that you brought into your house and want to make a priest is a Jew, Don Carlos. A Jew. And that half of me that is Jewish pulls against the half that is Catholic. I can never become part of the Opus Dei."

There was a long silence, a perplexed expression on the

older man's face. Juan thought that perhaps Don Carlos had not understood what he said.

"This is a trick of the liberals," said Don Carlos finally, an icy glare in his eyes. "They have won, and I have lost, and now you torture me by telling me lies. No, you will not be a priest, because there is a baseness in you that will not accept Christ into your heart as your true savior. You have been seduced by the forces of Satan. There is nothing I can do to combat him for your soul."

Juan gazed at him, marveling at Don Carlos' self-delusion in refusing to admit that he had housed a Jew all these years. He stared in wonder at his mentor, who preferred to continue railing against the enemies of Christ rather than confront what for him was an obscene revelation.

One evening in the second week of Juan's imprisonment, the guard came to his cell and told him that there was a visitor to see him, and no, it was not the elderly gentleman with the thin face. This man had hair that covered his head like a windblown bush, and he was tall, very tall.

He stood smoking a cigarette when they brought Juan into the visitors' room. The man's hair was streaked with gray, but his eyebrows were fierce and black above his piercing dark eyes. He seemed to fill the room with some inner ferocity. He looked like no one Juan had ever seen, and yet he was staring at Juan as though he knew him.

"Juan Lepanto?" said the man, shaking his hand.

"Yes."

"I'm Tonio Katakis. Don Carlos Mendes de Salceda suggested I come to see you. Has the lawyer arrived yet?"

"Don Carlos didn't tell me he was sending a lawyer."

"No. The lawyer has been retained by me."

Juan sat down in the chair, completely bewildered.

"Are you eating well? Should I send some food in for you?"

"No, I don't eat well," said Juan. "But who are you, and why are you here and so interested in my health?"

"I told you my name. Tonio Katakis. I'm a fellow Jew. I've come to get you out of jail."

Juan laughed. He looked at the guards and then back at the big-shouldered man with the fiery hair, and he laughed again. He was face to face with a Jew, someone like him. And he had looked at him and had not known it. Contrary to what Sister María Blanca had said, he had not recognized a Jew when he saw one. This was a mystery even more enigmatic than Don Carlos' dedication to his mystic visions. Suddenly Juan's laughter turned to tears. Never had he been known to cry before. He had always emulated Don Carlos and the men of Valdepeñas in such things. But he wanted to cry now. For León and Sandor, for his never having seen a Jew before. And while he wept, Tonio Katakis, the stranger, the man who had called himself a "fellow Jew," waited and smoked his cigarette.

XXXII

Helene arrived in Berlin in the early afternoon. A taxi driver near the entrance to the train station pulled his car alongside the curb, but Helene waved him away. It was a brisk February day, and she wanted to walk the streets of Berlin to the Tiergarten, to see Grandmama's house before she met with Frau Fleischer. She tucked her silk scarf more securely into the collar of her navy wool coat and began to walk. It was 1955, and Berlin and she had both recovered somewhat from the effects of the war. Helene no longer wore makeup, as she had before the war; but her face as she entered her forties had a certain delineation, a striking presence, and her brown eyes turned away from nothing. Men looked at her more now than they had when she was in her twenties and had the soft, unaware gaze of the young wife.

The streets were clean, and the passersby appeared to be well dressed. But important buildings were missing. The theater where she and Erika used to see films was gone, as was the Schiller Schule, where Helene had studied the piano with Madame Steller. New buildings had taken their place. She had thought she would be afraid here. She had told Tonio that she might finally collapse in Berlin, when she found herself surrounded by so many Germans again. But she wasn't collapsing. If anything, she felt her strength more keenly here. She had thought that the sidewalks would cry out the names of all the victims, or that the faces of all the Germans she met would be the faces of the guards at Ravensbrück. But these were the faces of ordinary people on their way to do ordinary things on a February day in a metropolitan city.

Grandmama's house was gone, along with the park in the

Tiergarten and the shops that had bordered it. Helene felt her heart pound as she stared at the brick apartment buildings that stood on the grounds of what had been the Rosenzweig estate. The rose garden was gone. There was nothing left. She searched the skyline for a glimpse of the Italian cupola of Grandmama's house. Perhaps it still stood within the maze of utilitarian buildings. But now there was only squareness and asphalt, young trees and new grass.

"Do you need some help, *Fräulein*?" asked an old man in work clothes with a rake in his hand.

"The Rosenzweig estate," said Helene. "I was looking for the house of Magda Rosenzweig."

"Bombed," said the old man. "Nobody was killed. They'd all left with the rest of the Jews. Are you looking for Jews in particular?" He was now looking at her strangely. "Because if you are, you won't find them here." He pointed toward the southern part of the city. "Used to have some living over there, beyond the Mitte."

"When was that?" asked Helene, clutching at straws.

"Let me see." The old man thought for a while. "1938. Yes, it was 1938."

"Yes, I remember that, too. Thank you very much."

Frau Fleischer was nervous with Helene. "As you can see, with such a small apartment there is no longer any need for servants, even if one had the money to hire them," she said after she had greeted Helene and taken her coat and hung it in the spacious closet next to the door.

Frau Fleischer prepared tea in the kitchen alcove off the sitting room. The apartment was not luxurious, but it was in an elegant old building, and whatever damage the war had wrought had been covered over with plaster, fresh paint, and new wallpaper. There was a feeling of gentility in the furnishings. Helene recognized a few things that had survived the war: an antique Chinese charger on a rosewood stand, two delicate French end tables.

"The cookies I made myself," said Frau Fleischer. "I have learned to do many things for myself."

"Your apartment is very comfortable," said Helene as she accepted the cup of tea and held one of the chocolate cookies in a napkin. Frau Fleischer had once had a collection of Georgian silver to rival Grandmama's and furs that were the talk of the Berlin opera season.

"Erika has seen to it that I don't suffer too much."

The tea service was the Meissen that Helene had always admired, but the lid of the teapot was cracked, and the cups had tiny chips on their rims.

"I am so glad to see you, dear Helene," said Frau Fleischer. "I have often thought of you, wondered what had become of you. But it was difficult during the war for me, too. As you can see, I am in much reduced circumstances. My husband was captured by the Russians, and, of course, I never saw him again. I sold almost everything I had during the war just to survive. And then the bombings, my God, I'll never forget the bombings. Such a catastrophe. Let us hope that nothing like it ever happens again."

"Yes, it was a catastrophe," said Helene, watching Frau Fleischer closely. It was so different sitting here with her now. Frau Fleischer in an apartment, instead of the baronial mansion that she and her husband had lived in before the war. Serving the tea herself on chipped Meissen. Wearing a silk dressing gown, but the diamond studs that she always wore missing from her earlobes. Lines in her face and her hair gray. And nervous with Helene.

"Do you remember how close you and Erika were? My goodness, sometimes I thought I had another daughter. There was almost never a time I saw Erika that you weren't with her."

"Yes, I do remember."

"And you live now in Barcelona, you said. And your family? You didn't tell me anything of your family."

"There is no one left but me."

"But Maurice? And David and the baby, Miriam . . ."

Frau Fleischer held her head in her hands in silent grief for long-gone children. Helene wanted to touch her gray hair, now so like Grandmama's had been. She wanted to hold Frau Fleischer and be comforted by her as she had been as a young girl. Do you remember when my mother's sister died, Grandmama's beloved Lena, how you talked to me and soothed me and told me that I would be happy again, that Grandmama would be happy again? But Helene's hand did not move toward Frau Fleischer's shoulder. She could not bring herself that close to Miriam and David. She would lose control.

The woman's eyes were filled with tears when she looked up at Helene.

"It's all right now," said Helene. "Many years have passed. I'm married again, and I have an adopted daughter, Sara. She was in the camps with me. We survived the war together."

"What can I do, my dear Helene? I am devastated. I have nothing to give to you, nothing."

"Please, don't," said Helene as her hand went out to touch Frau Fleischer's.

"*Gott im Himmel, Gott im Himmel,*" murmured Frau Fleischer as she took Helene's hand in hers. Helene sat stiffly, feeling a pain so deep that it numbed her entire being. The tears rolled down her cheeks, but she did not utter a sound.

"I remember your family with such fond memories," said Frau Fleischer. "It is incomprehensible to me that all of this has happened. How could we have known that it would happen, Helene? If you could tell me the answer to that, I perhaps could reconcile myself to life again." Frau Fleischer's face was contorted with anguish. "I would give up my life if we could go back to the way that it was before the war, if I could bring your children back to you, your family back to you."

Helene withdrew her hand and took a napkin from the tea tray and wiped the tears from her face. "You mustn't feel guilt over this, *gnädige Frau.* You have always been the kindest, the most compassionate woman. You could have done nothing. It was beyond your ability to alter anything that has happened to me."

"Then you don't blame me?"

"No, I don't blame you. If I were to start to blame people for what happened, there would be no one left in the world unblamed, including myself."

"Thank God that you don't hate me, Helene." She blew her nose into a linen handkerchief that she pulled from the pocket of her dressing gown. "I must show you pictures of my granddaughter, Alexa," she said, her eyes brightening. "The birth of Alexa was the only good thing that happened to me during the war."

Frau Fleischer walked into the bedroom and returned with an envelope of photographs. She sat down on the worn sofa next to Helene and held out the photographs one by one.

"She's beautiful," said Helene, looking at the photographs.

"You have come very far to have tea with an old woman and look at pictures of her granddaughter. Tell me about your life now, Helene. I hope that you have found some happiness with your new family."

Helene stared at the last picture of fifteen-year-old Alexa, sitting on a horse, gazing at the photographer with a sweetly innocent smile.

"My husband is a good man. He was very active in behalf of the Spanish Jews during the war. He saved me and Sara from death in Ravensbrück. He saved many others also. And now he and I work together."

"You work together?" said Frau Fleischer, smiling again. She poured some more tea into Helene's cup and then lifted her own teacup to her lips. "What kind of work do you do?"

"We are part of a network of people throughout the world who search for Nazi war criminals."

The teacup trembled in Frau Fleischer's hand.

"Don't be afraid," said Helene. "I know you were not a Nazi."

Frau Fleischer's eyes filled with tears again. "You were like a daughter to me, Helene. I could never have done anything to harm you. I never saw you as a Jew, never."

Helene flinched at the innocent remark. "Please, Frau Fleischer, I'm not accusing you of anything."

"But you come here for a reason, don't you?"

"Yes."

"I have no information to give you. I know nothing of any Nazis."

"You do remember Count von Kirchner, Karl von Kirchner?" asked Helene quietly.

"Of course. And his mother, Countess Mathilde von Kirchner, God rest her soul."

"It is the Count that I have come to talk to you about."

"The Count? Are you saying that he is a Nazi war criminal?" She shook her head vehemently. "No, I don't believe it."

"I am witness to the fact that Count von Kirchner killed women and children with his own hand, at close range with a pistol, and when they fell, they were picked up by others, who carried them to the crematoria to be burned."

"Please, please. I have not been well. My heart. I am not to have any unnecessary excitement. The doctors tell me that there is something wrong with my heart."

"Dear Frau Fleischer, I am so sorry to upset you in this way. I only recite facts. Sometimes I don't realize the effect that my facts have on the listener. Of course I will refrain from retelling the details. But, as you can well understand, Count von Kirchner is on our list of wanted Nazis. Commandant Koegel, the first commandant at Ravensbrück, was arrested and committed suicide in his cell in 1946. His successor, Commandant Suhren, was executed by the French in 1950. There are so many who are wanted that it seems almost a waste to spend much time and attention on one man. But I was at Ravensbrück when the Count was the co-commandant. I have a special interest in him. Others, including my husband, are very occupied with tracking down and capturing Stangl of Treblinka or Baer of Auschwitz. I help in that also. But it is with Ravensbrück that I am most occupied. And with the Count."

"I feel quite sick, Helene. I would not have agreed to see you had I known the purpose of your visit. I cannot speak for the Count. I remember him only as he was before the war, a cultured, refined, well-born man. The war did many things to many people. People became deranged. Now that things are quiet, let life go on. For you to live with such hate must be worse than to have died in the concentration camp. I am sorry for you and for your children and your family. But I am sorry, too, for myself and my dead husband."

"I have no hate, Frau Fleischer. It is only a mission that I have undertaken to perform. And as for your suffering, I'm sorry for it, but it was the Germans, not the Jews, who were the murderers. If I cause you to remember unpleasantness, then it is necessary. We have reason to believe that the Count was in touch with Erika and Gunter in Italy throughout the war and that there is a possibility they can give us clues as to his friends, the ones who helped him escape from Germany."

"No, no, it is not possible. I cannot help you in this matter."

"Why? It is a simple thing that I've come to ask. You know where Erika is. I want you to tell me that."

"I cannot. I have not seen her since 1939." Frau Fleischer had become very agitated.

"Why are you so frightened, Frau Fleischer?"

"It is that Erika and Gunter have asked that I not reveal their whereabouts."

"They have told you that they left us in Rome without resources, haven't they? That they took the gold and diamonds and left us with nothing? Is that why they don't want you to tell anyone where they are?"

Frau Fleischer's eyes were circles of fright. "Erika has told me only that they left Rome because she and Gunter were invited to stay with Countess Ciano and that she has felt guilt over leaving you and your family behind. But she has never said anything to me about gold or diamonds. I know nothing of such things. I do not believe that Erika would take anything that did not belong to her. That they left you because they could save themselves is all I am aware of. But you must understand and commiserate with their position at the time. It might have been you and Maurice who left them behind had you not been burdened with two children."

"I am no longer burdened," said Helene.

"Forgive me, Helene," said Frau Fleischer in dismay. "I spoke without thinking."

"It is I who should ask your forgiveness for intruding upon you in this way," said Helene. "If I have any interest in knowing where Erika and Gunter are, it is only because of my determination to find the Count. I want no harm to come to Erika or Gunter or your granddaughter. I am very sincere in that. I have thought about Erika over the years. I have tried to understand her position, to understand Gunter's position when we were all in Rome. You say that they left us only because there was a safe place for them to go and there was no room for four more people. I accept that. Perhaps there were things I didn't know at the time. Perhaps the Count took the diamonds that were meant for us. Only Erika and Gunter and the Count know what truly happened. And to say that because we were without the gold or diamonds is the reason Maurice killed Miriam and himself—"

Frau Fleischer gasped in horror and lay back on the sofa, her hand to her heart.

"Please, I am so sorry," said Helene. She held the cup of tea to Frau Fleischer's lips. "There now, drink slowly," she said. Frau Fleischer's eyes fluttered gratefully as she sipped the tea. Helene fluffed the sofa pillows up around Frau Fleischer's back and waited until the older woman's breath had changed from agonized wheezes to more normal respiration.

"I'm sorry, Frau Fleischer. I sometimes forget when I talk about Maurice and Miriam that others are unaware of what happened."

"Such a tragedy, such a tragedy," said Frau Fleischer breathlessly.

"Yes, it was a tragedy," said Helene. "I try not to dwell on it. If I were to dwell on it, I would be unable to function."

"Yes, I understand," said Frau Fleischer.

When the older woman had recovered and was sitting up once again, Helene continued talking in a conversational tone of voice. "No more revelations, Frau Fleischer. I promise you that. We know that the Count and the Ciano family were in contact during the war, that Erika stayed in Countess Ciano's villa in Rome, and that sometime afterward Gunter was arrested and taken to Auschwitz. There seems to be some connection between the flight of Nazis from Europe and the Ciano villa in Rome. Eichmann we know was helped with a passport and a new identity through the Franciscan monastery in Genoa, but we have no information as to the method by which Count von Kirchner escaped."

Frau Fleischer looked relieved. "Then you have forgiven Erika and Gunter for leaving you in Rome?"

Helene took a bite of cookie and then a sip of tea, feeling the chocolaty bits melt in the warm liquid in her mouth.

"I forgave them a long time ago."

When Helene returned to Barcelona, it was past the supper hour, and she took a taxi from the train station. Tonio had the light on in the office. Through the window Helene saw Sara in a chair behind her desk. Tonio sat facing a young man across his desk. She would not bother them now. She was exhausted and wanted to take a bath. Then she would have a cold supper, and by that time Tonio would be through with his business with the young man.

Helene entered the apartment quietly and walked up the stairs to their living quarters. Their apartment was in an old building in the Gothic Quarter, where Helene could look out the window and watch the priests walking through the square to the cathedral. It comforted Helene to be here near the cathedral. Sara had a room and a bath downstairs between the kitchen and office, and upstairs overlooking the cathedral were Helene and Tonio's bedroom and bath and a small sitting room. Helene walked to the window and looked below. What did she hope to see by surveying the square so regularly and diligently? The cathedral was the first place she had gone when Tonio brought her and Sara home from the displaced persons camp. She had not yet recovered her health, and Tonio had pleaded with her to wait until she was stronger. He had said she was in no condition to be put through the ordeal of searching for David while her own health was so fragile.

"I will rest later, I promise, but my heart is bursting with excitement. I must go, Tonio. I have to talk to the priests at the cathedral. Please don't keep me from David any longer."

But the priests were of no help to the thin, anxious-eyed woman.

"His name was Juan Lepanto. I left him sitting on a stone bench. He was three years old but grown-up for his age, hardly a child at all," she said in a rush of words, as if to make up for all the years of silence.

"*Lo siento mucho, señora.* I am so sorry for you. There were so many children. There were the children of the Republicans who had been orphaned, there were the children of refugees passing through. There were so many children that we despaired of finding enough homes for all the children who were left in our care."

"But he was an intelligent child. He might have told someone that his name was David. Yes, I'm sure he would tell them that his name was David. I called him Juan Lepanto only so that the Church would take him in. He was not really a Catholic. He is a Jewish child, my child. Surely there is a way to find him. Don't tell me that there is no way to find him." Helene had begun to sob and then was seized by a paroxysm of coughing. The priest called for a nun to come to the refectory. The nun brought water for Helene to drink and a wet cloth to place across her fevered brow.

"I'm sorry," said Helene listlessly.

"You have not been well?" asked the priest solicitously.

Helene shook her head. "I have not been well."

Helene moved away from the window. It was growing dark now, and she could no longer make out the figures below in the square.

After she had bathed, she put on a robe and walked down the stairs to the kitchen. Sara had placed the remains of their supper on a plate and put it in the cooler. Cold beef and rice. Too much food when she was so tired. She poured herself a glass of milk and put two slices of beef on a plate, then sat down at the kitchen table. She could hear their voices in the office down the hall. Tonio was telling the visitor about the war. Helene had heard him tell the stories before when he wanted to enlist help for their work. The stories no longer made Helene cringe. She could listen to them now at a slight remove, almost as though all the terrible things had happened only to others and not to her. She had once talked to a psychiatrist from the United States who had visited them to inquire about finding a lost brother. He had been amazed at her equanimity in the face of what she had been through. He had even suggested that it might not be healthy to keep her emotions so walled off from the pain of the events. Denial, he had called it. She practiced a form of denial.

"Can it hurt me?" she had asked.

"Possibly, if the feelings that you have buried deep inside you are unrelieved, in time it could hurt you."

"Would it be better if I screamed and cursed the world for what happened in my life?"

"Possibly."

"I can't."

Helene finished her meal and walked through the hall toward the stairs. The young man was asking questions now, unbelieving of what Tonio was telling him. Where had he been, this young man, who knew nothing of what had happened to the Jews? He could not be a Jew himself.

She stopped at the foot of the stairs and turned around and walked toward the office. Tonio saw her standing in the doorway and looked up at her and smiled. The young man turned toward her. A nice-looking young man, dark eyes in a weathered face. Not more than nineteen or twenty. He was quiet and poised as he sat opposite Tonio. Was he Jewish? Helene couldn't tell by his face. Tonio and the young man stood up.

"We have a guest for a while, Helene. This young man has been involved in a political crime. Two of his friends were killed. Of course I told him we would help him."

Then he was a Jew, thought Helene. Tonio did not bring home everyone who was involved in a political crime. She walked toward the young man, who was smiling at her in such a charming fashion. He extended his hand to her, and she grasped it. "Juan Lepanto," he said. At the sound of the name, she felt her knees giving way beneath her. A small boy, sitting on a bench in the Cathedral La Seu, had had the same name.

She looked toward Sara, who had been listening quietly.

"Sara," she said, holding out her arm. Sara got up from the chair and ran toward Helene as she began to fall. Tonio and the young man were now on each side of her, helping her onto the sofa.

"Tonio?" she asked, looking into his eyes.

"Yes, Helene, I've found him for you," he said.

The young man had moved away from the sofa, but he was staring intensely at Helene.

"No, don't go away," said Helene. "I didn't mean to frighten you. Don't go away!" Her lips started to tremble, and then she was sobbing, but she didn't take her eyes off the young man who stood there, so isolated in his bewilderment.

She reached for him, and he moved slowly toward her. He held his hand out to her, and she took it in hers and pressed it to her cheek.

"David," she said. "David."

XXXIII

All along, first with Martita, then with Don Carlos, and even at the university, Juan had known there was a part of his life that was missing. He would speculate on what it meant to be a Jew. When he thought about Jews, it was with curiosity. The history books said that they had been expelled from Spain in 1492. Don Carlos referred to them as Satan's agents. And the Spanish newspapers told of the German concentration camps, of what the Europeans did with their Jews.

"Why have you stayed in Spain?" Juan asked Tonio.

"It is my home now. It is Helene's home now, and Sara's," Tonio answered. "And we are able to do our work more effectively here. There are still many Nazis to be searched out, and Spain hides them as well as any country in Europe. As for our Jewishness, we don't shout it from the rooftops. We are, after all, still in Spain."

Helene talked to Juan carefully, as though he were still a stranger to her. They were mother and son, but too many unknown things had happened to each of them. Juan knew that she was watching him in order to understand what kind of man he had become.

"What shall I do about the Catholic Mass?" he asked. "I am a baptized Catholic."

"If you are comfortable attending Mass, then that is what you should do," answered Helene, watching him with eyes that tried to see his child's face.

"It is a habit," he said. "It is something I must think about."

"You will still be a Jew, no matter what you do," said Tonio. "Your mother is Jewish; therefore you are."

Sometimes Helene asked him quiet questions about the past. "Were you treated well?"

"Martita was good to me," he answered.

"You must visit her often," Helene said. "And Don Carlos?"

"He is difficult to understand, and he would like me to believe that he has no feeling for me."

"Does he?"

"Yes."

And Tonio was different from the men that Juan knew. He did not preach as Don Carlos did. He did not preen in Spanish arrogance. He looked at you in a direct way and talked simply. He was gruff at times, and sometimes impatient, but loving, too, in a way that Juan had never seen in men. Tonio loved Helene. David saw it when they were together. Tonio touched her hair or slid his fingers across her arm, and sometimes he just gazed at her in the evenings when the day's work was finished and it was quiet in the apartment.

And Helene. Carriage so straight, face and eyes still lovely to look at. But nothing soft in her, only steeliness. Still, she smiled in delight when Tonio entered the room. And now when Juan entered the room.

Juan knew something of Jewish life from his secret readings, but he wanted to absorb all of Jewish history and suffering into himself so that he could understand what his mother had suffered. There was such strangeness in the word. *Madre.* Mother. Why did you leave me?

"I want to understand what it is to be a Jew. I want to fill in the part of me that I've lost," David said to Helene.

"Don't try to understand everything at once," said Helene. "Don't try to become a Jew at once. Don't try to become a Jew at all. I accept you as you are."

She accepts me as I am. *Madre.* Mother. Is that the meaning of the word?

And Sara. Helene said that she was a Gypsy, the child of Gypsies. Black hair and dark skin, shy, with the face of a wild child and a fiery brightness in her brown eyes. She was small but not petite. Her breasts and hips were full, and her naturally curly black hair usually escaped the combs with which she bound it back from her high forehead. She was content to observe quietly, to have no attention paid to her. The animation and excitement of others dissolved in her quietness as a red liquid in a black glass. She had a stillness in her that was close to lifelessness. There was none of the joyousness that Juan had seen in the Gypsies of Spain. And she worried him in the way that she stared at him.

"Sara suffered much," said Helene. "Perhaps she thinks of you in ways that are new to her. It will pass."

And his name. Names meant many things to the people who owned them. They incorporated a past life, a history, a treasury of encounters with other human beings. He thought long and hard about his name.

"What do you prefer to be called?" asked Helene.

"I don't know," he answered. He thought about it in philosophical terms. What did it matter what name others called him by? He remained the same. And yet he was not the same. Life as a Jew would never be the same as his life with Don Carlos had been.

"What did you feel when you gave me to the Church?" Juan finally asked his mother.

Her expression did not change when she answered him. "Happiness," she said. "I have never felt more happiness than that day. I knew you would survive."

After several weeks had passed, Juan said to Tonio, "Helene seems not to care what name I am called."

"She cares," answered Tonio. "But she does not ask for favors."

"Was her suffering that great?"

Tonio did not answer.

One day Juan said, "I feel myself changing."

"You don't need to change," said Helene.

"He will change if he feels the need to," interjected Tonio.

"I want to be called David," said Juan.

David watched Sara and Helene together. They were as one person. A glance between them seemed to be enough to communicate what each was thinking or feeling. At times he thought that Sara must be Helene's natural child and he the orphan.

He felt conflicting urges toward Sara. One moment she was his sister, and the next moment he wanted to put his hands against her bare skin, to touch her full breasts, to kiss her and hold her dark head close to his. But always there was the jealousy.

"Will you stay with us for a long time?" Sara asked him late one afternoon as they sat opposite each other at the kitchen table. Helene and Tonio were out, and Sara had not turned on the light in the darkening kitchen. Rain pelted against the windows, and David felt a tremendous sense of comfort and belonging sitting next to Sara.

"Do you want me to stay?" he said.

She turned away. "Helene wants you here with her."

The curve of her neck tantalized. Did the pulse that beat so rapidly there beat for him?

"I want to help in the work," said David, his own heart thumping. "There is no point in returning to the university. All that the university prepared me for was to become a priest."

"Are you sorry?" asked Sara.

"No. I could never have become a priest. I had no vocation, no calling. And I knew I was a Jew."

She turned toward him. "I'm happy that you're here, David."

Tonio had told him how Sara had lived for three years beneath the floorboards in Ravensbrück. That, too, was mixed up in David's feelings toward her. She had experienced the incomprehensible. She shared it with Helene. With his mother. *Madre.*

"Helene never speaks of Ravensbrück," said David cautiously.

"It is because of me," said Sara simply. "She has put it behind her because of me."

He leaned toward her, searching her eyes for a contradiction to her words. But her eyes were clear and black. There was nothing hidden in her eyes. "Do you remember it?" he asked.

"I remember the dark. It was very dark. I don't remember anything more."

David sighed in relief. "I'm glad," he said. "I've read the books and looked at the pictures. I'm glad that you don't remember."

The kitchen was dark now, and he could no longer see her face. Were her eyes as clear and black as they seemed? Was there nothing hidden in them at all?

"I'll turn on the light," said David.

"No, not yet," she said. "Would you ever marry a non-Jew?" she asked.

"That's a strange question. I have never thought of it before. Do Jews marry only other Jews?"

"Yes."

He was silent for a while. Then he said, "I have always thought I would never marry at all."

The small brick building that housed the mikveh stood on a parcel of land not far from the synagogue. Rabbi Theonikis was waiting for Sara at the door to the building. It was the first time in the months he had tutored her that the rabbi had seen Sara so animated. She wore a two-piece suit and a red and blue scarf over her black hair, and her face and eyes were as radiant as a new bride's.

The two men who, with the rabbi, would constitute the beth din were in the vestibule of the small brick building when the rabbi and Sara entered. The men were elderly and wore hats and prayer shawls around their shoulders, and since there were no chairs or benches in the vestibule, they stood, prayer books in hand, while Sara was led to the room where the immersion would take place.

In a small dressing room at the side of the pool, a woman attendant helped Sara remove her clothes. The woman stared disinterestedly at the voluptuousness of the young girl. Sara blushed as she stood naked before the strange woman.

"Come," said the woman, leading the way toward the pool, which was fed by an underground spring. Sara walked down the steps into the heated water until her shoulders were submerged.

The woman, whose voice could be heard by the men in the vestibule, said, "Are you ready to recite the benediction?"

"I am." Sara let her hands float atop the water. She felt as though she were in the womb, ready to be reborn, the child of another mother.

"Blessed art Thou, O Lord, our God, King of the universe, Who hast hallowed us with Thy commandments and commanded us concerning immersion."

Sara's voice was full and clear. She imagined herself being reborn beneath the swirling water as Helene's child. Only through Helene had she lived. Between them was a deep bond of shared suffering, and beyond that was the love that Helene had lavished on Sara as her only child. There was no memory of another mother, yet when she saw Gypsies on the street with their bright kerchiefs and full petticoats beneath long skirts, their wrist and neck jewelry jangling in mixed harmonies, she thought that her mother must have been like them. But when the Gypsies spoke to her, she did not understand them and did not feel one of them.

Helene had told Sara as much as she knew about her mother. Francesca had said that she was a pretty woman whose husband was a musician, that they had traveled with a band of Gypsies who wandered through Eastern Europe, that her mother had been pregnant when she and Sara came to Ravensbrück, and that she had died of infection shortly after the child was born. No one knew what had become of the child. The stories of her mother and of the Gypsies and of the dead brother or sister were all the past that Sara had, except for the darkness beneath the floor in Ravensbrück.

Sara had told David she did not remember, because she did not want to see the fright in his eyes that she had seen in other people's faces when she told them what she did remember. It was not such a terrible lie, telling David that she did not recall the horror.

"You may get dressed," said the woman, helping Sara up the steps out of the mikveh. When she had dressed, she was brought again into the vestibule, where the beth din, the pious witnesses, were waiting.

"I have witnessed that she has immersed herself in the mikveh and is ready to be questioned," said the woman.

Rabbi Theonikis said to the two men, "Sara is mentally and emotionally stable enough to take this step. She is an adult, having attained the age of twenty-two years. She has stated to me that there is no romantic reason she desires this. She does not do it for the purpose of marriage to a Jew, which would not be acceptable. I have pointed out the negative aspects of being a Jew, those being the persecution, the anti-Semitism, the difficulties of living a Jewish life in a Gentile society. I have also told her of the beauty of Jewish life. She has been taught about the Sabbath, about the Jewish home and the rituals of Judaism from birth to death. I feel that she is ready to be questioned."

One of the men asked, "Do you of your own free will seek admittance into the Jewish faith?"

"I do."

"Have you given up your former faith and severed all other religious affiliations?"

"I have."

"Do you pledge your loyalty to Judaism and to the Jewish people amid all circumstances and conditions?"

"I do."

"If you should marry and be blessed with children, do you promise to rear them in the Jewish faith?"

"I do."

"Your name, Sara, is like the biblical Sarah, which means 'princess.' You will now also have the name of Shayndel, which in Hebrew means 'pretty.'"

Sara nodded, feeling the tears beginning to flow down her cheeks.

"You may recite the Shema, Shayndel," prompted Rabbi Theonikis gently.

"Hear, O Israel: The Lord our God, the Lord is One."

Her voice was trembling. God would forgive her not telling Rabbi Theonikis of her love for David. God had guided her all her life. He had sent Francesca to her in Ravensbrück, and when Francesca had died, He had sent Helene. And He had made the darkness of the hole in which she lived bearable because of Helene's goodness. No, she would not blaspheme against His commandments, but hadn't Helene always told her that love was the thing that made us human beings, that joined us to others, that made life worth living?

Her voice was steady now. "And thou shalt love the Lord

thy God with all thy heart, and with all thy soul, and with all thy might. And these words, which I command thee this day, shall be upon thy heart; and thou shalt teach them diligently unto thy children, and shalt talk of them when thou sittest in thy house, and when thou walkest by the way, and when thou liest down, and when thou riseth up. And thou shalt bind them for a sign upon thy hand, and they shall be for frontlets between thine eyes. And thou shalt write them upon the doorposts of thy house, and upon thy gates."

XXXIV

Tonio and David stood in front of the building that headquartered the Mandelbaum Archives, the organization that coordinated the international hunt for Nazi war criminals. It had been a year since David and Helene had been reunited, and this was the first time that David would meet Elias Mandelbaum, the driving force behind the Mandelbaum Archives. Tonio pressed the buzzer of the modern gray building on the thirteenth-century *Ringstrasse* in Vienna. The day was cold and blustery, and Tonio blew on his hands as he waited for someone to respond to the buzzer. David stood behind Tonio and a little to the left and looked up at the windows of the five-story building.

"You will see nothing by looking up there," said Tonio. "They stay safely away from the windows."

David nodded and pushed his wool scarf more tightly into the collar of his jacket. Tonio touched the buzzer again. There was a two-second delay, and then the outer door opened. Tonio motioned for David, and the two of them walked into the small cubicle that was formed by the outer door and the locked inner door. There was the sound of static over a loudspeaker, and then a voice asked in German, "State your business, please."

"Tonio Katakis and David Gelson," said Tonio in a loud voice. "We are here to see Elias Mandelbaum."

There was another buzzing sound, and the inner door opened, and a man wearing a sweater and a handgun in a shoulder holster stopped them.

"A formality," said the man. "Raise your hands above your heads, please."

David looked at Tonio questioningly.

"It is a precaution," said Tonio. "Do as he says."

David raised his arms above his head, and the man with the gun patted his body looking for weapons. When the man had checked Tonio, he pointed toward the staircase. "The third floor, on the right."

As Tonio and David walked up the three flights of stairs, David asked, "Why couldn't we use the elevator?"

"The elevator is inactive. They can control the location of everyone in the building better by not having elevators moving between floors."

When they reached Elias Mandelbaum's office, he greeted Tonio warmly. "My dear friend," said Elias, hugging Tonio's big body to his own slender one. All the furniture was placed away from the windows. A loudspeaker monitor hummed atop a filing cabinet, its light static interrupted ocasionally by the sound of the footsteps of the guard in the downstairs lobby.

"Elias, this is David Gelson, Helene's son."

David and Elias shook hands. The older man's eyes gleamed with interest as he looked at David. Mandelbaum's head was almost bald, except for a few wispy hairs at the sides and at the crown, but he had a lush growth of gray beard that hung untrimmed almost to his shirt collar.

"So, David, I have heard much about you from your mother and Tonio. All good things. All good things." Elias stroked his beard and contemplated David's face. Then he turned to Tonio. "You didn't tell me what a good-looking boy he is."

"And intelligent," said Tonio, smiling at David's embarrassment.

"Ah, intelligence, Tonio," said Elias, "the main thing." Then, as if David were not there, "He understands the purpose of this visit?"

"We discussed it," replied Tonio.

"And he is willing to participate to the limit?"

"Ask me," interjected David, speaking in German.

Elias turned toward David, his face no longer jovial. "All right, then, I will ask you. Are you willing to participate to the limit of your abilities in this matter?"

"I am," said David in a clear, firm voice.

"Why?" asked Elias.

"Why?" David turned to Tonio for help.

"Tell Elias what you have said to me," prompted Tonio.

"All right, then. It is because of my mother's suffering, because of her pain when I was young. It is because I can't give her back my father and my sister, and because I cannot erase her time in the camps." He paused. "And it is for me, too. I must understand what happened." David's voice faltered.

Elias looked away for a moment, moved by what David had said. After a few seconds Elias turned back to Tonio. "You didn't tell me he speaks German."

"He speaks with Helene. Many things have come back from his childhood. It also comes easily for him. He has a natural linguistic ability."

"I see, I see. That is all to the good also, don't you think, Tonio, to have someone who speaks German?"

"Yes," replied Tonio, "it is all to the good."

"One further thing, Tonio," said Elias. "The matter of Helene. She is willing that he participate? Of course she is aware of the dangers involved, since they are the same dangers that we all face."

"She is aware of them. Helene is a stoic, Elias. You know that."

"Yes, good. Well, that is out of the way, then, and we can now talk about the details. Come, we will go to the archives room. The material is there."

David and Tonio followed Elias into the corridor and across the hall to a large room that was filled with book shelves and filing cabinets. "Please sit down."

Tonio and David sat down at a conference table in the middle of the room.

"Here we are," said Elias. He placed two file boxes on the conference table. Alongside the files he put two large reels of film in metal containers. He patted the files as he spoke. "Everything is in here, David. Read it and familiarize yourself with it. It is a complete dossier on Don Diego Manero, Franco's Minister of the Interior. I am told that you have met him, that you know him through Don Carlos Mendes de Salceda."

"Yes, I have met him many times, both in Barcelona and in Valdepeñas. He has visited Don Carlos there."

"Good. Before we go further," said Elias, "I must tell you that we have no suspicion that Don Carlos is aware of Manero's activities. But, of course, there is always the possibility that he may be more knowledgeable than he appears to be. Would that affect your work, knowing there is the possibility that Don Carlos may be involved?"

"I have thought about it," said David slowly. "No, because it would be impossible for him to be involved."

"How can you be so certain?" asked Elias.

"Because he is a man of God."

One of Elias' eyebrows went up. He had heard men described in that way before, and with the same conviction. But David's information tallied with his own. Don Carlos was said to be a fanatic, but a fanatic with integrity.

Elias sat down in a chair across from David. "Manero was trained in interrogation methods by the Germans during the Spanish Civil War. He was so efficient at questioning prisoners that he swiftly rose from police captain to commander of the Guardia Civil and then to the cabinet post he now holds. He is the Spanish link in the Nazi escape network. He moves Nazis and their money and stolen treasures in and out of Spain to various countries around the world. He believes himself safe from scrutiny in Spain. And Franco protects him. Franco lets no one question Manero's connections to the Nazis during the war." Elias interrupted himself and turned to Tonio. "The matter of the pamphlets and the shooting has been dismissed?"

"Everything has been cleared," replied Tonio. "Because of David's age at the time, and with Don Carlos' influence, all charges against him were dropped."

"Good. I want no complications in this," said Elias. "Now, David, tell me how you propose to get close enough to Manero to observe his methods."

"I know the meeting times and places of the Opus Dei. Don Diego Manero is a member. I'll observe the meetings as best I can without being seen. Don Diego also lectures at the university, which is a short distance from his home. I know the hours that he is in his office at the Interior Ministry. Throughout the day I will be able to follow his movements."

Elias laughed. "You were right, Tonio. He is intelligent." Then he said to David, "But not foolhardy, are you? This is not a childish game you are entering into. These men are clever and in deadly earnest."

"And I am in deadly earnest," said David, his eyes meeting Elias' eyes.

"Good. Then that is settled," said Elias. "As I said, study the dossier, the pictures of people who are suspected of being part of the network. We need to identify them, to discover the pattern by which men and money are moved across international borders and whose help is required to accomplish the operation. We want to know the mechanics of obtaining false passports, what the links in the Spanish bureaucracy are. There need not be any confrontations. We need you for a close-up look, an unimpeded view of their operations. I can't even be sure you'll find out anything. They have been so cautious that it was only by luck we discovered that Manero was one of the Spanish links in the network."

"I'll do everything I can," said David solemnly.

"I know you will," said Elias, equally solemnly.

He turned to Tonio. "Now for the films. I was able to get a copy of the war crimes trial of the Viennese People's Court in Vienna in 1949. Obersfehrin Ilse Blucher is very plainly seen in about five minutes of the film. But that is not the name under which she was tried. And for lack of witnesses the prosecutor was forced to let her go free."

"But she was positively identified as Blucher?" asked Tonio.

"Positively," answered Elias. "Now, the other film was taken approximately two months ago in Calgary, Alberta, Canada. It is a film of a woman named Patricia Williams. She is an assembler in a bottle factory. The face and hair are different, but our informant tells us that Patricia Williams, who is married to a Canadian postal inspector named Ray Williams, is in reality Obersfehrin Ilse Blucher."

Tonio stroked his lips with his fingers as Elias spoke. "You need Helene to identify her," he said quietly.

"Yes."

Tonio reached across and touched the containers of film. "This is very close," he said. "Helene has never been this close to her past before."

"It is always difficult in these cases," sympathized Elias. "It is never easy."

XXXV

Helene strolled down Las Ramblas, her purse on one arm, her shopping bag on the other. A crusty loaf of French bread stuck out of the top of the shopping bag, and beneath the bread was a honey cake. She felt no urgency to get home. Tonio and David would not arrive back from Vienna until late in the afternoon, and Sara had said she wanted to prepare the evening meal. She had told Helene that it was to be a special dinner.

"A beautiful living tree in your home," said the sidewalk vendor as Helene stopped to look at the potted plants that the vendor had arranged in a semicircle on his square of pavement at the side of the promenade.

"A tree is too big," protested Helene, smiling at the thought of carrying a living tree through the Gothic Quarter to the apartment. "A small bush would be nice," she said, touching the glossy leaves of the miniature gardenia bush. One of the buds on the plant was open, and as Helene's hand touched it, the fragrance of gardenia filled the afternoon air.

Helene paid for the plant, the vendor wrapped it in several layers of tissue paper, and Helene placed it carefully next to the bread in her shopping bag. She walked on down the promenade, watching the people, listening to the music of the caged birds that were for sale up and down the avenue. She felt like any other housewife out for an afternoon walk, perhaps to do some shopping or to pay a friend a visit.

Helene sat down on a bench near one of the bird stalls. She felt at home in Barcelona. She spoke Spanish well enough now and could make herself understood in Catalan. At times she felt perfectly normal, even happy. Tonio made her happy. David and Sara made her happy. She sat on the bench and thought quietly of her good fortune, of her happiness. If she sat just so, with the sun shining and the colorful plumage of the birds before her eyes, she would not look deeply into the dark, walled-off portion of her memory that stayed obediently, unobtrusively behind her happiness. People said she had magnificent self-control, power of will; they said it was nothing if not miraculous that after all she had been through, she was still able to make a new life for herself. She bent her head toward the tissue-wrapped gardenia bush and breathed deeply of its fragrance. Perhaps she was unusual. What would they have her do? She could not, like some survivors, let the dark pools of pain and longing and remembrance overflow and crush her. They must stay within their boundaries. She did not want any part of bitterness or revenge or hatred. She wanted justice done, not vengeance.

She stood up and began to walk again. David had survived. That was the miracle. The years lost must not be cried over. She would not do that to herself or to him. And she would not be fearful for his safety. And if she were, she would never show those fears to him. He was part of her life again. That was enough.

When Helene got home, the apartment was dark. Sara had been so secretive the past few months about the appointments that took her away for several afternoons a week. Helene walked into the kitchen and put the bread and honey cake on the table. A pot of food simmered over a low flame on the stove. Sara was home after all and had prepared dinner. "Sara," she called. There was no answer. Helene walked up the stairs to her bedroom. She took off her shoes and hung her coat up in the closet, and then she lay down on the bed and closed her eyes. She would rest awhile before Tonio and David came home.

Tonio's lips on hers woke her from her nap.

"I meant only to rest," she said, putting her arms around his neck and feeling the cold of the early evening on his face. "Did you accomplish what you wanted to in Vienna?" she asked.

"Elias gave me films for you to see, and he gave David the dossier on Manero and his friends."

Helene sat up and slipped her feet into her shoes. "Then it starts for him in earnest now," she said.

"I think he's prepared, Helene. He is a strong boy. He is a strong man. He will do well. He no longer questions the necessity of searching out and finding the Nazis in their hiding places. You're not afraid for him, are you?"

"No, I'm not afraid, but I don't want him to think that we are as cruel as those we look for," she said. "I don't want him to do vengeance in my behalf. It isn't healthy. I'll send him back to Don Carlos if I think that is what he is doing."

Tonio held his hand out to her. She stood up, and he pressed her to him, his wild hair mingling with her own. "He is your son, Helene," he murmured in her ear. "There is no question of that. There is nothing vengeful in him."

Sara was standing in the dark dining room when Tonio and Helene walked down the stairs. David stood at the door to the dining room, his back to them.

"It has begun to get dark. Why are the lights off?" asked Helene. David turned toward her momentarily. "It's Sara."

Helene dropped Tonio's hand and ran toward the dining room door. "She's all right," said David, stopping Helene's path at the entrance to the room. The table had been set, and there were carnations in a vase at the center of the table. Sara stood between two chairs and faced the table. A large white shawl covered her dark hair. She lit a match, and in the glow of the flame, Helene saw the outlines of a pair of brass candlesticks. The match licked the tips of the white candles in their holders, and Sara's face glowed serene and beautiful in the candlelight.

"What is she doing?" whispered David. Tonio walked up behind Helene and put his arms around her waist as she swayed momentarily in the doorway. "Do you feel all right?" he asked Helene in a low voice.

David turned suddenly. "Are you ill?" he asked his mother.

"No, no," she murmured, "I'm not ill."

David turned again to watch Sara, whose eyes were closed. She passed her hands, palms down, over the tops of the lit candles in a circular motion, as though drawing the fire toward her.

"It's the Sabbath, David," said Tonio. "In this way she is the bride of the Sabbath, greeting it, welcoming it into the house."

"Why has she done this?" asked Helene, turning in Tonio's arms to look into his face.

"You will have to ask Sara," he replied.

Sara placed the flat of her open palms against her eyes, and her body swayed from side to side. "Blessed art Thou, O Lord, our God, King of the universe, Who hast made us holy by Thy commandments and commanded us to kindle the Sabbath lights."

David watched in fascination. Helene looked at him and then back at Sara. She felt helpless, powerless. So Sara had spent all those afternoons with the rabbi, preparing to become a Jew.

Sara's prayers were over. She removed the shawl from her head, folded it neatly, placed it in a drawer in the sideboard, and then looked at David and smiled. Helene noted the smile carefully. It was sweet and not knowingly seductive, but her eyes shone with the reflected candlelight as she gazed at David.

When Helene walked out of the dining room, past the kitchen and into the office, Tonio followed and shut the door behind them. She sat down at her desk. "There was my answer," she said. "It is because of David."

Tonio bent over Helene. "Is that what makes you so angry, Helene?"

"I'm not angry. How can I be angry over such a thing? That she loves David?"

"Perhaps you're angry that she loves God," said Tonio quietly.

"She was with me in Ravensbrück, Tonio. She cannot love God." Tonio took her hand in his. The expression on Helene's face was one of confusion. "We were together in Bergen-Belsen," she said in dismay. "If I cannot believe in God, how can she, Tonio?"

Tonio shook his head. "She has to believe in something more than us, Helene. It is only a sign that what was dead in her has come to life again."

• • • • •

David and Sara talked all through dinner about her conversion.

"You're more a Jew than I am now, Sara," said David.

"Am I?" she asked.

"Of course," he said. "Now I can ask you all the questions I would ask Helene or Tonio."

"I would like that," she said.

Helene alone did not talk through dinner. When the meal was finished, Sara cleared the table, and Helene helped her in the kitchen while Tonio and David set up the film projector in the office.

"You're not happy over what I've done," said Sara after five minutes of silent dishwashing.

"I'm not unhappy. In some ways it makes me proud. But it was a foolish thing to do."

Sara turned off the water. "Why is it foolish?"

"Because you don't have to be Jewish. I have to be Jewish. David and Tonio have to be Jewish. You don't have to be. I want to spare you any pain that could come to you in the future because of it. You have suffered enough without adding this to your burden. And it accomplishes nothing in the end, because you are Sara and nobody else. Nothing changes."

There were tears in Sara's eyes. Helene put her arms around her. "Shh, Sara, don't cry now. Remember what I've told you, that you mustn't cry. All the sadness is past." She patted Sara's thick dark hair and kissed her forehead.

"I am a Jew," said Sara through her tears.

"Of course you are," said Helene, holding her close. "Of course you are."

The film danced unevenly on the screen.

"There, she is there," said Helene as Ilse Blucher's figure appeared on the screen. There was no sound track, only voiceless figures moving through the courtroom, lips forming soundless words.

How do I feel? Helene asked herself. After all these years, seeing her, how do I feel? The woman was young, blonde, her figure slim and athletic. She was wearing a pretty dress, a dress that a young woman would wear to go to work in an office. It came to mid-calf, and the long sleeves were banded in white to match the round white collar at the neckline.

David looked intently at the film, saying little. Helene's eyes followed the blonde through the film, not seeing anyone else but the slim young woman. "She murdered people for sport," said Helene without emotion.

Tonio looked at Helene. "Perhaps we should watch the film tomorrow."

"No, it's fine. Don't touch it," said Helene. "I want to see her face. I want to study it carefully. I never had the chance before to study her face this closely. It is a fascinating face, don't you think so, David?"

David nodded. Sara got up from her chair and came and bent over Helene. "I can't watch," she whispered, her eyes averted. "I remember too many things when I look at her."

Helene patted Sara's face without taking her eyes from the film. "It isn't necessary for you to see this."

"Good night," said Sara to David.

He looked up at her in surprise and smiled. "You're going to bed?"

"Yes."

"I enjoyed the Sabbath dinner," said David. Sara blushed and then left the three of them to watch the film alone.

The blonde woman in the film laughed a lot. Her teeth were always in evidence. Tonio came over to Helene's chair and sat on the arm of it. Helene felt her breath coming more easily with Tonio close by, where she could feel the warmth of his body next to her.

The film ended. David jumped up and rewound it, then placed the second reel on the projector.

"Elias says that this woman lives in Calgary, Canada," said Tonio as the film began to play. There were shots of a factory, of workers coming out. Then the camera closed in on the face of a woman. Her hair was dark, and her figure was stocky.

"It is eleven years later now," said Tonio. "Can you see any resemblance?"

Helene got up and approached the screen. "Can you stop it a moment, David?" she asked. The film stopped, and Helene stood staring into the face of the woman factory worker, her forward momentum frozen on the steps of the plant, her coat buttoned against the Canadian autumn, her mouth closed so that the whiteness of her teeth could not be seen. Helene stepped back from the screen and sat down again in the chair with Tonio next to her.

"Go on," said Helene.

The film continued. The woman was in a car now, a man driving. "That's her husband," said Tonio. "He's a Canadian citizen."

"It's so hard to know if it is her," murmured Helene. "She looks so different. People change. But perhaps there's been a mistake." Helene looked up at Tonio in alarm. "It could be a horrible mistake, Tonio. We could follow her and torture her as they did us, and maybe she is innocent after all. Maybe it is not Ilse Blucher at all."

"That's what Elias needs you for, Helene, to make absolutely sure."

Tonio watched Helene undress. He lay in bed, a cigarette between his lips, and watched her remove her slip and then her bra. Her body was young-looking, the breasts well shaped and full. Nothing of her past life showed on her body. Except for nights like tonight, nothing of her past life was evident in her personality either. She turned to look at him. She was standing nude, a quizzical expression on her face, still lost in the films, in the question of the stocky Canadian woman's guilt or innocence of the charge of being Ilse Blucher. "I keep asking myself how I feel about seeing her face again. I don't know whether I'm angry or sad, whether I want to hurt her, whether I hate her. It puzzles me, this mix of feelings that I'm having so much trouble sorting out."

She walked toward the bed, oblivious of the desire he felt for her when he saw her naked before him. He inhaled the smoke of the cigarette, let it out slowly, and then stubbed the butt out in the ashtray on the bedside table.

"You don't hate her," he said. He reached out toward her, his hand tracing a circle around one of her nipples.

She touched the back of his hand with her own. "I think what it makes me feel is alive, Tonio," she said. She leaned over him and kissed him, and his hand moved slowly down her stomach and between her legs. She shut her eyes and pressed against him. "Only when I'm with you, Tonio, do things become clear."

He pulled her toward him, onto his stomach. His legs encircled her body. "My Tonio," she said, kissing his face and his thick eyebrows. "How could we live without each other?" she asked, her body trembling slightly. His grasp tightened on her. He was within her now, exquisite sensation joining them. He had no existence separate from hers.

Afterward she lay atop him, her head resting in the bend of his neck. He caressed the smooth skin of her back.

"Things are always better after we make love with each other," she said. He smiled and smoothed the hair away from her forehead.

She was a living miracle to him. Not a day went by that he didn't think of the emaciated woman he had plucked from the refugee camp in 1945, who at eighty-five pounds was hardly bigger than the child whose hand she would not let loose.

"You salvaged me, Tonio, from the dung heaps of Europe. Did you know that, Tonio?" She kissed him on the lips. "The dung heaps."

"I told David that you weren't bitter, Helene. He couldn't believe that you could not be bitter."

Helene looked at him silently for a moment, and then she said, "I will not disappoint him, Tonio. I will not be bitter."

XXXVI

The Interior Minister, Diego Manero, was easy to follow. David set up a routine, as he had seen Helene and Tonio do. Certain days David followed Manero's movements during the daylight hours, to Manero's office off the Plaza de Cataluñia, to his favorite restaurant in the Barceloneta, to an apartment of a woman listed on the apartment registry simply as Matilde Aragón. On other days he followed him in the evening. Manero's evening schedules were more difficult to anticipate, and it was harder for David to keep out of sight. The people who crowded the streets and pedestrian walks during the day were scarce in the evenings, and he had to allow greater distances between him and the portly figure of the Interior Minister.

After three weeks of surveillance David had seen none of the men whose photographs and descriptions were in the cardboard folder that Elias Mandelbaum had given him.

"Keep your camera in your pocket, and when you get the opportunity, take his photograph," Tonio advised. "Whether you see someone you recognize or not, later, when the photographs are studied, there may be something in them that you were not aware was there at the time."

David followed Manero to Madrid. He sat on the train in the compartment behind Manero and his secretary. Nothing unusual occurred on the train trip, no one came from any other compartments to speak to Manero, and no notes were passed to him that David could see. When they arrived in Madrid in the afternoon, Manero and his secretary were met at the train station and taken by limousine to the Royal Palace. David followed by taxicab and managed to take a few pictures of Manero entering the palace portals before he disappeared inside. Manero emerged from the palace at six o'clock in the evening with a man whom David didn't recognize. Manero, his secretary, and the unidentified man got back into the limousine, and David hopped into a taxicab and followed them to the Hotel Wellington, where they went directly to the hotel's salon and ordered drinks. David checked with the clerk at the desk. Yes, the Interior Minister was registered at the hotel.

"Do you have a single room available?" asked David.

"*Una noche?*" asked the clerk.

David thought a moment. Manero's visit could be only overnight. His schedule tomorrow afternoon included the visit to Señorita Aragón's apartment in Barcelona. Manero had not missed his twice-weekly rendezvous since David had begun to follow him.

"*Sí,* only tonight," replied David.

The clerk gave him the key to the room, and David took the elevator up to his floor. He had brought nothing with him but his camera and shaving kit. He ran his hand over the stubble of his beard. He would shave in the morning. He lay down on top of the single bed, his arms behind his head, and he stared up at the ceiling. He was twenty-one years old. He felt very old and very wise. He no longer had the joyous, impulsive feelings he had had when he was in Valdepeñas riding his horse and trying to outwit Don Carlos. He felt himself bifurcated now, two people, a Catholic and a Jew. He had told Martita when he visited Valdepeñas in April that he no longer knew where he belonged.

"That is God's test for you," she had said.

On the same visit to Valdepeñas, Luisa had told him that she planned to marry a tavern owner in Toledo.

"I cannot wait forever for you to make up your mind," she had said as they lay in bed together in the small room in the Hotel de Valdepeñas. "This man cannot live without me. He tells me so," she had said, hoping to make David jealous.

"My life is different now," David had said.

"How is it different? You go away to Barcelona, and you come back as always to visit. Only now you stay in the Hotel de Valdepeñas instead of in the house of Don Carlos."

"That isn't what's different," David had said, surprised at the relief he felt that she was to marry someone else.

"I have no interest in your new life," Luisa had said, sitting up on the edge of the bed and pulling on her stockings. "But I tell you now, Juan, that when I marry Gilberto, I will not be able to sleep with you so easily."

David had stroked her soft back and smiled. "That isn't what you should say, Luisa. You should say that if I don't marry you, then you won't sleep with me at all."

She had looked at him, a puzzled expression on her face. "But why should I say that?"

It was too early to sleep. Perhaps he would go down to the bar and sit in a corner where he could watch Manero and his companions. Manero regularly ate dinner at nine-thirty in the evening, and he was able to consume many glasses of wine before dinner without becoming drunk. David looked at his watch. He got up and pulled the blinds open and looked out on the street. He thought of the photographs of the concentration camps that Tonio kept in albums in the apartment office. The evidence was there. How could one deny that it had happened? Since he had seen the photographs, David had begun to have feelings of guilt. Guilt that Helene and Sara had been there and he had not. Guilt that he could not really understand their experience, nor in any way make up for it. Not by giving up Catholicism. Not by becoming a practicing Jew. Not even if he married Sara.

He sat down in a chair by the window, folded his hands on his lap, and stared at himself in the mirror of the bureau opposite him. A handsome young man, Elias had called him. And intelligent. The week before, Sister María Blanca had sat with him in the cathedral after Mass, and she had asked him if he still felt the holiness of the liturgy.

"I feel it as I have always felt it. A peacefulness," David had answered. "But now I have begun to question also."

Sister María Blanca had waved his words away with her hand. "You will analyze your soul until there is nothing left of it, Juan. Peacefulness is a nice thing to feel at the Mass."

He had looked at her questioningly, wanting to gather into himself the serene faith that filled her to overflowing. "I live my life as a Christian now more than ever," he had said to her, trying to understand, "but I am a Jew."

"And our Lord was also a Jew. There is room in your heart for peacefulness, for love of the Mass, and for being a Jew."

"Don Carlos doesn't agree," replied David.

Sister María Blanca's black eyes snapped, and for a moment the same spirited look that Martita had was in her face. "Don Carlos is narrow in his thinking. His narrowness is like that of the Church leaders in the Civil War. He did not come from poverty as I did. He sees things in only one way. His way. If he were a true Christian, he would see things in many ways."

David had not thought that anything Don Carlos believed could really be of importance to him. But he missed the ramrod-straight little man with his passionately wrong-headed ideas. David had visited Don Carlos once in Valdepeñas. Don Carlos had received him cordially, but he had asked him nothing of his life. They had sipped a glass of sherry together, and Don Carlos had inquired after his health. The conversation had lasted little more than fifteen minutes, during which time Don Carlos spoke of the olive yield that year and of the unseasonably dry weather and of Graciana's difficulties with her arthritic hip. When David rose to leave, Don Carlos had remained seated. Graciana had limped painfully into the room and removed the wine glasses, and David had known that that was the end of the visit.

In the kitchen Graciana had embraced David. He could feel her tears on his neck. "You must come often. He feels your absence very much, Juan."

David had shaken his head. "He feels nothing."

David washed his face and put his suit jacket on. Manero might be getting ready to leave the bar. He must not forget why he was here in Madrid. Sister María Blanca was right. He must not analyze his life so much. He must not let his loyalty to Helene and Tonio make him feel that he must marry Sara because of what had happened to her at Ravensbrück. He adjusted his tie in the mirror and then dropped his eyes away from his image. When he thought of Sara, he felt a rush of passion for her, but there was something in him, a stubbornness that he could not confront, and it was that stubbornness that would not permit him to love her.

When David entered the bar, Manero and his secretary were sitting alone. David sat down at a table near the folding French doors. The secretary picked up her purse and a stenographic pad that lay on the table. She said a few words to Manero, and then she, too, left. David watched, waiting to see whether Manero would leave also. Suddenly Manero lifted his head and looked in David's direction. There was nobody behind David, nobody to his side. Manero was looking straight at him, and even at the distance they sat from each other, David could feel the hatred in his gaze.

"He knows I'm there, Tonio," said David when he arrived back at the apartment the next day.

"That sometimes happens," replied Tonio.

"But how can I find out anything if he knows I'm watching everything he does and everywhere he goes?"

"But he doesn't know that," retorted Tonio. "You give up too easily. You are a man of little patience. So he has seen you. So what? If he thinks you are after him for something important, he will just be more careful. And you must do the same. You must become more careful. Make sure he doesn't see you again. Do you understand? It is not in the watching, David. It is in his seeing you when you are watching." Tonio's eyes bore into David's. "Elias has entrusted you with a great responsibility. Can you do it?"

"I'm not afraid," said David. "I just feel that now he won't reveal himself."

Tonio shook his head. "No, David, you're wrong. He will reveal himself. Have patience."

That afternoon David arrived at the apartment house of Señorita Matilde Aragón. He walked up the stairs to the fourth floor and then walked to Señorita Aragón's apartment door and listened for the sounds of voices within. He could hear nothing. The *señorita* was alone and waiting for Manero. Today David had varied his routine. He had not followed Manero here and waited out on the street while Manero entered the apartment building and disappeared upstairs for two hours. He had come an hour early so that he already would be upstairs in the corridor when Manero arrived, and perhaps that way there would be an opportunity to catch a glimpse of Señorita Aragón from the inside corridor and to find out what kept the Interior Minister so faithful.

David walked back to the staircase, sat down on the steps, and waited. Soon he heard footsteps coming up the stairs from below. He jumped up and ran to the next landing, where he could see down to the fourth floor without himself being seen. The footsteps were light and made a rasping sound on the stair treads. It was not the heavyset Manero. David could see the top of the woman's head of black hair. He darted out of his hiding place at the upper landing, ran down the steps, grabbed Sara's hand, and pulled her up the stairs and away from the fourth-floor corridor.

"You shouldn't be here, Sara," he said, not wanting to lose his temper with her.

Her black eyes were innocent as they looked into his. "I haven't seen you all week. I want to keep you company while you wait."

"I'm not waiting for a train, Sara. This is very serious."

"And I'm very serious, too." She smiled conspiratorially and reached into her handbag, bringing out a paper-wrapped sandwich, which she handed to David.

He grinned at her. "You knew I was hungry. How did you know that?" he asked, biting into the cold-meat sandwich.

Sara touched her finger to her temple. "I can read your thoughts."

"Then tell me what I'm thinking," he teased.

"Let me see," she said, closing her eyes to think more deeply. She opened them again as though she had had a revelation. "You are thinking that when Señor Manero comes to see Señorita Aragón, I can knock on the door, and when *la señorita* answers, tell her that I have the wrong apartment; and while I have her attention, you can take her picture from the corridor."

"That is what I was thinking?"

"Weren't you?" she asked.

"No. It's too dangerous."

"You're afraid of what Helene and Tonio would say," said Sara, "but I think it's a good idea."

"I think it is, too," said David.

When the hour for Manero's rendezvous was a few minutes away, they heard the sound of the elevator stopping on the fourth floor and the metal clanging of the old-fashioned mechanism that opened the elevator doors, and then Manero's body came into view, his large belly swathed in a worsted double-breasted suit.

"He's brought her a box of candy," whispered Sara.

Manero took out a key and opened the door and disappeared inside the room.

"When shall I do it?" asked Sara eagerly.

"Now," said David.

Sara walked across the hall to the apartment that Manero had entered. David stationed himself against the wall across from the apartment. He took out his camera, ready to take the woman's picture when the door opened. Sara knocked on the door. After a few seconds the door opened. Sara had her mouth open, about to ask a question, when a man's arm reached out and pulled her into the apartment. David stared at the closed door. Then he dropped the camera and began to pound on the door with his fists.

The door opened. Sara was standing next to Manero in the sparsely furnished living room. There were three men sitting around a paper-strewn table, in addition to the man who had opened the door for David. All were well dressed. All were speaking in German. There was no sign of a Señorita Aragón.

David had never seen in anyone's eyes such fear as he saw in Sara's. She looked as though she might die of fright.

"Why do you follow me?" asked the Interior Minister in Spanish.

"You're mistaken," answered David. "I follow no one."

"You were in Madrid. I saw you there last night," said Manero. "And I've met you before. I don't remember where."

"Let my friend leave, and I'll explain it to you," said David.

"But we're not holding you or your friend," said Manero genially. "It is you who misunderstand us."

The candy box that Manero had had in his hand lay open on top of the paper-strewn table. Colored stones glittered in the cellophane compartments in place of chocolates.

David reached his hand out toward Sara. "Then we're leaving. Come, Sara."

Sara had closed her eyes and looked as though she might faint. "Come, Sara," he repeated. She didn't move.

David looked at the faces of the men around the table and the one at the door. If he were allowed to leave with Sara, he would remember their faces forever. He did not need the camera to record their faces.

"You have not told me why you follow me in Barcelona and then in Madrid also," said Manero. Two of the men at the table got up and walked toward David. One of them held him around the neck while the other one pulled his arm behind his back. There was a sudden wrenching movement and a flash of pain as the second man dislocated David's shoulder. David sagged forward, and Sara screamed as he fell to the floor. The man at the door ran toward her as the steady scream continued to come from her mouth. He put his hand over her mouth and nose and held it there. David was doubled over in pain on the floor. He couldn't move his upper body. And Sara's screaming had stopped.

"Who are you?" Manero shouted at David.

One of the men bent close to where David lay on the floor. "*Jude,*" he shouted in David's ear before he broke his ribs with his boot.

"Don Carlos," David said through his pain. "Opus Dei, Don Carlos."

The boot was about to strike David's chest again when Manero shouted to the man in German, "*Lass ihn zufrieden.* Don't touch him."

Doors slammed. Men ran through the apartment gathering up boxes. David could see the men's shoes moving back and forth across his field of vision. Nobody was paying attention to him any longer.

"Opus Dei," said David again, savoring the words as a life-giving talisman, and then he fainted.

• • • • •

"It's the shoulder," said David, lying very still, his eyes dark with pain. Sara sat on the floor next to him, holding his hand while Tonio looked into his face, talking to him from his crouched position on the floor.

"They'll be back," said Helene, turning away from the window and kneeling down beside Tonio. "We're lucky to find you alive," she said, a look on her face that David had never seen before. A hard look, as though she had removed herself spiritually and only her physical presence remained.

"It's my fault, my fault," said Sara, holding David's hand and crying.

"It is no one's fault," retorted Tonio. "It is the risk, that's all." He turned to Helene. "If you hold his other shoulder, perhaps I can move this one into place so that he can walk."

Helene nodded. "We must take him away from here, and no ambulance or doctor. It is the only way. Manero has many friends in the militia. If they find David, he will simply disappear forever." She moved her face closer to David's. "You will have a lot of pain if we do this, David, but you cannot stay like this. We must get you out of here before they return." David nodded and held Sara's hand tighter.

"I'm ready," said Helene as she moved to David's other side and grasped his arm and shoulder in her strong hands.

The pain radiated from the ribs through the shoulder joint into David's head as Tonio pulled on the dislocated shoulder.

"No," screamed David at one point as the socket resisted receiving the shoulder joint.

"A moment more," said Tonio, perspiration running down his forehead. "I feel that it's ready to slip into the socket. Bear with me, David."

Tonio waited a few seconds, watching David's face for signs that he was ready to try again. David closed his eyes and then opened them and blinked the perspiration away. "Go on," he said.

"Brave boy," said Tonio as he took hold of David's arm again.

"I feel it tearing," said David, breathing rapidly.

"No, it has not torn," said Tonio.

"Aaaah." David screamed as his shoulder moved past bruised tendons and torn ligaments and slipped into the shoulder socket. Helene released his other arm and leaned over David and wiped his face with the hem of her dress.

"Rest a minute," she said. "Then we'll help you up."

David rolled carefully onto his back. He touched his right shoulder with his left hand, not moving his neck in either direction. "It feels numb."

"That's to the good," said Tonio. "Numb means that we can get you to your feet."

After a few minutes of lying on the floor on his back, staring up at the ceiling, David reached toward Tonio with his left hand. Helene and Sara put their arms around David's waist, and gently Tonio pulled David to his feet. The two women held fast to him as he stood between them, unsteady on his feet.

"Your job is over for now," said Tonio as they walked David slowly to the door of the apartment.

David winced in pain with each step, now feeling the pain of the broken ribs.

"He cannot stay in Barcelona," said Helene.

"What do you mean?" asked David through his pain.

"She means that you cannot stay in Barcelona," said Tonio. "She means that it's too dangerous now for you and for us to have you remain here."

David asked no more questions. Helene and Tonio would do with him what they would do. He could concentrate now only on bearing the pain of his injuries long enough to help remove himself from the apartment. Suddenly Germans and Nazis had become very real and personal to him. The man who had kicked him had called him "*Jude.*"

Helene opened the apartment door while Tonio held David upright against him. David glanced at her. He did not know her at all, so impersonal and strong had she become at this moment. Sara walked ahead of them down the corridor. Helene was back at David's side to help carry him out of the building. Life was making up its mind for him, he thought as his feet stumbled along with their help. Tonio and Helene and events would carry him with them, no matter whether he agreed or not.

XXXVII

The doctor in the Hospital of the Foreign Colonies in Barcelona taped David's ribs and examined his shoulder. "Ribs and tendons heal quickly in young men," the doctor said.

"Will he be able to travel?" asked Helene.

The doctor looked puzzled. "And where will he travel to, *señora?* He is certainly not able to venture too far. His body has been badly bruised and beaten."

"Is Valdepeñas too far?" she asked. David was startled, but Helene was listening intently to what the doctor had to say and did not notice the expression on David's face.

Later, in the apartment, while Helene packed, David asked, "Then we are going to Valdepeñas?"

"We are going to Valdepeñas," answered Helene. "It's all arranged."

Helene and David had a sleeping compartment on the train. David lay in the bed and looked out the train window at the passing countryside, dark and rainy, the storm clouds hanging over the plain in jumbled swirls of gray.

"Are you hungry?" asked Helene as the train descended into the plateau country of southern Spain.

"No," David replied, not turning away from the window.

"Then you're angry with me," Helene said. "You haven't spoken for two hours."

"I'm not angry," said David angrily.

Helene moved from the train seat and sat on the edge of David's bed. "You think that I treat you like a child, perhaps, that I wish to banish you, to send you back to Valdepeñas and away from Barcelona because I fear for your safety and because I'm your mother and naturally fearful. It is not so," Helene said. "It is that you have not had the experience I have had with the people who beat you in Barcelona. What they did to you, David, was a love kiss, a gentle tap, a sweet warning. You think that it was merely an isolated incident, never to happen again." She turned David's face toward her own with her hands. "Look at me," she said. "If you were a stranger to me, I would say to you that your life is in danger, that you have entered into the jungle and that you don't know the nature of the animals that will stalk you there. That will want to kill you there. I do not shelter you because you are my son."

He looked into her eyes, at the coldness in them as she spoke, and he saw Ravensbrück mirrored there.

"But I feel that I am a man now and able to take care of myself," he said, his tone softer.

"You *are* a man," she said emphatically. "A young one. I want you to live to be an old one."

Martita and Helene walked the path behind the cottage toward the olive groves. Martita pointed toward the house half hidden by the olive trees. "The house of Don Carlos, where Juan lived when he left my house. And the fields to the left, where Don Carlos taught Juan to ride."

Helene listened to Martita's words, and every once in a while she turned to look at the dark-haired woman who walked beside her.

"Juan can stay here with me as long as he must. He is a son to both of us, eh?" Martita laughed a little nervously, feeling strangely ill at ease with the well-dressed city woman.

"He is a son to both of us," replied Helene seriously.

They stopped at the rough fence that enclosed Don Carlos' fields. Martita put one foot up on the rail and leaned her buxom upper body against the top planks of the fence. "Do not think that because we live in Valdepeñas and the harvest is harvested in the autumn and the rains come with some regularity, there is no tragedy here. There is tragedy. My husband was killed in the Civil War. My brother was executed by Franco. Luisa and Isabel and I almost died of starvation."

Helene looked out over the fields in the same direction as Martita's gaze. "I know you suffered. David has told me."

Martita chuckled. "To you he is David. To me he is Juan."

"He is still the same son," said Helene.

"What pain you must have had when you gave him up to the Church, eh?" asked Martita.

"Great pain," replied Helene.

"You were wise. Many times I have thought of the wisdom of your actions and marveled at your thinking in such a time of crisis."

Helene turned to look at her. "You marvel at me, and I look at you with a gratitude that I cannot express."

Emotion closed Martita's throat. She coughed loudly. "And now he's in danger again, and you bring him to me yet again."

"I bring him to you again," repeated Helene. She felt a great love for the other woman. She could not explain it, even to herself. She touched Martita's rough hand with her own smooth one, and then their arms were around each other, and they clung silently together, each coping with her own feelings, not talking. After a few moments they moved out of the embrace, but now there was a palpable sense of communion between the two of them. They had joined together, both of David's mothers.

Helene looked up at the grand house beyond the olive grove. "What kind of man is Don Carlos?" she asked, breaking the silence.

"He is not a bad man," answered Martita. "He is not like the others, although he would seem to be at times. He is a useful man to those who know the way of him."

"He raised David well. I'm grateful to him."

"Tell him so," said Martita.

"I don't know that he would welcome me in his house," said Helene. "I will do nothing that would make him uncomfortable."

"Do you fear him?" asked Martita, a sly look in her eye.

Helene turned, her back against the fence now. "I have not come to Valdepeñas to see Don Carlos. I have come to hide David from the Nazis once again."

Martita waited for a reply.

"No, I do not fear him," Helene answered.

Graciana showed Helene into Don Carlos' study, and while she waited for Don Carlos to appear, Helene walked slowly past the rows of books on the shelves, stopping every once in a while to pick up one of the leather-bound volumes and leaf through its pages. One in particular interested her. She carried it to the window, where she could read its yellowed pages in the morning light. *El Camino* (*The Way*) by Monseñor José María Escriv de Balaguer y Albas. "Obedience is the surest way. Obey your superior blindly. This is the way to holiness." She closed the book as she heard the door to the study open.

"Don Carlos," she said, standing where she was near the window.

Don Carlos bowed quickly. There was no smile on his pale face. She noted his quick movements, the stiff carriage of his elongated head on his slender shoulders as he offered her a chair. She sat down, the book still in her hands. She placed it on the dark mahogany pedestal table next to the chair.

"It is an interesting book," said Don Carlos. "If you would like, I will obtain a copy for you."

"I would like that," answered Helene.

"Why have you come to see me?" he asked, withdrawing the hand of friendship as rapidly as he had extended it.

"There are many reasons," Helene answered. "To thank you for being a friend to David."

"David? I know no David," said Don Carlos. "I know a Juan, a baptized Catholic, a child whom I raised to become a priest. I was deceived by Martita. She knew the true circumstances."

"I will not say I'm sorry, Don Carlos, because I'm not."

"Then you have come to gloat over my gullibility."

"No, no, that's not why I have come. David needs you as a friend now, just as he needed you before. Maybe more."

Don Carlos' face reddened. "I did not take him into my home out of friendship."

Helene looked up at the wall of books, searching for a way to pierce his armor. She looked at the book that lay closed on the pedestal table next to her. She picked it up again. "This is the book of the Opus Dei, is it not?"

"It is one of them."

"What does it mean to be a member?"

Don Carlos stiffened in his chair. "Why do you ask me questions? You have come here with motives that are not clear."

"I have no motives. I merely want to understand you. If I understand you, then maybe I will understand the others."

"What others?"

"The ones who attacked David and almost killed him."

Don Carlos' face contorted in anger. "We in the Opus Dei are men of God. We do not hurt, we do not kill. We serve God."

"Explain to me how you serve God, Don Carlos," asked Helene quietly.

Don Carlos hesitated, and then he said, "The Church of today is not the Church that it should be. The Jesuits of today talk of politics and land reform. Only we of the Opus Dei believe that the Church has an obligation to the faithful to return to Spain the glory that was hers in the sixteenth century. We are the ancient Jesuits in modern dress, come to help restore what has been lost through secularism. When Spain locked her doors to the Protestant Reformation in the 1500s, the ascetic spirit that was the spirit of Christ in man asserted itself. On Good Friday thousands and thousands of hooded penitents, heavy chains at the ankles of their bare feet, would painfully retrace the route of Calvary in villages throughout Spain. It is that faith we will capture once again in Spain."

Don Carlos' words rang out in the high-ceilinged room. Helene waited a moment before she spoke.

"All of your members believe as you do?" she asked.

"All. We are in the world but not of it. We have renounced worldly gain for Christ's gain. Spain will not be great until liberalism and rationalism have been destroyed and we have replaced them with the blood and body of Christ," said Don Carlos with vehemence.

"There are Nazis within the Opus Dei," said Helene, watching his face closely.

"What?" He looked startled and confused, and then he muttered, "You speak nonsense."

"Interior Minister Manero was a member of Odessa when it was active in helping Nazis escape to South America," continued Helene. "Odessa ended in 1952, but its framework still remains in another form. It now calls itself the Kameradenwerk and deals primarily with transportation and safe houses for Nazis who are still trying to evade capture. David was following the Interior Minister in order to learn who his other contacts are within the organization. It was Interior Minister Diego Manero and his friends who attacked David."

Don Carlos' finely chiseled jaw grew slack. "It isn't possible."

"It is possible, Don Carlos. It is also a fact."

Don Carlos' shoulders stiffened. "There are explanations," he said. "David has been in trouble before. He is a radical. He has radical ideas," protested Don Carlos.

"Interior Minister Manero is a Nazi, Don Carlos, whether David is a radical or not," said Helene gently, feeling that behind Don Carlos' imperious manner he was in acute discomfort.

"The war is over," snapped Don Carlos. "There are no Nazis."

"The war is not over," persisted Helene, "and Diego Manero is a Nazi."

Helene got up from her chair and walked toward Don Carlos. She held her hands out to him.

"You are very presumptuous," he said.

"I have had to be, Don Carlos. Please let me thank you for David's life with you."

Don Carlos looked as though he were going to turn away from her. Helene's hands remained outstretched toward him. He clenched and unclenched his thin fingers on his lap.

"I won't let you turn me aside," she said, and bending toward him she clasped him in her arms and held him to her. She felt him shudder slightly in her embrace. Before she let him go, she said in a low voice close to his ear, "Many people have helped David and me, Don Carlos, and I am unable to tell them what is in my heart, but I am here with you, and for all of the others who have sacrificed so that David and I might live, I give thanks to you, to your God, in all their names. There is no way to repay you, there are no words to thank you. You are a good man, Don Carlos, and you love David as I love him, and I know that you will not protect those who would kill the Davids of this world."

Don Carlos did not look up at her when she turned to leave. He was lost in whatever thoughts Helene had stirred within him.

XXXVIII

"Are you very cold?" asked Tonio as he and Helene sat in the rented car on the side street near the A-1 Bottle Company in Calgary, Canada.

"It's bearable," replied Helene. They had sat in the car for an hour during the height of the snowstorm, not wanting to miss seeing Patricia Williams as she exited the bottle factory at the end of the day shift. Now the snow had stopped falling, and the warmth of the idling engine was beginning to melt the blanket of snow on the hood of the car.

Helene rubbed her gloved hands together and then opened the dossier that Elias Mandelbaum had accumulated on Patricia Williams. She studied the pictures that had been prepared by a photographer who had spent a month in Calgary during the preceding autumn. Tonio watched out the left window while Helene was engrossed in the picture album.

"He has caught her in every possible situation," said Helene. "Here she is hanging clothes in the yard of her house. And another one of her and a man—I suppose her husband—walking past some animals in a cage. It must be a zoo of some kind." She turned the page. "He has photographed her face in every kind of light and at every angle."

"Do you recognize her?" asked Tonio, not turning his eyes away from the steps of the factory.

"If it is Blucher, she has dyed her hair," replied Helene.

"Easily done," said Tonio.

"And her figure has thickened." Helene turned the album sideways to study a photograph more carefully. "And she is very serious in these pictures."

"You remember her as happy?" asked Tonio.

"I don't know if it was happiness," answered Helene reflectively. "It was more of a joyousness, as in one who has found her perfect vocation." Helene rubbed her eyes with her gloved hand, letting the smooth kid leather rest against her lids momentarily, imagining she saw Obersfehrin Ilse Blucher before her across the muddy field of Ravensbrück, her hand on her hip, her blonde hair blowing in the afternoon breeze, her rippling laugh echoing across the years.

"A maniac, perhaps," said Tonio. "They, too, are joyous."

"No, not a maniac. Too controlled and disciplined for a maniac," replied Helene.

Tonio turned toward Helene. "How was it possible that you came back to me from out of that fire?"

She raised her eyes from the album to look at him. "I don't know," she said simply. He leaned toward her and kissed her, pulling her close to him. "Put your hands inside my overcoat," he said, "against my chest. It will warm you." He opened his coat, and Helene slipped her arms around his body, and the two sat there looking out the window toward the factory.

"How could it be the same woman? How could we find her here, working in a bottle factory, the wife of a postal employee?" asked Helene.

Tonio stroked her hair and said, "Where would you expect to find her now that her perfect vocation no longer exists?"

"Nowhere. I would like to think that it was all a dream, that it never happened," answered Helene. "And yet I know as precisely as anyone can know anything that she existed, that it all happened, and that it is possible you would not be able to tell her from anyone else."

"As David has found out," commented Tonio.

"Yes. But David still is outside it. He is fighting against the idea of evil as a living presence in the world. He plays games with it. Runs after it, theorizes about it, but when he is face to face with it, he minimizes its capabilities. He didn't want to stay in Valdepeñas. How could he believe that they wouldn't want to harm him further if he returned to Barcelona now?"

"He's young, Helene."

"And naive."

"Yes, but I see him learning all the time."

"I don't want his innocence to betray him," said Helene. "I don't want to discover that the weakness that existed in Maurice somehow is in his son also."

"He has not collapsed as Maurice did," responded Tonio. "He is strong like you."

"Then why will he not listen to me? He turns away when I tell him of the dangers."

Tonio kissed her forehead and wrapped his coat more snugly around them both. "You are both alike. He resists you because he knows that what you say is true. Have patience with him."

"I love him," said Helene. "I love you and Sara, but I love David in a way that is different. Not better or more deeply. More sadly, I suppose. There is nostalgia and longing and sorrow in the love that I feel for David. Since we have found him, my dreams are full of the camps. I relive each death as if it were David's. I visualize Miriam's sweet baby face as she lay dead alongside Maurice on a hotel bed in Rome, and I can feel Francesca's thin dying body in my arms in Ravensbrück and hear her last faint breath as she died, so soft a sound that it was hardly recognizable as a human breath at all. I had hoped that I was finally at peace with my dreams, but now I see that I am not."

"You associate David with loss, and even though he didn't share your experience, you expect him to understand what you understand," said Tonio.

"Yes."

"He can't."

Helene sighed. "I know he can't."

A whistle blew, and within a few minutes people began to exit the ugly brick factory building. Helene sat up, her attention on the faces and figures of the people who were walking down the steps and filling the sidewalks in front of the factory.

Tonio opened the car door, got out of the car, and stood beside it.

"The woman in the pictures," said Helene, pointing to a stocky woman in an old fur coat that reached almost to her ankles. The woman started to wrap a green scarf around her head, but not before Helene had seen her dark brown hair and her face—the same face that was in the photograph album.

Tonio opened the door wide so that Helene could get out. The woman walked along with the other employees, and Tonio and Helene fell into step on the sidewalk behind her. From the back Helene recognized nothing as familiar; she saw merely a heavyset middle-aged woman on her way home from her factory job.

The sidewalk was slick with frozen snow. The people hurried along, jostling one another as they rushed to get out of the cold, some heading to the parking lot behind the building, others to cars that waited at various places up and down the street. Helene moved slightly ahead of Tonio and started to pass the woman. As she did, her left shoulder touched the woman's arm. The woman looked in Helene's direction, no sign of recognition in her blue eyes. But she had been startled by the bump of shoulder against arm. The pavement turned to ice, the woman's shoe slipped on the glassy surface, she was falling to her left, reaching her hand toward the sleeve of Helene's coat. Tonio caught Helene in his arms as she started to go down with the woman onto the frozen snow.

A few people stopped, but Tonio knelt down to where the woman sat, her leg twisted beneath her. Helene picked up the woman's purse, which had slid a few feet down the pavement. She handed it to the woman.

"*Danke,*" said the woman. Helene backed away from her. Tonio looked up at Helene's face, then back to the woman's. There was only pain on the woman's face, nothing more.

"Do you think you can stand up with my help?" asked Tonio in German.

Now there was more than pain in the woman's face. The blue eyes darted from Helene to Tonio.

"No, no, I can get up myself," she said in heavily accented English. She got to her knees and slowly stood up, breathing heavily from her exertions, her cheeks red from the cold. She and Helene stared at one another for a few seconds.

Then the woman smiled, showing her even white teeth. "I am a Canadian," she said. She brushed the snow off her fur coat and turned and walked away.

The next day was bright and clear. Tonio and Helene parked again at the same location, and when the factory whistle blew, they got out of the car and waited until they spotted the woman coming down the steps. Then they followed her along the sidewalk for a while, and when the crowd of people had thinned, Tonio moved to her left side and Helene to her right.

"You have no right to harass me," said the woman. "My name is Patricia Williams. I'm a Canadian citizen. My husband is a Canadian citizen. We have done nothing wrong. We are entitled to live in peace in Canada."

"Your name is Ilse Blucher," said Helene. "I know you from Ravensbrück."

The woman stopped walking and turned to Helene. "Leave me alone. You're a liar. I have told you who I am."

"You have changed your face with surgery," said Helene, "you have dyed your hair, but you are Ilse Blucher."

"Where is your proof?" demanded the woman.

"My proof is that you stand here and deny it," said Helene.

The woman's face showed no fear, only arrogant self-assurance. "Who are you?"

"It's cold here," said Helene, ignoring the woman's question. "Let's walk to the café at the corner. We can talk there."

"Jews," said Ilse Blucher, "are all the same. They follow me, take my picture, badger me on the street, but they are ineffectual; they have no power over me." Her tone was conversational as they sat at the rear table in the white-tile-floored café, cups of steaming hot chocolate in front of them.

"I have power over you," replied Helene in a low voice.

"You? What connection do you have to me?"

"I was at Ravensbrück. I am a witness."

Ilse Blucher blanched, the red color in her cheeks disappearing suddenly. When she spoke, her tone of voice was conciliatory. "You see, I am only a woman who wants to live her life in peace here in Canada. I have no quarrel with anyone anymore. My life is changed. I attend the Lutheran Church here with my husband. My neighbors think well of me. My employer at the factory is satisfied with my work. The Canadian government will protect me. I hardly remember the past."

"I remember the past," said Helene. "You will not enjoy the luxury of forgetting. I'm here to remind you. Others will be here also to remind you."

"The Cold War is ending," said Tonio. "Witnesses can be found to testify against you now. It won't be as it was in Vienna."

"There have been attempts to extradite me before," said Ilse Blucher coldly. "They have all failed. Why do you think you can succeed?"

"We have not talked of extradition," replied Helene.

"Then what do you want of me?"

"Explanations," said Helene. "We want to know the workings of the organization that arranged for your transit visa to Canada, who arranged for the safe houses you were taken to, how a passport was secured for you. We want to know all that you know."

Ilse Blucher looked at Helene suspiciously. "You haven't come on behalf of the War Crimes Commission?"

Helene shook her head. "Ours is an independent organization. We have no authority to arrest you or to detain you in any way."

"If I tell you what I know, will you leave me alone?"

"We'll leave you alone," replied Tonio.

"It's too simple," snapped Ilse Blucher. "It's Jewish trickery."

Helene's eyes were steady. Tonio glanced at her. There was no sign that Ilse Blucher or anything Ilse said was having any effect whatsoever upon her. She was calm and deliberate in her manner, giving no indication that anything that was being said touched her personally.

"I must have guarantees," said Ilse Blucher.

"That is not our province," said Tonio. "You have our word that we will not alert the authorities or put any pressure on the Canadian government to extradite you. Beyond that we cannot guarantee anything."

The woman thought awhile. She was pleasant-looking, eyes clear, forehead unlined, the features purposely indistinct, the product of the plastic surgeon's knife.

"I cannot," Ilse Blucher said finally. "It would mean my death. Better extradition than death at the hands of the agents in the Kameradenwerk."

Helene leaned forward on the white enamel table, listening intently. Tonio pulled a cigarette out of his pocket and lit it.

"I can't tell you anything more," said Ilse Blucher.

"There is one thing more," said Helene. "Count von Kirchner, Karl von Kirchner, where is he?"

Ilse Blucher's eyes darted nervously. "I have not seen the Count since I left Ravensbrück."

"But you know where he is, don't you?" persisted Helene, noting the woman's hesitation.

"I know nothing about where he is."

"Who does, then?" asked Helene. Ilse Blucher did not answer.

"I will stay in Canada," said Helene quietly. "I will take a house on the street where you live. Every day I will follow you to and from work, and every day I will ask you the same questions."

Ilse Blucher put her hands up to her ears to shut out Helene's voice. "It is impossible for me to remember that long ago."

"We have time," said Tonio. "Think about it."

Ilse Blucher looked longingly at the door to the restaurant.

"We know that Count von Kirchner had friends in Italy who helped him escape," said Tonio. "All we need from you are the names of those friends."

"All I can remember is that Count Ciano was a friend of his."

"Count Ciano was executed by the Italians before the war ended," snapped Tonio impatiently.

"Count Ciano had a villa on the outskirts of Rome," said Ilse Blucher.

"And what about Count Ciano's villa?" asked Helene eagerly.

The woman looked panicked. Tonio leaned toward her. "You have our guarantee," he said reassuringly.

"People stayed in the villa. It was a safe house. After the war they were taken to safety in the United States."

"Who?" asked Helene. "Who was taken to safety?"

"I'm not sure."

"Have you ever heard the names of Gunter and Erika Liebermann?" asked Helene.

Ilse Blucher stared at her. "I have heard the name Erika."

Helene felt as though her head would burst with the import of what Ilse Blucher was revealing. "Erika and Gunter Liebermann were friends of mine in Berlin," said Helene. "They had a million dollars in diamonds in their possession in 1939. Did Count von Kirchner ever tell you anything about them in connection with Count Ciano's villa?"

"I've said enough," replied Ilse Blucher.

"An address in the United States where we can find Erika and Gunter Liebermann?" prodded Helene. "Anything. Any information at all that you have about them."

"They can be found easily enough," said Ilse Blucher with a shrug. "It is of no consequence now."

Tonio stubbed his cigarette out in the ashtray. "It is of consequence to us."

"I will have to find the address," said Ilse Blucher.

"When?" asked Helene. "Tomorrow?"

"It will do you no good to have it," said Ilse Blucher. "They won't lead you to Count von Kirchner."

"We'll determine that for ourselves," said Tonio.

"Then tomorrow," said Ilse Blucher. "I will have it for you tomorrow when the shift is ended."

The next afternoon, when her work shift ended, Ilse Blucher met Tonio and Helene in front of the A-1 Bottle Company and handed them a piece of paper with the address of Erika and Gunter Liebermann, as she had promised.

"You won't bother me again?" asked Ilse Blucher.

"We're through with you," replied Helene.

The following morning a picture of Ilse Blucher was on the front page of the *Calgary Tribune.* The headline alongside the picture said, "Nazi Criminal Evades Extradition," and the story accompanying it read:

> Patricia Williams, a Canadian housewife, has been identified as the infamous Ilse Blucher of Ravensbrück concentration camp in Germany. Mrs. Williams has been implicated in the murder of 12,000 women and children prisoners during World War II. Mrs. Williams, the wife of a Canadian postal employee, has been the subject of several unsuccessful extradition attempts instigated by the U.S. Justice Department's Office of Special Investigations in Washington, D.C. It has just come to the attention of the Calgary Tribune that Mrs. Williams' entry into Canada was secured through false statements on her application for immigration.
>
> When advised by the Calgary Tribune of the crimes alleged to have been committed by Mrs. Williams, Donald Berg of the Canadian Department of Immigration said, "Mrs. Williams' entry into Canada is being looked at closely, since it has been brought to our attention that there were falsehoods on her application for immigration. If it is true, as the Calgary Tribune has informed us, that Mrs. Williams was tried in Vienna in 1949 for war crimes and that she concealed that fact from the Canadian government when she applied for entry into Canada, then it is possible that proceedings leading to the deportation of Mrs. Williams will be instituted.

The airport lounge was crowded, and the Canadian officers kept Mrs. Williams in an adjoining private waiting room. Newspaper reporters and newsreel cameramen milled around in the lounge, waiting for a glimpse of Mrs. Williams and her husband. When the flight was finally announced, everybody rushed toward the door of the private waiting room. In a few seconds the heavy figure of Ilse Blucher emerged, an officer on each side of her. Her husband walked behind her, accompanied by two lawyers. The reporters shoved microphones and cameras at Ilse Blucher as she passed by.

"Ilse, over here," shouted a reporter from *The New York Post.* "How do you reply to the charges that you kicked and trampled old women to death and helped to select the women and children who were to go to the gas chambers?"

As Ilse looked up, the flashbulbs went off, and the cameras whirred. She blinked rapidly but did not answer.

The man from *Movietone News* ran after Mr. Williams and the two lawyers as they followed Ilse Blucher up the ramp to the plane.

"Do you have a comment on your feelings, Mr. Williams? Did you know about your wife's past when you married her?"

Ray Williams turned around, his face purple. "She's a good woman, a fine wife. If she did anything, then it needed doing."

The reporter bore in closer, the camera up against Mr. Williams' bland face. "You mean that the women and children deserved to die?" asked the reporter. One of the attorneys tugged at Mr. Williams' jacket and tried to pull him along up the ramp.

"I mean that it's the goddamn Jews who are behind this. My wife is a fine Christian woman who is being persecuted by an international conspiracy of wealthy Jews."

The attorneys had Mr. Williams firmly by each arm now and were walking him rapidly away from the reporters. "Vultures," Mr. Williams shouted at them over his shoulder. "Goddamn vultures."

In April David was fully recovered from his injuries. Tonio arrived in Valdepeñas on a fragrant spring day.

"I'm restless," said David as he and Tonio walked through the budding olive groves.

Tonio put his arm around David's shoulder. "You have been very patient."

David looked at him. "I'm returning to Barcelona, then?"

Tonio shook his head. "Not yet. First we need you to do something very important for us." The red earth was spongy beneath their feet as they walked. David studied the fissures that the irrigation water had created in the soft loam.

"I'm ready," said David.

"We want you to visit a family in the United States. The Liebermanns. Helene has told you about them."

David nodded, remembering everything that Helene had said about what had happened in Italy, about Gunter and Erika and Count von Kirchner.

"Helene has sent a letter to them about your arrival. She has told them simply that you need to leave Spain for political reasons."

David looked at him. "But that isn't the reason, is it?"

"No. You'll be gathering information. We want to know by what means they escaped Europe," said Tonio. "This is as important as your surveillance of Interior Minister Manero was. The Liebermanns may have a connection with the Kameradenwerk. That may have been how they were able to get to the United States. If so, you can see how invaluable your trip would be."

"But the Liebermanns aren't Nazis."

"No, but they could possibly lead us to others who are."

"You don't think they will suspect why I'm there?"

"I don't think so. I think you're clever enough not to reveal yourself. What happened to you in Barcelona has taught you much, I'm sure."

"I'm ashamed that it happened at all. It never should have. And because of it Sara was in danger as well."

"Barcelona was the beginning of your gaining wisdom, David."

"Does my mother want me to go to the United States?" There was a wistfulness in the question.

Tonio stood back and looked at David, tall and healthy, both shoulders straight and strong once again. "Helene worries that you don't understand her. She doesn't want you to do this if you feel that you can't. She doesn't want to force you to do anything against your will."

David put one foot up on the fence rail and then swung his body so that he was sitting atop the fence. "I feel sometimes that I'm not her son, that perhaps Sister María Blanca was mistaken, that it was another child who was left on the bench." David looked out over the green fields.

"To become someone's son takes time," said Tonio. "Will you go?"

"I'll go."

"Helene in her letters has attempted to re-establish the friendship she once had with Erika Liebermann," said Tonio. "To write to Erika and her husband took a great effort on her part, and she hopes that you can disarm them further when you're there. Your mother has told me that she thinks you have great charm."

David looked at him curiously. "She said that?"

Tonio smiled. "Yes. She says that your charm reminds her of her grandmother."

David blinked rapidly. "She doesn't say things like that to me."

Tonio patted him on the shoulder and then walked closer to the fence and put both of his strong arms on the top post. He breathed deeply of the sweet spring air. "Another spring, David. Was there ever such a promising time as spring?"

April 2, 1956

Dear Erika,

I have tried to locate you for several years, and I'm sure that your mother told you of my visit to her in that regard. Despite my assurances that I bore you no ill will, she would give me no information about you. I fully understand and appreciate her protectiveness toward her only child. It was through other means that I finally secured your address in the United States. My fond memories of our friendship in Berlin and of our years as musicians together prompted me to try to find you. Do you still play the piano and perform? I, who once could not live without music, no longer play.

I hope that through this letter the fear and mistrust that has existed between us for seventeen years will come to an end.

Helene

April 10, 1956

Dear Helene,

All these years I have hoped that one day we would be at peace with each other. There is nothing that has been in my heart more. Whatever happiness I feel in my family has always been shadowed by feelings of guilt over your fate and that of your family. When Mother told me of your visit, I was overjoyed to hear that you were alive and well.

Gunter and I live a very isolated life here in Arizona. Alexa is away at boarding school part of the year, and it is then that I wish we did not live so far from a city. Gunter has been changed by his experiences in the war and wants no company but mine. It is a difficult life at times, but I must not complain. Do you remember the movies we saw when your grandmama thought we were at our piano lessons? Does it seem as far away to you as it does to me?

You told Mother you wanted to locate Karl. I can give you no information as to the whereabouts of Count von Kirchner. I'm sorry.

I kiss you and hug you, my dear friend.

Erika

April 21, 1956

Dear Erika,

I have no desire to punish you for the past. I want nothing more than to be at peace with it. As for Gunter, I, who shared the camp experience, can understand perfectly well what his feelings are, and I will not inflict any more suffering on him.

If you say that you don't know the whereabouts of Count von Kirchner, I will accept that as the answer I was seeking from you.

When I visited your mother, I wasn't aware that my son David was alive. Now we have found each other again after all these years of separation, and I cannot describe the joy I feel. There is sorrow for what has been lost, but no longer any hatred for anyone. We have Sara, who is a daughter to me in every way. She was in Ravensbrück with me. She has converted to Judaism, a religion I have never consciously practiced nor really appreciated. Her conversion astonishes me, and yet I understand it, too.

Tonio and I plan to send David on a trip to the United States. It is the last refuge I have for my son at this moment. Barcelona is not hospitable to young people such as David, who are filled with a longing to change things. We were sisters, Erika. The past is the past. My love for my son erases whatever bitterness I once felt over your actions in Italy. Let David stay with you for a while, and perhaps those in Spain who would do him harm will lose interest in him.

I'm sure you will not turn my plea to you aside.

Helene

1956: Katie

XXXIX

The sound of the tractor awakened Katie from sleep. She rubbed her eyes with her hands and yawned, not wanting to get out of bed yet, wanting to savor a few more minutes of sleep. But the unaccustomed roar of the tractor's engine reverberated through the still morning air and was magnified in the vast noiselessness that existed beneath the parapets of the canyon walls.

"I give up," she said aloud. She reached for her bathrobe on the chair next to the bed, put it on, and then walked to her father's bedroom. The door was open, and a note lay on the Indian blanket that covered the iron bed. "Gone to Williams to pick up Senator Lacey. See you at supper."

Katie dropped the note on the bed, went into the cramped bathroom of the wood-frame house, and washed her face and brushed her teeth. She used her fingers to pat down the honey-blonde curls that were cut almost to her scalp around her face and which, despite frequent wettings and pattings down, insisted on forming ringlets around her tan face. The long braid she wore down her back had come loose as she slept. She pulled the strands apart, and peering with blue eyes half-closed into the medicine-cabinet mirror, she rebraided the wavy hair. Then she went into the kitchen and put a slice of bread into the toaster and poured herself a cup of coffee from the enamel pot that sat simmering on the stove. She sipped the coffee in a daze, not yet awake. The April tourist calendar was thumbtacked to the cupboard door over the sink. "Monday, April 18, Levine group in. Three adults. One elderly, but can ride: Elgin. Thursday, Levine group out: Elgin. Friday, April 22, pick up Senator

Lacey at train station in Williams. Monday, April 24, Yuba City Boy Scout troop in. Eight and scoutmaster: Roscoe."

A light knocking on the window above the kitchen table interrupted Katie's reading. She looked up to see Lee Jones' face staring back at her, unsmiling, his straight black hair falling forward under an Indian headband, a lightweight T-shirt on his slight but muscled upper torso. They stared at one another for a few seconds, then Katie downed the rest of the coffee in her cup and rinsed it out in the sink. She took the slice of toast out of the toaster and spread it thickly with the peach jam that sat in a covered crock on the sink-top. When she opened the kitchen door, Lee was sitting on the stoop, hunched forward, drawing pictures in the red dust with a willow stick. He turned, and Katie held out her hand with the heavily coated slice of bread flat on her palm.

"I have to get dressed," said Katie as he took the bread and began to eat. When she returned from her bedroom, wearing a checkered gingham blouse with a matching ribbon on her long braid and heavy cotton pants tucked into her riding boots, Lee had finished the toast and was standing waiting for her with his own horse and Mandy.

"How's it going, Mandy, huh?" Katie asked her horse as she patted her mane. Lee had saddled and bridled her and had brushed her coat until it glistened like the Indian's own hair. Lee held Mandy's rein of woven cloth in his hand while Katie mounted the horse. Taking the reins from him she whistled to Mandy, and the horse started a gentle canter through the dirt toward the freshly plowed fields that surrounded the small house. The shining new tractor that had been brought down the horse trail piece by piece and reassembled in the village sat at the edge of the field, silent now, while two unbridled horses nibbled at the grass and weeds that had been turned up in the early-morning plowing.

In the morning sunshine the canyon walls were a rich red, and the air was filled with the smell of fresh earth and honeysuckle vine. Lee mounted his horse and followed Katie toward Main Street, the cottonwood-shaded dirt path that led out from the village toward Hualapai Hilltop. They passed the little white schoolhouse and the agency buildings.

The dirt square in front of the tribal council office was deserted, except for a few nondescript dogs that rolled in the dust and chased each other around the empty buildings.

"It's a great day, isn't it?" Katie said to Lee as they galloped side by side out of the village. If he answered, his reply was lost in the sound of the rushing waters of Havasu Creek. The canyon was still wide at this point. Mud-and-brush hogans sat out in the open fields. Closer to the trail were the pastel-painted wooden houses put up by the Bureau of Indian Affairs.

"Race you," shouted Katie as she spurred Mandy ahead through the dry wash at the end of the village. Soon the two of them were flying along the trail, Katie's laughter interspersed with the sound of Lee's clicking noises to his horse.

When they had ridden for two and a half hours, the trail narrowed, and Katie took the lead again. Mandy grunted and foamed as she picked her way carefully along the steep, rocky path. Lee was close behind, his horse's mouth occasionally brushing against Mandy's rump in an effort to take the lead away from Mandy.

"Look at him," Katie said with a laugh. "He won't keep his place. He thinks he can bully his way past Mandy."

Lee made a few more clicking noises, and his horse dropped back again into a plodding, steady gait. The trail continued its steep ascent for three more miles and then leveled off. After riding for four hours, they reached the end of the trail and were on sloping pastureland.

"Git, Mandy," said Katie. Lee rode close and slapped Katie's horse with a switch that he had taken from a low-hanging cottonwood tree. Mandy snorted once and then tore across the pastures, past the brook, and down the slopes of the Liebermann ranch.

Katie sat on the edge of the bed and watched Alexa as she sat at her pink-organdy-flounced dressing table carefully tracing her lips with cherry lipstick.

"You're only going to eat it all off at lunch," said Katie, her tongue following an imaginary glossy line on her own lips.

"It's the newest color at the Owl Drug in Flagstaff," said sixteen-year-old Alexa, turning to show off her bright-red lips in her sunburned face.

"I can't stay for lunch," said Katie, looking at her dust-covered boots.

"But you've got to stay. Daddy will be back from showing David the cow barns, and Mommy says you must stay. So you must, then," retorted Alexa with the logic of a spoiled child.

"I've only come to get a look at him, that's all," said Katie. "Lee is waiting with the horses near the brook. He won't come nearer to your house than that. And I can't keep him sitting there all day. Besides, I don't think your father would like it if I stayed."

"Pooh, you're my friend. Mother says what goes on between your father and my father is their business and has nothing to do with you. Has Daddy ever been nasty to you or said anything to make you feel bad?"

"No. It's just the way he looks at me. It makes me feel uncomfortable."

"Well, you shouldn't. He likes you. He's told me so a thousand times," said Alexa unconvincingly.

The door to the bedroom opened, and Erika stood in the doorway, dressed in a skirt and blouse, her gray-streaked blonde hair done up in a sleek pompadour. "Your father and David have come back," she said in her thick German accent. "Alma is taking the bread out of the oven now."

Alexa stood up and squeezed Katie to her. "Oh, I am so excited to see what you think of him." She closed her eyes and leaned her head back. "Oh, he makes me swoon just to look at him."

"Enough of that, Alexa," said Erika sharply. "You will stay and have lunch with us, yes, Katie?"

The house and its European furnishings and Dresden figurines made Katie shy and ill at ease. She felt confined when she was at the Liebermanns', and out of step, as though she had to say exactly the right thing or she would be turned unceremoniously out of the house. She worried that she might slip and mention her father and that Gunter Liebermann would be furious with her and say something mean about Will. Although Erika was unfailingly polite, Katie sensed that she felt exactly as her husband did about Will and that the dislike was transferred to Will's daughter.

"She's staying, Mommy. Tell Alma she's staying," Alexa insisted.

Erika nodded and shut the door again.

Katie came to the Liebermann house only because of Alexa. They had grown up the only white children for a hundred miles, and Katie's mother had taught them, along with the Indian children, until they finished the sixth grade. Then Alexa had gone away to boarding school, and Katie had gone to live with Peggy in Flagstaff.

"Don't look so serious, Kate. Smile. Nobody is going to bite you, I promise," said Alexa.

"What should I talk to him about?" asked Katie.

"Anything," replied Alexa flippantly. "He speaks English very well. I don't know how long he'll be here. No one says anything about it."

"How do your parents know him?" asked Katie. "I mean, did they ever live in Spain?"

"It's all so mysterious," said Alexa. "It has something to do with his mother and father and the war and all that stuff. Daddy says that David is in some kind of trouble and he owed David's parents a favor. And Mommy said that his mother was her dearest friend. Like you. I suppose if you had a son and he showed up on my doorstep, I'd let him stay for a while. At least until I got tired of him."

"You are a silly goose," said Katie. "What do you think the real reason is that he's here? Come on, you know more than you're telling."

"Real reason?" said Alexa. "Well, if you want to know what I think the real reason is, I think it's because he's a spy."

"A spy?" Katie laughed. "Who's he spying on?"

"Us. My parents. He asks me lots of questions. I don't mind, though. I like it."

"What kinds of questions?"

"Oh, who comes to visit the ranch, what Mommy and Daddy do out here all by themselves, stuff like that."

"That doesn't sound like spying to me," said Katie. "It sounds normal."

"Maybe. Maybe not. You asked me what I thought, didn't you?"

There was a murmur of men's voices in the hall, and Erika's high-pitched musical voice mingled with them.

"Just don't steal him from me," said Alexa as they walked out of the bedroom. "Remember, I found him first."

"Did you enjoy the tour of the ranch?" Erika asked David pleasantly as Alma cleared away the lunch dishes. Katie looked down at her hands in her lap. It was the second time Erika had asked him that question, but the conversation over lunch had been so awkward that she had probably forgotten which polite questions she had asked and which ones she hadn't.

"It reminds me of some places in Spain," said David. "It is dry there also. And the earth is also a rich red color as this is."

Katie had hardly spoken except to say, "How do you do," when she was introduced to David. She glanced at him furtively during lunch, assessing his good looks and his foreignness and the way he handled himself. He fit well in the Liebermann home, with his slacks, shirt, and tie, his black wavy hair combed neatly back, and his formal manners. He spoke English with an accent that was heavy but not like Erika's or Gunter's. He appeared to be comfortable, not intimidated by being a stranger, and in his ease and sophistication he made Katie feel like one of the Liebermann ranch hands who had wandered into the dining room by mistake. Only his eyes when he caught her looking at him were lively and seemed to say that he thought she was pretty.

"Katie rides beautifully," said Alexa while they ate their custard pudding dessert. "She flies over the desert and through the gullies just like an Indian."

"You live nearby?" David asked with interest.

"In Havasupai Village with my father," said Katie.

And as soon as the words "my father" were out of her

mouth, she saw the look on Mr. Liebermann's face, and she stopped talking. David saw it, too, thought Katie. Otherwise, why was he looking at her so strangely, as though he knew all the answers to the questions before they were even asked?

"If you were to see her on Mandy, you'd swear she had Indian blood in her," said Alexa, pushing past the impasse.

"I ride in Spain," said David. "I have ridden since I was ten."

"You have?" asked Katie, looking directly at him for the first time.

"I had an accident, and I have not ridden for a long time, but I enjoy it very much," he said.

"Would you like to ride to Havasupai some time?" asked Katie, feeling emboldened by his directing the conversation to her. Alexa fidgeted in her seat.

"With permission of Mr. and Mrs. Liebermann," he said, looking at Gunter.

"There is nothing to see in Havasupai Village," said Gunter. "There are only shacks and Indians and white men who are little better than Indians."

"Gunter," exclaimed Erika, a look of horror on her face. "Katie is here at your table."

Gunter nodded at Katie, who stared red-faced down at her half-eaten custard.

"Maybe we will talk about it another time," said David diplomatically.

"It is only a horseback ride, Gunter," said Erika, as though remonstrating with her husband for his rudeness to their guest.

"It is of no importance to me if he rides into the Havasu Canyon or does not ride into it." Gunter rose from the table, an imperious-looking man with an immovable quality about him. He walked out of the dining room.

"I think you ought to stay here," said Alexa to David. "Daddy's right. There's nothing much at Havasupai but horses and Indians."

Katie kicked her under the table.

"And Katie, of course," finished Alexa.

XL

The powwow at Frazier Wells lasted from dawn until the midday sun was high and blistering in the sky. Then the Indian women started the fires under their camp stoves and heated oil in large black pots to make the fry bread for the meal that would mark the end of the gathering.

"The Hualapai are blood brothers to the Havasupai," said Will, standing, his face flushed with excitement and intensity. "The Hualapai should speak for their brothers down in the canyon, who are being squeezed to death in the narrowness of five hundred eighteen acres. Before the white man came, the Havasupai were able to feed themselves. They didn't need our houses and our charity. They hunted the deer on the high plateaus and made their own deerskin garments. Now boxes of old clothes come from the Philadelphia Indian Society. Cast-off clothes to a proud people. This is a great canyon. There is room for the National Park Service and the hotels on the north and south rims of Grand Canyon. The Havasupai take only what they need from the land. They kill only to eat. They are preservationists. The Grand Canyon doesn't need outside preservationists to save the canyon from the Havasupai."

For a long moment Will looked around him at the mix of white and Indian faces. Then he sat down on the Indian blanket next to Senator Lacey in his brand-new Stetson hat.

"Very well said, Will," the Arizona state senator declared.

Katie leaned toward her father from where she and Lee and Elgin sat cross-legged on the adjoining blanket. She squeezed Will's hand, and he smiled back at her.

Darryl Wekogie, chief of the Hualapai, who had given the land on the high plateau as a meeting place for the powwow, now stood in the middle of the encampment, his arm upraised for silence. "It is the turn of the Grand Canyon Wildlife Preservationists," he said.

Gunter Liebermann stood up. The wind ruffled his thinning brown hair and plastered his linen shirt against his body. David sat near him on the ground, along with the men in the uniforms of the National Park Service. Gunter adjusted his glasses and looked around him for a few seconds before he began to speak.

"I have been accused of hating the Indian. It is impossible that I could hate Indians." He pulled back his shirt, exposing the blue numbers on his arm. "I know persecution and hate from my own experience. In my lifetime I have been hunted like an animal, and there were those who wanted me dead. In that way I am an Indian," he said, waiting for the effect of his declaration to settle over the crowd. There was a shifting of bodies on the blankets, but the Indians made no sound in response to his words. Gunter continued, his face impassive but his voice louder to compensate for the hot winds that had begun to blow over the plateau. Dust swirled up around his boots, and horses whinnied nervously in the background. "But there are many others who are involved here. There are those who speak for the Indians. I speak for the beauty of the Grand Canyon, for the animals and the plants and the trees. Without being restricted in their movements, the Indians will harm the terrain. And who is to say that they will stay in the canyon plateaus and not hunt on private lands? Who will police them?"

Will leaned toward Senator Lacey and in agitation said, "You see the crux of his argument, Senator? He doesn't give a damn about the birds and the animals. He wants to grab the private lands for himself. He's already bought two thousand acres this year to add to his existing ranch lands. If the Indians prevail, the land will be protected. He'll no longer be able to buy it for five dollars an acre."

"I see," said the Senator, stroking his handlebar mustache thoughtfully.

"We do not wish to persecute the Havasupai," continued Gunter. "We would propose that the government spend more money on them, even, than they are doing. Give them a subsidy to feed themselves. There is surplus food in government warehouses. Give it to the Indians."

There was no sound, not even the shifting of bodies on the blankets, only the rustling noise of grasses being riffled by the wind. Gunter stood silently now, looking into the stoic faces of the Indians on the ground before him. Katie turned toward Will, waiting to see if her father would respond to Gunter's words. Then she felt, rather than saw, Elgin slowly getting to his feet next to her. She turned to look at the middle-aged Indian, his face prematurely lined by the sun, his unplucked chin whiskers reaching to the top button of his checked cotton shirt. All faces turned toward him as he faced Gunter across the no-man's-land of the encampment. Katie could see no emotion behind the blackness of his eyes. His son, Lee, sat, eyes downcast, shoulders quiet, an alertness in the way he held his back, waiting to see what his father would do.

Elgin raised his arm to the sky. With his outstretched fingers he pointed toward the distant buttes of the canyon. Then he moved slowly in a circle, pointing to the trees and then to the canyon walls and then to the gorge beneath the plateau. Out of the stillness of passivity and the years of patience came Elgin's voice, sure and steady as the canyon walls themselves. "I am the Grand Canyon," he said to the wind.

"Daddy, this is David. He's visiting from Spain," said Katie. The pots were packed onto the horses, and there was the scuffling sound of boots and moccasins in the earth as the powwow broke up.

Will had been walking toward the pickup with Senator Lacey. He stopped and turned toward Katie and the tall, dark-eyed, serious-faced young man at her side.

"Weren't you with Liebermann?" he asked sharply.

"He's visiting from Spain, Daddy," said Katie. "He's never met an Indian before in his life."

"How old are you?" asked Will suddenly.

"Twenty-one years," answered David.

"Spanish Civil War, 1939. Were you there?" asked Will.

Senator Lacey looked uncomfortable with the conversation and walked on ahead to Will's pickup.

David nodded. "I was raised by a Spanish woman. But I am a Jew."

"You always tell people you're a Jew the minute you meet them?" asked Will, unbending slightly.

"Being a Jew is something new to me," replied David, feeling more relaxed as he saw Will's face soften.

"How do you know Liebermann?" asked Will.

"He and his wife were friends to my parents in Germany before the war."

"Did your parents survive?"

"Only my mother."

"Oh," said Will, seeing the entire scenario of David's life suddenly before him.

Katie took her father's arm. "I don't want to go back to Flagstaff today, Daddy. Lee brought Mandy up from the canyon this morning, and David has permission to ride one of Mr. Liebermann's horses. I promised I'd show him Havasu Canyon."

"Your mother'll worry," said Will, looking from Katie to David.

"You could call her from Williams and tell her that I'm staying awhile longer. Would you, please?" asked Katie cajolingly. Her father never refused her anything. He had learned indulgence of children from the Indians.

Will hesitated a moment, but the expectant look in Katie's face prevented him from saying no.

"Lee will be with you, won't he?" asked Will.

Katie turned around. Lee stood at the edge of the camp clearing holding the reins of Mandy and of his own pony.

"Yes," she said, turning to look at Will again.

"Then go ahead," said Will, bending his head to be kissed on the cheek.

"What did you think of the powwow, David?" asked Gunter as he drove the station wagon along the bumpy road back to the Liebermann ranch.

"It was an interesting spectacle, the coming together of two cultures in a truce of sorts."

Gunter laughed. "Yes, that is so, isn't it? Americans are very fond of confronting their enemies and talking with them. They believe that talk accomplishes much."

"It is better than killing one another," said David.

"I'm not so sure that we won't end up doing that, too, by the time this thing is over," said Gunter. "But, then, you know about politics. Your mother spoke of your involvement in the politics of Barcelona. Did that come to violence in the end?"

David swallowed before he answered. "Yes, it came to violence."

"So you have already learned that it is difficult to resolve differences peacefully."

"But I was not a committed activist in Barcelona," said David, "merely a compliant accomplice."

"That's what we need more of, David, compliant accomplices."

"But I am afraid I would not be on your side in a fight with the Indians."

Gunter glanced at him quickly and then looked back at the road again. "The Havasupai are a primitive people who have not learned to adapt to modern society. Problems arise in the dominant culture when that happens. I saw it personally in Europe. I am a casualty of it."

"Then you should have sympathy for them," said David. "Thomas Paine said that man does not enter society so that he may have fewer rights than he had before, but so that he can better secure the rights he has."

"Ah, the 'Rights of Man.' Surely you did not study Thomas Paine with the Jesuits in Spain. I would hardly think that individual freedom would be a concern of theirs."

"I have read on my own also," said David soberly. "They set me on the path of philosophy—"

"And you then became a philosopher."

"No, I am not a philosopher any longer."

"Well, David, my reading has gone more toward the ancient Greeks and their notions of democracy. The Greeks were aristocrats and understood the need of some to be ruled by others."

"Then you are not interested in negotiating with the Indians?"

"How can there be negotiation? Our interests will never be compatible."

"Don't Jews believe that all men are equal in the sight of God?" asked David after a pause.

"Show me where to stand so that I may be in the sight of God, and I will stand there. You have much to learn about life, David, much to learn about the superiority of some men to other men. You do not see me mingling with the descendants of East European Jews who live in this country. They are a superstitious, uncultured lot. What would I have in common with them, me, a German Jew? So it is with the Indians. What does the white man have in common with the illiterate, uncultured Indian?"

"They are Americans, too," said David.

"No, they are Indians," said Gunter emphatically. "They understand that, and I understand that. In that way we are compatible, after all. Socrates has said that he who allows himself to be taken prisoner may as well be made a present to his enemies. I surrender nothing to the Indians. Whether they will surrender to me is yet to be seen."

"And if neither concedes to the other?" asked David.

"Then you will see the violence that I have talked about."

Katie and Lee were waiting at the boundary of the Liebermann ranch when Gunter's green station wagon rode out of the dust and stopped at the stables.

"I will not notice their trespass today, David," said Gunter as David got out of the pickup. "You are a guest, and I want you to enjoy the ride. There are some things of beauty to be seen along the trail to the Havasupai, and you will enjoy them. But you see how the Indian takes advantage of the situation." Gunter motioned toward Lee. "You see how arrogantly he sits his horse? That is what I have to contend with, that Indian arrogance."

"I will be staying in the canyon for a few days," said David as he stepped down from the pickup.

Gunter smiled and waved at him. "Enjoy yourself," he said.

David rode Gunter Liebermann's hunter as he and Katie headed out across the plateau with Lee following on his pony.

"We're going down the Liebermann ranch trail," said Katie as they rode. "No one uses it but Lee and me. Everyone comes down from Hualapai Hilltop. This way's steeper, but it's quicker than cutting across the plateau to the Hilltop."

"Mr. Liebermann doesn't like Lee near his ranch," said David.

"Lee knows that. That's why he's so careful to stay behind the boundary lines. A few years ago Daddy showed Lee where he could safely go and where he wasn't allowed. Lee pretty much knows his place."

David sat his horse well. Some time between the day Katie had met him and today, he had bought some different clothes. The shirt and tie were gone, and in their place were Levis and a checked cotton shirt, and he had tied a red-and-black kerchief around his neck. He rode confidently, even on the unfamiliar and narrow trail. Katie thought it strange to see someone with such a tall body ride so effortlessly. She was used to Lee, with his rangy frame seeming to grow out of the horse's back. When David rode, it was a purposeful but natural pairing of horse and rider.

Lee kept at a distance from them. At times, when Katie turned to see how close behind her David was on the rocky path, she thought that Lee had disappeared, until the next switchback, when she would look up above them and see him coming down the trail.

"How did you know about this trail?" asked David, riding close behind Katie.

"The Liebermanns used to use it when they came to visit my parents in the village."

"Then they were friends before they were enemies?"

"Very good friends. Alexa and I were like sisters. I guess even an outsider can see what happened."

"Only that your father is on the side of the Indians and Mr. Liebermann is not," said David.

"It's pretty much like that, I suppose. Daddy came to Havasupai to take pictures of the Indians. He had come back from the Second World War with what my mother says the doctors called battle neurosis. He couldn't think of anything but the war and the concentration camps. Sam Wickes, who used to be the Indian agent in Havasupai, broke his leg and couldn't ride in and out of the canyon, so Daddy kind of took over for him. It was going to be only temporary. My mother took over the school. That was going to be temporary, too. But Sam's leg healed crooked, and he began drinking with the Indians on mail nights, so the BIA asked Daddy to take over as Indian agent."

"And your mother?"

"She stayed for a while, until Daddy got so political that there was no talking to him without arguing. She moved to Flagstaff when I was twelve. She and Daddy are real good friends, though. I can't say that I've suffered because they don't live together. They never did get a divorce. Mom teaches school in Flagstaff, and I'm starting at the University of Northern Arizona in September."

The trail widened out so that David could ride parallel with Katie. He glanced at her every once in a while as they rode. She could feel his eyes on her breasts as they bounced free beneath the loose shirt that she wore.

"But you are here often with your father?"

"I come and go between the two of them. I feel comfortable both places. My father's a little strange at times, so it's hard for people to understand him. They don't really know him like I do. His heart is so big that I think he dies a little over every injustice he comes across. That's what kills him about Mr. Liebermann, with him being a concentration camp survivor and all and then not sympathizing with the Havasupai."

"What more do you know of the Liebermanns?" asked David.

Katie laughed. "I think Alexa was right. You are a spy."

"She says that?" said David, startled.

"You should be careful with Alexa," said Katie. "She has a

vivid imagination. I guess that's because her parents kept her with them so much when she was growing up. They've always worried about her safety, like if she got on a horse, she might fall off, or if she took a long hike, she might tumble into an abandoned well. She used to fight them, but she finally gave up."

"But your father does not worry about you on a horse with no one to watch you?" asked David.

"Oh, there's always someone to watch me—Lee." She turned her head, her long honey-colored braid flipping onto one shoulder, and looked at Lee as he came down the last switchback behind them. "Lee never lets me out of his sight. Some people think my father pays him to watch out for me. But I'm here to tell you that my father doesn't pay him."

"Perhaps I would do as he does if I lived here and you were here also," said David, looking at her.

The trail opened into a series of limestone escarpments. The horses picked their way slowly from one level to another. When they came down on the other side of the steep slope, they were at the river. Katie's horse waded into the moving stream, and David's followed. In the middle of the stream, the horses stopped and began to drink.

"It is beautiful here," said David, looking up at the red cliffs that towered two thousand feet above their heads as the blue-green river flowed around the horses' legs.

Katie handed her canteen to David. He opened it and took a few swallows and then handed it back to her. She drank deeply, then tucked the canteen back into her saddlebag.

"Here it is different from Spain," said David thoughtfully. "There is great beauty in Spain also. But it remains the same. It must not be touched or altered in any way. Here the unexpected, the unusual man like your father, is accepted even though he is trying to change the way things are. In Spain those who try to change the way things are must run for their lives to America."

"When I'm here, there is no outside world," she said, turning in her saddle to look at the cliffs that surrounded them. David watched her, not speaking. Her skin was scrubbed and clean, with a sprinkling of freckles across the bridge of her nose, and here in the canyon, away from the stuffiness of the Liebermann dining room, she was at home and at ease. She flirted with him as they rode along the trail, but not with the coquetry of the Spanish girls he had known. He understood that it was because she had seen him looking at her breasts and that she expected something would happen between them.

The horses finished drinking and moved slowly out of the river and up onto the dry trail toward the village.

Elgin unlocked the small frame building that served as hospital and guest hotel. The smell of iodoform floated out as the door swung open. Elgin pointed to an iron bedstead in the corner near the pharmacy cabinet.

"There is water in the canteen at the bedside," said Elgin. "Nobody is sick, so you will have the hospital to yourself. You will not be disturbed by noises while you sleep."

Elgin left, and David was alone. He undressed and lay atop the bed, which was covered with a thin Navaho blanket and a lumpy pillow. He lay awake and listened to the sound of the trees brushing against the roof of the building. The United States was different from anything he had ever known before. The week before, when Gunter and Erika had taken Alexa back to boarding school, David had gone along, and they had stopped in Phoenix to do some shopping. In the bright, clean air David had been able to look across the city and see the low-lying mountains beneath sunny skies. Everything was new, the buildings sparkled in the sunshine, and there was a sense of roominess, of not being crowded. The store owner from whom David bought his riding clothes had noticed his accent, and when David told him he was from Spain, the man had invited him to supper the following Sunday.

"I'm in Phoenix only for today," said David.

"Well, if you come around this way again, come in. You don't have to buy anything. Just say hello. I'll buy you a cup of coffee. I like to make visitors to Phoenix feel welcome."

It would have been unthinkable in Spain to have been invited anywhere by a shopkeeper. It would have been unheard of to accept an invitation from a shopkeeper. Distances between people were rigidly maintained in Spain, and every man and woman knew what those distances were. On the trail today David had wished that he were Lee, with his hair grown long over his ears and his body unfettered by stiff clothes, riding, hunting, and fishing in the streams and cooking supper over open fires. He would not have to hunt Nazis or be hunted by them. He would not have to worry about Sara anymore. If he stayed in Havasupai very long, he knew that he could become like the Indians, as Katie and her father had.

"I have not seen Lee behind us since you left me in the village yesterday," said David as Katie spread the blanket on the grass beside Havasu Falls. He undid the picnic basket she had tied across the saddle, and he placed it on the blanket.

"He's there," said Katie nonchalantly. "Elgin and he hunt the high plateau in the winter, and Lee has learned to stalk without giving himself away."

David sat down on the blanket. "I thought that they could no longer hunt on the high plateaus. Isn't that what they fight about now?"

She opened the basket. "I forgot the hard-boiled eggs," she said. And then seeing the puzzled look on David's face, she explained, "Elgin and Lee do it secretly. No one is supposed to know. Elgin wanted Lee to know the ways of the hunt for that day when their lands were returned to them."

She handed David a napkin-wrapped sandwich. "We all have secrets," said Katie.

When they had had lunch, they lay down on the blanket on their backs and looked up at the sky.

"You said you were raised by a Spanish woman. Are you close to your mother now?" asked Katie, turning her head to look at David's profile.

"I live with her and her husband, Tonio, and her adopted daughter, Sara. Sometimes I feel close. Other times, no."

Katie leaned on her elbow and watched him as he spoke.

"We were apart for too long, and I will never understand what she suffered, no matter how many books I read or how many pictures I see," he said.

"That's the way I feel with Daddy. I look at all the old *Life* magazine photographs, and in my head I'm saying, 'Oh, my God, no, how horrible, how awful, how could people do this to other people?' But then I shut the magazine, and I go ride Mandy, or I take a swim, or I just lie against a tree and don't think of anything at all."

He turned his face toward her. "Then you understand how I feel."

"I suppose I do. This girl Sara, do you think of her as a sister?"

David shook his head. "No. I try not to think of her at all. She suffered very much in the concentration camp where my mother found her. I feel an obligation."

"An obligation?" asked Katie. "You mean like marrying her?"

"I think that is what my mother and Sara want," said David.

"Oh," said Katie. She turned her eyes toward the waterfall that cascaded down the moss-covered cliffs into the blue-green water swirling beneath the falls. While David watched, Katie began to undress. First boots and socks, then jeans and shirt, until she stood naked before him, her small upturned breasts and her stomach and boyish hips the same golden tan as the rest of her body.

"The water isn't as cold as it looks," she said, with no embarrassment. Before she ran toward the water, she stood and stared defiantly up at a figure on the narrow footpath above the falls. Then she dived beneath the water and swam to where a fallen cottonwood tree lay across the connecting pools like a floating raft. She clung to the tree for a while and watched David shedding his clothes on the bank. "This way," she yelled as she turned and swam away to the opposite side of the falls, where she climbed out of the water and stood near the caves alongside the falls. David dived into the water and swam across to the tree, then came up sputtering and looking around for her.

"I'm over here," she called from beneath the misty veil of water that bathed the mouth of the cave. Then she turned and walked through the spray into the dark cave, which smelled strongly of the gardenias that grew wild at its opening. At the rear of the cave a blanket was spread on the damp earth. She took the cup that sat in a niche in the rock wall and held it out to catch the clean water that flowed from the falls past the cave opening. She drank the water and then replaced the cup in the niche.

"Katie," called David from the opening of the cave.

"I'm here," she said.

What light there was was at his back. He walked cautiously as his eyes slowly became accustomed to the dark interior. He shivered in the dampness of the cave, droplets of water glistening on his naked body.

She touched him, and he stopped. "You're so cold," she said, touching his skin with her lips. He fell to his knees on the blanket in front of her. He could see her now, sitting Indian-style on the blanket, smiling a small smile. He kissed her and pressed her back against the blanket, his body over hers, her cool, smooth legs against his.

"Come into me now, I need your warmth," she said, pulling the hardness of his penis into her moist opening.

"God, Katie, I want you so much."

He kissed her breasts and her stomach and held her slim hips in his hands, and then they turned so that she was atop him and he was stroking her breasts as she sat outlined in the light of the cave's opening. Her braid had come undone, and her blonde hair enveloped them in its shimmery waves.

Later they lay side by side, his hand lingering on her breast, touching her skin.

"Are you worried about my father?" she asked.

"No."

"Then what are you thinking about?"

"About this place, this cave, the blanket."

"Girls make love in Spain?"

"Yes, peasant girls."

"Then I am a peasant girl," she said with a laugh. She curled into his arms and kissed his lips. "Alexa told you I was like an Indian maiden, didn't she?"

"Yes."

"The Indians make love very easily, David. That's why Lee follows me even though I no longer want him."

She felt his body tense against hers. "I want you now, David."

XLI

Erika's gray and golden hair caught the light of the kerosene lamp on the glass patio table as she and David sipped their lemonades on the terrace of the ranch house. She was a striking woman, not beautiful in the conventional sense. She held herself gracefully, and the blondeness of her skin and hair was a delicate contrast to the Arizona landscape of craggy mountains and rugged terrain.

"We have enjoyed your visit, David," said Erika. "Gunter is sorry for all the times that he has been absent while you are here, but there are often things that he must take care of in Phoenix." She spoke in a lilting English-German accent, and her small nose wrinkled when she talked.

"Is he in Phoenix now?" asked David casually.

"Why, yes, he is," said Erika hesitantly. "He is very interested that the Grand Canyon lands will stay with the people. It is the only reason that he will leave the ranch."

"Then he has people in Phoenix he talks to about the Indians' claim?" asked David. Her clear blue eyes were guarded now, as they always were when David asked questions about anything personal.

"He has friends there, yes," she answered. She sipped her drink and stared out at the star-filled sky. "Your mother has asked that you find out certain things about Gunter and me, no?"

"She is curious, yes," he answered carefully.

Erika laughed. "It is more than curiosity, David, when she wants to know in what way I came to America and who it is that Gunter speaks to in Phoenix."

"I am here because the Spanish government thinks of me as a dangerous student, as a terrorist," said David warily.

"When it is safe for me to return to Spain, or when I intrude on your hospitality too much, then I will leave the United States."

"I'm sorry, David. I did not mean to accuse you of anything. It is only that Gunter and I have become naturally suspicious of everyone. Questions of any kind remind us of Germany during the war, and for that reason I am perhaps too sharp with you in my answers. For that I am sorry."

David was quiet, listening to the sound of her voice, which revealed nothing of herself but was always politely restrained.

"I am too reticent," said Erika finally. "There is nothing mysterious about the way we are and the way we live. There are things that Gunter and I are ashamed of, that we did not stay and help your mother and father. And there were diamonds that belonged to the group of us who left Germany together. They were not ours to take, but Gunter persuaded me that your father was near to a mental breakdown and that your mother would never leave him. The diamonds were meant to be used for all of us, but there was no time. You must understand, David, what it was like in Italy at that time. It was a place where we were safe but not safe. We had lost all protection in the world. We were nothing more than hunted creatures, trying to find a small burrow in which to bury ourselves until the war was over. Gunter and I had friends in Italy who were willing to help us for a very large price. We did not think for a moment. They offered help. Gunter had the diamonds in his possession. And so we did what we did."

"But the diamonds didn't protect you. Mr. Liebermann went to Auschwitz anyway."

"We did not know it would turn out that way. We had no choice but to accept the promises of those we turned to. And we were helped somewhat, because when I found I was pregnant with Alexa, Count Ciano's mother took me into her home in Rome. They could not prevent Gunter from going to Auschwitz, but I was safe with Alexa until Gunter returned from the concentration camp."

David nodded, hoping by his silence to keep her stream of conversation going.

"That is all there is to tell, David. Your mother's stories are far more exciting than mine."

David looked at her in surprise. "Exciting? She was in Ravensbrück and Bergen-Belsen."

Erika appeared to falter. Her cheeks grew red as she groped for the appropriate words. "'Exciting' is not the word I should use. It is that nothing happened to me that can compare to your mother's experience."

"Mother has mentioned a man who attempted to help all of you escape during the war."

"Count von Kirchner," said Erika. "I have not seen him since we left Italy."

"Then you did see him during the war?" asked David carefully.

Erika had by her innocent recitation of the war years opened up the subject that David had been unable to broach since his arrival at the ranch. Now, from the expression on her face, he could see that she was looking for a way of extricating herself from any questions that went beyond that recital.

"We did see him, Alexa and I. He and Count Ciano's family were very close friends. When he was in Rome, I did see him, yes."

"You knew he was a co-commandant at Ravensbrück?"

"I did know that, yes."

"And that he killed people with his own hand?"

"One hears all kinds of horror stories. Not everything is true."

"Did Count Ciano's family help Count von Kirchner leave Europe after the war?" asked David recklessly.

Erika stood up and picked up the tray of lemonade. "I have talked so much, David, tonight. I don't know what has made me talk so much. Perhaps it is your good company, no?"

She turned and walked toward the door to the house. "Gunter will be back soon from Phoenix," she said over her shoulder. "Don't sit out too long, David. You will get a chill."

During the night, from his room in the guest wing of the ranch house, David could hear the sound of men's voices coming from the main portion of the house, but he could not tell what language they spoke. He pulled his Levis on over his pajamas and walked into the hallway to listen. They were speaking in German. He walked quietly along the carpeted passage until he was next to the living room door. By standing close against the wall, he could see the floor-to-ceiling slumpstone fireplace that covered the far wall of the room. Gunter Liebermann was standing with his back to the fireplace. He had a drink in his hand. The man with him sat on the sofa in front of the fireplace so that David could not see his face. David's German was not good enough for him to understand everything they were saying, but it had something to do with travel permits and money. He heard the name Elias Mandelbaum mentioned several times. Suddenly Gunter stopped talking and looked toward the hallway. He put his hand up for silence, and the other man stopped speaking. David turned and walked quickly back to his room. In the morning both Gunter Liebermann and the man were gone.

XLII

Katie woke early and dressed in shorts and a light shirt. There was the feel of summer in the air, and the fields from the kitchen window were an undulating blue-green, like the waters of the adjacent Havasu Creek.

"You're up early," said Will as he walked into the kitchen in his flannel bathrobe, his thinning red hair an explosive tuft atop his head.

"David and I are going to picnic at Mooney Falls today," she said, packing the last sandwich into the backpack.

"He comes down into the canyon an awful lot lately, Katie. Something special going on?"

Katie placed the thermos of milk in the backpack, along with some paper napkins. "It's just my last free time before school starts. We're having fun, is all."

"Nothing more than that?"

Katie smiled. "It's too soon to tell."

"Your being so close all of a sudden to the Liebermanns doesn't make me too happy."

"I'm not close to the Liebermanns, Daddy. I'm close to David." She hugged her father, and with her arms still around his neck, she looked into his face and asked, "You do like David, don't you?"

"I don't know him well enough to dislike him. He seems okay. The only thing wrong about him is that he's staying at the Liebermanns'."

Katie dropped her arms from Will's neck. She unwound her blue sweater from the back of the painted wooden chair in front of the stove and put it on, then picked up the backpack and headed for the kitchen door. "Will you be home tonight?" she asked as she opened the door.

"I'll be up at Williams most of the day. Senator Lacey is bringing some fact-finding people in tomorrow to meet with the tribal council, and I'm going to arrange a meeting place at Jeff Harlan's Pancake House. I can tell you, Katie, things are really looking up with the Senator. I've got a personal commitment from him that he intends to introduce legislation in the coming session of the Arizona senate. If it all goes the way we think it will, the Havasupai tribe is going to regain its hunting lands."

Katie ran back to her father and hugged him. "The Havasupai should make you chief if you pull this off, Daddy."

"I don't want to be chief," he said. "I just want to be—"

"I know, an Indian," finished Katie.

When she left the cottage, she walked past the storage yard where the tribe kept the things that were judged too valuable to throw away yet not valuable enough to warrant space in the storage shed. There were cracked toilet seats, broken sinks, and a few doors that had been delivered by trail sled but had split down the middle on the way down the trail into Havasu Canyon. Beyond the storage yard Katie walked past the white wooden schoolhouse, down the path toward the creek. Two stout Indian women, their long apron dresses scuffing up the red dust as they walked, greeted Katie shyly, their black eyes friendly beneath the thatches of long black hair that cascaded over their foreheads and down their backs in oily profusion. The women, on their way to the willow trees to gather sticks for basket-making, had large burden baskets hanging from their shoulders.

The village square was deserted, except for an elderly Indian man in an old Army uniform, who was picking up paper wrappers and debris from alongside the wooden door to the post office. Katie stopped at the bulletin board next to the post office. The Bureau of Indian Affairs had posted a notice that a new schoolteacher for grades one to four would arrive in September and that volunteers to pull the weeds in the school yard were needed. Beside it was an announcement of a movie on alcoholism to be shown at the Saturday night movie in the meeting hall, and next to that a small typewritten note about foot races in the field near Havasu Falls. On Sunday there would be a visiting preacher from

Salt Lake City; somebody was needed to repair the church bell in time for the services.

Katie walked off the trail now and cut across the field in the shadow of the red rock pinnacles that the Indians called the Prince and Princess rocks. She hadn't ridden Mandy for two days. Lee always took care of the horses, seeing to it that they had food and water and that they were brushed and exercised.

As she approached the corral, she spotted Mandy up against the opposite fence and felt a thrill at seeing the animal again. She put the backpack down on the ground beside the corral fence, and as she put her hand on the latch to open the gate, she heard Lee's voice behind her. She turned and looked up at him on his pinto. He wore chaps, and his chest was bare and painted red with ocher. He had lined his face with ocher and tied back his full black hair with a headband made of braided strips of buckskin.

"Mandy has not seen you for two days," he said.

"I know, and I miss her," said Katie, unlatching the gate.

Lee reached down and caught Katie's arm in his hand as the gate swung open.

"Lee, the horses will get out," she said impatiently.

He jumped down from his horse and shut the gate to the corral. Then he stood facing her.

She squinted in the morning sun and pulled at her braid nervously. "Why are you painted up like that?" she asked.

Lee bent down and picked up the backpack and handed it to Katie, who took it in her two hands. "Where will you meet the white man today?" Lee asked, standing close to her, his hand holding the reins of his pinto.

"At the wash," she answered, backing away from him. As she backed away, he walked toward her. "I will take you to meet him," he said.

He clucked his tongue at the pony, who stamped his feet a few times in place. Lee released the reins, and the pony stood motionless next to the corral fence.

"No, Lee, I'll ride Mandy," pleaded Katie. "It's a picnic, that's all."

Lee put his hands around Katie's waist and lifted her up

into the pony's saddle. Katie dropped the backpack to the ground and kicked the pony with her heels and whistled at him. "Come on, boy, let's go, come on."

"You know he will not listen," said Lee as he picked up the backpack from the dust and tied it onto the saddle. Katie began to cry. "Come on, boy, damn you, come on." The horse remained standing, not turning his head or even flicking his tail as Katie beseeched him to move.

Lee looked up at her on the saddle, the tears running down her face. "Your face is painted with tears," he said. He put his foot into the stirrup and sprang onto the bare back of the horse, behind Katie. He put one arm around her waist, took the reins from her hands, and gave a low whistle to the horse, who began a spirited gallop away from the corral.

They rode all morning, but not in the direction of the wash and not in the direction of Mooney Falls. They followed an old half-covered Indian horse trail that led up to the forbidden plateau. Lee helped Katie off the pony. In the shelter of a natural rock overhang, Lee had built his mud-and-thatch hogan. There was dried deer meat on a pole, and in a basket were piñon nuts and dried corn. A rubbing stone lay on a blanket next to a Moki bowl and an earthenware pot. A smoothly finished bow and arrow leaned against the center pole of the hogan next to a Civil War repeating rifle.

"You could be put in jail for hunting up here," said Katie as she looked into the hut.

"I am in jail already in the village," Lee retorted. "There is a stream a hundred yards east of here that is clean and pure. I will wait here for you," he said, sitting down on the ground before the opening of the hogan.

"I'll run away, Lee," said Katie.

"There is no place to run. There are mountain lion here among the scrub oak and juniper trees. The Grand Canyon rattlesnake hides beneath the ponderosa pines. The tarantula and the scorpion will also keep you from going far."

They looked at each other without speaking for a few seconds. Then Katie turned and walked in the direction that Lee had pointed. Through the tangle of brush she could hear the sound of running water. She urinated in a small opening in the brush and then continued on toward the water. She lay down on the ground on her stomach, drinking her fill and letting the cool water run over her sunburned face.

A red-tailed hawk circled in the sky over her as she looked up from the stream. She shielded her eyes with her hand and watched the hawk's effortless glide through the canyon. Was Lee telling the truth about the mountain lions, or was it as safe here as it was in the village? A turkey vulture swooped down from the sky behind the hawk and disappeared into the dense brush. Katie looked down at her legs, bare except for the shorts. She was not dressed for an all-day hike through uncertain terrain. She didn't have a compass, and she had not paid enough attention to Will's lessons on celestial navigation to trust herself to get back to the village on her own.

She wiped her wet hands on her shorts and walked back in the direction of the hogan.

"You can eat dried deer meat or the food in your pack," said Lee when she stooped and entered the low-ceilinged dwelling.

"I'm not hungry," said Katie, sitting down on the blanket next to the earthenware pot. A string of cedar beads hung around Lee's neck, and he was drinking something from a buckskin flask.

"My father will be looking for me, Lee," said Katie.

"Yes," he answered, taking another drink from the flask. He wiped his mouth with the back of his hand and offered her a drink. She took a sip from the flask and spit the liquid out on the ground.

"It's terrible. What is it?"

"It is liquor made from the juniper berries that grow on the plateau."

"How long are you going to play this game, Lee?" She stared at him as she leaned back against one of the hogan's supporting poles.

"No game," he said, taking a deep swallow of the juniper liquor.

"Your keeping me here isn't going to change anything, you know."

He didn't look at her as he continued to drink.

"Daddy told me this morning that the Arizona legislature is probably going to give the hunting lands back to the tribe."

"They cannot give back what is ours already."

"You won't have to sneak up here in the wintertime. Doesn't not having to sneak around mean anything to you? My God, Lee, the Havasupai will be able to live like they lived before the white man came."

Lee put the flask down on the ground. "We will never live like we lived before the white man came," he said, his eyes shadowed by the darkness of the hogan. "Will you go with the white man when he leaves?"

"What white man? You mean David?"

"Yes, I mean David."

"I'm enrolled in the fall semester at UNA. I haven't got plans any further than that, Lee. I just don't want complications in my life, that's all."

"David brings complications. You sleep with him now."

"So I sleep with him. So what? I slept with you. You were the one who told me that to sleep with someone was a natural thing, not a thing to be avoided. You told me that you found only Indian women beautiful, that the fair skin and light eyes of white women lacked fire. And now you follow me wherever I go and watch what I do."

"I'm going now," said Lee, standing unsteadily on his feet.

"Going? Where are you going?" she asked in a frightened voice.

"I'm going," Lee repeated. He stooped to exit the low doorway of the hogan. Katie ran after him and stood watching as he mounted his pony. "There is a gun inside," he said. "Don't use it. It is old and can explode in your hands. If you see a mountain lion, there is the bow and arrow."

"I won't see a mountain lion," said Katie defiantly, more upset at his leaving her than she was at the prospect of encountering a mountain lion.

Lee whistled to the horse, and the horse snorted once, reared his head, and then galloped away from the hogan.

David waited for Katie in the dry wash until the sun was hot and blinding overhead and then he moved for protection from its rays beneath the sandstone canopy on the terraced slope above the wash. He drank water frequently from his canteen and listened for the sound of Katie's horse clip-clopping through the shale and rocks of the dry riverbed. When he dismounted from his horse and sat in the shade of the overhang to wait, he thought about Katie and Americans in general. Living with the Liebermanns had given him a constant frame of reference for considering Europe and the way Europeans lived. Erika and Gunter had not become Americanized. They never would. They could not be like Katie and Will, comfortable in America, at home wherever they were. Will, a much-talked-about *Life* photojournalist, happy to truck supplies into Havasupai Village and to fight for Indian rights. And Katie, with her no-nonsense approach to people, her lack of falseness and absence of trickery. What to make of her? He hadn't decided yet. She seemed to be headed nowhere, intent on nothing, while maintaining the busyness and activity of someone who had a definite destination in mind.

Erika and Gunter could never be Americans like Katie and her father. They had brought old ideas to a new country. It was clear why Gunter wanted the Havasupais to remain deep in the canyon and not come up on the plateau lands. The Indians' presence would disturb the neatness of the terrain. Gunter's neatness was not actually a desire to keep things straight, decided David, so much as a desire to keep himself separate from the Indians. In Europe we are always trying to keep ourselves separate from the Indians, he thought, leaning his dark head against the red sandstone wall. Jews, Freemasons, Marxist-Leninists, Carlists, anarchists are the Indians of Europe.

David slept awhile in the heat of the canyon, and when he awoke, Lee was standing over him. Lee's pony stood untethered next to a redbud tree.

"Where's Katie?" asked David, seeing the controlled hostility in the young Indian's face.

"Katie is with me," said Lee in a even voice. "Stand up."

David put his arm against the canyon wall to get up from his seated position, and then he saw the knife in Lee's hand.

David stopped his upward movement and tightened in a half-sitting, half-standing pose. Lee took a cautious step forward, leaning his body toward David, the knife held loosely in his palm in striking readiness. David suddenly feinted to Lee's right, and the knife blade flashed past David's shoulder. David kicked furiously with one booted foot and caught Lee on the upper thigh with his heel. Lee groaned and fell to one knee, and David sprinted toward his horse as Lee knelt, clutching his upper leg. David's horse started forward as Lee recovered and jumped to his feet.

"Aieee," screamed Lee, his knife still in his upraised hand.

"*Vámonos,*" yelled David at the horse, kicking the animal with his heels. In seconds the horse was in a full gallop up the wash toward the trail. After a short distance David pulled at the horse's reins, and suddenly they were off the trail and hidden by trees and limestone boulders. David waited until he heard the sound of hoofbeats going in the opposite direction, then he turned his horse around and followed in the direction of the hoofbeats.

Lee knew that he was being followed. He turned every once in a while, looked back at David, and waved his knife at him.

David did not believe that Lee meant to use the knife on him, only that he meant to frighten him into staying away from Katie. But David was here, and so were Katie and Lee. Things would have to be resolved, thought David, following behind the Indian as the pony tore up the ancient trail to the plateau. When David reached the uplands, he stopped his horse to let him rest. He could still see the pony, and beyond the pony were the sandstone escarpment and the mud-and-twigs shelter. David got off the horse and walked the rest of the distance to the hogan. He had come all the way from Spain to play cowboy to Lee's Indian.

The pony stood guard at the door to the hogan. David cautiously leaned down and looked into the opening of the dwelling. "No knives, Lee," David yelled into the hogan. The Indian sprang out of the hogan, screaming a string of Havasupai expletives at David, but there was no knife in his hand. The two grappled with each other in the dirt, Lee's hands around David's neck, David's hands pushing at Lee's face. Katie had come out of the hogan and was watching the two of them, a helpless look on her face.

David got a lock on Lee's bare upper body with his forearm, and he began to drag the Indian along the ground until Lee managed to twist in his grasp and punch David in the stomach, and then the two of them hit the ground and rolled over and over down the rock-strewn trail.

"Kill each other. I hope you kill each other," screamed Katie. David got up first and pulled Lee to his feet. Lee kneed him in the groin. David went forward onto his knees, and while he was bent over, Lee reached for him. Then David suddenly brought his doubled fists up under Lee's chin, knocking him down again. They battered at each other on and off until the sun began to go down over the rim of the canyon. Finally they both lay in the red dust, not moving, staring up into the sky, their chests heaving with their exertions. When they had not moved for some time, Katie took the Moki bowl and the earthenware pot from the hogan and walked to the stream and filled them with water. She walked back to where David and Lee lay, and she placed a bowl of water next to each of them.

David sat up first and held the bowl of water in his lap, flicking the water into his face with his fingertips. Then he lifted the bowl to his mouth and drank deeply of the water. Lee lay in the dust, his black hair powdered by the red earth. He watched David from the corner of his eye.

"Someone must win," said Lee from his prone position.

"Only in the movies," said Katie at the entrance to the hogan.

Lee sat up and touched his bruised face with his hands and grimaced with pain. "You are a worthy opponent," he said grudgingly.

"I didn't want to fight you," answered David, getting up slowly.

The two stumbled into the hogan and lay down on the blanket and fell asleep. They awoke when it was dark. Katie opened the backpack and spread the sandwiches on the blanket, and they ate together in silence. Lee's right eye was swollen shut, and David had two gashes across his forehead, and his shirt was dirty and torn. Katie had started a fire outside the door of the hogan, and in the firelight the two men looked at each other respectfully as they ate. When they had finished, Katie said, "It's too dark for David to find his way back to the main trail, Lee."

"Are you able to ride?" Lee asked David.

"I can ride tonight. I don't know if I will be able to tomorrow," answered David.

Lee got up on his haunches. The ocher paint had been worn off in the fight, and his dark body shone in the light of the fire.

"I will ride with you to the wash, then," he said.

David glanced at Katie, who had turned her face away from him. Without saying anything more, Lee and David left the hogan and mounted their horses for the ride back to the main trail.

"It is different in the dark," said David as they rode side by side. "I would not recognize anything."

"Yes, it is different," acknowledged Lee. "Only the Havasupai, who have lived in these canyons and plateaus, can find their way both in the daylight and the darkness."

"I didn't come here to cause you trouble," said David.

"But you did. The white man never wants to cause us trouble, but he always does. The white man brings radios and electric lights and refrigerators to the canyon, and the generators to run them. And when the generators no longer work, the white man says 'Do what you did before the white man came.' And when they tell us we are citizens, and we can fight in their wars, we say, 'Then we want to vote,' and they tell us we are illiterate."

"It is like that in Spain," said David thoughtfully. "We are educated, and then when we try to think for ourselves, we are jailed for subversion. And if you are a Jew, as I am, you can never be a European first. You will always be a Jew first."

Lee looked at him in the darkness. "Jews and Indians."

"Yes," said David, "Jews and Indians."

Gunter met Will at the Hualapai Hilltop. The stars filled the clean Arizona sky over their heads.

"There is no deal to be made, Gunter. Senator Lacey is introducing the legislation at the opening session, and that's the way it's going to be. The Indians are going to win this time around. They've never had such a powerful ally as Senator Lacey before this."

"I will cede the fifty acres of pastureland for a herd of cattle. They can graze cattle on my pastureland if the legislation is not pursued," said Gunter.

Will laughed out loud. "Keep your goddamn charity, Liebermann. The Indians are going to get the whole plateau back, and you're not going to be able to do a goddamn thing about it because you and I know something that the Park Service and the Immigration authorities would love to know."

Gunter's face contorted in anger. "You are a nettle in my hair."

"You mean a burr in your saddle, don't you, Liebermann?"

The stars twinkled over the canyon, and Will's laugh was deep and satisfying to him. He felt it floating free over the disputed Indian lands. Gunter lunged toward him, pushing as hard as he could with both his hands. Will looked surprised for a moment, then the laughing stopped as he sailed backward, tumbling head over feet along the crags and buttes he had photographed so many times. The air rushing by him was cold, and the descent was endless. Dreams of falling filled his head, and he heard himself screaming. Gunter watched from above, from the Indians' treasured plateau land, and now he was smiling.

Lee did not speak, only pointed to the rim of the canyon as their horses rounded the rise on the Hilltop. David stopped his horse behind Lee's pony, and the two of them watched the men outlined in the clear moonlit sky.

"What are they doing out there at this time of night?" asked David.

"Will Mathison's white pickup is parked up top," said Lee, watching the figures at the edge of the canyon.

"And Gunter Liebermann's station wagon," said David. "I

don't believe it is possible that the two of them are together, talking. It can't be."

"I know them by the shapes of their bodies. The taller one is Mr. Liebermann," said Lee. "Something bad will happen between them. They have not talked together for seven years."

"Maybe they are meeting to make peace," offered David, not taking his eyes off the solitary figures on the Hilltop.

"Peace? Look," said Lee. And in that moment the men's positions altered almost imperceptibly, the taller man reaching toward the shorter one. There was a blurring of shapes as the night's shadows obscured the rocking motion of the shorter man. And then there was only the figure of the tall man standing at the edge of the precipice, facing into the gorge.

David and Lee sat atop their horses, not speaking, not moving. Then Lee made a soft clucking noise with his tongue, and his pony began the long trip back to Katie.

When Lee reached the hogan, he walked his pony to the stream, and while the horse drank, Lee slid down onto the ground. He removed his pants and leggings and walked into the current, letting the cold water cover his entire body. He scrubbed at his black hair with his hands to remove the red dust. His heart felt heavy. The liquor and the fighting with David were past, forgotten. Only sad feelings about Katie's father remained. He soaked in the water. His skin tingled with pain where he had fallen again and again during the fight with David. Will was not like other white men. He did not steal what belonged to the Havasupai people. Will was not prepared for an enemy like Gunter Liebermann. He did not have the capacity to understand the force that his enemy could exert against him. He did not know that white men were as dangerous to each other as the mountain lion was to the deer that it stalked on the rim of the Grand Canyon. Gunter had stalked Will Mathison for ten years, waiting for the right moment to kill him. No mountain lion and no Indian could wait that long to destroy his enemy, thought Lee as he climbed up onto the bank of the stream.

He led the pony back to the hut, and holding his pants and leggings in his hand, he entered through the low doorway. The fire outside had died down to a few glowing embers, and in their soft light Lee could see Katie rolled up in the blanket asleep. He sat down cross-legged, facing her. Elgin had told his son that he played at being a man, that it was not enough that he could hunt for his own food and train horses to obey his every whistle and tongue cluck, or that he could beat the other young men in foot races. To be a man, his father said, meant that you knew what to do in times of sadness, that you were not only capable of killing your enemy, but able to comfort a loved one, too.

Lee reached out and touched Katie's shoulder where it showed above the fold of the blanket. His dark brown hand rested on her fair skin. She moved in the blanket. "Did you take David back to the Hilltop?" she murmured.

"Yes."

"I'm glad," she said.

"Are you warm in the blanket?" he asked.

"Very." She turned her head to look at him sitting naked on the ground next to her.

"Where are your clothes?" she asked.

"I bathed in the stream," he answered.

She unrolled the blanket and lifted the edge of it. He kneeled down beside her and looked into her eyes and then lay down alongside her in the blanket.

"You were foolish today," she said as his arms went around her.

"I was afraid of the white man for the first time when I saw him with you."

"Are you afraid now?"

"No." He touched her breasts under the cotton shirt that she wore, then put his hands inside her shorts. She unbuttoned the shorts and pulled them down inside the blanket. He held her and touched her softly and spoke to her in Havasupai. She turned toward him, her lips parted. He kissed her mouth. "You will stay with me here awhile," he said.

"Yes," she said, "I will stay with you."

He moved within her, murmuring comforting things to her and kissing her body so that she moaned with pleasure. "I have not had you since the white man came," he said, his back arched, feeling her softness.

"Have me now," she said, pulling him deeper into her, stroking his shining black hair with her hands. He held himself back, looking at her face, a light circle in the darkness. He would care for her. She would not suffer because her father was gone.

"Katie," he said as he climaxed, and they clung to one another.

He kissed her eyes and held her head in his two hands. "The white man has not come between us," he said softly.

She shook her head from side to side. "No."

He spoke to her in Havasupai and told her that her father had gone to join the Coyote in the Grand Canyon.

She looked at him in disbelief, and then he cradled her in his arms, and she cried, and he felt that he had comforted her well.

XLIII

On the long trip on horseback to the Liebermann ranch, David thought about what he had seen. He did not believe that Gunter Liebermann had seen him and Lee at Hualapai Hilltop, but he could not be sure of that. Clearly it was time to leave the ranch. The confrontation between Gunter and the Indians had culminated, as Gunter had predicted, in violence. But it was not an Indian that Gunter had killed, it was another white man. What had happened between Will and Gunter that could have brought Gunter to push him to his death?

As he rode, he mulled it over. He would have to notify Helene and Tonio immediately about what had happened, but first he would pack his belongings into his suitcase and hike from the ranch to Grand Canyon Village and start on his journey back to Spain. He would leave a note for the Liebermanns saying that he had had to leave unexpectedly and hadn't wanted to disturb them at such a late hour. He would thank them for their generous hospitality and promise to write as soon as he got back to Barcelona.

Who were these people Helene had sent him to? Erika, the serene, loving wife who had stood by her Jewish husband during the war only to—what?—stand by again while he persecuted American Indians. And the German-speaking man in the Liebermann living room who had arrived mysteriously in the middle of the night and disappeared before morning.

By the time David reached the ranch house, it was three a.m. Gunter's station wagon was parked in the drive that led to the cow barns. David took the horse to the stables, removed its saddle and bridle, and then entered the house by the door to the guest wing. He packed his clothes in the darkened bedroom, careful not to slam drawers or make any noise that would wake up the Liebermanns. He stood in the doorway to the bedroom, wondering if there was anything else he could have done. No. He picked up the suitcase. He was not sure that he had accomplished what he had been sent to the United States to do, but what he had seen tonight had changed forever his opinion of Gunter Liebermann. He was not merely a rancher who wanted to wrest land from the Indians, a Jewish refugee who had sought to make a new life in an isolated part of Arizona. Gunter Liebermann had murdered Will Mathison, and only Lee and David had seen him do it.

David hiked from the ranch up past Hermits Rest. When the sun had been up for several hours, he arrived in Grand Canyon Village and walked up the hill to the rim of the canyon, where the dark-wood-battened El Tovar Hotel perched. He registered at the front desk, then carried his suitcase up to his third-floor room, sat down on the bed, and stared at the telephone. He felt exhausted. He had not pushed himself like this since before he had been attacked by Manero's thugs in Barcelona. He felt his ribs with his hands. They were still intact. The gashes that Lee had put in his forehead were crusted over, but his ribs had not cracked again. The telephone sat, cold and black and impersonal. He could place an anonymous call. Man pushed over cliff by concentration camp survivor. David picked up the receiver. The operator came on. "The police. I would like to talk to the police," said David to the operator.

Harley Winokur, the Park Service ranger, sat in the comfortable chair across from the slumpstone fireplace in the Liebermann living room. Gunter sat in a matching chair next to the Canterbury magazine rack, which was filled to overflowing with magazines on cattle breeding. Erika had brought a tea tray with orange-iced cakes arranged in tiers on a crystal dish and had placed it on the low table next to the ranger's chair. Then she had sat down on the couch at the far end of the room and listened.

"Police Chief Beloit called me from Williams, Gunter," said Harley. "Damnedest phone call I've ever had, I can tell you that right from the start." The ranger was thin and pale, and his washed-out eyes were set far apart in his face so that it was difficult to tell which eye was focused on you.

"Beloit asked me if I knew you," continued Winokur. "Seems someone in the mayor's office in Williams had a write-up on you from the newspaper that told about how you were fighting the Havasupai and all for the rights to the Grand Canyon plateau."

"No, I don't fight for the rights for myself," said Gunter politely. "It is a preservationist effort."

"Well, of course, I know that. Haven't I been to every powwow ever held between the Havasupai and the preservationists?"

Gunter nodded.

"So this newspaper article is on the wall in the mayor's office. Has your name in the article, your picture. Even has a little story about how you came to the Grand Canyon in 1946, escaping from the Nazis and all that."

Winokur focused one of his eyes on Gunter's face. "Tell me when I'm stepping on sensitive history here, Gunter."

"It is all right," said Gunter, "but I don't understand how a newspaper article in the mayor's office in Williams has brought you here this afternoon."

"Coming to that, coming to that. The mayor was up in Phoenix for a few days, so Renee from the Williams police station is taking her calls in the mayor's office. Sort of doing double duty, as you might say. She'd jot down the mayor's calls, and in between she'd catch the emergency calls and cat-up-a-tree calls for the police station next door."

Winokur laughed and shook his head. "Gunter, I swear she says she'd have hung up the phone without another thing being thought about it." Winokur thought for a moment. "As a matter of fact, seems to me that she did say she hung up on the first call—guess it was along about noon. Someone called in, said his name was Lee Jones, a Havasupai Indian, said he saw you push Will Mathison off the Hualapai

Hilltop into the gorge." Winokur shook his head lower this time and laughed a little heartier. "Well, naturally, you know what she thought. She thought he had got too much of the hair of the dog and wasn't exactly thinking straight. She humored him a few minutes, took his name, and told him she'd report it to the police chief when he got back in. I guess you know where calls like that go, Gunter. I don't have to tell you. Right into the circular file. Don't stop to rest on the desktop long enough to gather even one coffee stain before they're deposited in ye old wastebasket."

Gunter was looking impatient with Winokur's story.

"I know, I know, I'm as long-winded as everyone says. But this is the darnedest story, Gunter. It just deserves telling right, is all I can say in my own defense." He took a gulp of air and continued. "So she hangs up on the Indian. Right? An hour goes by. The mayor calls from Phoenix. She gives him his messages. The police chief gets back. She looks at the messages, throws away the one from the Indian, and gives him the rest. He goes back next door to his office. No sooner is he gone than the phone rings. It's someone from the El Tovar Hotel at the south rim. 'I saw Gunter Liebermann push Will Mathison into the canyon up at Hualapai Hilltop.'" Winokur laughed more heartily than he had before. "So Renee says that right away she's thinking, 'My God, are they having a convention of loonies up at Hualapai Hilltop?' She starts writing down what the man on the phone is saying, and meanwhile her eye is on the wall facing the mayor's desk—where she happens to be sitting while she's taking the calls. You know, the telephone from the police station has a long cord, so she just dragged it along the hallway and under the door to the mayor's office, so the two phones sat there right on the mayor's desk. Anyway, while she's talking to this guy at the El Tovar, she's looking up at the newspaper clipping on the wall in the mayor's office, and there's the name she's writing down on the pad. Eerie. She said it was the eeriest feeling she ever had. Like when you have a dream, and then the next day the exact thing happens that you were dreaming about.

"Anyway, she sees this newspaper clipping pinned up on the wall. When she gets off the phone, she walks up to the clipping and reads the story about how you were a spear-header in the fight to save the Grand Canyon from the Indians. And right behind your picture, standing to your rear and a little to your left—or was it to the right?—anyway, there I am standing there bold as can be, right in the damn picture. Even has my name on there as head of the Committee to Protect National Parklands. I'm about to shake your hand or give you a plaque or some such thing, which Renee wasn't too clear about in the telephone call.

"Anyway, this time she keeps the message, walks next door to Chief Beloit, waits till he finishes the article in the *Reader's Digest* he was in the middle of reading, shows him the message from the guy at the El Tovar. Then they walk back to the mayor's office. She shows Chief Beloit the newspaper clipping on the mayor's wall. Come to think of it, I think she told me that about this time she fished the Indian's message out of the wastebasket, too. Anyway, Chief Beloit and I are pretty good friends. Great bass fisherman, Chief Beloit. None better. Wrote an article for *Field and Stream* on the art—and it is an art, I can vouch for that—of bass fishing.

"So Chief Beloit says, 'Call my friend Harley Winokur. If he knows this man, then I want him in on it.'"

"In on what?" asked Gunter blandly.

"Why, in on the investigation, of course," replied Winokur, one eye on Gunter and one eye on the top tier of the orange-iced cakes.

"Yes. I can see now why you have come," said Gunter.

"You can? You mean after that long-winded story you still figured out why I'm here?"

"Of course," said Gunter indulgently.

Winokur leaned over the iced cakes. He looked like he was going to pluck the topmost cake from the carefully arranged tier. But instead he looked earnestly into Gunter's face and said in a voice absent of any hint of comic relief or casual storytelling, "Tell me, Gunter. Is it true? Did you push Will Mathison off the Hualapai Hilltop into the gorge?"

XLIV

The telephone connection between Flagstaff and Barcelona was scratchy and intermittently absent.

"David? You are all right?" came Helene's voice, familiar but strangely ethereal across the distance.

"I'm fine. Can you hear me?"

"I can hear you," she said.

"Something has happened here," said David. "Gunter Liebermann is being investigated for murder."

There was no sound on the other end of the transatlantic call.

"Did you hear?" he asked again.

"I heard," she replied.

"He pushed a man off a cliff two thousand feet to his death. A Havasupai Indian named Lee Jones was with me when it happened. We both saw it."

"Come home," she said loudly and clearly as the crackling of the lines lifted for a moment.

"I can't. Gunter had a visitor in the middle of the night last week. I didn't see his face at the time, but they spoke in German. Yesterday, when I was interrogated by the Williams police chief, I saw Gunter Liebermann in an adjoining office with another man. It was Don Diego Manero."

There was a long silence on the Barcelona side of the connection. David waited, knowing that his mother had heard him this time.

"Then he knows you are there, too," she said finally.

"Yes. And he'll see me if I stay and testify at the grand jury hearing next week."

"Do nothing for the moment, David. I must discuss this with Tonio and with Elias Mandelbaum. Where are you now?"

"At the Desert Paradise Hotel in Flagstaff."

"Stay there. Give me three hours and then call me again. I will be able to tell you more then."

"The sun is so bright it hurts my eyes," said Sara, staring down at the Sky Harbor Airport from the window of the twin-engine DC-3. Helene had slept most of the time since they had changed planes at La Guardia in New York. At the sound of Sara's voice, she opened her eyes and ran one hand through her disheveled hair. She glanced at Sara, who had put on the rose-colored hat that she had carried in her hand since they left the airport in Madrid. The delicate pastel of the hat gave a glow to Sara's olive skin, and as she turned away from the window to look at Helene, her eyes sparkled with excitement. "We will be landing in a few minutes," she said.

"I must wash my face, then," said Helene. She stood up and reached for her beige merino jacket and put it on over her white blouse. She felt exhausted by the trip, by the loss of sleep, by the incessant worry over the danger threatening David.

Helene walked down the aisle to the lavatory. She closed the door behind her and turned the water on in the metal sink. "Enough," she had said to Elias Mandelbaum when she phoned him. "David and I have given enough. Let me bring him home. Let me bring my son home to Barcelona."

"I am not God," Elias had answered.

"And my son cannot save the world," Helene had retorted.

"Have I asked that he save the world, Helene? I ask for one thing only, that he stay longer so that we can make the connection between Gunter Liebermann and Don Diego Manero and the Nazi Kameradenwerk."

"And what if Don Diego remembers him? What then?"

"It is America, Helene, not Spain. Manero is a member of the Spanish Parliament. He will not attempt anything in America."

The water refreshed her. She held her hands tight against her eyes, letting the water clear her eyes of fatigue. Then she patted her face dry on a paper towel and looked into the small mirror above the sink. Tiny lines creased the corners of her eyes and rimmed her mouth. Hers was no longer the face of a young woman. At a distance, with her still trim figure, she knew she could pass for thirty-five. But the glare of the light above the mirror in the airplane lavatory was not so generous. She combed her hair back and let it fall unrestrained to her shoulders. Life never lets up, she thought. It holds you fast in its tentacles.

It was Tonio who had finally persuaded her that David must stay in Arizona awhile longer. "He is a man, Helene. He is giving you the courtesy of asking your advice, but you can no longer say to him 'Come home, go here, do this, don't do that.'"

"Then I will go there," she had said.

Tonio had nodded. "I cannot tell you not to."

"But you are afraid for me, too. You see what it feels like?" she said in anguish.

"I am not afraid for you," said Tonio. "I have never been afraid for you."

Helene closed the lavatory door behind her and walked back to her seat.

"Everything appears so flat below," said Sara.

Helene bent to look out the window. She touched Sara's thick black hair beneath the hat with her hand. "You look very pretty," she said.

Sara turned toward her, excitement in her eyes. "That's because I'm going to see David."

"I know." The fact that Sara had changed over the past year could be explained only by her love for David. How else to account for the happiness that was always evident in her face, or the eagerness for life that she now had? Sara's face shone with love, her eyes sparkled, and she laughed easily. She reminded Helene more and more of the Gypsy women when they first came to Ravensbrück, with their heads held so high, unafraid of the unknown.

"If you want David, you must tell him so," Helene had said before they left.

The airplane was only partially filled, and within minutes after they had landed, Sara and Helene were walking through the glass doors to the passenger arrivals section of Sky Harbor Airport.

"There, he is there," said Sara, spotting David behind the roped-off arrival area. "He is surprised to see me," said Sara. "I can see it in his face."

Helene smiled at him. He looked very tan and healthy to her, fully recovered from the beating he had suffered in Spain. He kissed Helene on the cheek and said words of greeting to her in Spanish and German. Then he took Sara's hand in his.

"Kiss me, too," she said, looking up at him, her eyes bright and dancing. She raised her lips to his. He hesitated for a moment and then kissed her lightly on the lips.

"I have an adjoining room reserved for you in the hotel," said David, leading them away from the arrivals area. "I didn't realize that Sara would be here, too, but it is easy enough to obtain another one for her."

"If we could perhaps have some lunch while we wait for our luggage," said Helene. But David hadn't heard. His eyes were on Sara's face.

"We're hungry, David," said Sara, laughing.

"Of course, of course," said David.

When they had sat down in the booth in the airport restaurant, Helene looked more closely at his face, then touched his forehead with her fingers. "You have been injured again."

"It is nothing," he said.

"It has nothing to do with Gunter Liebermann?" asked Helene.

"No."

"Tell me about Gunter and Erika," she said.

"Erika was very nice, very hospitable to me," said David. "She spoke of you in a loving way and tried to explain why she and Gunter had run away in 1939."

"Yes," said Helene, her eyes bright and alert as she listened.

"And Alexa is away at school most of the time. She comes home at holidays, and I've seen her on several weekends. They hold her away from themselves, as if to protect her from their lives. Erika and Gunter seem childless, except for the brief periods when Alexa is home."

"Go on," said Helene.

"Gunter is a complicated man, difficult to know and understand," said David. "He was always polite to me—I felt out of duty or for some obligation that he owed to his wife. Aside from the time that I saw the man in the living room with him, there were no other guests besides myself. But Gunter did go to Phoenix frequently. On business, Erika said."

"The murder, what about that?" prompted Helene.

"That is the most complicated story of all," said David. "Gunter had made an enemy of a man named Will Mathison. Will and his daughter lived with the Havasupai Indian tribe down in a small part of the Grand Canyon not far from the Liebermann ranch. Will's daughter, Katie, told me all about how the fight started, that Will had come back from his work as a photographer in the war, and that he had taken up the cause of the Indians to regain their hunting lands. He arranged the tourist business for the tribe on a lease arrangement and had built a few cabins near Havasu Falls. The Indians trusted him. Then Gunter and the National Park Service wanted to buy Will's lease away from him without letting the Indians know, which would have had the effect of narrowing the Indians' living space even more. When Will Mathison found out that Gunter Liebermann was using the National Park Service to preserve private lands for himself, Katie said her father seemed to go crazy. He couldn't understand how a concentration camp survivor could be so cruel, could treat the Indians as he himself had been treated."

"And for that reason, because of the fight between them, Gunter killed this other man?" asked Helene.

"It is the only reason I know of."

"And you saw it happen?"

"Yes. Lee Jones and I were coming back from—" David stopped talking and touched the scabbed-over lacerations that lay beneath the hair on his forehead. "Lee and I had had a misunderstanding. We had left Katie at Lee's hogan on the opposite plateau. It was dark, and Lee was helping me find my way back to the Liebermann ranch. Two men were at the edge of the precipice. Gunter's station wagon was parked up there alongside Will's pickup truck."

"But you are not sure it was Gunter?" asked Helene.

"I'm sure. Lee was even more sure than I was."

"But you did not see his face?"

"It was too dark and too far away for that."

"Because of the Indians' fight, you think that Gunter killed this man?" persisted Helene.

David was thoughtful for a while. "His property was very important to him. What other reason could there be?"

Helene's eyes were on her son's. "I don't know. I ask you that."

"I have no answer."

The waitress came, and Helene ordered lunch for herself and Sara in almost forgotten schoolbook English. David had a Coke and watched them while they ate.

"Why do you stare at me so, David?" asked Sara, a mischievous look on her face. "You have seen me before."

"I'm happy that you're here," he said seriously.

Helene drank her coffee and was silent.

XLV

"Is all of America like this?" Sara asked David as she walked with him through the picnic area near the Museum of Northern Arizona in Flagstaff. In the morning the sun had shone as bright and strong as it had in Phoenix, but by afternoon the skies had grayed over, and now there were snow flurries blowing across the picnic tables and through the pine trees. Sara wore new Levi's, a western-style shirt, and around her waist a Navaho belt with a large, rough-cut turquoise stone set into its buckle. David put his arm around her for protection from the snow, and the two of them ran for the cover of the museum's portico.

"I haven't seen all of America," said David, "but I want to."

The two of them stood shivering in the sudden cold of the six-thousand-foot altitude.

"You look like an American now," said David, "in those clothes."

Sara grinned. "Is that all it takes to make one an American?"

"Sometimes I think that might be the truth, as simple as it sounds," said David thoughtfully.

"Do you think that you could live here, David?"

"Very easily."

"So could I," said Sara emphatically.

She turned her face away to look at the snowflakes, buffeted by the wind and melted before they reached the ground.

"Snowflakes in the desert," said Sara.

"Yes, that is what I like in America," said David. "Nothing you expect to happen will happen. It is a country of surprise.

I think that someone like me, who fits in nowhere in Spain, could live easily in a place like America."

Sara leaned against the wall of the museum entry, feeling the damp chill of the stones through her shirt.

"It is easy to become an American," said David, watching the snow, his arms folded across his chest. "There is no book that says that an American must be only one way and no other. There is so much room here, no feeling of confined space. Even in Valdepeñas there was the feeling of confinement, of having to know who you were and where you belonged. Here people think my accent is quaint. Some people smile when I talk to them. But no one attempts to identify what kind of man I am by the way I speak or dress."

"It's very cold, David," Sara said.

"When the snow stops, we can walk back to the hotel," he answered. He turned toward her, sensing something inexplicable between them. The air around them was cold and charged with words they had not said to each other. Did she sense it, too? He was near her, almost touching her as she leaned against the wall. She turned her head, and he pulled her close to him, trembly with desire for her as he felt her body pliant against his.

"The snow has stopped," she murmured.

When they were together in Sara's room, they stood and looked at each other without touching.

"I have not slept with a man before," she said.

He moved toward the door, as if to leave, but she had begun to unbutton her blouse. Underneath was a brassiere of the palest yellow. In the dimly lit room he could see her face redden as she undid the bra and let it slip down over her full bosom. She removed the rest of her clothes and then walked toward the bed and sat down on the edge.

He undressed and stood next to the bed and touched the upturned nipples of her breasts with his hands.

"Have you made love, David?" she asked, staring up at his nakedness.

"I have made love," he said. He knelt beside the bed and put his arms around her waist and caressed her and kissed her perfumed hair.

"I have thought of us like this often," said Sara, her fingers touching his head of smooth black curls.

"So have I," he said, his eyes on hers. He held her in his arms and touched her body gently, stroking the skin of her inner thighs until he felt her relax against him. She lay back on the bed, and he knelt beside her and spread her legs apart and touched the softness there.

"You're not afraid, are you?" he asked.

"Not with you, David."

He held her in his arms for a long while, talking to her in a low voice, kissing her, and when he finally entered her, there was only a small cry of pain.

"Don't stop," she said, holding tight to him.

"I'll be careful not to hurt you again," he said as he pressed against the barrier. She moaned once more, and then he was past it, and she was kissing him and crying and calling his name.

She slept in his arms, and when she moved, his eyes opened, and then he touched her and she was awake.

"Why did you not see me before?" she asked.

"I can't explain," he said and held her tighter.

"Was it the concentration camp? Did you see the camp when you looked at me?"

"No, it was more than that," he said, his hand against her breast.

"What was it, then?"

"You and my mother, the two of you shut everybody else out. You share a secret together. And Tonio, he shares it, too."

"You don't want our secret, David."

"But it binds you together."

Sara turned in his arms, her large black eyes luminous in the darkness. "My David, my poor, poor David. Don't be jealous. How could you be jealous of the starving animal that I was?"

He tried to see her face more clearly in the dark. "You do remember the camp, don't you?"

"Of course I remember it, David. I am Sara because of it."

They made love again, slowly and languorously. "It doesn't hurt now," she said as he entered her again. She put her arms around his bare shoulders.

His head was against her breasts, the cool skin beneath his lips. "I don't want you to have pain, Sara, only pleasure, only happiness."

He put his fingers on her moist flesh, slowing his rhythm inside her. "Tell me how it feels," he said.

"There, David. It feels good there."

"I love you, Sara," he said, moving urgently now against her moaning. "I love you."

She trembled and cried out with pleasure at the touch of his fingers. As he saw the expression on her face, he ejaculated within her.

"Stay there. Don't move," she said as he lay atop her, his legs entwined in hers. "I want you to stay close to me."

"I'm here," he said. "I'm not going anywhere."

"I'm so happy," she said.

At four in the morning there was the sound of footsteps in the corridor outside their second-floor room. Sara woke from her pleasant dream and touched David's face. "I love you, David," she said as the explosion went off and lifted the bed and shattered the windows. Sara screamed as the explosion's brisance pulled David away from her and flung him through the plate-glass window.

David lay on the grass beneath the blown-out window, a dense fog in his head, and through the fog he heard sirens in the distance.

"David, get up, David." Helene was shaking him. He could hardly see her, so thick was the fog in his head. "Get up, David. Get up. Sara is still in the room."

Acrid smoke filled the air. David stood up unsteadily on the grass. The manager and his wife had rushed out of their apartment. The manager ran back inside and brought a pair of shorts for David to put on.

Sara stared down at them through the blown-out window. Smoke swirled around her and out onto the small balcony.

"I can't see her, David," said Helene in a low voice. "She's gone."

"Sara," screamed David, but there was no answering cry.

David spun around to the manager. "Have you got a ladder, anything?"

"I don't know," said the manager in confusion. "Let me think. Where could it be?"

"My God," howled David in despair as he saw the flames behind Sara. "My God." He sprinted toward the patio of the first-floor room and then began to climb up the trellis on the side of the patio. He reached toward the railing of the second-floor balcony where Sara had stood a moment before.

He stretched his hand out, and their fingers touched. She was there, her nude figure before him. He pulled himself up over the railing and held her in his arms for a moment.

"I can't jump. I'm afraid to jump, David."

David looked up at the patio above them. The hotel guests were watching them from the lawn beneath the burning second floor.

"The third floor has a door that goes to the roof," yelled the manager from down below.

"Will you trust me not to drop you?" asked David.

"I trust you," said Sara.

David grabbed onto the trellis and climbed up to the third-floor patio. He leaned over the railing, his hands reaching for Sara. "Now, Sara, I'll pull you up."

She stood on the small balcony of the room. The fire had ignited the drapes behind her. She reached up, and he took her hands in his and strained forward, pulling upward with all his strength, feeling that he would black out at any moment.

"You're touching the rail," he shouted. "Can you feel the rail?"

"Yes."

"Put your foot on it, and I'll lift you the rest of the way."

The weight on him shifted as she placed her foot on the railing and leaned toward him.

"Thank God," he said as he pulled her onto the safety of the patio next to him and then into the vacant third-floor room. The fire engines clanged down below, and men shouted at one another over the noise of pressurized water as it played against the building.

"The roof," hollered a fireman through his bullhorn. "Get onto the roof through the rear corridor."

The heat from the fire on the floor below had penetrated the third floor. "It's so hot, David," said Sara as he pulled a sheet from the bed of the empty room and wrapped it around her body. He lifted her into his arms and carried her across the radiant floor. The sheet covered their faces as David groped his way through the smoke to the rear corridor.

"David," she said in the darkness.

"I'm here, Sara," he said.

"Hand her up," said the fireman, fresh air and night stars at his back. Then gloved hands pulled them one at a time up through the exit and onto the roof.

XLVI

The grand jury met in secret session on May 2, 1956. The accused, Gunter Liebermann, sat on a bench in the corridor of the Federal Court Building in Flagstaff, his wife, Erika, on one side of him and his daughter, Alexa, on the other. The witnesses against him were called one by one from a private office into the grand-jury hearing room and were questioned by Mr. Bragg, the jury's attorney.

Harley Winokur, as part of the group of witnesses who would testify in Gunter's behalf, had arrived early and sat in the corridor drinking coffee from a paper cup and watching as the door of the grand-jury room opened and closed behind each new witness. At midmorning Leland Summers, the jury foreman, came out of the grand-jury room and walked toward the office where the witnesses were waiting. Harley got up, paper cup in hand, and followed Leland to the door and looked in over Leland's shoulder. "Haven't even touched this bunch yet. How come?"

"Been listening to character witnesses from the National Park Service," replied Leland, counting the people in the waiting room.

"Awful full house in here," said Harley. "Who the hell are they all?"

The foreman nodded toward the two Indians and a white girl sitting near the Coke machine. "Let's see, there's the Indian, Lee Jones; he's going next. His father, Elgin, next to him. Then there's Katie Mathison, the deceased's daughter. May call those two and may not. As far as we can see, all they've got is hearsay and a pretty good case of hate for Liebermann."

Harley motioned toward the three people at the far side of the table. "And those three?"

"That's the Spaniard who was supposedly up there with Lee Jones at the time of the alleged incident. That's his mother and a relative of some kind who've come here from Spain for God only knows what reason. He either saw it or he didn't. Can't see that their being here's going to change that no way."

"They aren't going to testify?" asked Harley.

"Hell's bells, can't see why they would. Couldn't tell us anything we want to know anyway."

"So Leland," said Harley, looking at him the best he could with his spaced-apart eyes, "which way's it going?"

"Harley, Harley, you sneaky old bastard you," answered the foreman. "You know better than to ask a question like that. I am the grand-jury foreman, sworn to uphold the secrecy of our sacred institution." And then Leland winked and closed the door.

Harley sat back down and shoved the now cold cup of coffee under the bench till it was touching the wall. The Liebermanns had sat together in the same spot near the door to the grand-jury room the entire morning, except once when his wife and daughter had got up to go to the ladies' room.

Now the door to the witness waiting room opened, and the foreign lady with the no-nonsense look about her came out of the room followed by the younger female relative. The two women looked somewhat alike, both with olive skin and dark hair, but the younger woman's features were fuller, her mouth more generous, her shorter figure fuller on top. The women hesitated for a moment at the door of the waiting room, then they began to walk toward where the Liebermanns sat. Harley thought he ought to go tell Leland that the witnesses were mingling with the accused, and then he remembered that Leland had said the two women knew nothing and were not going to testify. "None of my damn business anyway," he said, leaning his head back against the stone wall of the corridor.

• • • • •

Helene approached them warily, as she had in her imagination so many times before. She felt her footsteps springy beneath her, as though everything were in slow motion. Each sensation was intensified as the distance between them narrowed. Sara was close behind her, but the two of them did not speak. Their eyes were focused ahead of them toward the end spot on the bench. The Liebermanns. Erika's head, the same shape, but the blonde now washed with gray, coarser in texture than Helene remembered it. But it had been seventeen years. Whose hair did not lose its fine, youthful texture after seventeen years of living in this world?

There were no further steps to take. She could keep walking down the corridor, past them. They would not look up. She would not speak. It would be as it had been in her imagination before, merely an illusion. She would not ask the questions she had been burning to ask. She would not feel the sensations she was sure would arise. There would be no raw emotion, no need to compose herself afterward, no recrimination, no tears. She stopped walking.

"Erika," she said.

Erika looked up. Her hand went to her eyes as if to shield them from a too-bright light. Helene waited for Erika to compose herself. Perhaps Erika would wait later while Helene composed herself.

Gunter's hand went to his wife's shoulder. Alexa was looking at Sara and Helene with the clear eyes of innocence.

"I cannot speak," said Erika, holding herself stiffly against Gunter's arm.

"I have not changed so much, then. You do know me," said Helene. She stood before them, looking down at them. They had to lift their faces to look at her.

"This is your daughter?" asked Helene, giving Erika still more time to recover from the shock of seeing her.

Erika turned toward Alexa, who had a puzzled expression on her face. "Yes, my daughter. This is Alexa."

Erika's voice shook as she spoke. Helene glanced from Erika to Gunter. He had changed. She could not place the exact features that seemed different; she knew only that there was an aura about him that gave her a sensation of disquietude. He looked at her through wire-rimmed glasses similar to the ones that she remembered, although now the glass was tinted instead of clear. His hair was thin on top, in a crescent above his forehead, and beneath the jacket sleeve of the arm that rested on Erika's shoulder was the beginning of the blue numbers of Auschwitz.

"Helene," said Gunter in a low voice, his face expressionless. Hardly a line creased his smooth-shaven skin.

"It has been a long time, Gunter," said Helene in German.

"Yes," he said.

A torrent of words erupted from Erika. "It is not true what you think, Helene. Gunter is not a monster. He did not murder that man. It will be shown by the witnesses that there has been a mistake, that his car was taken without his knowledge. It was someone else, not Gunter."

Helene was startled by Erika's outburst. She looked back at Gunter again, and her head began to spin. Was it possible, she thought? Was it possible?

Sara had clasped Helene's hand in hers, and she could feel the trembling of Helene's body through her fingertips.

"I have forgotten what I wanted to ask you. Isn't that strange?" said Helene, steadying herself. "That things that one thinks are so important can so easily be forgotten? How our minds play tricks on us.

"Yes, I remember now," said Helene. "Don Diego Manero, I do not see him here. David has told me that he visited you, Gunter."

"I have many friends who visit me," said Gunter, his eyes steady on hers.

"You know that he is a Nazi, of course?" persisted Helene. "Has he told you that he and his men tried to beat David to death in Barcelona? Perhaps he did not tell you that, Gunter. Perhaps the two of you are too occupied with the business of the Kameradenwerk to talk of such ordinary things as that."

Erika gasped.

"Dear Erika, my old friend," said Helene gently. "Do not tell me that you do not know of the Kameradenwerk, of its work with Nazi war criminals. I would believe anything of you but that, anything."

"It can be explained," said Erika, her voice a whisper.

"What cannot be explained?" said Helene. "I defy someone to suggest a subject that is incapable of being explained somehow or in some way by someone."

"This is America," said Gunter.

Helene turned to him. "It has been such a long time, Gunter," she said, looking into his eyes hidden behind the glasses. "And now we meet again in America. Don Diego attempted to kill my children last night in America, Gunter. Not in Spain. In America."

"I know nothing of that," he said.

Helene then bent her head toward Sara, and the two spoke together for a few seconds in a whisper.

"Alexa, tell me, are you finished yet with school?" asked Helene in a kindly voice.

Alexa smiled, not understanding any of the conversation but intensely curious at the byplay between her parents and Helene. "I have one more year at boarding school," she said.

Helene pulled Sara forward. "I, too, have my daughter with me. You see, this is Sara, my daughter from Ravensbrück. I found her in Ravensbrück beneath a board, hidden in a dark hole with rats for playmates. Actually I inherited her from a woman who died. She bequeathed Sara to me. You are younger than my Sara, Alexa. You are, I would say, sixteen years old. Is that possible?"

Alexa was confused by the talk of Ravensbrück. If it was a camp like her father had been in, she had no knowledge of things like that. Her parents never spoke of the concentration camps. "I will not be sixteen until this October," she said hesitantly.

There was a look of surprise on Sara's face. She glanced at Helene. Helene had noted the answer carefully.

"You have a lovely daughter, Erika," said Helene, not smiling. "You must protect her from ugliness as much as possible. And you, Gunter, you speak so very little. Is it because you have nothing to say to an old friend such as I?"

Gunter turned his head away and stared at the door of the grand-jury room.

"Yes, you must watch the door carefully, Gunter," said

Helene. "You will never know who might come through the door."

Helene turned, and with her hand still in Sara's, she walked down the corridor, past the dozing Harley Winokur, and back into the witness waiting room.

XLVII

Early in the morning of May 4, 1956, the grand jury released a typewritten report of its findings. The last paragraph, after a summary of witnesses' testimony and a recitation of the accusation, stated: "Therefore, it is the finding of the grand jury, sitting in Flagstaff, Arizona, on this 4th day of May, 1956, that there is insufficient evidence to deliver an indictment of Gunter Liebermann in the above-described incident."

At two o'clock the next afternoon, three men, dressed in business suits and carrying attaché cases, deplaned at Sky Harbor Airport in Phoenix and were met by Harley Winokur. They had no baggage to claim, and in minutes the men were whisked away in the Ford station wagon that the National Park Service provided for Harley's use.

At four-thirty the same afternoon, Harley and the three men arrived at the Desert Paradise Hotel, where Helene was waiting for them.

Elgin looked through his binoculars, sweeping past the gray-blue cliffs streaked brilliant red by centuries of rainwater acting on limestone. Each morning when the sun lit the crevices and crags, Elgin and Lee had come to stand on the high plateau to search for Will's body. Now he trained the binoculars on a place between the Hualapai Hilltop and the San Francisco peaks.

"It is possible that it is only sage and rocks," said Elgin, handing the binoculars to his son.

Lee studied the carved-out gorge below. "That is far to have fallen," he said.

"He could have been carried there by animals," said Elgin, taking the binoculars once more to look again at the slant of sun on the place in question.

"It will be a day's ride," said Lee. Each day that they had come to the Hilltop to search, they had brought provisions for a three-day trip, as well as a sled made of willow branches, which Lee tied to the back of his pony.

Elgin took the binoculars from his eyes. "It is his body," he said.

"Then we'll go today," said Lee.

They rode the Havasupai Trail down to the gorge, where the mountains rose above them and ringed the plateaus and made the juniper trees seem like short grasses high above their heads. In the heat of the day, they rested in the shadows of the terraced rocks that hung apronlike from the sheer sandstone cliffs.

They reached the body before the sun had set. Elgin jumped from his horse and stood staring down at the remnants of twill pants and work boots that still clung to the skeleton.

"The coyotes have brought him far," said Lee, removing the wooden sled from the back of his horse.

Elgin did not answer. He sat down in the dirt and watched while his son covered the remains of Will Mathison with a saddle blanket. When that was done, Elgin and Lee prepared their camp for the night.

"He would want an Indian funeral," said Katie when her father's body was brought into the village.

"He will not be buried in the ground," said Elgin. "His spirit was Havasupai and must be free to join the rain clouds and to return in the summer wind to comfort you. Only in this way will he not moan when the plateaus are cold and not torment us with his voice when we sleep."

At dawn the tribe gathered in the sacred funeral grounds within sight of the Prince and Princess peaks. A blanket was spread for Katie to sit on, and two Indian women sat on either side of her to give her solace. The men had made a pile of wood, and atop the wood they placed all Will's clothing and possessions, and finally Will's remains, his face toward the rising sun, his combat camera at his feet. When everything was ready, Elgin walked to the pyre. From his headband he removed Will's journalist pin, then he bent down and fastened it carefully to the flap of Will's shirt. The pile was doused with petroleum.

Lee helped Katie to her feet. She was wearing a dress like the Indian women wear, and she had undone her braid so that her hair blew unfettered around her face. Lee lit a long match and handed it to her. Katie held it steadily in her hand. "Our Father, Who art in heaven. Hallowed be Thy name. Thy Kingdom come. Thy will be done in earth, as it is in heaven. Amen." The match had burned down as she said the prayer.

"Throw it, Katie," said Lee, pulling her hand toward the pile. She closed her eyes and tossed the match. There was a sucking-in of air as the petroleum ignited.

Elgin began to chant in Havasupai, and Lee took Katie's hand in his and raised it to his lips.

"He's gone," said Katie softly.

"Yes," said Lee.

"The white man must be driven away," said Elgin at the tribal meeting. "He has killed one of us. If he remains, he will bring rashes and death and destruction. Our houses will be set afire, and the crops will not grow. When the white man Liebermann is gone, then the spirits of the dead will return to us and bring prosperity. Our fields will grow green and ripe with fruit. There will be no sickness."

The tribal chief listened gravely. "It will give the white man excuse to keep our lands from us forever if we do this," he said.

"The white man needs no excuse to keep our lands from us," replied Elgin. "The Mohave and the Paiute believe that the Ghost Dance will rid the Indian Nations of the evil spirit of the white man. Gunter Liebermann is an evil spirit."

Harley drove the Ford while Helene and Sara sat in the back seat. David and the three men had left earlier in the day for the Liebermann ranch and were waiting when the Ford drove off the highway behind the grove of giant pine trees that shielded the ranch house from view.

"David thinks that Manero is in the house, too," said Lathrop, one of the Justice Department agents.

"Then it is too dangerous for David," said Helene. "I'll go."

Harley shook his head. "If what you say is true about him, then I don't think you ought to be in there alone with him either. I'll go with you."

Helene nodded gratefully. Sara kissed her and smoothed Helene's hair with her hand. "It will be all right," said Sara.

Lathrop handed Harley a pistol, which the ranger slipped into his pocket. "Arrest him in the house if you can. Don't shoot him," said Lathrop.

David walked with Helene along the path toward the ranch house. "Do you forgive me, David?" she asked, her face averted from his.

"Yes."

"We have not understood one another very well, have we?"

"I'm understanding better now," said David.

"You've grown into a good man, a strong man," she said. "Don Carlos and Martita did their work well."

David was silent.

"Sometimes there are choices in life. I had a choice with Sara. Either I would feed her, or she would die. And if she died, then my spirit would die, too. But with you I had no such choice. You were my little boy, and I left you in the cathedral because I wanted you to live."

"But after the war—you didn't try to find me after the war," said David.

"But I did. I tried everything, but it was no use, there was no way to find you, no one who remembered me, no one who knew where you had been taken. I feel the pain of it even now after all these years, but how can we change things, David? If I could have changed things, I would have saved Miriam. I held you from Maurice so that he could not get to you, but I could not help Miriam. Miriam was gone when I awoke. I could do nothing to prevent what happened then or what happened after."

There were tears on her cheeks, but she was not crying. She took David's hand in hers.

"Thank you for bringing me Sara," he said.

The ranger had caught up with them now. "Stay here, David," said Helene, drying her eyes with a handkerchief.

He smiled at her. "Again?"

"Again," she answered, smiling back.

David watched his mother and the ranger walk through the grove of trees along the path. She was composed now, and the hard exterior was once more in place. But she had revealed herself to him. She was no longer a stranger to him. He had seen her.

The path meandered behind the cow barns, and then it emerged in the clearing where the ranch house stood. Erika came to the door, and without a word Helene and Harley stepped into the house.

"Gunter," called Erika in a shrill voice.

In a moment Gunter appeared, accompanied by a stocky, dark-haired man. Gunter looked confused at seeing Helene and Harley Winokur standing in the entry side by side. The dark-haired man turned immediately and disappeared.

"Why are you here?" asked Gunter. "This is my home. You are invading my private property. I have been cleared by the authorities. You have no right to be here."

"You have no right to run Nazis in and out of Flagstaff either," said Harley carefully.

"Who has said that?" snapped Gunter.

"Well, just about every government agent who's called me on the phone the last few days."

"I smuggle no one. I raise cattle, and I have a right to be here in Arizona. I came here legally in 1946."

Helene had said nothing. Her eyes were fixed on Gunter's face. She seemed to be listening to him with special care.

"It would be nice to sit down somewhere while we talk, Gunter," said Harley amiably as he walked from the entry into the living room. In the living room he looked out the windows and behind the drapes and then sat down in a chair by the fireplace.

"We'll all sit down. It is more comfortable," said Helene, taking the chair next to Harley.

Erika and Gunter followed them into the room and sat on the sofa facing Helene.

"We do not want violence," said Helene. "We know that it is possible that with many men coming to your door, there is a chance for violence. Not from us, but from you. So the men are outside waiting. All you have to do is to walk outside with Mr. Winokur, and that will end everything. And I am sure that they will find Don Diego outside also."

"He has a visa. He is visiting me," said Gunter.

"His visa has been revoked," said Harley. "And as for you, well, Gunter, I don't believe I've ever been so bamboozled as I was by you. I believed you, with your damn story about being in the concentration camp."

"I was in a concentration camp," said Gunter hotly.

"When, Gunter? When were you in Auschwitz?" asked Helene.

Gunter glanced quickly at Erika, who sat frozen, all color gone from her face.

"First I was in Sachsenhausen," Gunter said. "Then, in 1942, I was transferred to Auschwitz, where I stayed until the Allies freed the camp."

"There is no need to continue as Gunter any longer," said Helene. "I see Gunter's face in my mind as clearly as I did seventeen years ago. At first, when I looked at you in the grand-jury building, I thought that you had changed because you had been in Auschwitz, and besides, time changes people's faces. But I knew even at that moment that it was not possible that you were the Gunter I remembered. It was in the movement of your body, the way you spoke my name, so cool, so correct, that I saw you suddenly in Berlin, your violin under your arm, looking at me in just such a way as you are looking at me now."

Erika got up and stood next to her husband, her arm protectively around his shoulder.

"I have knowledge of the Kameradenwerk and the means that they use to give Nazis new lives," said Helene. "They change names, they change faces. A Nazi can become a Jew. Especially when the Mandelbaum Archives have revealed now that Gunter died in Auschwitz in May of 1942." Helene sighed. "I could not believe that Count von Kirchner would be found in this way," she said, shaking her head in mystification. "But I said to myself over and over, how can a Jew who has been in the concentration camps be a man such as David describes to me in his letters?"

"You do not understand Karl," said Erika fiercely. "We were lovers in Berlin long before the war. Do you think for money he would have risked what he risked to help you and Maurice and the others?"

"Did he help Gunter, too, in the same way that we were helped?" asked Helene.

"Gunter was discovered and deported," said Karl. "It was not my doing."

"I am so glad that there are things that were not your doing, Karl," said Helene quietly.

"There is no point in this," said Karl. "If you have come to arrest me, Harley, then I would require that you state upon what authority you are here."

"God, Gunter—I mean Count—I got authority coming out my ears," said Harley.

"Why did you keep all of the diamonds and leave us without any resources?" asked Helene.

"There was no help for it," said Karl tersely. "Erika was pregnant with my child, and the Cianos demanded a great deal of money in order to care for Erika and Alexa during the war. All of the diamonds were needed for that. It would have been a waste to give any of them to Maurice. I could see the weakness in him and that you were tied to him. I could have predicted that he would do what he in fact did. What I could not have predicted was that you and David would survive."

Helene nodded. "We have survived. I am no longer the person I once was, but we have survived."

"You seem to be a better person," said Karl grudgingly. "Yet you are the same. So many years have passed, and still you want to ask questions and seek answers. You bring my friend Harley here to arrest me, but Harley will not arrest me, because he knows that you have told him lies about what I did during the war. Harley was a Marine on Guam during the war. He understands what is done sometimes in the midst of war."

Gunter turned toward Harley. "Have you ever shot a man, Harley?"

"I do have to admit I've shot my share," said Harley.

Gunter smiled. "You see. Harley has killed people, too. It is the context in which these things happen that we must be concerned about. We cannot dredge up the war so that you may punish me for your personal misfortune."

Erika was looking more relaxed as Karl spoke. She stroked his shoulder and glanced from him to Helene to Harley.

Karl patted Erika's hand.

"In what context do you shoot women and children, Karl?" said Helene.

"He could not have done that," interjected Erika.

"He did that, Erika," said Helene coldly. "Tell Alexa that I saw her father kill children. Not once. Too many times to remember."

Harley was fidgeting in his chair. "If you're innocent of the charges, Gunter, you won't have any problem proving it, I don't suppose."

"They are ludicrous," said Karl.

Erika's hand dropped from his shoulder.

"Now the pain shifts to Erika and Alexa," said Helene. "That does not make me happy, because Erika does not understand yet what you have done. She has been protected here in Arizona, and Alexa is innocent of everything. She is, after all, still a child. Perhaps that is your fittest punishment, Karl, that your wife and child will know what you have done. You see how Erika's hand drops away from you. She recoils in horror at what I have said. I know her. When she understands more, she will hate you more than I hate you."

Harley stood up. "They gave me a gun, Gunter, but I don't think old friends like us need anything like that, do we?"

There was a blur of motion. Karl shouted something in German and began to run.

Harley started after him, but Helene restrained him. "Leave him," she said. A door slammed in the rear of the house. "His journey will be short."

As a show of solidarity, members of the Navaho and Hopi tribes came to Havasupai Village to prepare for the Ghost

Dance with which they would help the Havasupai exorcise the devil white man from the Grand Canyon. The braves washed in Havasu Creek, and then they donned long white doeskin shirts that fell to their thighs and were tied around their waists with braided bands of buckskin. Their breechcloths were of rabbit skin, and their close-fitting leggings were of fringed buckskin.

"The Ghost Dance is symbolic," said Lee as he kissed Katie good-bye at the door to Elgin's house, where Katie had lived with Lee as his wife since Will's death. "The Ghost Dance is to make the white man afraid, to drive him away. We will not hurt him. My father tells me that since 1863, when seven Yavapai were killed trying to raid the village, no other intruders have been killed. We do not kill easily or often."

Forty-three braves dressed in their costumes of white doeskin rode out of Havasu Canyon on their horses, accompanied by twenty Indian women, who wore Navaho blankets over their shoulders and tied at their waists with cord. Elgin was in the lead, and he chanted the songs that he had learned from the Hualapai subchief, who had learned them from the Paiutes.

The Indians rode steadily, the dust swirling around their horses' feet and the noise of the horses' hooves echoing through the washes and gullies of the canyon. When they emerged from the canyon near Hermits Rest, the riders let their horses drink in the stream before they continued on to the ranch.

The wind was blowing across the field facing the Liebermann house when the braves arrived and dismounted. With hand shovels they dug a deep hole in the earth, and into the hole they placed the cottonwood pole that they had carried with them from the village. They put stones and rocks and debris into the hole and pounded the area around the pole until it stood straight and steady in the ground. When Lee climbed up to the top of the pole to test it, the pole swayed only slightly. He climbed down, took the belt of eagle feathers from Elgin's hands, and climbed up the pole again. To the very top of the pole he laced the belt of feathers, and while the braves danced a circle dance beneath him, Lee clung to the pole, his arms and legs twisted against the slickness of the wood. Elgin chanted the Paiute songs in a reedy voice for several stanzas, and then the women joined in the chanting, and over all was the accompaniment of bare feet stamping rhythmically on dry earth. Lee clung to the pole for an hour, until he fell to the ground in exhaustion.

Then another brave climbed the pole and wrapped his body around it beneath the belt of eagle feathers, and the dancing and the chanting continued. While a Navaho was taking his turn atop the pole, there was the sound of a car motor being started across the field near the Liebermann house. Elgin continued his chanting as he moved toward the house, leaving the braves behind him. He chanted and danced his way across the field in his white doeskin costume. He was an Indian and an American hero of World War II, who had his commendation from President Truman hanging on the wall of his wooden house in Havasupai Village. The women's voices had become hysterical behind him as the Navaho brave fell from the pole and spoke of having talked with the dead. The car was moving forward, leaving the house. There were two men in it. Elgin recognized one of the men as the devil Liebermann. Elgin approached the car, his hand up, chanting his song to the Deer-god:

Let it rain that the grass may feed the deer.
Let the white man be banished from the sacred canyons.
Let our home be prosperous once more.
Let us hunt on the high plateaus in peace.

Elgin stood before the car, his arms uplifted, his eyes closed. The car lurched forward, and there was the sound of cracking bones and trampled flesh as Elgin fell beneath the car's wheels. The Hopi atop the pole shouted to the Indians below. The car picked up momentum as Lee and the other braves mounted their horses and chased after it through the field. At the stream on the Liebermann ranch, the car stopped. The Indians on their horses blocked the car from going any farther. The doors of the car opened, and Karl von Kirchner came out of one side, Don Diego Manero out of the other. Don Diego had a gun in his hand and shouted at the Indians in German to back away and let them drive the car through. Lee reached for the bow and arrow that hung from his saddlebag. Manero looked up at him. "I have a gun, you crazy Indian."

But Lee did not understand German. He aimed the arrow and watched its trajectory, clean and smooth through the air. It pierced Manero's left eye socket and exited partway out of his right ear. As Manero fell to the ground, his right eye looked surprised.

Lee jumped from his horse as Karl bent to retrieve Manero's gun, and the two men grappled with each other on the slippery bank of the stream.

"You filthy Indian," screamed Karl as he grasped Lee's neck between his strong fingers. Lee pulled at Karl's hands until he freed himself.

Karl ran, stumbling and falling, toward the creek, fording in up to his knees, his arms flailing with the effort of running through the water to escape the Indians behind him. Lee picked up his bow and arrow and watched Karl moving away from him. The narrow creek glistened in the dappled sunlight, and there was the sound of birds loud and cacophonous against the silence of the Indians. The creek seemed to stretch in Lee's vision until it was a great expanse of water, blue-green in places and white where Karl's movements had disturbed it. Lee held the bow to his shoulder, bowstring taut, his eye on Karl's neck. He pulled back on the bowstring and let the arrow fly across the water. It sailed high and straight, and the diving birds twittered at the sight of the odd-looking bird that flew so cleanly to its destination. Karl's right arm was up, his left foot ready to touch the opposite bank. Lee could not see Karl's face, but he could imagine that it was triumphant. And then the arrow struck Karl's neck squarely through the spinal cord. The feathers of the arrow quivered for only a moment as Karl's body was held in midair by some invisible support. Then slowly Karl fell backward into the stream.

When Lee was a child, Elgin had recounted the stories that had been told to him as a boy. He had told him that many years before, when an enemy of the Havasupai was killed, they cut off the scalp and brought it to the village, and a dance celebrating the death of the enemy was given to honor the tribe's victory. Then the body was cremated, and everything that would preserve the rank or prowess of the enemy as a warrior was destroyed. Lee thought of the stories as his knife sliced into Karl's forehead.

"Don't do it, Lee," said Harley Winokur as he and the Justice Department agents ran to where the bodies of Count von Kirchner and Don Diego lay. "It'll just give ammunition to the preservationists," said Harley.

Lee ignored him. Karl's scalp already lay neatly on the ground, and he now removed Don Diego's and laid it beside Karl's. The other braves had brought wood and heaped it around the two bodies.

"This is the old way. This is the way of the stories that my father told me," said Lee, watching the flames lick at Karl's shirt. "He is the enemy. His scalp and that of the other man will hang in the village. It is a sign of victory. It is homage to my father." Lee tied the bloody scalps onto the belt of eagle feathers that had hung atop the cottonwood pole.

David moved closer to the fire. Lee's eyes met his for a moment before he mounted his horse. Harley walked toward the horse and looked up into Lee's face. "I'm sorry, Lee. Maybe if I'd believed you in the first place, none of this would have happened."

Lee nodded and turned his horse. The other Indians had placed Elgin's body on the back of his horse and were halfway across the plateau. Lee whistled to his pony to follow them. The pony began to gallop, and Lee raised an outstretched arm to the sky, the belt of eagle feathers in his hand, the scalps of Count von Kirchner and Don Diego Manero flapping and turning in the wind.

Epilogue

Sara and David stood beneath the huppah in the Barcelona synagogue, Helene and Tonio to the side, near the rabbi. Don Carlos had come, and Martita and her two daughters were there. Sister María Blanca and Sister Angelina sat in the second row, their pale faces hidden behind their stiff wimples. Helene could not concentrate on what the rabbi was saying. What could he say that hadn't already been said at every wedding that had ever been? Tonio's hand touched Helene's thigh as they stood so close together beneath the huppah. She turned to him and smiled. It was a dream. Ravensbrück had never existed. Karl von Kirchner had never touched her life. She had no life or memory beyond this moment. She and David had completed their odyssey, their separation from each other and their return. David did not hate her. He had forgiven her for leaving him. He understood now with the mind of an adult what had been demanded of her and what she had had to give. Now she could let go of Maurice and Miriam, she could let them rest in peace.

David's eyes looked with love at Sara's upturned face. David had some of Maurice's reticence about life in him, but he also had Helene's tenacity. And he had Sara, the daughter of her memory, the child who had replaced Miriam. A tear fell on Helene's cheek. What kind of person would Miriam have been had she lived? Would she have delighted and surprised Helene with her abilities? Would she have been a beautiful woman as she was a beautiful child?

David offered Sara a sip of wine from the goblet, and a tiny red drop rested at the corner of Sara's mouth. They had spoken of leaving Spain, of a desire to live in the United States. There was something to be captured here, something in the moment to remember, thought Helene. It must be stored away for the future. It could not be forgotten.